THE GENESIS EQUATION

KENNETH TAM

BECKETT LUPUS
GENERAL, EARTHER MARINE CORPS

THE GENESIS EQUATION

THE FIFTH EQUATIONS NOVEL

KENNETH TAM

Published in Canada by Iceberg Publishing, Waterloo

Library and Archives Canada Cataloguing in Publication
Tam, Kenneth, 1984-
The genesis equation : the fifth equations novel / Kenneth Tam.
ISBN 978-0-9865017-5-3
I. Title.
PS8589.A7676G45 2010 C813'.6 C2010-900087-0

Iceberg Publishing
55 Northfield Drive East, Suite 171
Waterloo ON N2K 3T6
contact@icebergpublishing.com
www.icebergpublishing.com

First pocket paperback printing: July 2006
Special international edition: January 2010

Cover Artwork: Wesley Prewer
Cover Design: Kenneth Tam

For
Mary Louise Barron,
my grandmother.

Rest in Peace.

Darymanis City
Bastion
Bastion
Bastion
Schaeffer Home
Express Superhighway
Civilian District
Spaceport
Bastion
Commercial District
Lake Darymanis
Industrial District
Bastion
N
Bastion
Bastion

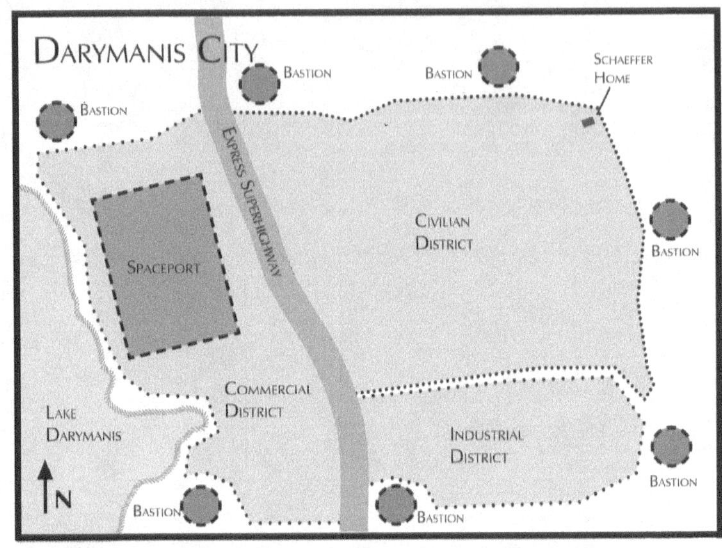

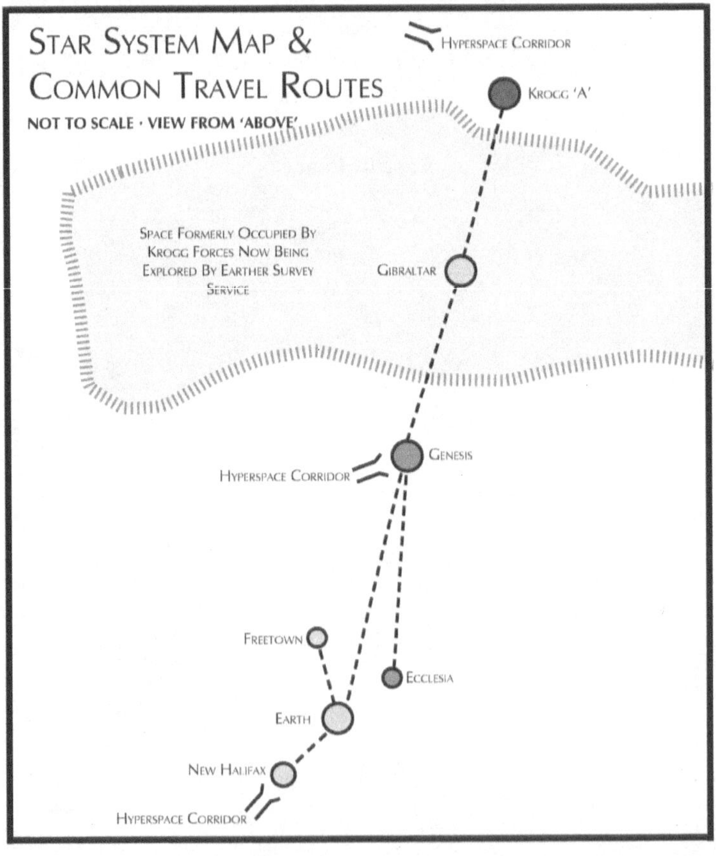

Star System Map & Common Travel Routes
NOT TO SCALE · VIEW FROM 'ABOVE'
Hyperspace Corridor
Krogg 'A'
Space Formerly Occupied By Krogg Forces Now Being Explored By Earther Survey Service
Gibraltar
Genesis
Hyperspace Corridor
Freetown
Ecclesia
Earth
New Halifax
Hyperspace Corridor

FOREWORD

When we were preparing *The Human Equation* for release in this special edition series, it was *The Genesis Equation* more than any other book that encouraged me to alter the way we began the journey. During the original drafting of the series, I knew this book would be coming — that we'd get a chance to examine the deep flaws of Genesis civilization — but in retrospect I wondered if we should get a clearer preview of these problems at the outset.

Now we've added *The Quest* novella to *The Human Equation*, so if you've read the special edition of that book, you'll be well aware of the history that must be overcome if the people of Genesis are going to live together in peace. For centuries, a false Church was enslaving half the planet's population, committing horrendous crimes against them, and forcing them into a war against the Larosians so that prophecy might be served.

And the Church, of course, is still around, because religions that well entrenched have a hell of a time disappearing, even if there's concrete proof that they're completely fictitious. The Faithful simply believe the Earthers are lying — demons trying to stop humanity from completing the Quest. It's an easy way to justify their completely defunct dogma.

The Naval classes, meanwhile, have power for the first time in centuries. Some amongst them are looking for revenge, while others have become complacent. None trust the Church, though after four decades, few are vigilant in monitoring their old overlords.

So we find two very polarized halves of a society, both feeling victimized in their own way, and both convinced that the other half is so completely misguided that it can't be saved. (Let's avoid making direct allusions to modern America, or any other place where people on the extremes are so entrenched in ridiculous positions that compromise seems impossible).

Historically, efforts to bring such deeply divided peoples together don't often turn out so well — particularly when religion is involved. Sometimes the efforts succeed, but from what I've studied, welded-together societies are often vulnerable to detonating at some point down the line.

And here we are, down the line.

The Genesis Equation begins the second half of the Earther saga, skipping us ahead forty years and letting us see just how the hopes and ideals of the Earthers and the humans have weathered the peace. The short answer: not well, at least for the humans. As you might expect, the Earthers continue to be too good to be true, though they're having an increasingly difficult time figuring out how to interact with their fellow Earth-born species. Hard to blame them.

Looking back on this book four years after its release, I have to say it is still one of my favorite *Equations* novels. For the first time, we really get to dwell on human society, and get Earthers down to Genesis. Human governments can be awfully dysfunctional, and I've enjoyed working on another series, Defense Command, because it spends so much time examining the flaws of our society, government, and character.

What's special about *The Genesis Equation*, though, is that we're not just looking at human flaws through human eyes: our dear friends the Earthers are still trying to figure out what to make of their Krogg War allies. And though they never judge or condemn, the Earthers are starting to realize the 'let them find their own way' approach might actually allow humanity to self-destruct.

When the Church starts to make aggressive advances, what can the Earthers do without overstepping their position? How much help can they offer to the privateers at Freetown, particularly when the Church has founded its own colony and is obviously trying to start a civil war? Is there any way at all to keep the human race from descending into chaos and destruction? It's no easy task, but as always the Earthers are willing to try.

The oldest enemy is returning to the fore, and they have to be ready to deal with it, no matter the distractions or political complications...

Entering the back half of the series, the same thanks still apply.

Though the Kroggs are absent from this story, the Larosians are on the periphery, as they struggle with their own challenges. Once again, then, I must thank Cody Herauf, the creator of both races. What becomes of these species will be interesting in the context of the developments on Genesis, and both will return in richer roles before the end of the series. Many thanks again to Cody for providing them to me.

More brilliant cover art leads off this book, and highlights Wes Prewer's continued, exceptional involvement in this series. We also get to see a little more of some of his characters in this book — Earther war heroes who, in the forty years since the defeat of the Kroggs, have moved up in the Navy, or found new jobs. It's a privilege to have these characters along, so my eternal thanks to Wes both for writing them in *Retaliation*, and for helping illustrate this in such an effective fashion.

We're on the cusp of seeing the true, evil, maniacal genius of my good friend Peter Caron. And I mean maniacal and evil in the most positive sense... anyway, we're not quite there yet. For now I'll avoid spoiling anything by restricting my thanks to his encouragement of the Freetown storyline from its earliest days. Without James Stanton and Audrey DeBrooke building their own society on that beautiful resort planet, this book would have been a hell of a lot more difficult to put together, and quite possibly couldn't have happened at all. Peter: thank you my friend.

If you're playing the home game, you'll know who gets the next round of thanks: my parents and business partners, Peter and Jacqui. Best. Ever. It gets tough to find new ways of saying that, but it's no less true now than it was in *The Human Equation*. If anything, their constant support getting to this point makes their 'Best. Ever.' status even more obvious. I am both lucky to have them, and absolutely indebted to them. And I'll keep saying so in every book along the way.

Finally, Atlas must be thanked. That dog's philosophy has guided the Earthers through forty years of peace, and now the real test begins. Because the chaos and agony that's in store for the universe might soon be entirely overwhelming. Let's see what happens...

PROLOGUE

The room was dark, aside from very brief flashes of light.

A circuit somewhere along the Warcruiser's corridor wall was constantly flickering blue — evidence of the sorry state of the vessel. This ship had seen much action. For a time it had even been a flagship, serving long and well under the guidance of Novash. But now that Admiral was on another ship, performing another duty.

Shanavorous was alone.

Indeed, it was the Warcruiser's solitary state that had appealed to the scientists now aboard. This was a ship they could afford to sacrifice — along with their lives — in a last desperate bid for victory.

In principle, this was the mission for which the vessel had been conceived. Praaxus himself had developed the ship class to survive great gun battles and to reach the heart of the enemy's lumbering battle line, to be the last bid against hopeless odds…

And yet the present circumstances were in no way similar to the battles he had envisioned.

Shanavorous was slowly coming apart, gently drifting through space without a ship's company or main power, near the Larosian homeworld, Laros. All that remained operational within its hull was this lab, powered by valuable portable energy reactors, and the large shuttle linked to a nearby airlock. That shuttle would be jettisoned if things went wrong.

The scientists who had developed the treatment for the plague that ravaged the Larosians knew that their lives depended on it working now — in an even more immediate sense than had previously been the case. If this attempt failed to produce a cure, the scientists might literally be driven insane before they could even escape the ship.

That danger, of course, left the question as to why Admiral-of-the-Fleet Narosh was aboard. Narosh was the most senior warrior left in any Larosian service, and the leader of their efforts against the plague. He'd orchestrated the quarantine of Laros, with the last remaining vessels of the great fleet which had forty years before helped destroy the Kroggs.

But of the thousands of ships he had brought back from that epic battle in Krogg space, only 300 remained alive. Attrition, infection, and simple mechanical fatigue were taking their toll on the scarred remnants of the once-great Larosian Navy, and with the outer systems and their resources gone, constructing replacements was as near impossible as it was futile.

The disease that had first appeared after the Battle of Genesis had spread with an insidiousness that *must* have been designed. Narosh, and all Larosian experts, believed the Kroggs had created this plague as a last weapon against the Larosians, though because of the quarantine, they could not travel to the other galaxy to confirm this possibility. No other races could be endangered by the sickness, particularly not those beings Narosh had in hindsight increasingly come to admire: the Earthers.

It had been forty years since he'd seen one, and when last he had he'd made Setter Caine, then their First Lord of the Admiralty, promise never to enter Larosian space. Or to let any Larosians leave. The plague *had* to be contained, and that required a ruthless quarantine.

The Larosians would either stop this themselves, or they would all die and hopefully take it with them. Narosh's people could — and *did* — accept that statement of honor.

With significant limitations binding them, they'd divined what they hoped was a cure. A weapon of ironic justice — one built from the rudiments of the Krogg DNA they had salvaged from hundreds of occupied worlds in their own space, keyed to work against a Krogg-devised biological weapon. The scientists now aboard *Shanavorous* had manipulated the pliable alien DNA, made it aggressive and compatible with general Larosian physiology, and geared it to attack the plague's own infectious cells.

If this failed, no hope of success remained.

Which again raised the question of why Narosh was aboard *Shanavorous*, when he was the master of Laros' defenses and irreplaceable.

He had no answer, beyond the fact that something in his *blood* seemed to tell him he had to be aboard, that his presence had a purpose.

But as a wise Larosian, he knew his *blood* hardly qualified as a source of good information. Only Earthers could rely on such things, and though an old injury had seen him treated with Earther DNA, it seemed a fruitless hope that the procedure would have caused him to develop any instinct.

The Earthers themselves were intuitive creatures — created by a mutation after a virus had wiped humanity from the planet Earth. They'd evolved from wolves, cats, and bears, and they'd grown in the span of 700 years to become as enlightened as Larosians and as deadly as Kroggs — the ideal balance, in retrospect. Humans had tried to retake Earth, but the Earthers had stopped the humans' destructive path and eventually they became allies, fighting alongside one another against the Kroggs. All this a galaxy away from where he now stood...

We will be ready soon, Admiral-of-the-Fleet.

The report startled Narosh from his musings, but he quickly acknowledged.

Very well. Wake the patient.

One side of the dark room was comprised of a glass, energy-reinforced wall, facing into the isolation lab. The lights were dim in the adjacent chamber, but as Narosh turned to the glass they brightened.

There was one Larosian in the chamber — one who had once served closely with Narosh. Captain Natosh had been infected with the rest of his ship when a plague pod had crashed into it at the behest of a maddened pilot. He'd managed to isolate himself in a lifepod as he was infected. With the last of his sanity, Natosh had keyed the pod's transponder to broadcast his infected state, and to declare his wish to be used for study.

Natosh. Perhaps that was another part of the reason Narosh was aboard. Natosh had been a friend...

Narosh halted all lines of thought, stilling his body and mind as he watched an almost clear gas begin to pump into the chamber, neutralizing the powerful sedative that had been carefully administered to Natosh days earlier. The Captain, lying on a medical bed, twitched to life, and screamed vocally.

Flinging himself to his feet, he clawed at his head and added a telepathic shriek to his vocalizations. Narosh would have winced at the wrenching sound, but he was not human, and Larosians did not wince.

Deliver the antidote soon... he ordered quietly.

This had to be the cure. The Larosians *needed* a cure. The plague drove them insane, destroyed their minds, and had come close to killing them all.

If this failed, it was only a matter of time.

CHAPTER 1

Someone was poking her in the arm.

"You're going to be late."

Sarah Manchester screwed her eyes shut and rooted herself more deeply under the covers, tightening her grip on the pillow to which she was clinging.

"Don't make me poke you any more. I'll get a bucket of water. I really will."

Sarah smiled and buried her head deeper into the pillow. He was bluffing, he always *said* he'd get the bucket, but he never did…

Then a cascade of cold water crashed over her head, and she shot upward.

"Gods damn — Pat!"

Pat Conroy was standing next to the bed with a big grin on his face, "Half done your shower now, aren't you?"

The big Irishman took a few quick steps back as Sarah glared at him, and then he pointed her towards the bathroom, "Go on then."

She scowled and went in search of hot water.

Finishing with the last of her jacket's buttons, Sarah slowly descended the stairs into their bright open living room, still a little angry. But she also smelled bacon. Ooh that Irishman knew how to get himself out of trouble…

Pat was whistling something upbeat in the kitchen as Sarah entered, holding a frying pan over the heating pad and gingerly flipping its contents. There were good smells coming from the quick-cook in the corner, and that was authentic Earther-grown, gene-modified bacon he was frying up.

Just as well — she'd need a good breakfast today. Another big day for her… just like most of the others.

Looking fleetingly at the calendar, Sarah mentally crossed another day off her count to liberation. Her term was up in 441 days, eleven hours, and six minutes, Genesis Standard Time. She'd be seventy-two when she finally got out, she was seventy now. But the Earthers weren't the sort to let age destroy a body — she'd gotten the first regen treatments from them over thirty years before, a human test case for Elandra Caine and the Earther Medical Industry. It had worked. Her aging process had been virtually frozen, and so she was still in her prime, with the promise of remaining so to the age of 220 or so.

Her life would be just a bit shorter than that of an average Earther — not too bad at all.

And she still felt about twenty-eight, which made things nice too, perpetual youth being that constant wish of humans, after all.

Of course, this fountain-of-youth deal had come with a catch: it had convinced her she could spend a couple of decades in politics without losing too much crucial living time.

And *damn*, she was sick of this job.

Genesis had come a long way since the Krogg War, a civilian government rising up to parallel the power of the Chancellors' Council. Essentially, the government had become three-pronged. The old nine-man Chancellory still held some veiled executive powers, and retained control of community Churches and a greatly downsized Crusader Army. A new civilian administration — headed by President Manchester — controlled the Navy and Naval Marine Corps, officially handled foreign policy, and oversaw municipal government operations. Both sides had the ability to propose legislation to the Congress, which was the third prong; a house of 441 democratically-represented officials, it was supposed to balance the two administrative powers, and to ensure fair government.

Unfortunately, the Church-loyal elements were gaining increasing sway in the halls of Congress, meaning Sarah's Presidency — and its supposed ability to guide Genesis into a new era — was losing political traction. The civilian and Naval groups had lost the fight in Congress to keep regen forty years earlier, so perhaps they'd never had as much traction as the Church let them think they had…

Well, it honestly hadn't been so bad back when Harvey Bingham had been Chancellor, but with his death fifteen years ago, and with Benjamin Argyle, his moderate successor, dead of a rather mysterious heart attack eight months after that, the Chancellors' Council had been growing increasingly militant over the past few years.

And it was getting worse.

Theoretically, the Congress should have been able to work with the President to offset the Chancellors, but the Chancellors' Council had bankrolled enough candidates of their own to get 204 seats — not enough for a majority, but enough to keep the assembly from overturning Church edicts affecting parish life, or even to resist some of their foreign policy initiatives that escaped the President's purview because they were alleged 'missions of faith' that supposedly did not directly impact foreign powers.

Perhaps more unsettling than the Church bankrolling of supposedly neutral candidates was the steady increase in the number of delegates being elected from the Theological Alliance Party — the Church's open force in Congress. Genesis had been officially integrated thirty years back, with all classes living and working together in every city. Yet beneath a pleasant veneer of suburban bliss, Sarah's intelligence people, and her gut, were well aware of an undercurrent of tension.

Team sports were carefully monitored and any teams with too much representation from organized Church or old technician classes were disbanded. Vicious rioting had been seen during the past decade for such ridiculous reasons as team sports, and Sarah had no desire to see it again.

So things were feeling slightly precarious. Which was one of the reasons Sarah missed commanding warships in the fleet. The divisive politics she'd seen within the fleet during the Krogg War were a joke next to what she was seeing now. She sorely missed having everyone under her charge working towards the same, or at least a roughly congruent, goal.

But that fleet was long gone. Her old flagship, *Pope Joseph Barron* was now laid up at New Halifax, purchased by an Earther museum in order to keep it from the breakers after the war. Aside from that Superdreadnought, none of Sarah's old ships remained in Genesis, and she missed them.

But that was useless nostalgia, and besides, she was saving up to buy *Joseph Barron* back from the museum. The curator, an old acquaintance by the name of Artemis Tigar, had told her in confidence that he'd sell the veteran ship back as a yacht for a criminal price.

Actually, he said it'd cost her and Pat a couple of drinks in a reputable Earther 'pub'.

The Earthers really had no need of money — their capitalist economy was nonexistent, they simply *shared*. She still couldn't grasp how it worked... it was essentially a system of distribution through private enterprise, except private businesses had to pay no overhead, customers had to pay nothing for products, and everyone took only as much as they needed. For free.

It seemed to be possible because of latent Earther reasonability combined with their incredible industrial capacity — two qualities Genesis simply lacked. Indeed, Genesis was entirely based on hard capitalism, with cut-throat corporate wars driving thousands to poverty and putting a strain on Sarah's new social safety net. But she didn't want to think about that right now. There were many, *many* other problems. And frankly it was more soothing for her to think about her allies.

The Earthers were generous with everything they had. They'd even provided regen treatments to whoever would take them — that's how she'd managed to secure them for some the best officers in the Navy back in the old days. But then, within the first year of the treatments being delivered, the Church had used scare tactics and a referendum to sway Congress into banning further use without license.

Now, the Church had actually managed to get a law passed that simply made it illegal to use the treatments. Punishable by life imprisonment, a threat with a whole new meaning when one's life had just been doubled. That's why so many of her people were leaving for Freetown these days. Leaving Genesis and not looking back.

Good living, *long* living, plenty of Earther support if needed and wanted, and no Church. If it wasn't for her stubbornness, Sarah would be there too.

But instead she had wanted to help change her world, and make society better...

Maybe she'd be able to, or at least maybe she could throw a roadblock in front of the latest plan for the Faithful.

The Commonwealth of Faithful Humans was the Church's 'holy mission' that supposedly didn't impact foreign policy. A backwater world sitting opposite the Freetown colony but nearer to Genesis, it was the Church's own world, a direct opposite and rival to Freetown, and thanks to an economic downturn after the Krogg Wars, numerous Church-folk had taken up residency there. Small numbers were still making the annual — permanent — pilgrimage, augmenting the Faithful armies of Templars.

Now the Commonwealth and the Freetown Republic were on the brink of war, and the Earthers were taking production contracts for Freetown-designed ships to build up a new, elite Freetown Squadron. Sarah had heard those new ships were better than anything Genesis had to offer, and she believed it. The Earthers were constructing them — albeit to Freetown plans — and Earther construction really couldn't be bettered by Genesis' starved private yards.

In fact, the Earthers were helping the Freetowners set up builders' yards of their own...

Sarah appreciated that fact, but it caused her a certain element of political difficulty. The Church's increasing sway in Congress had allowed them to gather support for a 'Defense of the Faithful Mission' bill, which offered much of the mothballed Genesis Fleet to the Commonwealth of the Faithful at prices to rival those offered by the Earthers to Freetown. Well, not to match Artemis Tigar's museum prices, but lower than the Freetowners would accept from the Earthers.

Freetowners insisted on paying for their ships, and paying reasonable rates. They didn't want charity, and the Earthers respected that, so they traded for some of the rarer minerals found in and around Freetown space. The Church simply sold the Faithful old Genesis ships in large numbers, and rumor had it they'd orchestrated the sale of a private yard or two.

But Sarah didn't actually have *proof* of that last sale, so she couldn't stop it.

The Church was arming the Faithful, the Earthers were arming the Freetowners, and if war broke out, that might make for sticky problems within the Genesis-Earth relationship.

And that lovely-smelling breakfast bacon already cost a lot to import, thanks to the tariff wall the Church had pushed through Congress to 'protect' local business against 'predatory Earther underselling and subsidization'. It had been impossible to convince Congress that the Earthers operating in a monetary-free society posed no danger to Genesis small business...

Sarah forced herself not to relive that maddening debate — she really didn't want things to get worse. She didn't get a nice breakfast every day, even on her salary. Presidents didn't actually make that much on a relative scale–

"*Shit!*"

Sarah blinked herself out of her contemplations and watched the bacon land on the floor. Pat turned red, dropped the frying pan onto the heating pad, then ran to the sink, dousing his thumb with cold water.

"Gods wept! Ouch!"

The pan, not really supposed to make contact with the heating pad, began to melt.

Watching as it turned into a puddle on the counter, Pat shook his head, "Second one this month. Sandwiches then?"

Sarah's head lolled forward and she sat at the counter, awaiting her cold breakfast.

CHAPTER 2

Captain Ed Jeffries was a big man, and generally well liked. His family tree originated in Kenya and his ancestors had come to Genesis by way of the United States, settling there long before the Omega Virus had wiped out Earth's human population. Through seven centuries of Church rule on Genesis they'd held onto at least some of their culture — not enough for him to even *know* what the native language of Kenya had been, or for him to understand any of the old African customs, but enough for him to still be proud of his origins.

What limited awareness he had was all the Church of Genesis would allow, even in the more liberal days after the Earther liberation and the Krogg War, so Ed was glad he'd left Genesis behind.

Actually, sitting on the bridge of the Freetown Republic's first newly-commissioned Battlecruiser, *FRS Savanna Felix*, he was *very* glad to be away from that planet.

He'd joined Freetown with his old Battlecruiser just after the war, and had since proved himself the best among his fellow 'renegades' in the realm of cruiser operations. He'd been an ArcColonel in the famed 444th Battlecruiser Squadron at the beginning of the war, fighting alongside Sarah Manchester and then Pat Conroy at Earth, and had been promoted to command another squadron right before Gibraltar. After the war, that record had made his decision to leave rather unpopular...

But now he commanded the most advanced Battlecruiser *anywhere*.

He always smiled when he thought of that.

Unfortunately, however, it seemed as if his ship was going to be tested on its first mission out of Freetown space. Granted, *Felix* had first been conceived of to fulfill the patrol-escort-combat role, and Ed wasn't reluctant to fight, but it was just annoying that he was going to have to.

Thanks to the Faithful.

"They're definitely looking to stop us, skipper."

Ed cocked an eyebrow, "Are they now?"

"Yessir, they've got their tubes open and they're prepping a shot across the bow of the lead freighter."

These new sensors were *wonderful*. Like many of the innovations contained within *Felix's* hull, they were the product of Earther R&D, made accessible to Freetown as part of the long-standing alliance between the Earthers and the small privateer republic.

Since the end of the Krogg War, Freetown's immigrant population had slowly been ballooning — first defectors with their ships, then simply people coming in on regular transports. There were now almost six *million* humans on Freetown, and they helped support a thriving mining economy based on the system's asteroid belt. Freetown's economy was strong, and it relied on freighters loaded with rare elements cruising back and forth to Earth.

Of course, the Earthers would undoubtedly have been the Freetowners' friends even without the trade — the Earthers had really taken a liking to the ex-Naval renegades who had founded and maintained the colony. Earther goods had helped repay Genesis for the ships that had left the Fourth Fleet to join Freetown during the war, and the Earthers were always glad to provide Freetown with whatever it needed... though the Towners preferred to earn what they got.

Either way, there was a strong bond between Freetown and Earth — strong enough that the Freetowners were naming their new class of Battlecruisers after the elite Earther Admirals, starting with the great, late, Savanna Felix. He'd been the first Earther to grant letters of marquee to renegade Genesis ships, and he'd been a hell of a ship fighter.

As far as Ed was concerned, the Battlecruiser *Felix* lived up to its namesake.

Which, right now, was a good thing.

"They're not signaling, skipper. Loading tubes one through forty."

Ed grimaced, "Stupid... Send to them to leave immediately. First Lieutenant, all hands to battle stations."

Felix had been maintaining a reduced level of alert since they'd left Freetown the day before, so it was a simple matter for its 1,100 crew to move to their action stations and bring weapons online. As the Faithful Battlecruiser came closer, it had no idea what it was getting into.

Appropriate — the Faithful never seemed to have a clue. Since the founding of their colony after the Krogg War, the Churchers who'd occupied the Commonwealth of the Faithful had stirred up trouble with Freetown, and in the same way the Freetowners were supported by the Earthers, the Faithful were backed by the Church.

While Genesis was now under a joint civilian-Church government, the latter still had enough clout to bankroll its pet colony, and to provide it with surplus ships at obscenely low costs. Now that the conservative elements of the Church were starting to press again in the Genesis government, the Faithful were getting more and more pushy.

Around a month ago, in this very sector of space, a Commonwealth ship had stopped a convoy of fourteen freighters, confiscated its cargo, and sent it home. It had been very nearly an act of war, but with only one of the new *Felix*-class Battlecruisers online, Freetown's leaders had rightly decided to wait before initiating any conflict.

But *Setter Caine, Andra Ursla*, and *Varnon Broadpaw* were all being delivered this month, as was another ship of even more significance...

So *Felix* had some latitude to work with this morning.

"All hands are cleared for action," the Cruising Master reported after a respectably short wait.

Ed nodded with a smile, "Alright... Signal Officer, send to him to withdraw *immediately*. Helm over to port 196... make your up angle thirty-two. Charge forward carronades."

Felix answered at the helm as smartly as any Earther frigate, and quickly its distinctive bow was aiming straight for the oncoming Battlecruiser.

"What're we looking at?" Ed came out of his chair and approached his bridge's main holo tank, the Battlecruiser's icon surging closer.

"A late model *Paladin*, skipper. Sixty tubes, max speed 3,100 pls."

A twenty-year-old ship against *Felix*, the most advanced Battlecruiser anywhere.

Ed *really* liked the ring of 'most advanced Battlecruiser anywhere'.

"No response coming skipper..."

"Hold on... missile separation! Warning shot coming out ahead of the convoy."

The little icon of the missile appeared in the holo tank, and Ed's eyes narrowed. These Faithful really were ambitious. And stupid.

"Shoot it down, carronades only. I don't want them to get a look at our missiles yet."

Like most things in *Felix*, the missiles were new and innovative.

But *everybody* knew how an Earther long-carronade worked.

A long energy lance slashed through space and contemptuously vaporized the flying missile. The Faithful Battlecruiser kept on its course towards *Felix*, but no second shot erupted.

"They answering us yet?" Ed turned to his Signal Officer, but she shook her head. Sighing, he shrugged, "If they want to be fools... Let's put a shot across *their* bow. Carronade number two, and fire from here. Remind them we have range on our side."

Long-carronades were no secret, but they were a hell of a lot more modern than that Faithful ship. They could fire their energy beams twice as far as old-fashioned carronades and lasers, and despite having been around for a few years, had yet to be matched in range by Genesis beam-weapon specialists.

So Ed could understand the Faithful ship's abrupt jerk to starboard and acceleration away as the beam sliced across its path.

"They're spinning up flux. Making a run for it, skipper."

Ed nodded, "Good. Send word of their interruption back to Freetown. Lieutenant, let's stand down. Master, back on station please."

Felix turned back into line with the convoy and continued on its journey.

CHAPTER 3

"It's guaranteed, sir, no melt. Could take a laser shot!"

Pat raised a suspicious eyebrow at the nervously smiling sales clerk.

Looking at the pan in his hand, he flipped it over and examined his face in the reflection. He still looked thirty, but damned if he wasn't a craggy old bastard on the inside. Well, not really, but he told himself he was because he was seventy-one.

A polite, slender young blond woman had just made an ambitious claim.

After a lengthy silence, this girl blinked a couple of times and frowned, "Um... sir?"

Pat's eyes narrowed and he looked up at her, "How old are you, miss?"

Her frown deepening, she tilted her head, "I'm 20."

"Weren't in the war then?"

She shook her head, "Of course not... my grandfather was though. He was an ArcLieutenant-General at Krogg."

Pat's eyebrow rose again. The store was empty on this Tuesday morning, with this lone sales clerk minding the counter, and by the looks of it reading a textbook on Interstellar Navigation. Despite the fact that his face had been plastered all over the place during the past decades, she didn't recognize Pat.

Big hero. Hoorah! Bah.

There was, of course, a logical explanation for that; he'd grown a beard and moustache, and always wore a hat and a scruffy old work coat. He liked the disreputable look, made people underestimate him.

Back to the point: there'd only been a dozen Arc-Lieutenant Generals at Krogg... and only two had survived — Graham and Pat. So who's kid was this?

"Who was that then, miss?" Pat wasn't really even thinking of the pan now. His brain was saying one thing: *Opportunity!*

"ArcLieutenant-General Bill Wallace; he commanded the cruisers for the Sixth Fleet."

Pat blinked twice, "Bill had *kids?*"

The sales clerk was getting increasingly suspicious, "I don't really see how that's relevant, I mean, the pan–"

"You said it could take a laser shot. What's the output on a type 105-c fleet laser?"

She frowned for a second, "Something like 44-ppx to the power of the barrel size."

Pat didn't visibly react to the correct answer, but he put the pan down, "That's right. But you're wrong about the pan. Melted one this morning when I was trying to make breakfast for the wife. What year are you in at the Academy?"

Again she eyed him suspiciously, "I'm in my final year... Look, I'm not really comfortable with you asking me all these questions."

Pat frowned... he was getting ahead of himself. First, he needed to introduce himself. Dragging his hat off, he looked squarely at the girl, "Do you recognize me?"

She slowly shook her head.

Pat grinned, "Hold on, I'm really good at this..."

His eyes quickly dashed over to the cash counter and eyed a few of the clerk's other texts stacked next to the navigation book... aha! *The Alien Equation: A History of the Genesis Action* was sitting there. He grabbed the book as the girl reached out to stop him, and flipped open the back page, holding the picture towards her.

"Look familiar?"

She stopped and squinted at the picture, then looked up at Pat's grinning face.

"You're... oh my Gods... you're him! Oh... oh... can you sign my book? Please? You're him right? You're Pat Conroy? The ArcGeneral?"

She became nearly giddy in a flash, and Pat smiled.

Still got it... now, go in for the kill...

"Of course, of course..."

She rounded the counter quickly and fumbled nervously for a pen, handing it to him with a slightly shaking hand. He opened the first page of his second-to-newest book, and under his name signed...

"To..."

"Christine Schaeffer."

"Chris... tine... Schaeffer..." Pat recited as he wrote, "from your Grandpa's old buddy... best wishes... there."

He handed the book back to her and she grinned broadly, "Thank you *so* much Mister Conroy... I mean ArcGeneral."

Pat held up a hand, "Three letters. 'P-a-t'."

She grew a bit wide-eyed... he loved having fans sometimes. Made getting what he wanted so easy.

"So, how about a discount on the pan?"

There was a pause and her wide eyes normalized. A thin frown formed over her brow... "I can't, I'm afraid."

Pat grinned, "Alright, one better. When's your lunch break?"

She blinked, "*Excuse* me?"

"Lunch. You eat after working, right? I presume you're off for summer and that's why you're not on campus..."

"Well, yes but, I mean, what exactly are you proposing?"

Pat frowned for a second.

What could a young woman be worried about from a craggy old basta–

Oh, right. Old men in young bodies inevitably would have insatiable appetites for young females, or so the gossip columns liked to posit.

Reaching into his pocket, he pulled out a mini computer, then smiled, "Nothing untoward, I'm three times your age!"

She still looked skeptical, so he pressed on.

"I'm writing *The Earther Equation* about the battles at Krogg, and I've been trying to track down officer families for a month now. Bill's record didn't show kids though, and I was having a hell of a time figuring out where to find any relations."

Christine's eyes brightened again, "He and my grandmother never got married through the Church, it was common-law. That's probably why the record wasn't complete."

Pat grinned, "This is exactly why I believe in luck... now, Christine... *lunch*?"

She blinked and nodded eagerly, "Can I ask *you* questions, too? There's a lot I wanted to know..."

"Of course!"

"Great!" she sounded positively giddy. "Okay... um... I'm off at 12:00."

Pat nodded, "Excellent, I'll meet you... oh wait."

Graham... *right*. Meeting him at noon. He was going to be one of the major sources for the book, and he was coming down from the fleet for lunch...

But there was no reason he couldn't get two birds with one boulder, as the old saying went. Hell, Graham and Bill had worked together for some long months in the Sixth Fleet, so the junior Manchester might think to ask some questions that didn't occur to Pat.

"I just remembered I'm meeting a buddy for lunch at noon... why don't you join us. We have a reservation at the *Disc*. You know, just up the road?"

She nodded eagerly, "You don't mind? If you do, I've also got some time tomorrow..."

"It'll be fine, trust me. Two birds with one boulder and such."

Christine Schaeffer nodded without really understanding the archaic expression and smiled, "Would you still like to buy the pan?"

Pat paused and then nodded, "Might as well."

She smiled and Pat went back and grabbed two.

As he laid them on the counter she frowned, "Two?"

Pat shrugged, "They might last me a month."

CHAPTER 4

ArcGeneral Graham Manchester sat back in his chair at the *Disc,* sipping water and ignoring the odd stares directed his way every now and then. The *Disc* was a fairly exclusive restaurant, generally frequented by celebrities, the rich and the otherwise successful. Despite the heady company, Graham's rank got him attention in what should have been a condescending place.

Well, hopefully it was his rank that was attracting the attention. The junior Manchester was all too accustomed to drawing disapproving stares from Church-oriented civilians who, despite all the progress of the past forty years, didn't seem to approve of his job. But that wasn't relevant right now; he was waiting for a friend.

Watching the clock, he counted as it rolled through 11:59:44... 11:59:46... Pat had fourteen seconds... thirteen... twelve...

"Graham!"

And of course, he was *just* early. Graham grinned as he stood, and extended his hand to his brother-in-law as the burly Irishman approached the table, "Patrick Conroy, you disreputable brother!"

The clash of the ArcGeneral's British accent with Pat's Irish one was noticed by a few sitting around the stylish restaurant, but they all looked away as the two men shook hands and Pat seated himself.

The waiter immediately came over and deposited some water on the table, "Your usual to start, sir?"

Pat and Sarah essentially *owned* this table — between Pat's research meetings for his history books and their relaxing dinners, one (or both) of them was here almost daily.

But today Pat could expect a new guest with *new research!*

The Irishman found it mildly perturbing how *peppy* the promise of new primary source material made him. Forty years ago, lunch with a pretty girl would have been exciting in other ways...

"We'll need an extra chair, Roy, and I'll skip the appetizer for now. We'll be talking a lot today..." Pat glanced to Graham for confirmation, and his younger sibling-in-law nodded in agreement.

"I ate before I got here anyway," Graham said without remorse.

The waiter paused and purposely glared at him, then nodded to Pat, "Very good, sir."

As the man went off to grab a seat, Pat draped his shabby coat over the back of his chair, "You *ate before you got here*? And then you tell the waiter of the best restaurant this side of Freetown?"

Graham grinned, "I command the fleet. He can argue with that."

Pat chuckled as a chair was pushed to the third side of the table, and Graham frowned, "Sarah slipping out of session to join us?"

Pat shook his head and took a swig of water, "No, someone more topical I met this morning. You'll see... anyway, how are you?"

Graham shrugged and a small smirk crossed his face, "Well, my personal aide just went on maternity, so I'm hunting for a temp. Interested?"

Pat cocked an eyebrow, and Graham chuckled.

"Anything else?"

Graham shrugged and took a longer sip of water. Laying his glass on the table, he leaned back and smiled, "Gillian's pregnant."

Pat blinked. Twice.

Then he grinned, stretching his hand over the table, "Well done! Ha, who knew you'd be the first father among the lot of us!"

Graham took Pat's hand but his face sobered, "Oh, I'm not the father."

Pat froze in mid handshake and his grin faded as Graham drew his hand back. Pat opened his mouth to scramble for some sort of back-pedal–

"*Ha*!" Graham stabbed a finger at Pat and laughed. "You're an idiot sometimes, you know."

Pat blinked again. Of *course* Graham was the father...

"You're a clever one, you bloody Englishman... Gods, you nearly gave me a heart attack."

Graham chuckled, "Yes, well, I don't think I'll try that on Sarah."

A smile crossed Pat's face again, "She'd have my *scalp*..."

Graham nodded, "So, how is she?"

Pat shrugged, "Tired. Wants to retire. Looks younger than she feels..."

Again Graham nodded, understanding the loaded nature of that last admission. The ArcGeneral looked twenty-eight but was actually sixty-eight. Regen took getting used to, but it also meant he and Gillian Hodge could start a family, despite being almost seventy. They'd wanted kids for many years, and now, as Gillian prepared to finish her tour with the marines and retire on pension, finally they had time.

It felt strange to Graham — not necessarily bad... but strange. He had been given the gift of a young body for *centuries*, but he still hadn't come to terms with it the way people might have expected him to. When he looked in the mirror, he saw a face that could all too easily be underestimated for its lack of years, not the worn and tired visage his mind subconsciously seemed to expect. One day, he was certain, he'd be pleased that he was so young in body and so wise in mind... for the moment, he still hadn't adjusted.

Not after forty years...

"I'm sure big sister can hold out," Graham concluded, his mind managing to grab onto the threads of the conversation. "Anyway, we're here for book talk."

Pat nodded — if they let themselves get off on a tangent, as they were known to do now and then, they'd get absolutely nothing done.

"*The Renegade Equation* will be on shelves next week, so I've really got to get going on *Earther*. My publisher wants the manuscript ready in fourteen months and I haven't talked to many people yet. I'm meeting with Beckett and Varnia on Friday, and I've got the archives to look through... and then there's writing the damn thing."

Graham grinned, "You're a thorough one."

Pat's research was by now well respected even in the most jaded circles of Genesis society. Both *The Human Equation* and *The Alien Equation* had been big hits on the Genesis bookshelves, and authoritative movies were being optioned — much better than the sensationalized ones that had been made about the Krogg War up to that time.

Pat shrugged, "I just make things sound good. I think the titles do a lot of the work though."

With a chuckle, Graham leaned back in his chair, "Ending every book with the title, I don't know..."

Pat shrugged again and smiled. He'd been stealing Caine and Ursla's title lines and using them right at the end of each book — it was all very convenient, though of course he'd taken some heat for being 'too cute'. But then, Pat was used to taking heat, and he knew he wasn't cute. Besides, the *Equations* were selling phenomenally; he wasn't about to toy with a winning formula just because it wasn't 'edgy' enough for a generation of readers who'd never fought a war.

So no delusions of grandeur there — he was right.

Of course, books selling well put new demands on his writing — readers wanted to know his take on how the Krogg War had ended, so *The Earther Equation* was already being anticipated before *The Renegade Equation* had even been released. That meant Pat had plenty of interviews to conduct, and archives to dig through. A good job required at least two years, not fourteen months... he'd wiggle the room out of the publisher.

His public could wait.

The thought of having a 'public' almost made Pat laugh.

"Sir."

Pat blinked. He was getting good at completely zoning out... though he always had been able to ignore reality when it served his interests...

"A young woman claims she is to meet you here."

Pat looked up at the waiter and nodded, then glanced at the chrono. She'd managed to cover half a kilometer in less than two minutes, assuming she hadn't left early... She'd probably left early.

"That'd be the extra chair, Roy. Go on man, bring her over."

The waiter smoothed his puzzled expression and left.

"You're inviting a young woman? This better be good, Pat."

The Irishman held up a hand to his brother-in-law, "Met her this morning when I was buying a pan at the Panatorium, actually. Hell of a coincidence, as it turned out."

"You met her in a cookware store and you're having lunch with her? This *must* be good."

Pat shrugged, "You'll see."

The waiter escorted a still somewhat wide-eyed Christine Schaeffer up the stairs from the main restaurant to the expensive tables and pulled out the chair for her. Pat and Graham stood as she set her briefcase on the floor and looked awkwardly at the waiter.

"She can sit down by herself, Roy. Go get more water," Pat shooed away the stuffy man.

The waiter nodded somewhat disapprovingly and left with a quiet huff, though Christine didn't take her seat.

"Recognize him?" Pat met Christine's eyes and bobbed his head towards Graham, and she turned to the man in uniform and frowned for perhaps a second before coming instinctively to attention.

She'd been too nervous at first to quite realize who he was.

"ArcGeneral, sir!" she snapped a very crisp salute.

Graham glanced at Pat who shrugged, "Well, she didn't salute *me*..."

"You haven't been in uniform since before she was *born*," Graham frowned at him, then extended his hand towards the perfectly-postured young woman. Christine frowned and took it nervously, and Graham smiled and nodded easily to her, "Pat hasn't introduced us yet, I'm afraid. I'm Graham Manchester... and I gather you're a cadet?"

"Yessir, at the Naval College. Fourth year, now, sir, off for the summer break."

Graham looked to Pat again, who shrugged, "I think we should all sit down before someone thinks we're stuck."

Graham nodded and waved Christine down. She obeyed instantly, sitting with a straight back and squared shoulders, and forgetting Pat entirely. Cadets knew how to stay quiet and out of the way, especially the good ones and especially in fourth year.

"This is Christine Schaeffer, Graham. Bill Wallace's granddaughter."

With those words Graham's eyes brightened, and he studied the young cadet more closely. He could see the resemblance... well, no he couldn't... but he allowed himself to believe he did...

"I realized I never proved that this morning, sir, but I have my Idacard with me if you'd like to check–"

Pat held up his hand, "Maximum speed achieved by a *Prophet*-class Battlecruiser prior to the Krogg campaign?"

"*Harbinger Bishop* on a scouting run two days out from Genesis towards Earth, before the Quest. You made 24.44 adjusted cee, sir."

"It's *Pat*, my girl. And that's proof enough for me," the Irishman looked across at Graham and they both grinned.

"Your grandfather and I served together," the junior Manchester said, and she nodded stiffly.

A slow frown formed on Graham's face, "Alright listen. Enough cadetishness, for Gods' sake. Drives me bloody nuts. I'm the one who served my bridge crew donuts on a bet, remember."

Christine blinked, "Really?"

Graham paused, then nodded, "I guess that needs to make Pat's book, doesn't it?"

She nodded quickly, a little of the excitement beginning to surface again...

Then a thought stopped Graham, "You've got your facts up to snuff, how are your marks?"

"Full 10.0s on all but one subject, sir," she replied, sounding more proud than nervous.

"Which subject?" Pat tilted his head.

She ground her jaw, "Protocol, actually."

Graham and Pat looked at each other again, eyebrows up, "They teach *protocol* now?"

She nodded.

Graham chuckled, "No wonder all my new officers are stiff as boards. I must look into that... well that doesn't matter, anyway. Doughnuts don't usually make the protocol list..."

"I pretended to accept an Oscar on *Bishop* once," Pat added.

Christine finally allowed herself a small smile at that particular fact — Pat's award-winning performance to fool the Kroggs *had* made the cut into *The Alien Equation.*

"Anyway... hmm..." Graham's eyes narrowed as he assessed the cookware cadet. "You work in a pan store?"

"Bill & Deb's Panatorium, sir."

Graham nodded once, trying not to smile at the name. 'Bill and Deb's'... he broke out laughing, probably inappropriately.

Christine frowned, "It's work sir..."

Graham started shaking his head, looking across the table at Pat, "I didn't put that together when you said it first... you shop at a Panatorium, Pat? You're still melting pots, aren't you?"

Pat shrugged innocently, and Graham sobered, his mind beginning to grasp more useful threads from the conversation. A very convenient solution to his organizational problems of the next couple of months appeared in his mind.

Glancing at Christine, he tilted his head, "What do you make now, Christine?"

She paused, "Um... $140 an hour, plus bonuses."

Graham winced. When he was young, he could have survived a week on $140. Inflation had been substantial since then... minimum wage was $120.

"Well, I'm probably just in a really good mood, but my aide lately went on maternity and I'm going to be a father, so I think after we're done here I'm going to bring you up to *Unity Genesis* and check you out."

Her eyes widened indignantly and Pat cleared his throat, "*His wife* is having the baby, it's *coincidence* that his aide is on maternity too, and your *file* needs checking."

Graham blinked and then totally cracked up. It took him a few seconds to get words out, "Oh dear me... yes, sorry about that. Feel older than I look with the regen and all."

She nodded slowly, then shrugged, "*Pat* did the same thing earlier. I thought he was propositioning me, actually."

Graham kept laughing, while Pat reddened at the frank comment.

"Oh I *like* you, you've got your grandfather's nasty wit!" Graham's laugh grew louder, drawing a few dark stares from people at nearby tables. "And my aide, even a temp for the summer, could make about $300 an hour. Nothing top secret... just stamp, fetch, carry, and occasionally deal with a coup."

Her eyes widened again, and Pat started laughing too, "Stop teasing her! She's still young."

Graham controlled his laughter with a sigh, "Ahh... I honestly can't remember what that felt like. Young... wow, we did have that period in our lives, didn't we?"

"Who bloody *cares*..." Pat sobered too. "Anyway, Graham, I need you to tell me what you remember about Krogg. Christine, I'll want family stories about Bill to add some color..."

Graham took another deep, cleansing breath, "Right..."

He glanced at Christine, who still seemed mildly shell-shocked at the latest development, "Don't worry about it, Miss Schaeffer. Who knows, this day might completely change your life."

She nodded slowly. Maybe it would.

CHAPTER 5

"They can't be serious."

Vice President Fred Thornton simply nodded, and Sarah heaved a sigh. This was ridiculous — there was no way this bill could get rammed through Congress. The Church was trying to force it, but there was no way the Congress could let itself be duped... Gods!

Sarah looked down and stared again at the pages resting on her desk. Despite her young Vice President's hopes, she had a much more realistic view of the short-sightedness of the elected house.

The Church had submitted a Naval Organization Bill — something that should never have even been *conceived* of by the Churchers, since the Navy reported directly to the President's Council — and she could almost see the fingerprints of the Faithful all over it. They wanted to catalogue every Genesis ship currently decommissioned in the mothball fleet, a gargantuan undertaking considering the hundreds of veteran vessels of Krogg War vintage that remained in orbit of some of system's outer asteroids. The Navy had lists dating back to the end of the War, but the Churchers wanted to determine the combat effectiveness of each hull, and its potential for scrap.

Which in reality meant the Churchers wanted a catalogue of ships they could bring before Congress and propose to sell for a profit. The reasoning was brutally logical: all these forty-year-old ships were of dubious military use, so why not sell them and pour the money into health care or education? That much made sense — except for Sarah's fear that one day those old hulls might be needed again — but the biggest problem was who might do the buying.

The roster would turn into a shopping list for the Commonwealth of the Faithful. The Church would wrangle cheap prices for the warships, and once sold as 'scrap', the veterans could be reasonably modernized to help the fanatics from Ecclesia overwhelm Freetown. It was perfectly clear to Sarah and her staff: this was yet another attempt to start a war with the privateers, and probably the Earthers too.

But would Congress recognize all of the implications? Many ex-Naval officers were in the house these days, and their numbers were bolstered by many bright-eyed new school politicians. Maybe they'd decide they wanted to see what famous ships could be found floating in the mothball yards — which heroic ships immortalized in bad movies and on stamps had in fact survived both the breakers' yards and forty years of micro-meteor impacts.

If Congress did vote this bill into existence, the Faithful would be putting in an order as soon as the report came back. The Church would rush another 'faithful mission protection' bill through, and the new schoolers, seeking to build unity, would go for it — because how could it hurt *them*? Four months, at most, and the Faithful would buy a brand new squadron for themselves.

Sarah leaned back in her office chair, took a deep breath, closed her eyes and ground her jaw. She wished she could just dissolve the Chancellors' Council, but there was still too much support for the old institution. If she tried to fight it openly, fully half the population would probably prove loyal to the Church, and there'd be civil war.

Things really were that dangerous these days — on the surface, in the press, on the movie screens, everything was unity, happiness and butterflies. But in reality the division ran deep, and it was beginning to occupy almost all of Sarah's thoughts.

So she couldn't do anything overt to block the bill — she'd have to fight it through channels or find a way to use it against the Church.

Maybe…

Sarah's eyes opened slightly, "Alright, they want to put together a catalogue of our ships… so we'll let them. But we know where this goes next — they'll run through a bill to start offering the ships for sale."

The Vice President nodded slowly, standing stiffly in front of her desk.

"So all we need do is make sure the Naval inspection teams have *very* exacting standards. They have to condemn almost every ship out there… perhaps we could make it look like a safety issue."

"That might still leave a hundred good ships, though," Thornton tipped his head sideways, and Sarah heaved another sigh.

"We can't help that… we *can* make sure the yards take a long time removing military equipment from any that are acceptable for sale. Rip everything out and fuse the relays, make sure when they hire crews to modernize them the work is maddeningly slow. We'll have to settle for slowing the process down, and send word out discretely so the Freetowners and the Earthers will have fair warning."

Thornton pursed his lips, "You don't think we can stop them altogether?"

Sarah shook her head, "There's no concrete proof confirming it, just our gut feeling that the Church is up to no good. Congress will want war museum ships for tourist revenue, and we've seen how much the new school politicians are trying to please both sides to stay in office. If we use our veto, we'll just lose any new school support we have left — we'll look like we're sticking with old prejudices… and we would be. No, no those ships will be ready for selling within six months."

"I'll go make some calls," Thornton bobbed his head in agreement, and

Sarah watched him leave her office.

Sighing again, she flopped further back against her chair and looked up at the ceiling. It was bright and white, like the rest of the office, but it was *annoying*. She'd spent many years looking at this ceiling, and now it was more a harbinger of doom than a piece of alloy covered with textured paint.

Bet the architect hadn't planned it that way.

Sarah was really beginning to hate this job. Liz had managed the position for twenty years, and Sarah had felt obligated to do the same. She had pointedly avoided asking Liz why she left Genesis and never came back after her term was over — she hadn't really wanted to know going in. Instead she was finding out the hard way, while Liz skippered an old Earther 64 for the Earther Survey Service.

It was all such a mess here. The Church and its followers, the old Navy caste… in his ten years Harvey Bingham had done a great deal to mix the people, bring down the barriers, open the floodgates of public thought… but it was going to take generations to overcome what Sarah could only term the 'hatred'. Seeing a movie where Churcher and Navy persons become friends despite the odds was nice, but hearing from your grandpa that the Navy betrayed Genesis to the demons was ultimately more compelling.

That was where the real threat lay. And it seemed that every day it was getting tougher to stop the Chancellors and their delightful plans. Sarah had a strong feeling that eventually the Church was going to make a bid to re-take control of the government… and she'd have to be ready for that. Hopefully, the attempt would never come.

Hopefully.

And again, there was *nothing* she could do to preempt such an action.

She was a civilian now, bound to serve the law and to *obey* it, even in the case of Crusaders and Churchers. She had no choice but to let them angle their pet colony towards a war with Freetown, and she had to hope the situation didn't somehow boil over into a war between the two great powers in this galaxy.

Well, the one great power — the Earthers — and whatever one could call Genesis. An almost-power, maybe… Even if Sarah had *wanted* to fight the Earthers, she knew she'd never win against them.

No one beats the Earthers…

Across the capital city, sunlight poured through the broad windows of the Chancellors' Chamber, warming the assembly of great Church leaders, and highlighting the beauty of the lush green world of Genesis, the gift their Gods had granted them.

High Chancellor Thomas Pious looked over the eight red-cloaked men who sat before him. He was the recently-selected leader of the illustrious Chancellors' Council, a role that identified him as the most devout man on Genesis, a servant of the Gods in every way.

And he was certain that soon he would be the faithful restorer of the Church.

Unlike Bingham and Argyle, he was not weak and would not be corrupted. He knew well how the Earthers had so blatantly deceived the humans. The story of 'Omega' and the self-destruction of the human race had been a ruse. The Earthers were demons, the last test, the final challenge to be overcome by the Church before it could reclaim Earth for all time.

Now, without arousing any suspicion, he was placing the Church in a position to make that move.

"Brothers, the bill has just been delivered to the President's Office. I imagine they are rather dejected at the moment."

He spoke, of course, of the bill calling for the survey of all mothballed Genesis Navy ships. This drew pleased smiles around the Chancellors' table — they had been planning the delivery of this bill for some time, waiting for the moment when the Faithful reported themselves able to take advantage of the opportunities that might arise.

Pious nodded to his brothers, "They will be aware they cannot stop this bill... but they will try to delay the speed of our mobilization, I can assure you of that. We must thus consider our next bill: one of modernization."

Smiles faded into confused expressions, "You mean upgrades to the old ships, Eminent Brother?"

Pious shook his head, his smile broadening. Even his brothers were not able to keep pace with his divinely inspired thoughts, "No, more clever. Modernizing old ships outright would be a clear statement of our plans. Instead, we must call for the further modernization of our *main* fleet. And in the reorganization, we must call for selling old ships or breaking them up."

It took a few seconds for that explanation to be digested around the table, but then it drew nods, "So we get rid of old ships to make way for new?"

Pious nodded again, "We do just that. It gives us more power and it gives our Faithful more as well. It is also something the Navy cannot disagree with. We offer them newer ships in the short term..."

"And when we eventually seize those ships, they will make us more capable of facing the Earthers," one of the other Chancellors joined immediately in the line of thought, the hands of the Gods caressing his mind.

Pious' smile grew even larger, "It is divine certainty, brothers... we may be in a position to assert ourselves in only eleven months, when the first of the third-line ships could be sold to the Faithful."

The Chancellors' faces sobered almost immediately. They had chosen Pious to lead them for his faith and his charisma. Was it possible he was so divinely touched that he could finish the work they had struggled with for forty years in just these few days?

"I know, brothers, it seems so soon. But you know as I do, our faithful men are out amongst the people, nurturing their families in the faith. The Gods have protected the minds of our followers from the propaganda of our enemies, and I, *I* have learned how the enemy thinks."

Pious felt the power of the Gods coursing through him, "Have no fear, brothers, we could launch our coup today, should we so wish it. But we will wait for the Commonwealth of the Faithful. We will wait for the Navy to be scattered. Then we will strike."

One of the Chancellors leaned forward, "Lord Chancellor, what if our arrangements are uncovered?"

Pious simply shook his head, "You do not hear me, brother. If we are discovered, we simply begin sooner, and right any wrongs we cause with our brothers of the Commonwealth after we are victorious. Here, on Genesis, we are ready now. We will only grow stronger while we wait..."

Thomas Pious was very sure of that, just as he was very sure the Navy was not ready for what he had to offer.

Sitting back in her office, Sarah thought she felt a chill... She was missing something, she knew she was.

But her concerns could wait — at least until the Earthers were made aware of the danger.

Whatever that danger *really* was...

CHAPTER 6

Ed Jeffries let out a relieved sigh as the last of the haulers decelerated from flux within the perimeter of the Sol system. In a way it was like arriving home... or perhaps more like arriving at a friend's house.

All the aid they provided aside, Ed was rather fond of the Earthers. Back during the war, he'd been very enthusiastic about working with them, and he'd very much liked the direction things had been going — towards a closer Earther-human partnership. Having just escaped the destruction of Pat's Pirates when he was transferred out to command his own squadron, Ed had been able to work with some excellent Earther flag officers...

But then after Krogg 'A' and the end of the war, the Church had slowly started forcing a gap between Genesis and Earth. When they stopped regeneration treatments, Ed had realized the chasm was only going to get wider, so he uprooted and headed to Freetown.

Now he got his cake, got to eat it, and still had another *whole* cake, as the old adage went. He lived under good government with people he liked, commanded an amazing ship, and worked with the Earthers. A long time ago he would have expected there to be a proverbial shoe to drop — *something* in this arrangement was too good to be true — but that was the great thing about working with the Earthers: there was never a second shoe. What humans called "too good" was just "average" for Earthers. They were good people to deal with.

That said, Ed always had to be sure they weren't trying to cheat him on the ore deals. He'd had it happen to him twice already; an innocent First Space Lord or First Lord of the Admiralty would slip an extra order of missiles in with the Earther shipments — more than the Freetowners had ordered or could technically afford, but virtually no loss to the Earthers.

The Towners didn't want more than they could pay for — they couldn't get into the habit of taking more than they were able to afford, it'd be *very* dangerous to self-sufficiency. All the same, it was hard to refuse a few extra crates of warheads now and then...

Though the Earthers had to be careful, too. Their giving nature had made them *very* unpopular with the Church, and the long-term peace between Earth and Genesis relied partially on Earther neutrality relative to the Freetowners, or at least to the appearance of balanced trade. The Church was arming the Faithful, but they clearly weren't afraid of being hypocritical and trying to provoke a fight by blaming the Earthers for doing the same.

And though the Earthers could beat Genesis senseless, peace was more desirable to everyone. The Krogg War's shadow still loomed in many ways.

Well, that was entirely beside the point now. It would take a week to load the shipments into the freighters, and after that it'd be another two-day haul back to Freetown, presuming no Faithful interference.

In the meantime, Ed and his crew would have to kill some time, right after they took care of the niceties...

"Signals, prep an e-hyper pod. Encode it with the telemetry from our little run-in and send it back to Freetown. Let them know what's gone on."

Ed wasn't about to worry himself with the politics of the Faithful — he wasn't the Governor or the Admiral of the Fleet. Some Captains made it their business to follow the political rumblings and to try to think for their governments, but Ed pointedly stayed away from those concerns now. His job was to do his duty as a ship commander; it was up to the founders of the colony to dictate foreign policy.

Something was beeping.

"Oh for the love of..."

James Stanton groaned and tried to roll towards the night table to key the comm, but he was blocked by Audrey DeBrooke, who was still sleeping peacefully between him and the key pad. Hefting himself up on an elbow, he reached for the key.

Almost... there... just another few–

"What the–" a sleepy voice grumbled.

Audrey tried to sit up, and things got tangled as James overbalanced and fell on her. His palm smacked the key as he fell, so the staff officer on the other side heard muffled swearing before a coherent answer.

"Stanton," James managed to grumble as Audrey pushed him off her.

"DeBrooke," she frowned and sat up.

"Governor, Admiral, pod just e-hypered in from Earth, marked from Eddie on *Felix*. Looks like he ran into a Faithful on the way out."

"We'll be down in ten minutes, Craig."

"Aye, ma'am, sir."

The comm cut and Audrey started to yawn.

James glanced at the clock, "It's 03:00. You'd think he could wait..."

He flopped back on the bed. Running a government wasn't all it was cracked up to be.

Audrey finished her lengthy yawn and lay back next to her husband, "You know you'd be annoyed if they didn't wake you for it."

"Of course I would... but did he have to send it *when* he did?"

Audrey smiled tiredly, "Stop playing martyr."

James' head tipped sideways to face Audrey, "Alright, let's get up then."
Audrey rolled over and closed her eyes again, "You first."

Eleven minutes later, the groggy Governor and Admiral entered Government House's C&C. Captain Craig Schwartz stood at the room's main holo tank, watching the camera footage of the old Faithful Battlecruiser hurtling down on *Felix.*

"Stupid bastard," a Lieutenant standing next to the senior staff officer muttered, and Schwartz nodded.

"Leave it to our Holy cousins."

Neither James nor Audrey bothered to announce themselves as they ambled to the plot. Audrey rubbed her eyes, "Well?"

Schwartz frowned, "You two look like hell."

James raised an eyebrow, "Pardon me, it's three *Gods-damned* o'clock. Normal humans sleep now, Craig. What's your excuse."

The Captain grinned and shrugged, "I'm above average."

James made the universal 'I'm going to throttle you' gesture and then winced at the holo, "*Felix* actually hit them?"

Schwartz shook his head, "Didn't have to, thank Gods. A long-carronade shot put them off their appetite, and Eddie didn't have to give up the missiles either. As far as we can tell, our Holy brethren got nothing more than a dose of common sense out of the exchange."

James grunted and Audrey 'hmmed'.

Schwartz frowned, "What?"

Audrey watched the approach of the Faithful ship, "They'll send more next time. If they actually have the Dreadnoughts our intel says they have, they'll use them."

The Commonwealth of the Faithful was indeed rumored to have two vintage Dreadnoughts on the line, as well as four old-style Battlecruisers. All bought at cost from the Church, probably with Church money.

Lovely universe.

At that moment the Freetown Navy — *Felix* excluded — had nothing tougher than a Battlecruiser, though most of what was on hand was upgraded and well maintained. Of course, that fleet lineup was changing thanks to Earther help, as *Felix's* fellows were being fitted out in Earther yards, and the new crown piece for the fleet was nearly ready.

But 'fitting out' didn't mean ready for war, only *getting* ready… and unfortunately it seemed war was getting very close.

Faithful attempts to stop Freetown convoys were edging closer to patent acts of war as it was. If they brought Dreadnoughts to play, not even *Felix* would be a gunnery match for them. Certainly, *Felix* would probably survive a hanging fire fight, though in rough shape. It'd almost certainly be out of action for a year, which did the small Freetown Navy no good at all.

So Freetown's fleet couldn't really hope to face the Faithful and all the ships the Genesis Church had handed over to that Commonwealth, until *Caine, Ursla,* and *Broadpaw* were brought online.

A month. The Freetowners needed a month.

"They might be waiting for the return trip," James said grimly. "If they try to catch us on a deep scan with more than we could pay for in the hold, they could accuse us and the Earthers of a conspiracy. And then they'd doubtless open fire. Trigger-happy bastards..."

Audrey nodded slowly — it was possible.

Quite possible, given the fanaticism of the Faithful. They were probably at least *aware* of the *Felix*-class and had to know Freetown would be tough to beat once modern Earther-built vessels joined the fleet. So the Churchers could be planning to attack sooner rather than later, and seeing free Earther war materiel moving towards Freetown might bring hostilities.

"They'd need an excuse just like that to fight, too," Schwartz's eyes narrowed. "If they claim they're battling a conspiracy, the Church can officially come in on their side."

This could potentially be the start of it, then. Admittedly, part of the rationale in sending *Felix* out with this convoy had been a test to see how far the Faithful would go. James and Audrey had just hoped things would have gone less belligerently than this.

Warning shots and that much implied aggression didn't bode well.

They'd have to send word to the Earthers that the finishing touches might need to be rushed at the yards, and they'd have to dispatch the crews for the four new ships to Earth immediately... no, *five* new ships — they'd have to blow the surplus and buy another *Felix*.

Well, they did have a contingency plan for all this.

"I'll get First Expeditionary ready to ship with the transports," Audrey heaved a sigh.

James nodded. A third of the Freetown Fleet, centered around the Heavy Cruiser *Grendelsbane City*, were detailed to escort the crew transports. The rest were to stay at home and protect the system, with the aid of orbital platforms.

They'd cruise to Earth and purchase the arms that would prepare Freetown for a war, in hopes of dissuading the Faithful from actually starting one.

CHAPTER 7

Sarah was sweating profusely.

She'd always been a committed fighter, sparring to remain in shape and to keep her temper in check. Back during the war she'd let the practice drop off — mainly due to exhaustion — and she credited that lack of a regular release with at least some of the blame for her personal issues during that period.

She'd had a rough time in those last months. It was no secret.

Now, with a job that *really* drove her out of her mind at times, she'd returned to her sparring. That was one of the benefits of the extended youth granted to her by Earther genetic treatments; though she was crawling past seventy, she was still *very* quick. Indeed, she was as quick as she'd been over forty years before when she had faced Beckett Lupus on a mat in *Cerberus'* gym.

And she was more experienced to boot.

As time progressed, she'd come to understand just how great fighters like Lupus achieved such amazing skill levels. Besides their fantastic physiology, the Earthers had *decades* to get things right — they lived long enough to experience virtually every imaginable type of opponent, and to advance themselves to a proficiency that was startling.

So Sarah was trying to do the same, though because her interest in regular sparring had admittedly lessened somewhat over the past decade, she'd increased the challenge by taking up a new weapon…

A dueling holo flipped across the open floor, rolling its sword in great arcs as it came. Sarah shuffled back slightly and rolled her wrist, bringing her own Earther-style, two-handed blade around in front of her to match. This was the new skill to master: swordplay.

After the Krogg War, the popularity of the sword had exploded. The Earthers' boarding actions and Lupus' stand on the surface of Krogg 'A' had been romanticized in popular myth with movies and pictures and all the other trimmings of the new free Genesis society, and the blades had become a symbol of the 'new' warfare.

Just about everyone on Genesis had rushed out and bought a sword for themselves, many even believing they knew how to use them.

The Earthers had proven quite partial to the weapons, though they had been less faddish about them. All flag officers surviving the battle at Krogg were given customized swords by the Admiralty, in recognition of their contribution.

Families of the deceased officers had been presented with well-crafted memorial blades as well. Some stayed on walls — like Pat's savage-looking, two-handed, straight-bladed, medieval-style broadsword that was hanging over this very sparring floor.

Sarah's was in her hand, and she'd gotten very used to it after a decade. Modeled directly on an Earther mass-production blade, it essentially took the shape of a Japanese katana, and it was as sharp as it needed to be to live up to its ancestor's reputation.

Of course, fencing with a holo didn't require Sarah to turn on the blade's atomic filament that would cause the sharp blade to act like a sub-molecular chainsaw. She could get away with the already honed metal edge. The holo's blade was sharp too, which made this training somewhat dangerous.

And satisfying. Because danger forced her to focus on matters that had nothing to do with running the planet.

Well, my half of the planet, evidently…

She winced — that sort of thinking was exactly what she was trying to avoid.

The holo was programmed to look like another human, with a blank expression. Hefting a sword like Sarah's, the simulation pressed closer now, and swung in fast from the side. Sarah moved with the agility she once used to back her fists, then smoothly intercepted her opponent's blade, parrying it ahead of her.

The holo made to lunge forward, but her sword narrowly deflected her opponent's, and she advanced, twitching her blade aside and making to stick it in the stomach. It backed away in time, squaring off at her advance and blocking her next attempt to reach it. Pushing ahead again, its blade blurred, and Sarah had to stop a slash coming down towards her head.

The parry left her stomach open and the holo drew back to take advantage of the gap in her guard. She dropped her wrist and her blade fell into the path of its swing, but she was forced back by the power of its strokes. Barely avoiding the assaulting strikes, she retreated across the floor and let the holo press on.

The thing's blade was moving with a quickness that seemed all too impossible, and it was whistling through the air as if it were real.

It advanced again, and Sarah continued to slide herself beyond its reach, changing the direction of her retreat to avoid the wall she was backing into. The holo moved to cut her off, and she tried pushing its defenses.

Her sword swung down but crashed against the holo's. Her wrist turned and an arching stroke brought her blade through a fast rotation that slashed up into what might have been an unguarded stomach — but the holo's sword was there to block hers. She still tried to force it back, and her blade flashed faster and rolled in blinding circles, each arc being punctuated by the clang of two colliding swords.

The holo reeled, its feet becoming more uncertain, but it recovered as Sarah eased off for less than a second to catch her breath, then came forward again. Sarah's blade now swung back to the defensive, trying to find an opening. She tracked back across the padded floor, through the brightly-lit sparring chamber of her home. The holo pushed harder, and she had to move with increasing speed to try to meet its strokes.

This was starting to look bad — she was literally getting forced into a corner as the holo spun and delivered a tough blow to her blade. Her sword fell from her hands.

The holo kept swinging, as it was programmed to, but Sarah dove handily out of its way, reaching fruitlessly for her blade. This didn't happen often, but when it did, it was damned embarrassing.

Only after *long* days did she get this careless.

She came to her feet but didn't stay in place as the holo came again. Dropping to one knee, she grabbed the thing's wrist, forcing its sword up and out of the way while her free fist drove into its gut. The projection staggered back, but as she came forward it took the sword in a single hand and swung it at her in a broad stroke, forcing her back long enough for its fist to find her jaw.

Knocked back in surprise, and tasting blood in her mouth, Sarah stumbled away from the holo and her sword, and made for the wall where Pat's blade was mounted–

It was gone.

Then Sarah saw a scruffy pair of shoes kicked off near the door, and a shabby coat on the bench. As she whirled back to the holo, Pat seemed to come out of nowhere. He *claimed* he never practiced with that broadsword, but he sure could move the meter-long piece of steel.

"I keep telling you," he roared in a huff, and Sarah realized he was yelling at her, "flashy moves get you bloody killed in here!"

Sarah was too busy catching her breath to bark back a comment, but she did watch as Pat steadied himself in one place on the floor, reducing his motions to their most abrupt and economic. The holo lunged forward at the new target, swinging in broad, glamorous arcs at a blinding speed, and Pat stepped back, parrying the blow that hurtled towards his left side, then recovering instantly and driving his broadsword straight through the projection.

"Simple!" he barked again, then ripped the blade out and let the holo drop to the mat and vanish. Breathing hard, he rolled his wrist up and laid the flat of the blade carefully on his shoulder.

Sarah straightened up a bit, "Thank you, dear."

Pat frowned, "I've said it a thousand times, stop the fluttery flashy stuff, it'll kill you. And for Gods' sake, you have to stop setting them on 'Grand Master of all deadly arts able to kill you with a glare'..."

He carefully hefted his sword and walked back to the wall, settling it into its wooden cradle, "Bad day at the office, was it?"

Sarah nodded jerkily, walking gingerly to the wall. She collected her sword carefully and set it in its slot next to Pat's, then leaned head-first against the wall.

"The Church wants us to catalogue the mothball fleet."

Pat cocked an eyebrow and let his shoulder rest against the wall, "A shopping list for our beloved Faithful?"

Sarah tried to nod, but with her forehead pressed against the wall it came out more like a shoulder wobble.

"So you come home and let a holo nearly knock your head off?"

She shrugged a bit, smiling despite herself, "Had to get the tension out... you know how I am."

Pat frowned, "There *are* other ways of getting rid of tension, Sarah."

Turning her head towards Pat she grinned, then rolled off the wall and moved closer to her husband, tugging at the shoulders of his shirt to straighten them a little, then looking up at him with a hint of mischief.

"Was that some sort of proposition, husband dearest?" she smiled.

"Gods *no*," Pat replied. "You've been fighting for Gods only know how long. You stink. Go shower while I make supper."

With that he turned away and walked to the door, collecting his coat and shoes. Sarah was left with an open-mouthed glare of surprise, directed fruitlessly at his back.

She didn't really smell *that* bad...

Well, maybe...

Hmm.

Shower.

CHAPTER 8

Christine Schaeffer had never before been aboard a Superdreadnought.

Her third-year training cruise had been on a Battlecruiser, and when she was a little girl, her father had taken her on a tour of a Dreadnought, but she'd never actually been aboard a *Super*dreadnought.

It was quite impressive, if something of an interruption to her day's plans.

She was actually supposed to be meeting friends to go see a movie… the latest hero film about the Krogg War — tripe drummed up for cheap entertainment, laden with inaccuracies that she and her buddies from the Academy would point out handily after it was over. This one was about an ArcColonel who supposedly fought at Gibraltar and somehow saved the day. The fact that every human ship at Gibraltar had been destroyed seemed to be missing from this dramatization, but then, what was history but something to get wrong in film? Tom Gillich was playing Graham Manchester in the movie, and Doug O'Keefe was playing Pat Conroy. Now she could say, with authority, that neither actor came *close* to the real characters.

Yes, she was going to be able to call all her friends to send her regrets about missing the movie, and then gloat mercilessly because she was on the *flagship*, hanging with the *real* heroes of the Krogg War…

And I might just be getting a job up here…

Well, she shouldn't assume too much just yet. She was aboard *Unity Genesis*, the biggest, best ship in the Genesis Navy, being assessed... the opportunity having come because she worked in the Panatorium where the greatest human Cruiser commander of all time came to replace a pan he'd melted making breakfast, and because her grandfather had known him and fought next to him half a century before.

It was barely believable. A circumstantial comedy that only an idiot would have come up with in bad fiction…

"Hmm… record looks alright…"

Christine was jolted back to reality and looked across the desk at Graham as he frowned at her file.

"One demerit in first year… what the hell is a 'Type Twelve'?" he looked up and she swallowed.

"It was nothing, sir… just… well, one of my instructors was being a bit… *stupid*. So I told him so."

Graham cocked an eyebrow, "Really?"

He laid the file on his desk and leaned back in his chair, steepling his fingers and examining her with slightly narrowed eyes, "Do tell."

She shrugged and swallowed nervously, "Well, it was ArcMajor Tremble... he taught strategy."

Frowning, Graham checked through his memory and came up blank, "Never heard of him."

A very brief smile crossed Christine's face and she nodded, "That's sort of the problem. He was telling my class he was in on the strategy at Krogg 'A', and he tried to take credit for the fallback deception."

Graham's eyebrows went right up. He hadn't been present when Caine, Ursla, and the other commanders had dreamed up that maneuver. He'd been told, however, that it had been at a meeting of senior strategists, and that certainly hadn't included some guy named Tremble.

"I checked into it after he said it, and it turns out he was an ArcEnsign on *Joseph Barron* at the time. So I sort of told him off in the middle of class."

"Aha..." Graham suppressed a smile at the young woman, "I see."

She ground her jaw nervously, not sure how the ArcGeneral was taking it.

"Well, nothing wrong with correcting a bit of misinformation, if you ask me," Graham leaned forward in his chair again and smiled. "I think that clears up your record."

A relieved smile crossed Christine's face, but before she could say anything, the office door opened and a woman in a marine's uniform stepped in, halting abruptly.

"Oh... sorry Graham..."

He was already on his feet, looking at his watch. Damn, he'd lost track of time. He rounded the desk, passed Christine, and smiled at his wife.

"I'm sorry I forgot! Didn't even realize the time..." he slid his arms around the waist of Gillian Hodge and she frowned curiously.

"You're in a good mood..."

His grin was infectious and it spread to her.

"What?" she tilted her head a bit.

Graham shrugged, "I'm going to be father... that makes me happy."

Gillian certainly got that sense, and she had to admit that despite the morning sickness, she was happy too. She was a good marine, but she'd spent the last forty years solely committed to that job. Now she had a chance to do start a family — and she *still* had the chance, despite being past sixty.

"We're going to have to celebrate then. Think we can get a reservation at the *Pulsar*?"

Graham grinned, "Most powerful human in space, dear. You know I can..."

Gillian was chuckling when she remembered the stiff-backed figure sitting opposite Graham's desk, "Um… am I interrupting though?"

Graham didn't realize what she was talking about for a second, then he blinked himself out of his fatherhood euphoria and glanced at Christine, "No, not at all… this is Christine Schaeffer, Bill Wallace's granddaughter. Christine, I'm sure you recognize my stunning, radiant, wonderful wife?"

Christine turned around awkwardly, "Good to meet you, ma'am."

Gillian, still smiling, nodded back, "No 'ma'am', I'm pleased to meet you…"

"She'll be filling in for Miranda for the rest of the summer," Graham inserted helpfully. "She's at the Academy, fourth year, and Pat ran into her this morning at a pan store."

Electing to ignore the confusing 'pan' reference, Gillian simply nodded, "Very good…"

Graham looked back to Christine, "There are forms you need to fill out. They'll be on my computer there. Password is 'donutchair'… d-o-n-u-t… no spaces. Fill them out, print yourself a Gold Pass and meet me here tomorrow morning at 08:30."

Christine, more than a little surprised at the abruptness and informality, tried to think of something so say, but Graham beat her to it, "Meanwhile, I'm taking my wife to dinner. See you in the morning."

Christine nodded very slowly, "Uh… yes, sir…"

Graham smiled and then motioned to the door, locking eyes with his wife, "Shall we?"

They left a rather shell-shocked Christine behind them.

What was a Gold Pass?

"Wasn't that a bit much to throw at her?" Gillian frowned at Graham as they walked leisurely through the corridor, his arm still happily around her waist.

He half-shrugged, "She needs to know what she's in for, so better she gets it sooner than later. And I think she has the right blood to get it sooner… now, about *names*…"

Gillian frowned, "What?"

"If it's a boy he's little Graham… a girl will be Grahamina."

Gillian laughed out loud, and Graham grinned.

"Maybe not…"

"He didn't bother to tell me!"

Pat was too busy chewing to look appalled, but Sarah dropped her fork onto her plate.

"He could have *called*. Left a *message*…"

Pat mused while he was still chewing, "I think he's a bit euphoric just now. I mean, he's hiring that Christine girl from the pan shop to replace Miranda, not that she's unqualified. But you know Graham, he's supposed to grumble and ruminate for days on matters like that..."

Sarah frowned, "Bill Wallace's granddaughter, you said?"

Pat nodded, loading more fish onto his fork, "The very same. Had some interesting family details to share that'll really work in *The Earther Equation*. Did you know he had a common law wife?"

"I honestly didn't know him that well, Pat," Sarah's eyes were beginning to glaze over at the history talk. She loved Pat dearly; history... not so much.

"Well he did. All through the war, and he didn't tell too many people about it. But he apparently wrote plenty of letters home, and Christine promised she'd send me copies. Hopefully Graham won't overwork her, I really could use those letters..."

Sarah tried valiantly to sound interested, "Oh yes, letters are very exciting indeed."

Pat shoveled the last of his food into his mouth and chewed with mock sulkiness.

"Well, if you want me to take my books elsewhere, I will."

Sarah dropped her fork and knife on the plate, "How about upstairs? I don't stink anymore."

Pat laid his own utensils on his plate and grinned, "No, you certainly don't..."

Things were happy on Genesis.

And then a thought struck him: happiness was never a good portent.

He was a historian, he knew that for a fact.

Oh well, it could be worse. *Unhappiness* could be a bad portent. There'd be nothing redeemable about the situation were that the case.

Right now, he was still living in a comfortable house, and working in a field he really enjoyed.

And then there was Sarah.

Very good indeed.

CHAPTER 9

Ecclesia was a lush jungle planet, with very little natural water above the surface, but plenty running through veins beneath the upper layer of bedrock. Ecologically, it was much like Genesis, which made it a natural choice as the homeworld for the new Commonwealth of the Faithful.

Its main city, Faithville, cut an even less subtle skyline against its surroundings than its name did on a map, dark buildings made of cheap but effective prefab alloys rising into the orange atmosphere. There was little in the colony that was not functional; it had been developed by its founder over thirty years before to be a perfect specimen of monastic faithfulness.

Now it was home to over a million faithful humans, all bent on the defeat of the heretics and heathen, and on the fulfillment of the Holy Quest. No sympathizers would be spared... no prisoners taken.

It was a simple and pleasant direction for the colony, its great mission as mandated by the Church. Free from the restrictions of Congress and the President's Office, it could act however it pleased to better the position of the true faith in this galaxy, and ultimately, would be the tool through which the Chancellors of Genesis could retake what was rightfully theirs...

Sooner than Chancellor Gregory Paine would have expected just a few days before.

He was a tall, slight man, with a pointed chin and a head of short-cropped, blonde hair. He had been born an Ecclesian, and now he led the colony as its Grand Chancellor. This was *his* world, *his* duty to the Quest. And unlike others, he would not be weak...

At thirty he was only a young man, but his youth came with a vigor that matched the fire of this colony. While he hadn't witnessed the corruption that had gripped once-Holy men like Harvey Bingham, he'd seen the fallout of their heretical practices — he'd watched the public destruction that had broken the Genesis Church and driven its faithful underground by the millions.

Gregory Paine would never undertake such monstrous misdeeds against the Gods. Indeed, the Ecclesia colony was, to him, the avatar of the *true* Church — the refuge of the true faith from the Earthers who sought to destroy it. The heathen Earthers and their human friends.

Paine's eyelids fluttered angrily as he pictured the heretic heads of the civilian government; soon enough, those non-believers would be removed. Very soon, indeed — sooner that anyone beyond Ecclesia might have expected. The direct rival of the Faithful was positioning itself to fight; the Freetowners were forcing the timetable, and Paine could not afford to hold back any longer.

Turning away from the tall window of Faithville's Main Council Chamber, he looked over his eight seated companions, assembled here to deal with this very issue. Each man was clad in the same kind of long red robe Paine himself wore, each was younger than his counterpart of Genesis. Together, they looked up at him with an appropriate amount of brotherhood and reverence — he was not the *High* Chancellor, for only a Genesis clergyman could be awarded that title, but he warranted respect over these lessers.

As was right, then, his fellows bowed their heads slightly as his gaze swept over them. He linked his hands behind his back and his eyes narrowed at the orange light flooding the room behind him, "We are certain it was one of their *new* vessels?"

He addressed the Chancellor of War, Thomas Leo, who bowed his head in acknowledgement, "Shaspa Karton was certain, Grand Chancellor. The ship fired a long-carronade at him, and was of a completely new design."

The War Chancellor keyed a panel before him, activating the wall screen opposite Paine, "The vessel, as can be seen here, is a bastard of Earther and Genesis design — precisely the sort of heathen ship we would expect of the Freetown pirates."

Paine nodded slowly and moved to stand at the back of his empty chair. While growing up, he had been taught to hate the humans of *Freetown*. They were the worst of the scum, servants of the devils who had not only accepted the Earther lies, but had also eagerly spread them.

And now they were being armed by even greater servants of the devils. The Earthers, with their dominant technology, veiled themselves behind a façade of innocence and geniality. Any faithful man knew that the image of a beast, no matter how well-dressed, remained just what it truly was — a savage creature, against all Godliness. There was nothing redeemable in the Earthers; they were monsters sent to keep Earth from those to whom the Gods meant it to belong.

But that, as yet, was not something the Faithful could concern themselves with. There was little the Fleet of the Commonwealth could do to weaken the Earthers aside from defeating the scum pirates... that and help the Church on Genesis start its coup. The Genesis Chancellors' Council had been planning that particular incident for thirty years now, at first behind the backs of moderate, corrupt High Chancellors like Bingham and Argyle, but now with the support of the entire Chancelleries of both Genesis and Ecclesia.

As was to be expected, the Navy remained woefully ignorant. They were but rustic and simple technicians, who had never learned subterfuge. Politics had been the province of the Church since the landing on Genesis; that skill would now restore the servants of the Gods to their place at the head of human civilization.

In any case, the time was now proving propitious for action, even though a year still remained until the ideal target date agreed upon long ago with the High Chancellor. It now seemed evident that the Freetown scum had become aware of the Dreadnoughts purchased by the Faithful Navy, and had moved to counter the reinforcement with the production of their new bastard-devil ships. These new devil-ships would potentially be able to stop the thrust of the Faithful armada.

But they weren't ready just yet.

Paine was a student of strategy. He had been instructed that the ways of war needed to be understood in order for the faith to be preserved. His education had taught him the ineptitude of the first Churchmen to face the Earthers — of Bactule and Bingham — so Paine had studied the art of war in order to protect his faith more fully.

The Krogg War had provided blessed examples from which to learn much, so he had examined each campaign carefully, noting the many instances of Earther evil and stupidity. He *knew* how to beat them, and how to beat the renegades. The solutions were in principle so very simple, it was only a matter of waiting until the moment was right.

But that latter point was moot: the Faithful would have to launch an attack before the Freetowners could marshal their new forces. The ships of the Gods would have to strike at the Freetown convoy, and then in secret, attack Freetown itself. Whatever was beyond the system would be wiped out, and then the system itself would fall to the force of the Gods.

"We will have to move before we had ordained," Paine related his thoughts dryly. "Chancellor Leo, will your Holy Fleet be able to intercept the Freetown convoy on its return from Earth?"

The War Chancellor bowed, "Our Battlecruiser remains on station near their expected route home. I can have the fleet join it in but a single day, including all three of our Dreadnoughts, Grand Chancellor."

Paine nodded, "Lead them to victory, brother Leo. But at the same time, we must send a message to our brother Chancellors in Genesis. They must know that we go to war before the planned time, and they must be ready to effect their coup."

"Will they be able to prepare at such short notice, Grand Chancellor?" another of the assembled asked humbly.

Paine took a deep breath and nodded slowly, resting his hands lightly on the back of his chair. His last words from High Chancellor Pious had reassuringly claimed that the coup could be launched at will, but that the longer the delay, the better the speed with which power could be seized.

There was no time now — no option to wait. To delay a year, even scant *months*, would endanger the Faithful's ability to defeat Freetown. So they had to move immediately, there was no other option.

This was the will of the Gods.

Freetown would fall, the evidence of Earther treachery would be made public, and as the civilian government on Genesis tried to halt conflict in the face of damning evidence, the Church would call to its loyal followers to rise up and destroy the heretics.

The Earthers were supplying arms to Freetown without pay; the civilian government was covering it up — or so it would appear. And so the people would rise, rally to the Church, and the great new ships of the Genesis Fleet would fly to Earth.

With their tremendously downsized Navy, and lulled by forty years of peace into a false sense of security, the Earther devils would be crushed before they realized the force arrayed against them.

Yes, that would be the way of it — the Gods would not be denied again. If necessary, Paine would give his life to see to that.

So the Grand Chancellor nodded to his fellows, “We must have faith. We will send our second energy-hyper cutter to Genesis to warn them. Our first will return to the Battlecruiser and inform it of war.”

The Faithful had only two cutters, both of Earther construction from the Krogg War. The crews were specially picked Holy warriors, chosen first for their faith in battling the evil of the devils’ machines, and second for their technical ability to keep those aged craft in operation.

It struck Paine as ironic: the Earthers would be caught totally unawares while the Faithful letters prescribing their doom traveled on their own vintage ships.

“Go in peace, brothers. Send word to our Faithful of war,” Paine’s words were soft as his mind wrapped around the concept.

The Earthers would be left friendless, alone…

Unprepared.

CHAPTER 10

It was a beautiful, bright, cold Antarctic day. Off to the east, a large body of Emperor Penguins eyed Antarctic Base curiously as a horde of the human-shaped animals milled about it. The penguins weren't capable of the higher thought required to understand the predicament of those upright animals — they knew them as loud but generally agreeable tenants on the Antarctic Plain, who'd cut the handy canals in from the coast, allowing fishing without too much migration. Now the animals were massing in considerable numbers...

Indeed, on the flanks of a massive elevated platform at the center of Landing Field Sixteen, some 10,000 marines of the Second (Heavy) Division were standing at attention, their khaki uniforms crisp and their rifles held in front of them in a respectful pose. In front of the platform, another 30,000 Earthers stood silently — civilians of all sorts who had been invited to the ceremony or had simply been interested in seeing the famed Earthers on the stage.

The Krogg War veterans tended to draw a big crowd wherever they went, Setter Caine particularly.

And he had to admit it actually made him a *little* nervous, something few people would have believed.

"Marines, stand at *attention*."

The order was given very softly from the podium by General Karyn Kudlee, the great bear herself a veteran of the Krogg War. Her words carried into the headsets of the marines and were simultaneously pitched out over the crowd by the powerful speakers on the stage.

There was an instant ground tremor and thud as the 10,000 marines of the Heavy Division brought their boots down in unison on the alloy-clad landing field. Rifle butts followed quickly, and in a smart, crisp, almost mechanical maneuver, the marines were locked into their most respectful parade poses. They'd done this for every speaker up to now — from Varnon to Andra — but this particular evolution seemed somehow crisper.

Kudlee stepped back from her podium and gestured to Caine, and he stood from his chair to spontaneous applause from the civilians. He smiled at the response and glanced at the big bear who'd been sitting next to him.

Andra Ursla shrugged in reply, then pointed at the podium, "Say something prophetic. Pat'll put it in a book."

Caine pretended to look thoughtful as he carefully crossed the platform, stopping briefly to shake Karyn Kudlee's hand and then nodding to the twelve Consuls of the Earther Consulate. Varnon Broadpaw — who'd just given his speech after his appointment as First Consul — smiled at Setter, then bounced his eyebrows up and down.

Good old Varnon.

Moving to the podium, Setter paused to look to either flank at the well-dressed marines. They really hadn't needed to assemble the whole Division for this...

But Varnon had planned the ceremony, and that meant it had to be showy, and public opinion seemed to side with the First Consul. Earthers enjoyed honoring their heroes.

I suppose that includes me...

Caine smiled and waved to the crowd, then stepped up onto the step behind the podium.

First Lord... oh wait, no, he'd given that up forty years ago.

First Consul... no, that was Varnon now.

Citizen Caine leaned forward slightly, and grasped the sides of the podium, "You're all too kind. Most people get a card for their retirement... this... well, this really is much better."

There were cheers from the crowd, and Caine smiled as he remembered his face was being enlarged in a massive holo projection behind the platform. He wanted to look happy and comfortable — this was probably going to be his last public address. He was retiring from the Consulate after thirty years at its head. He'd go back to his more relaxing interests and live out his last fifty years in peace.

Maybe he'd travel.

Well, whatever he decided to do, he'd enjoy it.

It wasn't that being on the Consulate had been that difficult — the Earther ruling committee was comprised of good people, and the population readily assisted it in making decisions and carrying them out. It was as harmonious as everything else in Earther society, but he'd been doing it for thirty years, to cap his twelve decades in the Navy. He'd spent a century and a half at work for the public, and he was now inclined to opt for some rest.

"I'm really not all that sure what I can say, aside from giving you my tremendous thanks. I know you'll be in good hands with Varnon, here–" he waved his hand at Broadpaw, who grinned, "–but other than that... well, I've never been all that good at speeches..."

"Oh come on!" someone yelled loudly from the crowd.

"We all know better than that!" another added.

There were laughs and Caine grinned, "Alright, alright..."

He paused again, his eyes sweeping over the thousands of Earthers before him, and then his smile broadened, "A number of decades ago we were at war...

and that's where I was, specifically speaking. By the end of that conflict, we'd lost many good people. We all lost someone close to us, and we all know what that was like. And yet here we are. We were told in no uncertain terms by our enemy that we'd bring destruction to a great many things. We were even left to question whether we were the kind of beings we believed we were."

Caine tilted his head very slightly.

"Well, we have our answer. We have grown but we haven't really changed, and that's a credit to all of you — and to all of us. We've faced our losses, we've dealt with some rather unfortunate circumstances, and we've begun to repair the damage caused by the war. We've even helped our old enemies find a way around the violence their Queen prescribed for them. And it hasn't been easy."

There were "hear hears," and a general murmur — albeit a loud murmur, given the setting — of agreement.

"I've had the benefit of watching this happen from the top, of seeing it *all*. Your efforts. Your struggles. *Our* struggles. And all I can say is that I'm proud to have been part of it. We've stayed true to ourselves over all these years, done what we said we would... And I am *fully* confident that we'll be able to keep that up, no matter what fate throws at us."

A great roar immediately rose from the crowd — drawing startled stares from a few thousand penguins — and Caine's smile reached its apogee. The Earthers in front of the platform waved and called out, "We'll miss you... best of luck... see you around..."

Caine waved back, "And don't get nostalgic yet. I'm not dropping off the edge of galaxy, I'm just retiring!"

A surge of laughter, "Where you going for vacation?"

Shrugging, Caine leaned forward a bit, "I've got an old crocodile friend in Africa. Took my leg off once. I think I'll go see him. And I promised my family a bit of travel. I think Andra's going to muscle in on that too..."

He turned away from the crowd and beckoned Ursla to the podium. She shook her head a couple of times but the crowd encouraged her to her feet. She walked slowly to the side of the podium and waved to the crowd.

"You all know I'm only retiring to keep him out of that croc's stomach!" she announced with a grin, her holo filling the air next to his.

The audience laughed and cheered, "You'll be back?"

Ursla smiled and shrugged, "I've been at the Admiralty since he's been with the Consulate... but yes, I'll probably be back. When Varnon decides he wants to retire. But this isn't all about me, is it? I got my retirement card at a nice little reception at Admiralty House, and Fox even gave me a gift basket. The presence of the Heavy Division means we're talking about this wolf — pester him, not me!"

Caine grinned as Ursla stepped aside, and he looked back out over the crowd, "Well, I'm not sure what else you can pester out of me..."

"We'll think of something!"

Caine chuckled, and the crowds roared with laughter.

"Alright then... I think I should leave you to think it over. Looks like the penguins are starting to get nervous."

There were more cheers and applause, and Caine held up a hand and waved, then carefully stepped back off the podium as Karyn Kudlee returned to close the ceremonies.

Caine and Ursla stood rather awkwardly, both waving.

Heroes were retiring.

CHAPTER 11

The post-ceremony reception was considerably less crowded than the Antarctic event — Caine's Newfoundland estate was only sixteen uncleared acres, and he didn't have enough food for tens of thousands of attendees.

Not to mention the marines.

Here he had about thirty guests for an informal get-together, including as many Krogg vets as could make it… and a few others. The veterans were the ones who had occupied most of his time during the gathering — everyone from Artemis Tigar to Ursla to Varnon were recalling the better memories from the old days, and eating heartily.

It was good to be in their company again…

Of course, many of them had new jobs; the First Lord of the Admiralty was Labrador Forepaw, the First Space Lord was Fox Magnus, and the Comptroller of the Navy Board was Dran Nightclaw, to begin with. Those three in particular now commanded and operated the Navy Caine had left decades before — the fleet that now had been so downsized.

Downsized. We've downsized.

Caine sat quietly at a picnic table as he thought of that decline in Naval strength, and the wind seemed to pick up with his thoughts. It would probably start raining soon, and then it'd be sunny until it snowed this afternoon… nothing quite like Newfoundland weather, as far as he knew.

"We'll have the last *Venerable* on the line next week…"

Looking up, Caine forced a small smile for Lab Forepaw, "I know that."

Lab shrugged, "Well, now you know even better. Mind if I sit?"

Caine shook his head and settled himself more comfortably onto the bench, "So that puts the fleet up to strength again. Six squadrons of *Venerables* and three of *Champions*?"

Forepaw nodded and set a plate of fish on the table, "We've finished moving the *Champions* back to the secondary duties on schedule, except for the squadron Chronos Claw has out at the Krogg corridor. Last of the *Chimeras* was put on reserve status yesterday."

Lab was the leading authority on the workings of the peacetime Navy. When Setter had retired, the Admiralty had decided to split the job of First Lord — Setter's job throughout the war — into two positions, thus reintroducing the post of First Space Lord. The 'First Space Lord' had responsibility for fleet operations and could spend ample time in space, while the 'First Lord of the Admiralty' stayed with the Admiralty on Earth and coordinated the entire war effort, being the senior Lord. During the Krogg War, the Admiralty had been forced to improvise with Setter's absence; that would no longer be a problem if another conflict drew the fleet away from Earth.

Under the new model, Lab Forepaw ran the Admiralty and the Navy with the same precision and judgment he'd demonstrated while in command of *Orion* forty years before, and no one doubted the validity of his rapid rise in rank to the First Lordship. He was probably the most respected officer in the fleet... and exactly the sort of paternal leader people expected a First Lord to be.

"What are you two doing talking about fleets without me!?" Fox Magnus was the other guy — the First Space Lord.

He was still the dashing young rogue who'd saved many a day during the war — first with *Flame* and then with *Atlas*. His style hadn't changed at all over four decades — a fact that surprised many human observers, but was no shock to most Earthers. Forty years sounded like a long time for short-lived humans; to Fox, it had just been long enough for him to shake the last shadows cast by his Krogg War days, and to win back his optimism. Because of the relative lack of out-of-system operations, he spent most of his time at home now, hanging around the Admiralty and tormenting Lab, just as he always had.

The Earthers wouldn't have it any other way.

Fox was charismatic and seemed plain *crazy* sometimes, whereas Lab was reliable and even-tempered. They were a very odd pair... but between them, they'd brought the Earther Navy to a level of quality never before seen.

And Setter was proud of them both.

"Don't worry, I only mentioned the *Venerables*."

Fox arrived at the wooden picnic table and swung himself onto the bench next to Forepaw, "Yep, all of them built now."

Caine nodded again, "Like I said, I know that."

Lab and Fox exchanged glances and the latter, smaller Admiral shrugged, "Alright."

"So what's the fleet standing at now?" Caine leaned forward, always interested in Navy talk, even if he knew the answers and was anxious about them. There was something dark coalescing in the back of his awareness... he could only assume it was the status of the fleet.

Things *had* changed. Decades ago, the Earthers had met the humans with 1,800 ships of all types, and then they'd finished the Krogg War with around 3,000...

"We've got 192 front line ships with the commissioning of *Colossus*, 112 secondary, and 256 ships in reserve," the numbers rolled easily off Lab's tongue, and Fox nodded in agreement, waving his hand in the First Lord's general direction.

"What he said."

Setter nodded and endeavored to smile, burying a sigh with some effort. The fleet had no reason to be overly large these days, even with the unsettling noises coming out of Genesis and the Commonwealth of the Faithful. Only 302 ships with full crews aboard, 256 ships at reserve status... 560 ships for a fleet that had once been over six times that size.

Though for all the difference in numbers, it was true that these were greater ships than those that had faced the Kroggs. After the war, the Carrier developments pioneered by Draco Maximane had been reassessed based on the suggestion he made just before his death at Krogg 'A', and more firepower became a big goal for new designs.

That need for gunnery power had combined with the long-standing problem of finding gunboats to cover ships of the line, and had resulted in three hybrid classes. The aged *Chimeras* were essentially *Engadine*-class Carriers with less deck space and an increased number of guns. The newer *Champions* were 100-gun ships with 60 boats each. Neither class quite lived up to the ultimate hope, so the Navy Board, under the leadership of Dran Nightclaw, had called for a ship that could better *Orion's* broadside by half, and could carry as many boats as an *Engadine.*

The result was the *Venerable*-class.

Nothing that had ever existed *anywhere* had the sort of firepower carried by a *Venerable,* and the Earthers had built forty-eight of the great ships. At 250 guns and 115 boats to a ship, they were massive, and with the advantages of new drives and more efficient reactors, they were able to maneuver at least as handily as *Orion* had, if not more so.

They were now the core of the fleet, backed by new classes of frigates and sloops which had seen similar growth and enhancement. So the 192 front line ships of the Earther Navy were, admittedly, more than a match for the 350-odd front line ships of the Genesis Fleet. But with that indiscernible dark feeling still eating at him, Setter wondered if they were enough.

Enough for what? After all, the Earthers were at peace, and Sarah Manchester was looking after the Genesis government... it wasn't as though war was over the horizon...

Still, Genesis had a massive mothball and reserve fleet. Something in the order of 1,600 ships to add to their active forces. Calling up their older ships, the Earthers would have only 560... quality was an edge, but against four-to-one odds, there would be plenty of needless blood spilled.

Well, maybe that was inevitable...

Lab cleared his throat, and Caine blinked.

Oh, right. He was at a party.

"I also got some interesting news this morning," the First Lord said, cutting a piece of fish for himself. "Ed Jeffries came in with *Felix* and a convoy. They had a little run-in with a Faithful Battlecruiser. We got a pod from Freetown shortly afterward, and they're sending Audrey and the First Expeditionary out to help escort the convoy home."

"And to order another *Felix*-class, and to bring crews for *Caine, Ursla, Broadpaw,* and *Republic,*" Fox added with a cocked eyebrow. "They want the yards to accelerate shakedowns. They're figuring on war soon."

Caine ground his jaw slightly and nodded, "Did they exchange shots — Ed and the Faithful?"

Lab tilted his head slightly, "Warning shots. Nothing struck home."

Well, that was something at least...

Perhaps this was the origin of the dark feeling unsettling Setter. War would put Earth and Genesis on opposite sides — at least in terms of who they backed. The Consulate had long recognized the dangers involved in supporting Freetown, but the risks had been ones rightly taken. The Freetowners deserved what the Earthers were giving them — as did the people of Genesis, but for the resistance of the Church.

War would obviously complicate things, as Freetown would buy supplies from Earther yards and factories, while the Faithful would buy from Genesis. Some of the more radical humans would demand that the Earthers be *forced* to stop supplying Freetown. And the Church would agree.

If things got out of hand, it could be war between the two great powers.

And that certainly had to be why Caine feared for the small Earther Navy.

Lab read that thought all over his old commander's face, "Don't worry."

Caine blinked twice again, "Why not?"

Glancing at Fox, the First Lord smiled, "This morning we ordered the unpacking of the First Provisional at Io. When I leave here, I'll order the unpacking of the Second at Mars. We're getting the modernization process going... just in case."

Caine cocked an eyebrow, "You ran that by Varnon?"

Broadpaw was standing behind Caine listening with a smile, "They did."

Craning his neck around, Caine frowned, "It could be seen as an act of war..."

Varnon held up his free hand, then forced the end of a donut into his mouth with the other, "Mmmph phdmfedumph mmphduoo."

Caine's head tipped, and Varnon swallowed, "It may be a deterrent instead. Remind the Church that the fleet that beat the Kroggs can be returned to space."

"And modernized," Fox added quickly.

That was true. Just as a precaution, the Earthers had left themselves a bit of a leg-up in mobilization — 1,500 of the best-kept survivors of the Krogg War hadn't been broken up, but had instead been disassembled and packed in rather large 'boxes' (storage crates) orbiting various Earther stations. They weren't easily assembled, but given a few months they could all be recommissioned with upgrades, as compared to the year or more it would take Earther industry to build the same number of ships from scratch.

Still, nostalgia aside, Caine didn't count on them too much. A war with Genesis could be over in only *weeks*. If it happened.

Either way, the Earthers *would* win, Caine didn't doubt that. His fear was for the cost in lives...

"Don't worry, dad."

The fifth Earther to enter the conversation smiled at the four old warhorses, "All of you stop making him worry... go on, Fox! Thena's been looking for you!"

The First Space Lord glanced between his fellows, "Right, better go find her..."

Lab grinned, "You married types."

Fox shrugged, "Be careful — could happen to you one day."

He climbed out of the picnic table bench and sauntered off. Lab looked at Broadpaw, "Well, we should talk about foreign policy, Varnon... us being in charge now and all."

Varnon nodded, "Frightening, isn't it."

Lab grinned and nodded to Caine as he too climbed out of the picnic table, "Very."

The pair wandered off, and Caine raised an eyebrow as his son settled in Lab's place. Phealan Caine was in his late forties now, and was just out of school, still shopping around for a career that would please him.

The younger Caine smiled and pushed a plate carrying a large slab of cake at his father. He didn't look all that much like his dad — he'd gotten his tan streaks from Elandra's side of the family. But there was no mistaking the eyes, and the same frank expression Caine so often used to wear.

"That for me?"

Phealan shrugged, "I think mom's cut me off. I ate one of the cakes by myself."

Setter chuckled, "*Right*. I ever tell you about that time at the Academy when I ate a double-decker alone?"

"Yes."

Caine frowned, "That's good, so you'll be right with me when I tell it again."

"I'm going to eat that cake if you start talking."

A mock frown crossed Setter's face, "Well in that case..."

He pulled the plate in closer and started hacking off forkfuls.

Behind him Ursla appeared with two pieces of cake, "Brought you some... oh."

Phealan waved at the blank spot on the table in front of him, "That'd be *mine*."

Ursla grinned and carefully sat down at the table, sliding the less generous of the two slabs of cake over to the junior Caine.

He grinned and started hacking into it.

It started to rain.

CHAPTER 12

Christine had a Gold Pass. And she had her paperwork filed. It was official, she was working for the legend — *the* Graham Manchester.

Graham was the father of the Genesis Carrier program. Commander of the battleships at Krogg 'A'. Head of the present Genesis Fleet. He wasn't the same sort of flash-and-bang officer as his sister — she had the ability to get into tons of trouble and still fight her way out. He was the more sensible one. And many of Christine's classmates believed he was boring because of that.

Well, that was *blatantly* untrue.

She'd already survived a day with him. He'd tested her to make sure she could handle the pressure, but hadn't been cruel about it. Things seemed to be falling into place — things that would be important for her career… and she was working with the *legend*, living aboard *Unity Genesis* as of last night.

It was *tiring*, but it was *great*.

And she'd get used to being tired, once she calmed down and got into her groove. But she was too excited to do that now.

So instead she was indulging in one of her hobbies at the ungodly hour of 05:20, practicing with the sword the Earthers had presented to her family for the services of her grandfather. It was a stylish weapon — a long and elegant saber, well suited for her hand, that had been left to her by her grandmother.

Christine had started fencing long before the Academy, and had been Captain of the Academy team since third year. It was both a hobby and stress relief, and she was really quite handy with a sword. She preferred the single-handed grip — probably because she'd grown up using it — and even though most one-handers could be beaten easily by a two-handed sword, her speed and ability allowed her to deal with the more powerful strokes.

That speed and skill was something she was demonstrating this morning. *Unity Genesis* was fitted with an Earther-designed sword program, complete with opponents of all sizes and shapes and blades. Christine had never actually been able to practice on a full simulator before — the Academy wasn't permitted too much new Earther tech, thanks to the Church regulations.

But now she was on the flagship, and with an hour until the next duty shift change, she was determined to work out her nervous energy by spending an hour vanquishing holo-foes in an abandoned gym.

•••

Graham swung his legs heavily out of bed and groaned. Gillian quickly capitalized on the vacancy to pull his share of the blankets to her side, and she snuggled down deeper against the cool air of the room.

Wincing at the chrono, Graham read '05:30' and 'harrumphed' at his punctuality. Thanks to what must have been an alarm clock buried somewhere in his psyche, he was able to wake up on time as a matter of course. Every night he decided when to wake up, and the next morning he woke up at exactly that time.

And on a morning like this, that meant at an unholy hour.

For crying out loud, it was 05:30 in the morning. Nobody since the Quest had set reveille that early — for a very good reason. Graham would never have allowed it. But this early hour was the only time he could regularly learn the art of swordplay without the crew seeing how supposedly bad he was with a blade…

"Oh Gods…"

He flopped back onto the bed and propped his head on his wife's side. She shifted her arm and nudged him, "You pretty much *begged* Beckett for these sessions. You can't leave him at the lock."

"He's a good guy, he'd understand…"

Gillian rolled back towards Graham, awkwardly sliding his head off her side and onto the bed, "Go on. I'll keep the bed warm."

Graham frowned, "Lot of bloody good a warm bed does if I don't get to crawl back into it."

No reply.

"Eh?"

Snoring.

"Ah for the love of–"

"Good morning, George."

General Beckett Lupus, as always, sounded quite chipper, despite the early hour. ArcEnsign George Rumpsfeld, on the other hand, didn't want to be awake, but he had the duty shift that made sure he was awake every Thursday night and Friday morning, supervising the airlocks linking *Unity Genesis* to *Genesis One*. An officer had to be on duty at the airlock at all times to make sure no undesirables drifted aboard — or more precisely, to make sure the spacers at the locks stayed awake.

And if a dignitary was coming aboard…

Well, by now, General Lupus wasn't so much a dignitary as a regular. He came aboard every Thursday, *very* early, so that he and the ArcGeneral could do some fencing. Fencing was the 'in' thing for senior officers, it seemed. Everyone had to know how to use a sword.

Rumpsfeld liked the pistol himself, or better yet, the *rifle*.

But he wasn't a flag officer, and he hadn't fought the Kroggs, so maybe he wasn't so qualified to judge.

And of course, no human was qualified to judge the General. Rumpsfeld had a number of friends who didn't care for the Earthers, and he knew a lot of people who didn't trust them, but personally, he thought rather highly of them. They were literally *awesome*, in the original meaning of the word.

As he always told the many skeptics, you just didn't doubt them once you'd met one, even just briefly. Especially when that brief meeting was with one the caliber of Beckett Lupus — the most battle-tested marine officer alive. He'd been in almost all the big battles of the Krogg War, and his reputation with his sword had been much-heralded in the old war holos.

And he was really quite friendly.

"Good morning, sir," it was a much-delayed response to the General's greeting, and the gray wolf grinned at the young human.

"Only forty-five more minutes, George. You can hold on."

The ArcEnsign suppressed a groan and Lupus patted him on the shoulder as he walked past, "I'm off to see the ArcGeneral."

"Yessir," Rumpsfeld slouched against the frame of the airlock as Lupus vanished down the corridor.

Graham was still trying to wake up as he came out of his cabin... and walked straight into Lupus as the Earther stopped at the door. Their collision came with a dull thud, and Graham looked up.

"Oh. Mornin', Beckett. How are you?"

Lupus grinned and stepped back, "We can start doing this in the evenings, you know."

Graham heaved a long sigh, "I have meetings. And I'd be embarrassed if anyone else saw me."

Pulling on the second glove to his fencing garb, he blinked a couple of times and waved down the hall, "After you, my good General."

Offering a mock-bow, Lupus set the pace through the abandoned corridors of the Superdreadnought. Like Graham, he wore what had now become the standard Genesis sword-practice gear: an all-white suit that fit neatly but not restrictively, formed out of a fiber meshed with alloy to stop sword strokes.

In Genesis space, the practice of sparring with Earther shields had gone by the wayside a couple of decades before, when shields had become especially hard to get — thanks to the Church (shields were supposedly endangering local body armor industries, so a prohibitive tariff barrier had gone up).

Graham, wearily putting one foot in front of the other as they paced down the corridor, let his hand settle on his sword's hilt.

Wait.

No, maybe he put his hand in the wrong spot.

"Oh Gods. Forgot my sword again."

He turned back around, and Lupus suppressed a chuckle, "I'll meet you there."

Christine scrolled through the catalogue of opponents in the computer database, looking for something she hadn't faced before. She wasn't familiar with the interface that provided the higher-level opponents, so it wasn't going as smoothly as it should have.

A few screens back she'd managed to access the Earther database — that in itself was a considerable accomplishment. In her previous training facilities, she hadn't been able to even look at a database of Earther opponents, and she had to admit she was eager to see how she'd fare against one of the much-vaunted fighters. Or at least a simulation of one.

Now she just needed to pick a species, skill level, and the armament! Ooh — that was a novel feature. Options included a long sword, two short swords, daggers, bare hands… the Earthers really did have some impressive holo technology.

This was so much better than her Academy simulator.

She'd have to choose something mid-range, then — for all her confidence Christine was not insane. A three-meter bear with a two-meter sword would not be forgiving. Cats were supposed to be very sly and hard to get a fix on. That left wolves — generally regarded as a healthy blend of the qualities of the other two, at least in the books she'd read.

Hmm.

Skill level 'Easy'. No point disillusioning herself on the first try.

And weapons… she knew best how to fight a single long sword, so that would be it.

She tapped the screen a few times, and the holo generator began to hum. Flipping her blonde pony tail over the shoulder of her white fencing suit, she tugged her helmet on and hefted her sword.

Then the holo computer made a disagreeable sound, and red words flashed across it. She frowned and turned to check the floor. There was an Earther standing there, so whatever the problem was didn't seem to be affecting the holo.

Taking a deep breath she walked away from the panel, watching the Earther as she closed with it. He was wearing the traditional Genesis fencing garb and had *two short swords* in his belt. Ahh, that must have been the glitch.

Christine slowly approached the Earther with her blade dipped towards the matted floor, then instinctively raised the saber's hilt to her visor in salute. The Earther seemed to frown as it watched her — as if trying to figure out why a human would be seeking a fight.

Excellent programming.

Nothing to do but have at it then...

Christine drew her saber up overhead into a hanging guard, then lunged forward with a few testing cuts. The Earther actually looked shocked—probably because he was set on easy — and he leapt backward, quickly drawing his two short swords and bringing them into a defensive position.

She hadn't faced too many double-sworded opponents before... well, she'd have to attack, keep the initiative...

Again she lunged across the floor — quickly, with quite a lot of deceptive grace — leading with the point, then rolling her wrist up to an outside guard as the Earther dropped back. He was moving just as quickly, and she realized coming straight on probably wasn't going to work. She backed off slightly.

The Earther came forward with just as much speed, and a good deal more force. His two swords blurred in a counter-strike before Christine managed to get more than two steps back, so she instinctively traversed to the left to keep her blade edge toward him. As the holo came forward with complementary swings from each sword, she lunged, slicing upward, hoping to catch him off balance.

He dropped back smoothly, making her feel rather clumsy as his feet slid across the floor.

Christine's steps carried her forward towards her target, her guard switching to the inside position and her other arm coming up behind her to maintain balance. The Earther advanced with a lunge, and this time she was able to parry sideways — only to watch the sword in the wolf's second hand slicing for her stomach. She didn't turn but instead leapt backward, her sword climbing high with the blade aimed down again.

She was suddenly stuck on the defensive. The Earther came forward with a force and a personal presence that was fundamentally frightening. His blades flew, and every time she got her sword into parrying position, the power of his strokes threatened to knock her saber from her hands.

And the whole time he looked so calm. She fell back, parrying and rolling her saber into a guard every time it was batted away. Her hasty withdrawal carried her across the mat, and the Earther pursued with serene determination. His swords came from opposite angles in economic arcs... If she could just disrupt the rhythm...

Instead of backing away, she suddenly traversed right, and her saber flew up at what should have been the Earther's unprotected back. But one of the two short swords had returned to the defensive, and the other was whistling at her.

She ducked and the blade missed her narrowly. She fell back a half-dozen meters, and took a second — a *literal* second — to think.

Time for a new plan.

Releasing her more rigid traditional posture, she leaned forward just slightly and squared herself. Her sword wrist rolled and her blade swept menacingly through the air, a challenge to the Earther. He stood with a raised eyebrow and a bit of a surprised look, his two swords hanging lazily in his hands.

She went forward again, and with a different tactic.

Her feet still moved lightly, but this time it was the edge of her blade that the Earther faced with his blades. She swung in fast and hoped to catch him off guard, but one of his swords was there, and the other was already driving her back. So much for that idea.

Turning her torso away from him again, she hauled her saber back up to the hanging guard and stayed put. She needed to try to dictate the tone of this fight — she'd let him come to her.

The Earther sunk slightly at the knees, then in dramatic and seemingly impractical fashion he raised one short sword over his head and pointed the other directly at her, guard outwards.

He came forward in a blur she couldn't entirely follow.

Christine traversed away immediately, circling and trying to stay out of range with her light steps. The Earther followed with heavy, impossibly fast strides. Every few seconds he taunted her with a possible strike — a lunge or a slash that she could choose to parry if she wanted to get closer... and every time she backed off. This wasn't going as she'd hoped.

She had to strike back... she just had no idea of how to get in past the guard of two blindingly-fast swords.

So she'd bitten off more than she could chew.

She angled back toward the panel, hoping to let the Earther's momentum drive them both that way. As the wolf continued to press forward against her defense with his controlled power, the plan seemed to work. The gym spread before her as she neared its corner. The panel had to be nearby...

She'd just have to step off the mat for the holo to stop.

And... there. Her careful balance allowed her to negotiate the edge of the mat rather handily.

Then her sword was gone and she was pinned against the wall with a blade pointing at her throat.

Oops. Maybe the malfunction was bigger than she thought.

Her hand flailed along the wall and found the panel. She slammed it with her palm, not entirely sure where the off button would be.

"Looking for this?"

Despite the point of the blade, Christine was able to crane her neck to see the frowning face of Graham Manchester. He pressed something on the panel and the holo hummed.

Christine let out a sigh of relief and turned back to watch the hologram vanish.

One appeared in the middle of the mat instead, and the Earther pinning her to the wall cocked an eyebrow, "I think we've had a bit of a misunderstanding."

Completely terrified now, Christine froze.

The blades came away from her throat and chest — that was good — and slid back into the Earther's belt. He offered a hand, "You're quite good. I take it you took me for a holo?"

She nodded very slowly and nervously pulled off her helmet. Graham took a long and half-astonished gape, and Lupus smiled politely.

"Beckett Lupus. Pleased to meet you..." he leaned forward slightly in search of a name.

Christine felt a *lot* of blood rush to her face. This couldn't be happening to her. No... that couldn't be the same Lupus...

"G... *General* Lupus?"

Beckett nodded, "So they call me. I'm afraid I still haven't caught your name, though."

Graham retrieved Christine's sword from the ground and quickly examined its hilt. The gold guard was engraved: "In honor of ArcLieutenant-General William 'Bill' Wallace, Sixth Fleet (Genesis) of the Allied Navy, Krogg 'A'." He studied the blade, then handed it back to Christine — who was by now completely red.

"This is my new aide, Beckett. Christine Schaeffer. She's Bill Wallace's granddaughter."

There was an undertone of pride beneath Graham's words.

Lupus' eyebrows rose notably, and Christine swallowed, "I am *so* sorry General... I should have realized..."

Lupus grinned and Graham couldn't fully suppress his smile.

She wasn't sure whether that was good or bad, but Graham took the initiative on her behalf, speaking to Lupus, "Pat met her a couple of days ago... rather long story, actually."

Lupus chuckled and nodded, "I imagine it is. Don't worry Christine, I haven't actually had a real workout in this gym before. Only been fencing with *Graham* you see, and I'm always glad for a change of pace."

Christine's eyes widened at the remark, and Graham frowned.

"You just took a shot at me," he looked up at Lupus, and the General shrugged.

"Well, since that holo is standing out there so lonely, I'm going to go warm up," Graham added. "We'll see who gets a workout!"

Taking his helmet from under his arm, Graham turned away from Lupus and looked to Christine, "Since you're here, would you give me a hand with this?"

She nodded eagerly, her complexion moderating again.

As the helmet dropped over his head, Graham leaned a bit closer to his aide, "Don't be fooled, I'm really quite awful with the damned sword."

A smile crossed her face and he went to face the holo.

Lupus turned to Christine again, “Now tell me, where did you learn to do that? I haven’t had that sort of bout with a human since I sparred with Sarah Manchester aboard *Cerberus*.”

She blinked a couple of times and shrugged, “Um. I just picked it up, I guess.”

Lupus frowned in a fatherly fashion and put a reassuring hand on her shoulder, “Don’t worry. You’ll get used to our ways.”

She tilted her head skeptically.

On the mat, Graham — who actually wasn’t as bad as he made himself out to be — easily disarmed the Earther holo.

CHAPTER 13

Something had been wrong with the delivery system for the antidote, the supposed cure. That was all Narosh could remember as he lay, slowly regaining consciousness, against the cold deck of *Shanavorous*.

A world of pain and terror came next… followed by punctuated thoughts.

Had the scientists escaped? Or had they perished? Probably that. Perished.

Narosh knew his head was pressed up against a wall. The pain was acute in his neck, and in his chest.

He felt sane, but there was so much pain. Interesting… was this the feeling of the plague?

No, he was in control.

But *Shanavorous* was under the control of something else.

The deckplates were humming as the Warcruiser drove through space.

What had happened?

He labored to haul himself upright. It was a painful proposition, and his head seared in agony. The room was dark; he couldn't immediately tell where he was.

A blue light flickered in the distance. It could be the lab.

Something in his chest continued to deliver sharp pain as he struggled to rest his back against the wall. His eyes narrowed in the darkness, and through the flickering light, he saw the broken glass of the containment room.

It had been broken.

Yet he was not infected. Perhaps he had not been exposed long enough. Perhaps the cure worked somehow.

His chest was swelling inside his armor, he realized. It was a natural Larosian reaction… but the feeling under his skin was not purely Larosian. He had been wounded before, but never had it felt like this, like something under his skin was *working*…

Was it the plague or the Earther immune-cells he'd acquired forty years before? Or both?

Whatever it was, he wasn't infected yet. The lab was destroyed, the scientists were gone. The cure, the last chance, had… failed? But he was still lucid.

And *Shanavorous* was under power… perhaps the plague had driven Natosh to use it against Laros itself…

As his mind grew clearer, Narosh struggled upward to his feet, steadying himself with a hand on the console near him. His equilibrium was relatively stable... mainly through the strict control of his mind. He stumbled painfully to the lab door.

The corridor was black too, but Narosh's eyes were adjusting. He found an arms locker nearby, and withdrew a short sword and a hand light. The hall was thus illuminated by the unsettling blue of the portable lamp, and he gingerly ambled through it.

Lifts aboard the Warcruiser had long since failed, as they had in many ships of the battered Larosian Fleet. But the shaft was intact, and common practice had become to shield each lift shaft from the gravity of the rest of the hull, making inter-deck transit relatively simple.

He made his way to the nearest lift, and stepped into the weightlessness with some relief.

Shining the blue light first below him and then above, he saw that the way to the bridge was clear, and with rough hand holds on the wall, he began to cautiously move himself upward.

He let go of the blue light, and it tumbled briefly, flashing his eyes before he clutched it in the zero-gee. The flash reminded him of the flash that had come when the glass in the lab had shattered.

Pausing in his ascent, he tried to focus his mind sharply against the pain and confusion.

He had been standing with the scientists when a black mist had overwhelmed the maddened figure of Natosh. For ten minutes it had seemed to be working, as the Captain collapsed into unconsciousness with stable vital signs, and the madness had seemed to ebb away.

Then the Captain had stood with a *smile*, and opened eyes that had turned all black... and punched through the glass that should have been *impenetrable*.

Narosh had moved forward to stop the escape, with only a piece of lab equipment as a club...

But Natosh had driven a fist into the Admiral-of-the-Fleet's chest, with such force that it slammed him back into the wall. And he'd blacked out.

That was all he could recall.

Whatever had happened, someone now had control. And judging by Natosh's new-found strength, that likely wasn't the scientists.

Narosh winced at the pain in his chest and pulled himself upward again. He was a good swordsman, but not a great one. In his weakened state, a conflict with an abnormal Natosh would do him no good.

But if the infected Captain was not stopped, this new insanity which had clutched him could be spread to Laros itself...

Narosh stopped again. Why had he not himself been affected?

Perhaps the feeling in his chest was the reason... or perhaps he would turn soon as well.

Then he had better make haste.

Climbing quickly in the weightless shaft, he came to the top and found the door partially open. He pulled himself upward until his feet could safely touch the deckplates, then painfully pushed himself into the gravity.

The blue light revealed nothing in the black corridor. He pressed on down the hall towards the bridge hatch, moving the sword into position before him as he arrived. His thumb keyed the atom-edge, but the blade did not hum to life. It must have been damaged... or perhaps it had simply worn out with age.

Still, it was all he had to defend himself.

He stopped before the hatch and scanned the wall around it, hoping to find a working keypad. There was only a torn space of alloy where the control mechanisms should have been.

So this would hurt even more...

He pushed the hatch with the tip of the sword, but the door did not move.

Taking a centering breath, he squared himself and drove his leg into the hatch.

It flew open, and leading with the hand light he scrambled ungraciously inside.

Red emergency lighting illuminated the silver cavern and its mostly-shattered controls.

Narosh keyed the light off and dropped it to the deck, hefting the sword in both hands with more than a little difficulty.

He edged into the bridge and let his eyes and mind reach out for Natosh... who seemed not to be there.

No, wait–

The hatch slammed behind him and as he tried to turn, a quick fist propelled him over a bank of tactical consoles. He fell back-first onto what had been a Captain's chair, pain erupting in his chest as his armor buckled. He could taste blood, but he wasn't dead yet.

Clumsily rolling off the remnants of a chair, he hauled himself upright against a nearby panel, and stared into the face of Natosh.

The Captain stood black-eyed and grinning... his skin seeming to undulate from beneath.

Why... it's the heroic Admiral!

Narosh winced but stared, his breathing accelerating. *You're sane again?*

Strictly speaking, I've always been sane... it's just the host who went berserk. No, I'm quite alright, I promise.

That made no sense.

Ha! Leave it to a Larosian. Too illogical, eh? Thought it would be wise *to inject Krogg DNA into a plague carrier? Desperate, weren't you?*

Narosh glared silently, and Natosh laughed audibly now.

"You in too much pain to reply?"

"I won't give *whatever* you are the dignity."

Funny, the scientists were obliging. But all they were required to do was scream as I dissected them. Alive.

Narosh's eyes hardened.

"Ahh yes… that was fun. I managed to keep one of them alive without any of his appendages — he lasted a whole day."

"Why not me then?"

Natosh — no, not Natosh — rounded the tactical consoles and closed with Narosh, "Because you're unique and I need a specimen to study, one who has Earther immunities. It seems they've saved you from me."

And the scientists?

"Infected as they died — how else would I keep them alive? This piece of rust you call a ship barely has propulsion."

Where are you taking us?

Natosh… *it*… grinned.

"You'll see, Narosh… or maybe not… or maybe *partially*."

Before he could realize what was about to happen, something had pierced Narosh's right eye, and then a solid blow to his head knocked him out.

Squishy… Natosh smiled.

CHAPTER 14

As always, Pat's table at the *Disc* was reserved, and again two chairs were facing him, though the occupants hadn't yet arrived.

Today his guests would be Beckett Lupus and Varnia Lupus — the latter formerly Varnia *Broadpaw*, of the famous family. They lived together here in Genesis space, serving as the ambassadors of the Earther consulate as well as heading up both halves of the Earther armed services. *General* Lupus commanded the marines, *Rear Admiral* Lupus had *Renown*, and together they were entrusted with the representation of Earther interests in the system.

Their postings meant Pat could contact them for research more easily than he could Setter, Andra or most of the other Earthers. The Irishman would have to catch up with all those old friends and many others in due time, but for now he couldn't get to Earth, so he'd get started with just Beckett and Varnia.

Well, 'just' was hardly a fair word — between them, these two had been in every major battle of the Krogg War, and specifically at Krogg 'A', they'd been in both the space and ground actions. Lupus had been the last to take orders from Andros Grieve, Varnia the last to speak to Savanna Felix. From a historical perspective, they were an invaluable couple.

Added to that, of course, was the fact that Beckett had saved Pat's ass.

No, there wasn't a more polite way to put it.

Had the once-Sergeant saved the Irishman on only a single occasion, it could count as saving 'bacon' or something. But Lupus had been with Pat at Antarctica, and then he'd saved the survivors after *Bishop* had gone down. They were extremely good friends.

Beckett and Varnia arrived at the table right on time, the waiter who escorted them taking a moment to stare rather rudely at the backs of their heads before he turned and sauntered off.

Pat tried to ignore the discourtesy — Earthers still got some strange reactions, even in places like the *Disc*. It was well that they didn't get offended easily, or problems might have ensued.

"Right on time, as usual," the Irishman smiled, standing and extending hands to both of the uniformed Earthers.

Varnia smiled and shrugged, "You know us, punctual to the last."

Both wolves chose to ignore the obvious looks they were getting in the restaurant — every human who thought she or he was stealing a secret glance was obvious to both Earthers' instincts — but the atmosphere was more charged than either of them would have preferred.

Pat grinned as the trio took their seats, and he settled himself directly across from Beckett, "All's well then, I take it?"

The wolves buried any thoughts of their surroundings, and Beckett nodded, "Not too bad at all. Had the usual session with Graham this morning, keeping up to date with Earth. There's been word of something brewing with the Commonwealth, but I don't have anything more than some cryptic wording from the father-in-law to go on."

Varnia grinned and shrugged, "Dad said to keep our ears open."

Indeed, Varnon had sent that suggestion... perhaps all these looks were somehow connected.

Pat hadn't noticed the more discreet looks from the people around them, and he cocked an eyebrow and leaned back in his seat — Gods only knew what the warning could mean. But he'd pass the word on to Sarah anyway. No telling what it could be...

"Well, that should be interesting to hear about," Pat shifted slightly and frowned at Beckett. "You meet Graham's new assistant yet?"

Another waiter approached from the side and interrupted Beckett before he could reply, "Would you care for a beverage, sirs, ma'am?"

That polite question, at least, didn't seem forced.

"Waters all around," Pat spoke, and the Earthers nodded. "That'll be it for now."

The waiter nodded and turned away, "Right away, sir."

"Have to love the service around here," Pat settled back in his chair, and Beckett raised an eyebrow, smiling thinly.

"I prefer a buffet, myself," he made the statement loud enough to get an unshielded glare from some of the staff.

Varnia — who appreciated turning the tables as much as Beckett did — still had a sense of propriety about these things, "*Behave.*"

Beckett shrugged and Pat just laughed. The drinks arrived immediately.

As the waiter left the table, Pat eyed his old friend, and Beckett narrowed his eyes a bit in reply, "What?"

The Irishman shrugged, "Remembering the good old days, back with *Bishop*, before the crash."

Beckett nodded slightly, "Aha. Wave of nostalgia?"

"I'm a *historian*, professional courtesy only," Pat smiled briefly. "Ran into someone the other day — Graham's new assistant now, actually."

Beckett's ear twitched and his eyes flicked quickly to Varnia, who nodded so slightly Pat didn't notice.

"Anyway, met her in a Panatorium of all places. Bill Wallace's granddaughter!"

Beckett donned a convincing frown, "She's Graham's aide now?"

Nodding, Pat laid his glass on the table, "Yep. Taking over part time until his regular comes off maternity. Christine Schaeffer's her name."

Varnia nodded and gave a 'hmmm', "Bill Wallace's granddaughter, you say?"

Pat nodded and picked up his glass for another drink, pausing to speak just before, "Yes indeed. You didn't meet her this morning, Beck? While you were fencing with Graham?"

He started to drink, and Lupus nodded.

"Yes, actually, she tried to kill me."

Pat listened, then it registered, then he tried to say something.

But he was drinking, so it didn't work out so well.

He coughed loudly as water tried to enter his lungs and he slammed the glass on the table, sloshing its contents indelicately over its rim.

"Excuse— *cough* *—what?"*

Lupus grinned, "If I hadn't been paying attention she'd have cut me to ribbons."

"Would've been very impolite," Varnia added with a solemn, slightly telegraphed nod.

Pat's eyes narrowed suspiciously, and his eyes shifted between them.

"You both need to stop being funny."

The Lupuses chuckled, "But you set yourself up so well."

Pat leaned back in his chair, "So you *did* meet her."

Beckett nodded.

"But she didn't try to kill you."

"No, she did..." Pat started to say something but Lupus held up his hand, "she mistook me for a holo in the gym."

Pat blinked and started to chuckle, "Poor girl's having a rough first week."

"Well she nearly gutted me. Pretty impressive for a young one, I found."

"Full of surprises, I suppose," Pat nodded slowly, looking at his glass and thinking of the last time Lupus had thought highly of a human opponent's skills. Sarah, forty years ago, and she was still at it...

"Well, anyway, I must complete my book research. And you two are witnesses for the Krogg 'A' battle... and Varnia you were at 'C'."

The Lupuses nodded slightly and glanced at each other, "True enough, what do you need to know?"

Pat grinned, "You know better than to ask. I want everything, just like last time... and the sordid details of those days coming home on *Algenon* might be fun too. I hear Varnon wasn't happy."

Varnia might have blushed if not for her sand-colored coat, "Dad was a bit miffed. Me having meals with a roughshod marine and all. Beckett being twenty years older than me..."

Pat grinned, "Aw, but when you live to be 250, what's twenty years?"

Varnia shrugged, "That's what we finally convinced dad of... but enough of that. You're giving Savanna a chapter, right?"

"A third of the first half of the book, I figure. He deserves it. So I'll need all that, too."

Beckett shifted a bit in his chair as he started to think back. Those hadn't been the best few days, the ones just around Krogg. Not *the* day especially.

"Andros gets a third of the last half too, Beck," Pat continued, and the General nodded.

That was good — both Savanna Felix and Andros Grieve had gotten their jobs done, and paid the ultimate price.

And in the process Lupus had experienced a moment of blind fury that had completely consumed him. On Krogg 'A', when the humans with them had been literally shredded by the Kroggs...

He blinked himself free of the memory and tuned back into Pat.

"...so accounts from both of you. And ladies first, so we'll start with you Varnia."

They talked, and people kept watching.

CHAPTER 15

"A cutter arrived last night from the Faithful's world, Chancellors."

The Holy room was silent, and all eyes turned to Thomas Pious. The High Chancellor's face was resolute, and the light from the window backing him enhanced his stature. The presence of the Gods in the room was undeniable — the power was palpable, and as was appropriate, it was focused on the single figure of the High Chancellor.

"It waited to make the journey until it could slip past the detection satellites of the Navy, and I believe it did successfully arrive unnoticed. This cutter carried important news."

The Chancellors' gazes remained fixed on Pious, and as he met each stare from his loyal brothers, he nodded slowly, feeling that they had silently come to the same conclusion he had. The Gods had blessed them all with such insight, they understood without words and simply bowed their heads in return. They waited now for his confirmation of their revelation, as he was the *High* Chancellor — the first *true* High Chancellor not corrupted by the devils. Not like the Bingham dynasty, not like Argyle, not a *heretic*.

"The Grand Chancellor of Ecclesia has informed me that an incident has occurred, and that war with Freetown is imminent."

There was a long pause, as these words were digested by the men at the table. This was perhaps not what their revelation had led them to expect…

"They were to wait and obey *our* timetable..." one of the Chancellors cast his gaze upward at Pious and spoke with firm words.

The High Chancellor nodded sympathetically, "They have set their course too soon brothers. But they have cause."

Further silence spurred Pious to key the wall screen, and all eyes turned to it as an image of a strange vessel appeared. The picture was moving, and its scan tags indicated that it had been recorded by a Faithful Battlecruiser.

The ship on the screen fired a long-carronade across the Battlecruiser's bow, forcing it to reverse course.

"This is *Felix*, named appropriately for the heathen. It is an advanced Battlecruiser, the first built by the Earthers for the Freetown heretics. With ships like these, Grand Chancellor Paine is certain the unbelievers will be able to overcome even his Dreadnoughts. He seeks to destroy their fleet before its main forces come online at Earth."

Unlike the inept Chancellors of yesteryear, these Holy men had been groomed in the ways of war, and they all nodded with understanding of the strategic significance of this problem. Another of them looked up at the High Chancellor, "The Earthers will involve themselves?"

Pious nodded slowly, "They already have, brother Timothy. They supply these ships to renegades, and are not stopped by our civilian counterparts in government even when they ship more arms than the Freetown government can possibly pay for."

Every Chancellor at the table looked up slowly at those words, one saying what all were thinking, "Our civilian government is allowing the Earthers to arm the renegades of Freetown? This is a gift!"

"The faithful people will not stand for Earther interloping!" another thundered, and there were loud sounds of agreement.

It was brother Timothy who said the words that were truly on all their minds: "Here is our reason for a coup."

Pious let a small smile cross his face at the enthusiasm of his brothers, then nodded, "With ships such as these, the Freetown scum are too dangerous to ignore. They must be denied such power until they have declared their loyalty to Genesis, or they will become a pawn of the Earthers and a threat to our independence. Who knows how many sympathizers they have in the civilian government — this could be the first step in an attempted *Earther* coup on our planet. The people will not stand for that."

"Can we bring this information to the people directly?" one Chancellor put the question in sober tones, and Pious' eyes narrowed as he shook his head.

"We must appear reasonable. Our loyal followers will rise to arms for us no matter the circumstances, but too much of the population is undecided. We may only count on their support if we demonstrate that the Earthers are meddling in our affairs in a way that threatens our liberty. We must thus demand a statement of loyalty from Freetown," Pious' words resonated and drew nods from all at the table. "Then, when Manchester refuses, we may call her out as a traitor to her people. It will take some days to arrange, but I believe with our agents spreading the word on the ground, and with our loyal news outlets, we may turn the undecided to our side."

Another of the Chancellors looked to Pious, "So all we need do is accelerate our plans. Less *finesse*, as they say it, and more preaching. Our men in the cities will spread the word, we will reveal the truth, all one year in advance of our plans?"

Pious and the Chancellors each nodded in turn at the question, themselves reflecting on the preparations that would need to be wildly accelerated. The commanding Crusaders and sympathetic Naval commanders were all aware of the Council's long-term goals — they would not need to be convinced, only ordered. The remaining year had been intended to be one of propaganda — to sew seeds of hatred and to win the loyalty of the half of the Genesis population that was largely undecided on the question of loyalty between Church and state.

And, it was true, it was also to have been a year of military maneuver, as Crusader battalions rotated into their garrison posts in the major cities. It was customary for major and minor garrisons to change hands between Naval marines and Crusaders every two years, to avoid the establishment of military influence in any single locality. The Naval marines presently held the bunker fortresses that ringed every city, the Crusaders maintaining their standing army only at their bases across the main continent of Genesis. Had the coup waited a year, the positions would have been reversed, making the changeover easier...

But it would still succeed. The time was *now*.

"We shall have to be ready to move in a matter of days, brothers. You each know your duties, I suggest you prepare your followers. Perhaps the Earthers will take some overt action when Grand Chancellor Paine begins the war... we need only a vid of some heathen beast overstepping his bounds to ignite the divine fury that will cleanse this world. You must cut away any superfluous operations. Secure the arms we need, and the men and even women. All loyal followers must fight. We *must* seize this opportunity, before Manchester can somehow preempt it. Send forth your agents, and go forth yourselves, and victory will be at hand!"

Graham frowned at the screen and ground his jaw, "By Gods you're right. How the bloody hell did it get through?"

Unity Genesis' Sensor Chief matched Graham's frown and shook her head, "We have no record of their arrival from Satnet. I'm betting they timed their jump to one of the gaps in the network, then went straight into cover... which would mean some Churcher told them our cycle schedule."

Sneaky bastards. Graham could still recognize the signature of an Earther e-hyper cutter anywhere, even though the Earthers hadn't used them in decades. The small ships were simply too dangerous for even Earther crews to handle, but the Faithful fanatics had bought the two used ones from the Genesis mothball fleet after the Krogg War.

Graham had once 'enjoyed' an adventurous ride on one of those cutters — though in all honesty it hadn't been so much fun. Not that that mattered at the moment. What did the Faithful have to tell people on Genesis that everyone on the planet couldn't hear?

"I'm guessing they're not dropping off recipes for grandma's cookies," Graham glibly answered his own mental question, then leaned back from the monitor and turned to the Comm Chief who sat nearby, "Think you can hack in and get their dispatches?"

A cutter like this one would inevitably have old computers — the Faithful would never have gone to the Earthers for a modern upgrade of the on-board systems.

The Comm Chief was already smiling when Graham's question came, "And... *done*, sir. They didn't change the lower registry passwords from when it was in our service, so I pulled them from the database. They don't even know I went in."

Graham grinned — no matter what asses like Pious tried to say, there were some lessons the Churchers just didn't *learn*, "What have we here, then?"

The Comm Chief keyed a few buttons and Graham turned to face her. The screen changed from a view of the witless cutter to a new-looking ship...

"Aha, *Felix*, if I'm not mistaken," he glanced back towards his chair to Christine, who'd been sitting quietly on the bridge, not sure if she was supposed to make her presence the least bit known. "Ever read about those?"

Christine swallowed at Graham's question, then shook her head, "Not familiar."

Graham glanced back to the screen just as a bright long-carronade shot slashed across the bow of what he presumed was a Faithful ship.

"Our friends in Freetown designed them. The way I hear it, they're close to a match for an Earther Fifth Rate, easily a match for a *Templar*-class, and more than a match for one of the Commonwealth's old *Prophets*."

"First of its line?" Christine's curiosity bested her fear of exceeding her place.

Graham nodded, turning away from the screen, "Named for my old dear friend, Savanna Felix. I hope it deserves it..."

She returned his nod in understanding, and he directed himself to the Comm, "Any message with it?"

The Chief cocked a confused eyebrow, "Just text: 'Only Days, Brother.' Signed 'Grand Chancellor Paine.'"

Graham's brow lifted, "Cryptic. Nothing scrambled in the lower bands?"

Frowning, the Chief scratched her head, "I'm going to have to do some looking, sir. If it's buried, it's buried much better than... well... I'd expect of our Faithful friends."

"Look, just in case. We did get at this quite easily..." Graham glanced back at Christine, and she felt compelled to nod in agreement.

The surface message could mean anything.

But 'anything' included the possibility of *trouble*, so Graham would definitely distribute warnings about it through the family: to his wife, soon not to be head of the Naval Marine Corps, and his sister, soon not to be President.

"Pass it on to the usual contacts... and start keeping an eye on Crusader activity planetside. Let me know if you find anything in the lower bands."

"Aye sir," the Comm Chief was already devoting her attention to the screen.

Graham turned to Christine with a bit of a frown, "I think we need to weed the fleet."

She tilted her head with some confusion, and he smiled, "Come on, I'll show you."

They left the bridge of *Unity Genesis*, and as they did, the Comm Chief looked witlessly past three buried messages in the lower bands of the feed — bands the Faithful couldn't *possibly* know how to use. Suspicion of the Church had so long ago become a joke among the regular Navy rankers that the new generation lacked the will to dig deep.

CHAPTER 16

Ed Jeffries leaned back in his chair and crossed his arms, staring at the forward view screen with some trepidation. The haulers were loaded up, and he would be happy to get them moving, but a drone had arrived two days before notifying him that Audrey DeBrooke and the First Expeditionary would be on hand to back him up for the return trip.

The government was understandably expecting trouble.

Loaded with orders of new missiles, Earther wares, and a few mini-industrial plants, the convoy was a rich one — and if the Faithful got wind of just exactly what it contained, they could complain their way to war… literally.

Felix was primed to deal with every Faithful Battlecruiser known to the Freetown Navy — all at once. But if the rumors of Dreadnoughts were true, well, that could be troublesome. No matter how advanced, *Savanna Felix* was still only a Battlecruiser, and the missile hurricane that even an old Dreadnought could fling would cripple Freetown's shiny new ship.

So Ed was waiting. Once the First Expeditionary arrived with its Heavy and Light Cruisers, there'd be a better force balance — even if it was only a precarious one…

Audrey had been due in Earth space some four hours ago, but she seemed to be running late, and that was starting to make Ed nervous. The First Expeditionary, by itself, lacked the punch to handle a strong Faithful force… what if they'd run into a Church fleet and been beaten apart…

Ed cradled his chin in the palm of his hand, his elbow planted on his chair arm. His first duty right now was to the convoy, not to First Expeditionary. His orders still called for him to protect these haulers at all costs, and even though he knew exactly what the greater political situation was, he couldn't afford to be cavalier about interpreting Fleetcomm's orders.

So he should get the cargo ships home on his own; he could not allow himself to worry about the whereabouts of First Expeditionary.

The convoy was on a schedule. Being late wouldn't do all that much harm… no, the concern was less about what happened when he reached Freetown and much more about actually making it *to* Freetown.

Four hours was a long time for cruisers to be overdue. If the Faithful were out there somewhere, his best shot at slipping the convoy past them would be to leave immediately, before they had a chance to settle into a blockade.

It was a bloody dilemma. He needed some intelligence about the Faithful's disposition...

"Signals, send to the Admiralty House... I need to speak to... *somebody*."

Lab Forepaw leaned back in his chair and, with some difficulty, hefted his legs up onto the desk. Dran Nightclaw, once commanding officer of the famous 111th Flying Squadron and Ursla's former Flag Captain, sat at the other side of the desk and frowned slightly.

"Do you do that often?" the panther asked smoothly, and Lab Forepaw frowned.

"Do what?"

"Put your feet on the desk?"

Forepaw grinned and shook his head, "Never used to, but Andra suggested it when she signed over this office. This is only try number four."

Nightclaw wasn't the smiling sort — he tended to be calm and conservative in appearance at all times. Now he simply tilted his head, "How many times have you thrown your back out?"

Forepaw shrugged, "Twice."

"Andra's legs are longer than yours, you really shouldn't listen to her posture advice."

Lab shrugged again and laced his fingers behind his head. He was the First Lord of the Admiralty now, and that meant his office was further up the hall from where it had been when he was Second Lord, and bigger by a square meter. Since he hadn't been in the job for very long, he was still enjoying the new privileges just a little.

This, of course, was *sort of* a meeting, so perhaps it warranted a little more decorum.

He slowly hauled his feet off the desk and leaned forward.

"Alright then, Dran, let's talk shop."

Nightclaw's eyebrow arched again, "You seem awfully happy, Lab."

Forepaw paused with another slight frown, "Maybe. But that's irrelevant, let's talk. How's life at the Navy Office?"

It was an ages-old question in the two-office Navy — one that confused the hell out of Pat and other human historians, but worked well for the Earthers because of their cooperative nature. The Navy Board, headed by a Comptroller — in this case Dran Nightclaw — was the Admiralty's right hand. While the Admirals would make decisions about deployment policy, approve new designs, and retire old ones, the Navy Board was the separate structure that ensured the fleet's blood continued to pump.

Nightclaw's office oversaw the distribution of supplies, equipment and non-commissioned personnel to the arms of the fleet, while Forepaw's Admiralty appointed officers to their posts and sent the fleets around. There were, in some areas, very fine lines of jurisdiction between the Board and the Admiralty, and in some cases there was clear duplication in responsibility. Shipyards were co-directed, as were repair and orbital stations. If the Comptroller and the First Lord didn't get along, there could be massive problems in the infrastructure...

But all Earthers tended to get along quite well, all the time. That's why it worked.

In any case, that close and intricate connection between Admiralty and Navy Board was the reason Nightclaw was Forepaw's first meeting of this day, his third as First Lord of the Admiralty and the first he was able to take with people outside Admiralty House.

"We're doing fine. We're starting to organize the reservist ratings and spacers in case your partial mobilization turns out to be more than a drill. Other than that, business as usual. By the looks of it you like your new office."

Lab grinned again, "A whole extra *square meter*. A view two degrees west of the one I had in my old office. And a different color carpet. It's alright."

Nightclaw opened his mouth to say something, but Forepaw's intercom buzzed. The wolf frowned apologetically to his comrade and then keyed the comm active, "His Lordship speaking."

"Uh. Lab?"

Forepaw grinned, "Yes, Rawden. Just getting used to title..."

"Riiighhhttt."

Rawden Coggs was the longtime chief of staff at Admiralty House — in charge of ingoing and outgoing information. An intercom buzz from him meant something interesting was happening.

"Well, anyway, Mister Lordship, I have a signal from Ed Jeffries standing by on Fleetcomm Four. He's not asking for anyone in particular, but I thought you might want it."

"Anyone else around?"

"Nope. Fox is on maneuvers and no one else is in yet."

Forepaw glanced curiously at Dran, and the panther nodded slowly, "I've got all morning. It's probably important."

Nodding again, Lab looked at the little intercom speaker, "Pipe it to my desk."

Ed watched another minute tick by on the chrono, and then looked back at the main tank. The crest of the Earther Admiralty was being proudly displayed, accompanied by some nice music. He was on hold.

For a while now... maybe the Admiralty was busy dealing with a situation... Or *not*.

The screen clicked active and a holo transmission came through, kicking in *Felix's* AI and generating a life-sized, 3D projection of Forepaw behind his desk.

The First Lord. Well… straight from the emu's mouth, as the saying went.

"Good morning, Ed," Forepaw smiled and nodded, and the human straightened himself in his chair.

"Good morning… um… Lord Forepaw. Your Lordship."

"Haven't been made a royal, Eddie, I'm still *Lab*. What's going on?"

Jeffries fidgeted somewhat awkwardly, "The First Expeditionary's four hours overdue, and I'm trying to figure out whether to leave or wait. You don't happen to know where the Faithful Fleet is, do you?"

Forepaw frowned slightly, tapping a few keys on his desk and looking away — presumably to another display in his office.

"None of our pickets have picked up any sign of them recently. I'm sending you what we have… I'll transfer you down to Rawden Coggs if you like, and he can give you a straight tap on our sensor logs."

Ed sat up even straighter, "That'd be great."

Forepaw nodded, "Good good… hmm. Well, as for advice, it looks clear on the road to Freetown for now. But that's based on readings a few hours old… You should probably get moving while the coast is clear. You might run into Audrey on the way."

Ed scratched his neck thoughtfully, then nodded, "I was thinking much the same. Alright then, we'll boost as soon as we link to your sensor grid."

Forepaw nodded, "I'll transfer you down there. Safe journey."

"Thanks… I hope so!" Ed smiled and Forepaw nodded again.

The screen flashed back to 'hold', and Ed leaned back in his chair.

Friends could really be useful sometimes.

Dran looked across the desk at Lab with a suspicious expression, "Faithful might be causing trouble… you're not just letting them go out alone, are you?"

Forepaw shook his head and keyed the intercom, "Communications, signal the First Space Lord to shift his maneuvers."

As the Signal Officer on the other end of the line began hunting for *Venerable's* signal antennae, Forepaw put his hand over the intercom microphone and met Nightclaw's eyes, "Think Audrey's just late?"

Nightclaw paused thoughtfully, "I wouldn't expect it of her."

Forepaw nodded and relayed his message for Fox through the Signal Officer.

CHAPTER 17

"Bob, you're not making me very happy."

Commodore Bob Enid shrugged and looked back through *Grendelsbane City's* main monitor, "What the hell am *I* supposed to do about it? She was due for an overhaul and we had to pull her out in the middle."

Audrey DeBrooke was past excuses just now—the entire First Expeditionary was sitting in open space, eight ships of cruiser size or less floating around a core of four heavy transports that were similar in age to *Grendelsbane*.

One of those transports — the *Theban Chariot*, whatever that name referred to — had been completely dead in space for over *three* hours. They were just out of sensor range of the outermost Earther pickets, putting them about two and a half hours out of range of Sol's communications, but to send a ship into range to let Ed Jeffries know what was happening could prove very ill-advised.

The day before they'd picked up a signature that had almost certainly been a Faithful Destroyer shadowing their force. That meant that splitting the First Expeditionary now might be suicide — if the Faithful were paying attention, they'd pounce on the lesser part of the Freetown Squadron. Old-fashioned divide and conquer — Audrey couldn't take the chance.

Coming out to meet the convoy was seeming less like a good idea than it had days earlier.

The heavy transports, relatively slow and cumbersome, lacked any capacity for self-defense, so the First Expeditionary, with only two Heavy Cruisers making up its combat core, was tied to a slow-moving anchor of four ships.

If only the transports could get to Sol... somehow Audrey knew the Earthers could have the rest of the advanced Battlecruisers and the bigger *Republic* up to spec in no time...

But that was irrelevant because right now Audrey's first responsibility was to get to Earth. Once there, she could worry about bringing every possible warship home to Freetown as quickly as possible. Speed was crucial, as an attack on the privateer world at this moment could be a serious problem. James had six old Battlecruisers, including the enhanced *Archangel Sword*, as well as a number of Heavies, Lights, and Destroyers. But against a Dreadnought group and lacking in the coherent and purposefully organized fast cruiser group Audrey commanded, the Freetown Fleet might not survive.

"Audrey?"

She blinked. She'd zoned out again…

"How *long,* Bob?"

"Another hour. I'll light a couple of fires under the ones I've already lit, just to make sure, alright?"

Audrey nodded somewhat sourly. She really couldn't blame Bob Enid, the Navy's Transport Commodore. She had literally hauled *Theban Chariot* off the stocks so she could move the full crews for the new ships out of Freetown. Apparently someone had left some pieces out when they'd hastily reassembled the transport's engines.

As the screen blanked, she toyed again with the idea of sending a Destroyer forward to Earth, or to start looking for an Earther sloop on patrol. But she was under threat — she had to assume the Faithful knew where she was — and with every one of her ships being so valuable to the tiny Freetown Navy, she couldn't take too many chances.

A few hours wouldn't make a difference… Ed Jeffries wouldn't ship out without her…

"Just clearing sensors of the outer pickets, skipper. Still nothing on our scanners."

Ed nodded and turned from the Lieutenant of the watch with a belated frown. He hated clichés, but this was all too damned quiet.

After his past encounter with the Faithful, it seemed certain they would try to get some measure of revenge. They had their chance now… *Felix* was alone with a slow moving convoy. The question was where they'd be coming from.

And that was the fun part, because it could be anywhere.

Life is good…

"Skipper! Eight ships on long-range scope. Two Heavies, two Lights, and four Destroyers… with four transports."

Here we go.

Ed's frown deepened a bit, "On an intercept course?"

There was a pause, "Stopped Captain, warships clustered around the transports."

"Do we know who they are?"

The natural assumption would be that they were the First Expeditionary, experiencing engine trouble with the transports. But things were still too quiet. This could just as easily be a trap set by the Faithful to lure him in…

"Coded IFF coming in. It's Admiral DeBrooke and the First Expeditionary!"

And I'm officially ignoring my instincts for the rest of the flight.

"Signal convoy to stand by for deceleration. Get Audrey on the horn."

"That's *Felix* ma'am."

Audrey tapped her foot on the deck with a mixture of irritation and relief.

The convoy and the new Battlecruiser were still almost fifteen minutes away, but with the new Earther signal systems built into *Felix's* hull, communication was already possible.

Energy comm pulses lanced ahead of the advanced Battlecruiser and reached *Grendelsbane* at faster-than-light velocity, prompting the Heavy Cruiser's Signal Officer to look up, "Hail from Captain Jeffries, ma'am."

"Well put it up!" her mood was either about to improve or topple...

Well, topple was the safer bet. She was supposed to be rescuing the convoy after all, now by all appearances it was rescuing *her*. And they'd all have to go back to Earth together — to make sure the crew transports got through alright. Then they'd have to come all the way back with the cargo haulers...

This wasn't running as smoothly as she'd envisioned First Expeditionary's first potential combat operation.

Oh well, at least they hadn't been blindsided by the Faithful.

Yet.

Audrey ground her jaw as Ed appeared and smiled kindly, "Uh. Hi."

"Get into formation, Ed. I'm *really* not in the mood."

He grinned, nodded, and disappeared.

His ships were still a quarter hour away.

Others were closer.

Others were closer still.

Chancellor Leo flew his Holy banner from the post-Krogg War Dreadnought *Illustrious Faith*, one of a new breed of tough ships brought in a year after the war to offset decommissioning losses. The theory had been sound — replace entire squadrons of old Dreadnoughts with single, far more formidable vessels. The Earthers had their *Venerable*-class, Genesis had their *Unity*-class. Both were vastly superior to *Illustrious Faith*, but in turn, *Faith* was far tougher than its two Krogg-vintage Dreadnought consorts.

Technically, the *Faith*-class Dreadnoughts had never made it to the open sales market. The Faithful certainly shouldn't have been able to get their hands on one — it was far too powerful a vessel to entrust to a small Navy. With fighter bays for twenty of Genesis' first small combat craft, 118 tubes and twelve heavy lasers, *Faith* was more than a match for a Krogg War Superdreadnought. And the Faithful had not even paid full price for it.

The ship had been sent to the breakers yards after defects had been found in its power plants — or so the story went. But *Faith* had truly been technically excellent. Another ship had taken its place at the breakers, and the Church of Genesis had successfully hidden that fact.

Now *Illustrious Faith* was lying in wait, behind energy jamming that rendered it and its squadron invisible to the ailing First Expeditionary. Chancellor Leo just had to time this correctly — he'd waited hours for the two heretic squadrons to combine so that he could destroy them simultaneously. He would not attack until the new heathen ship was close, though, as *Felix* was reputed to be very fast, and thus would have to be well within the missile envelope before the Faithful struck.

The two heathen groups would unite in fifteen minutes. *Felix* would be irredeemably within range of its death in just seven. Within the reach of the Holy Restoration Fleet. Three Dreadnoughts, four Battlecruisers, two Heavy Cruisers, two Light Cruisers, and eight Destroyers. More than a match for the First Expeditionary.

And the other half of the Faithful's Naval force remained at Ecclesia — ready to move against Freetown at Leo's order. He would wait until he was certain this group of renegades had been eliminated, then send word that the Redemption Fleet — identical to the Restoration Fleet but with a single Light Carrier instead of three Dreadnoughts — could depart to attack Freetown...

It was a plan far more sophisticated than anything the Church of the Quest could have conceived of — proof that the Church truly had learned the lessons of past defeat. They had at last drawn the Freetown force into the open, and using advanced technology bought at a great cost in lives and funds, had given the heretics no inclination of the true strength of the power of faith.

This would be a quick victory, won before the new bastard ships left Earth space. Freetown would never have the chance to even pretend to pay for those Earth-built vessels.

And at home in Genesis, the coup might be sparked...

Freetown was being secretly armed by the Earthers, after all.

"Ten minutes now, skipper."

Ed Jeffries nodded and kept both eyes on his sensor console. He wasn't seeing anything suspicious. Despite all the chaos, the Faithful might well have just been blowing smoke.

That was good, Freetown would be ready for them soon...

CHAPTER 18

Audrey watched the ETA for *Felix* tick under six minutes and ground her jaw, half expecting the alarms to start blaring…

And then they did.

Before she had a chance to react, the main screen flicked from a squadron camera view to the main sensor plot, revealing the presence of a Faithful fleet.

A big one.

Damn… she'd been counting on First Expeditionary's speed to avoid trouble this whole time. But the Churchers had been hoping for this sort of chance — they *had* to have been.

But *Felix* could still turn away and escape unmolested… no, it couldn't.

She scowled at the screen while her bridge crew gaped in mild disbelief. It was a well-executed action, certainly. Better planned than any of the crew — most of them veterans of the Krogg War who had taken regen treatments and spent decades discounting Church tactics — could have expected.

The Faithful had put a superior force in just the right place to kill every Freetown ship not at home, and they'd done it without tipping their hand. There'd been no warning whatsoever.

Audrey concluded almost instantly that she and Freetown had been played from the start of this little series of incidents, and within five seconds of that realization, she decided she'd been impetuous. She shouldn't have divided the fleet.

Too late to worry about that now, however. She had to save the situation somehow…

The four Faithful Battlecruisers were her problem. She had one — *Felix* — and it wasn't near her yet. First Expeditionary, built around *Grendelsbane City*, featured another heavy and two *Light* Cruisers, as well as four Destroyers. That meant they had enough speed to get out of the Dreadnoughts' way — forgetting the crippled *Theban Chariot*, as seemed inevitable right now — but not enough to escape the Faithful Battlecruisers. Those four Battlecruisers would *finish* her — her lighter hulls simply couldn't hope to withstand their larger cousins in an open-space shootout.

But she didn't have much of a choice. It was run or die, and at least *some* of the transports might make it to the Earther pickets if the run option was taken.

Of course, if the escapees didn't run straight into an Earther picket ship, they'd die just as easily within the Earther sensor frontier as they would have outside it. If only she'd found a sloop out here, the presence of an Earther vessel might dissuade any attack… would the Faithful go so far as to attack the *Earthers*?

No way to know… no time to care.

Grendelsbane and the other cruisers would have to make a stand, delay the Faithful long enough to let the transports run. That was it — her life was forfeit, along with the lives of her crews.

She didn't even bother to reflect on the unsettling calm she felt at the decision — it was too cliché.

"Destroyers break formation and move to escort mobile transports. Enter flux *right now*, make for Earth at unreasonable speed. Cruisers form line abreast. All ships to general quarters, load tubes immediately and stand by first volley."

Ed Jeffries swallowed hard and felt the very slight shift in gravity as *Felix* angled away from its charges and headed directly for the Dreadnoughts now looming nearby. The convoy was already making its own clumsy bank away, trying to get enough speed together to make Earth space and avoid destruction.

Fully laden with Earther cargo, it didn't appear likely that any of them could work up enough speed to escape.

The Faithful seemed to be holding their fire for an awfully long time — though Ed realized it had actually been less then a minute. Even *Felix's* superior speed wouldn't get it out of the envelope of those Dreadnoughts before a *lot* of damage was done. There was no point running. Better to protect the transports that were carrying crews for a squadron of ships like just *Felix*.

That was a fair trade.

Missiles cycled into *Felix's* tubes and its long-carronades charged. Crews sprinted through corridors to their action stations, some half dressed and others better prepared.

"Carronades now report cleared for action, sir."

Jeffries nodded, "Dump our data logs into a pod, stand by to send to Earth. Get another one ready for Freetown. Record our telemetry until we're under heavy attack, then send both."

"Aye, sir."

"Deep scan, *where* did they come from?"

There was a pause as the Sensor Techs at the sensors station bustled around inside their little ring of consoles, then their supervising Lieutenant looked up with a baffled expression, "Based on where they appeared, they must have been tracking the First Expeditionary… but their jamming was enough to let them slip past us even at point blank."

Jeffries nodded slowly — if *Felix* couldn't see them, no one probably could have. Earther-built sensors were the best anywhere, though he had been hearing things about new jamming fields and similar sorts of camouflage. He hadn't taken it seriously, which in retrospect appeared to be a mistake.

Even if that sort of stealth technology existed, he definitely wouldn't have expected the Faithful to have it.

"Maybe if we'd been closer sir… but then we'd have been dead as soon as we saw them. Before even…"

"Enough commentary, Lieutenant. Is there anything else in the area?"

Another long pause.

Jeffries was about to take the silence as a no, even as his mind tried to figure out why the Faithful weren't already hammering him with missiles.

"Wait sir… *something…*"

Chancellor Leo slammed his fist into the arm of his chair, "*What happened to our targeting solutions? Hells swallow you, answer me!*"

The commanding Shaspa's eyes were wide, "I don't know, Eminence… the… the solutions were suddenly blocked. The AIs believe there is a field of energy interfering in their scans. They cannot establish solid target locks."

Leo roared and came to his feet, "Then fire *blind*! All ships *fire*!"

The order to fire processed immediately, and Earther-built sensors picked up the minute shifts in energy output as the mag-launchers on the tubes prepared to hurl the Faithful missiles out of their tubes for ignition.

Fox Magnus was torn between a triumphant smile and a look of grim displeasure. Audrey had been caught unawares, and that was perturbing enough, but that it was the *Church* — or more precisely, the *Faithful* — who had done the catching was downright disturbing.

At any rate, the game ended now.

Things had come a long way since Fox had first pioneered the system of stretching a ship's energy drive field to seemingly dangerous margins for the purposes of stealth. *Flame* had nearly shaken itself apart under the strain of such risky acts during the Krogg War. *Venerable*, however, had been built specifically with such techniques in mind. *Venerable* and the seven others of its class now with Fox's command. *And* the eight *Cerberus*-class frigates with him, too.

Their fields drew in at a rate which once would have been *very* dangerous, but which reactors could now handle. In literally two seconds, the First Battle Squadron and the First Flying Squadron of the Earther Navy were returned to their material state. The third second saw gunports cracking open. By the fifth second, when the missiles left Faithful tubes, and their drives ignited, guns were run out.

The Earther guns were loaded — as they always were in situations like these

— with canister.

And there were plenty of guns.

Between the eight *Cerberus*-class — not to be mistaken for Ursla's older, much smaller ship called *Cerberus*, of the *Hades*-class — and the *Venerables*, 1,160 guns fired their canister in a single wave.

The missiles were removed handily from space.

There was no need to roll ships for the next volley — the newer Earther guns were far smaller than the old ones, occupying literally a third of the space but packing the same punch, and taking a proportionally shorter length of time to recharge.

Four seconds before the next missiles entered the Faithful ships' tubes, the Earthers were ready to fire.

But Fox wasn't about to give that order.

Chancellor Leo was frozen.

He'd laid a very good trap, but he'd been duped — the First Expeditionary had been bait, and not even his force could withstand sixteen modern Earther vessels. Even their *frigates* outclassed his Dreadnoughts.

"Stop all firing — *right now!*"

The second salvo didn't hit space.

Audrey's heart stopped beating for a particularly long second, and her brain certainly didn't register in time to order her cruisers to reverse course and *not* charge nose first into the unengaged broadsides of the *Venerables*. The shipboard AIs were actually forced to override the helms of each of the Freetown cruisers to stop them short of collision. There was particular and wholly understandable shock on every human bridge.

Ed's jaw had dropped conspicuously, but he quickly recomposed himself. Leave it to someone like Fox, with a flare for the dramatic...

"Give me a channel to the lead Faithful ship."

Fox's voice took on a forceful, cool edge, and the Signal Officer routed a broadcast to the largest Dreadnought. The main holo tank filled quickly with a red-robed human, and Fox's eyes narrowed.

"Is there a problem here, sir?"

Leo glared at the flat image of Fox Magnus on his screen. He was well aware of the Earther's reputation — and his prowess. The Chancellor was incensed by the Earther intervention. Of course he'd hoped to destroy their civilization, but what gave them the right to interfere in this?

For the moment, the fact that he was trying to use Earther interference as an excuse for a coup escaped him. The shock of what had just happened stopped his thought process.

Eight ships of the line proved a positively *icy* bucket of water.

"This is not your space, Admiral Magnus. I demand you remove yourself immediately, or I have authorization to declare you a hostile force!"

Magnus cocked an unamused eyebrow and his gaze fixed on the Chancellor, "It's *First Space Lord* Magnus to you, sir."

Leo glared.

"Now, there's something you might want to consider before you act hastily. I'm sitting on sixteen of the best ships in the galaxy. You've got a handful of vintage trash. I've got 2,500 guns and a thousand boats. You've got old tubes and twenty fighters, by the look of things. I think you need to ask yourself a question: do you feel lucky, sir? And I mean *very* lucky."

Fox had stolen that line from a human movie, thought he'd taken out the reference to 'punk' — he wasn't sure what that word meant. Still sounded good.

Leo actually asked himself that question. He'd felt *very* lucky a minute ago, but that hadn't worked out for him.

To lose half the Faithful Fleet when the Earthers seemed to be offering him an out was... *unwise*.

"This will not go unanswered, heathen," he spat, and Fox's head tilted slightly, his eyes hardening.

"I'd be truly shocked if you claimed anything else. Now oblige me and leave."

The link cut and Leo nodded angrily to his Shaspa, "Return to Ecclesia. *Now*."

He didn't realize it for some minutes, but he already had all he truly needed to make the venture a worthwhile one.

Fox let out a nice long breath as the Faithful ships turned away and hastily entered flux. He could have backed up his threat, but he was just as glad he didn't have to. War was averted, at least for now.

"Send to Audrey and Ed, we'll escort them back to Earth."

CHAPTER 19

"War? You've got to be kidding."

Sarah shrugged on the monitor and Graham sat back in his chair, steepling his fingers in his lap, "They'd be insane. Bloody bunch of *Churchers*, Sarah! I don't care what surplus they have, they couldn't crack the Towners."

"They're *Faithful* Graham, of course they're *insane*."

Graham took a few seconds to think and then let out a sigh. With the secret arrival of a Faithful cutter, they all had reason to be concerned. Sarah was worried trouble was coming that might pit Genesis against Earth, but Graham wasn't so sure. Surely they wouldn't be fools enough to think that the civilian government would allow any such campaign — if the Faithful started something, they'd get no Genesis support, and the Earthers would wipe them out. They *couldn't* be planning to try anything…

Then again, as Sarah said, the Faithful were a pretty 'special' group of zealots…

Sighing, Graham bobbed his head in a nod, "Fair point. Crazy bastards. Bloody hell."

"My thoughts exactly."

With another deep breath, the younger Manchester leaned forward again. Perhaps the Church had some other means of supporting the Faithful — sending volunteers, or defectors... The Faithful didn't necessarily need the sanction of the entire government. But would anything less than full support be enough to stop the Freetowners and Earthers? It didn't seem likely… the Church would have to rally part of the Genesis Fleet to have any chance of dealing with Earther ships, and even they'd have only a slim chance.

But they might try anyway, so he had to be careful.

Which was why he'd done his weeding. Oddly enough, all the while as he'd been explaining to Christine the ways in which he could isolate the Naval officers he didn't trust, he hadn't seriously believed it necessary. But he'd done it, which was the key.

Pulling a pad from his desk, he looked up at his sister, "Well, Christine and I just finished sending out the orders to my Church-loyal officers. They're all moving out on picket duty towards the hyperspace corridor and Gibraltar. We've kept them well split up — I'll detail our squadrons to deal with them if things get… *messy*."

The Genesis Fleet maintained some 450 ships, of which approximately eighty had substantial bodies of officers and crew loyal to the Church. His first thought would have been that they could have been a coup threat. Now, with the evidence that the Faithful were keen on war against the Towners, it seemed far more likely they'd try to defect to the aid of the Commonwealth.

With eighty modern ships — even with *ten* — the Faithful would be able to offset the advantages the Towners had with their new ships and excellent crews.

That possibility really gnawed at Graham.

"They could still be planning something here… try to destabilize the government or something along those lines," Sarah made the suggestion on the screen, and Graham nodded absently.

"Yes. I'm sure our man Pious is capable of that. Just as well as Harvey Bingham pulled off his fleet coup in Earth space, no doubt."

"I've asked that the marines be put on alert… *subtly,* anyway. I'm not too concerned," Sarah wasn't buying those last words even as she said them, but then what she was 'buying' was of no consequence… "Gillian agrees with us though; the Church can't have pulled plans together under our noses. And even if they did, why wouldn't they wait until their garrisons held the government centers at end of term?"

Graham nodded, "Indeed. Alright. I'll keep my eyes open. Top Flight hush-hush, eh?"

Sarah smiled thinly and nodded, "You know better than to ask."

The screen blanked and Graham looked away with raised eyebrows, "What security clearance do they give cadets these days?"

Christine Schaeffer nervously shifted her weight onto the balls of her feet, "They let us out on weekends. Usually without a chaperone."

Graham nodded, lifted another pad from his desk, and tossed it to her. She caught it awkwardly, then frowned at the screen, "What's 'Top Flight'?"

"A little something from the Church days. Pat kept it out of the books so we could keep using it. Means you have clearance for more than just the Naval matters. And that I trust you."

Christine opened her mouth ready to give a glib reply, but then looked up and met Graham's suddenly hard eyes, "This just stopped being a temp job for you, Christine. When Miranda gets back you're her assistant."

"Wha–" it wasn't the sound she wanted to make.

Graham stood and slowly rounded his desk, "This might boil over, it might not. You just heard Sarah say things that aren't Presidential, they're *Naval*. And there *might* be a coup. At the very least a defection of Church-loyal ships to the Faithful cause. I can't be without an aide I trust if that happens. So you'll need to be ready to step in. Which means you accept that–" he pointed to the pad "–and stay here. And if it blows over, and when Miranda rejoins, you stay with my staff until you get promoted through. Which shouldn't be long."

Christine was fairly certain her lungs had stopped working.

Graham turned back to his desk, pulled yet another pad, and tossed it at her. It hit her in the chest and fell loudly to the deck.

"I'm... you're... what about... I'm a *cadet*."

With a raised eyebrow, Graham pointed to the pad at her feet. She bent down slowly and hefted it — *hefted* it because she felt rather weak.

Her head was *swimming*. She was a temp, not a top-secret-flight-conspiracy-aide on the fast track under patronage protection of the elite Navy class she'd idolized since she could speak.

No, actually. The pad said she was an ArcLieutenant.

A *full* ArcLieutenant, three ranks from where she would have started if she had actually *graduated*.

"But you can't... I mean... I haven't graduated..."

Graham leaned against his desk and folded his arms, "Remember who signs things around here. I could name you Queen of Sheba if I wanted to."

"Sheb... uh?"

Graham held up a hand, "Go walk it off. Breathe. You look like you might faint. I know it's a lot to take in quickly, but trust me, taking it in is the easy part. The hard part's going to be staying up to speed with me."

She nodded a bit more normally — her head was *just* beginning to clear. *Just*.

"Now, we're done for this evening. I suggest you go home and have dinner with your family. There's a protocol script attached to the Top Flight pad, download it into their house AI. It'll grant them marine protection in case they're targeted. Tell them as much as you can *absolutely* trust them with — I'll leave that to your judgment."

Christine blinked and swallowed, "Yes... yessir. Anything else...?"

Graham sensed her considerable tension.

Rightly so, this was all too abrupt for him as well. He'd thought this sort of situation might come up, and while he liked the way Christine was fitting into his daily rhythm, it was very quick to bring a cadet to a position of such responsibility.

But circumstances demanded drastic moves. He did need an aide, and he was certain Bill Wallace's granddaughter wouldn't let him down.

That all said, she was as pale as a ghost — he needed to ease the tension. Donut time.

"Now, you'll also want to learn the secret handshake..." Graham put on a calming smile that set Christine slightly at ease. She nodded and turned to go.

"...and start carrying a sidearm."

She stopped in mid-step, nodding again, "Yes, sir."

Then she walked out very awkwardly.

Graham watched the door close behind her, leaned back over his desk and tapped the monitor back on. The comm had stayed open with the picture shut down, and Sarah was still waiting there. As Graham turned the screen to face him from his high angle she looked skeptical, "You sure you want *her*?"

Clenching his jaw slightly, he nodded, "I don't like coups, Sarah. She's so bloody fresh nobody can have gotten to her, and given the way she got here, I doubt she's a plant. Nobody starts an agent at the Panatorium in hopes she'd run into Pat and that he'd introduce her to me and that I'd hire her as my personal aide because mine got pregnant."

Sarah attempted to smile at the remark, but her attempt failed.

"I *am* going to start screening all my upper staff again, just in case. But it can be damned near impossible to identify Church sympathy these days. We've managed to integrate society *just* enough to make it tough to distinguish a Churcher from a civilian."

Sarah nodded slowly, "But you're sure she's Top Flight quality?"

Graham nodded a bit more fervently, "I *trust* her Sarah. And you should trust me. Pat likes her, Beckett likes her, and Gillian likes her. She's Bill Wallace's granddaughter. I think that adds up to as safe as it gets."

"Alright. So long as you're sure."

"I am."

So she'd made it into the inner circle — Top Flight, as they called it.

Graham had made a *big* mistake. Because as soon as Christine Schaeffer reached her cabin, she betrayed Graham's confidence in her.

Or at least she felt like she did.

She threw up.

Twice.

She wasn't meant to do covert world-saving stuff. She'd never be good enough to help the likes of Graham. It was impossible...

How had this all happened anyway? This wasn't *normal*. It was a *summer job*, and now she had a tag for her family's home so that they'd get special marine protection in the event of a *coup*?

Christine dropped onto her bed and tried to breathe deeply, calmingly. She read the Top Flight document that had been written quickly by Graham himself. To her. Personally.

You better believe she threw up again.

There were names on a list in that document. A lot of important people — politicians, celebrities, officers, and techs. And a Church official or two. People planted all across Genesis who were loyal to the civilian government and the Navy if the chips came down.

And there was her name.

What the hell was she doing on a list like that?

Just when she'd been settling in fine.

Damned Church.

She read the list of names again, then tapped one, inadvertently opening Graham's notes on the person — what they did, how they could be contacted, and what they were available for. Pat, for instance, was listed as a good guy to play poker with — deep pockets, bad luck, and a good conscience when it came to money.

Well, she wouldn't be calling *him*.

Scanning down the list again she settled nervously on her own name. She had to call her parents. No, she should go home instead. Yes, calling would be impertinent and improper.

She pulled a kit bag from her closet and started throwing in clothes, and her frayed nerves finally receded enough to let her stomach settle down. As she packed, she activated her wall screen and checked departure times. If she hurried, she could catch a pinnace heading down to Darymanis City — her hometown — in fifteen minutes. She could make it if she ran.

And she felt like running.

Beckett Lupus left the *Pulsar* with Gillian Hodge.

"So they've gone on alert?" he asked softly, and she nodded.

"Not high. Just *aware*. Trusted officers know there might be something brewing, the rest are being told there's a threat of militant terrorism."

Lupus clenched his jaw — he'd feared something like this would come up. The Church had rolled over rather easily at the end of the Krogg War, and while he'd trusted the leadership of Bingham and Argyle, Pious was by no means good-natured.

The name was something of a clue, for starters.

"We're thinking it's far more likely they'll move to help the Faithful than attack here, though. Wouldn't make sense to try an uprising — we've been watching closely enough and have them all accounted for."

Lupus nodded slowly. That meant there'd be an attempt to go to war with Freetowners, and then to drag Earth in. Not surprising considering the resolves of the old Church…

"I'll talk to Varnia, get her to send word back to Earth. Just a heads up, in case they aren't already suspicious. Sounds like the Faithful will be the first movers in this plot…"

Gillian shrugged, glancing nervously around for anyone who might be listening, "Anyway, I'm heading to my office. You going back to *Renown*?"

Lupus nodded, getting the subtle 'be quiet' hint, "Indeed, see you later."

They parted, and Lupus walked silently through the corridors of *Genesis One* towards the *Venerable*-class *Renown*, the mobile embassy of the Earther government assigned to Genesis. Docked in the slot next to *Unity Genesis*, the

First Rate was a popular destination for human tourists, who came aboard daily between 14:00 hours and 16:00 hours. They'd need to increase security just in case...

Lupus approached a corner in the corridor, not really noticing the open service hatch in the wall ahead. There was always maintenance going on aboard *Genesis One*, and all too often the human maintenance staff took their breaks halfway through a job, leaving panels open and tools out. Lupus never understood that attitude, and he'd trained himself to ignore it, as he did here.

Suddenly he thought he heard something, and looked left. Nothing there... odd...

Then a small-statured female came round the corner at a blistering pace and ran right into him. Owing to his greater size and weight, Lupus stayed upright while the momentum reversed and knocked her back towards the open hatch.

Lupus blinked back into reality and reached out to help right her, but it was too late even for someone with his lightning reflexes.

She slammed into the wall below the hatch, and then her head whipped back into the opening.

Lupus grabbed her, but again too late.

There was a brief flash. Ever so brutally brief.

He recognized her immediately, "Christine!"

Her eyes were open, but they rolled back into her head. He pulled her forward off the wall, hearing her kit bag hit the floor as her muscles began to spasm.

Time slowed as instincts Lupus hadn't used for years abruptly reasserted themselves.

Trying to be careful and fast all at once, he lowered her to the deck, then took her wrists in his hands as she began to convulse. He had to do something.

Then he realized there was blood pooling under her head.

He *had* to do something...

Lupus keyed his comm to *Renown*, "*Renown*, Lupus, medalert blue, *Genesis One* corridor just around the corner from lock six. Get here fast."

"Signal director here, sir. Scrambling."

Exactly forty-nine seconds later a team of Earther medics was next to Christine, applying a fast patch to her wounded head and injecting her with UDRC to keep her system going.

How the hell did this happen?

The medical team was comprised of marines of the Second Battalion of the 54th Regiment — the same unit that had been on Krogg with him forty years ago. In fact, this head medic was the battalion surgeon herself, a veteran of the battle.

She met Lupus' eyes, "Heavy dose of radiation... she might as well have stuck her head in an unshielded reactor. This is fatal if I don't give her full regen. Right now."

What maintenance crew would leave such a dangerous current unshielded? More importantly, how had Beckett — best fighter in the Earther Marine Corps — managed to allow this?

Something had distracted him...?

Lupus blinked at all those questions, "*What*?"

"We have to give her regen, General. Not local, I mean the full treatment. She hasn't had any and whatever radiation connected with her head in there is cooking her brain. She's minutes from the end — the local will only preserve her pathways that long."

For a second Lupus wasn't sure what the surgeon was saying, then his brain reasserted itself. Thanks to the Church, it was a *crime* for humans to get the full life-extending regen without special dispensation from the government.

But aside from lengthening lives, regen also strengthened human conditioning when it came to self-repair. And right now, it was Christine's only chance of surviving the run-in...

"She hasn't been informed. She can't *decide*..." Lupus swallowed as he said the words. He'd heard some humans didn't like the thought of outliving their friends and the like. But then, if Christine ever wanted to *see* her friends again...

He nodded after a lengthy — that is, two-second — pause for reflection, "Give it to her. Crash treatment?"

The surgeon nodded, drawing an injector from her case and keying it to formulate regen compound, "We're going to have to give it to her all at once, and that'll put her into cardiac arrest. But we can bring her out of that."

Lupus nodded, watching as a status bar on the injector's screen slowly crawled along towards completion. It occurred to him he should call Graham. He keyed his comm and asked *Renown* to put him through.

What would he say?

CHAPTER 20

Graham stood with crossed arms, watching *Renown's* doctor coax Christine's heart into restarting with some sort of gentle energy pulse. That was the third time her heart had stopped since he'd arrived, apparently the seventh time since she'd been injected with regen. The treatment was supposed to be spread out over a month; she'd had it all at once.

Lupus was rigid, grinding his jaw as he stood next to the younger Manchester, "I should have been paying attention… I mean, when *don't* I pay attention to every damned thing around me…"

Graham patted him on the shoulder, "You can't see around corners, Beck. She was probably on autopilot. I'd just dumped Top Flight on her. Full load."

Lupus looked slowly over at Graham, "I gave her a hell of a welcome to the Flight. 'Welcome to the club. Allow me to knock your head into an open conduit as a greeting….'"

The doctor approached the pair as the monitors showed Christine's vitals leveling off again, "I'm pretty sure the regen is now supplementing her immune system. The brain injury is already healing, but a lot of the pathways were burned out by whatever radiation she was in contact with. I'm not sure how… well, how she'll turn out with so many new ones being grown for her. Either way, at this rate she should be awake in a few minutes and on her feet in a couple of hours."

Graham was nodding solemnly, until he actually processed what was said, "*Minutes? Hours?* She just had her head cooked!"

The doctor frowned, "Yes, and she had a massive dose of regen treatment right after. The repair is going very quickly as the Earther cells overrun her system. It should plateau in the next hour, and after that she'll be physically alright…"

"You should keep her for observation, though. What complications might there be from the crash regen?" Graham's words weren't delivered in a cool tone.

The doctor tilted her head, "In a few hours we'll know. If it works, she'll be herself in that time, and I'm guessing if I tell her to stay for observation when she's feeling herself, she'll object."

Lupus nodded slowly, looking at Graham, "What would you do if you felt fine and wanted to get home, but we said you were spending the night with us?"

Shrugging, Graham elected not to actually say anything.

"I'll definitely put a monitor on her, I can use it to track her vitals no matter where she is in the system, if you like," the doctor offered smoothly.

"Yes. Yes do that," Graham said, still trying to get a grip on everything that had just taken place.

"Good," Lupus leaned in towards the junior Manchester, "and don't worry, Doctor Lazarus here was at Krogg 'A' with us, Graham. She's the one who worked on Narosh when he crashed."

Graham frowned at the reference, but nodded, "Okay then."

Lupus took another deep breath — how had this happened? He didn't just blaze around corners into people… well, evidently he just had. But at least she'd *survive*.

Did something distract me? No matter... walk slowly...

An energy-hyper cutter launched itself from Ecclesia space at full speed, its emissions indicating a reasonably stable translation to those who were watching its departure from the planet's surface. Already the witnesses to that ship's exit were being surrounded by chaos in the Faithful Command and Control center, as the third legion of Faithful Templars was being called from reserve duty by the order of Grand Chancellor Gregory Paine.

The Templars were the ground forces of the Commonwealth of the Faithful, and were directly related to the much more numerous Crusaders of Genesis. In point of fact, the five legions of Templars maintained on the Holy colony had been built around 'retired' Crusader legions that had simply transplanted piecemeal from Genesis to Ecclesia over the past ten years. These warriors were well trained and equipped with state-of-the-art human weaponry; the Freetowners had nothing that could face them on the ground.

But the Templars were indeed secondary at this moment; it was the fleet that most concerned the Grand Chancellor and Chancellor Leo. The Earthers had let the Faithful ships they had entrapped survive, and that arrogant oversight would be their downfall. Never again would the ships of the Faithful Fleet be surprised — they knew now how efficient Earther camouflage could be, and they could avoid it.

With that in mind, the Faithful ships planned to drive straight towards Freetown. They would leave just as soon as the Fleet could be reinforced by Leo's returned ships, and loaded with its cargo of four battle legions of Templars. The total force would be considerable: 100,000 Templars escorted by three Dreadnoughts, a provisional carrier — built out of a cargo hauler, though armed with reasonably modern fighters — as well as eight Battlecruisers of varying ages, three Heavy and four Light Cruisers, and fourteen Destroyers. This force would strip Ecclesia bare of all but its defensive satellites and the ground defenses of the Fifth Legion, but the risk would be worth it.

Freetown would fall within the week — unless the Earthers intervened.

But that danger was part of the scheme, and Paine had accepted it. He had hoped that, by pouncing on the Towner convoy near Earth, Leo's forces would have drawn fire from Earther vessels. It had not worked out that way, but what had been recorded would indeed be enough to allow High Chancellor Pious to raise the people of Genesis.

And this had been secured *without* the loss of the valuable Dreadnoughts of the Faithful Fleet. It was almost ideal.

The cutter that had just departed Ecclesia space would reach Genesis momentarily, and would provide Pious with the recordings of Leo's conversation with the Earther Magnus. He would spread word of it, show it and explain it to his people, and his supporters would cry out, there would be rioting, and, at long last, a coup.

The Navals would be unprepared, the Earthers even less so.

The Church would reign again.

Christine sat up slowly and felt the room spin.

Ugh. Had she been drinking or something? She'd done it once — at the demand of her roommate — and since then had never touched alcohol. She hadn't liked the blackout and the vomit all over the place.

But the current headache suggested that's what she'd been doing, as did the inability to get her eyes open. And she'd had the strangest dream about Graham Manchester and Beckett Lupus, not to mention Pat Conroy. She'd ended up in their inner circle of confidence. Top Flight… ha! She was reading too many history books. Dreaming about being the aide to a flag officer while in a drunken stupor… said a lot about why she had no social life…

Maybe she was late for work at the Panatorium… oh sh–

"How many fingers?"

There was a blur in front of her face and she frowned, forcing her eyes to open and blinking twice to clear her field of vision.

Well, she wasn't late for work.

"Um, six."

"*Two*," Graham leaned over her and lowered his hand, squinting a bit at her eyes, "No damage to the retina, right doc?"

Lazarus shook her head, "No, but her visual cortex was massively reconstructed. It'll clear up as soon as her brain gets used to the new imager."

"I'm very sorry," this time it was Lupus leaning over Christine. "I wasn't watching where I was going and I barreled right into you. You went head-first into an open power conduit… backwards… fried a lot of your brain matter..."

He sounded incredibly guilty, and Christine's first instinct was to courteously take the blame, "Well I was running… wait… what? What about a conduit and my *brain*?"

"Very fluke accident, Christine," Graham's voice couldn't hide his concern. "There was maintenance left undone and it was in exactly the wrong place when you and Beckett collided, and your head went into the power conduit. He pulled you out immediately, but the radiation from the relay you went through..."

Christine's hands clumsily flailed up to her head and started patting it, "My hair doesn't feel burned..."

"Weren't in there long enough, the current just ran from ear to ear. You're lucky we were close enough — 2/54th's surgeon got to you in less than a minute, or you'd be brain dead," Doctor Lazarus wasn't in Christine's view, but her words were soothing enough to let the young human's hands drift back down to her sides.

I was critically injured by a fluke... and saved...

She could count her lucky stars that this had happened the way it had, then. Earther T-Cells had regenerative capabilities that were nothing short of remarkable when it came to application in humans. The original Earther DNA sequences had been adapted by the Omega plague to be quite similar to human strands, presumably to allow for easy infection. The result, probably not intended by Omega, was that Earther DNA was easily made to work with human genetic material...

"Well... ahem," Graham cocked an eyebrow and nodded to Lupus, "tell her about the... *complication...*"

Lupus frowned, "What compl... oh. Yes."

Christine's head was clearing enough for her to start worrying at the ambiguous introduction. Her blood tingled.

Wait, her *blood* tingled — when did her blood ever tingle?

"To keep you alive we had to give you a crash regen treatment. The whole suite in the course of a few minutes. Killed you something like ten times before your system leveled off."

Christine didn't process the words for a second.

Graham half-hissed at his compatriot, "*Subtle* next time, *maybe*?"

Lupus shrugged, "I'm a marine. No tact. Me blow up stuff... you know..."

The inappropriately light comment got one of Graham's rarely-seen lethal glares, and Lupus shrugged, "Your head clearing, Christine?"

She nodded slowly and absently rubbed the back of her head. Her hair still didn't feel charred — how could it not feel burnt or even frizzy?

Then she stopped.

"Wait, you said *regen*?"

Both Beckett and Graham nodded slowly, and her eyes revealed her shock.

"The long-live one... with the 250 years of life... and the healing properties?"

Again, slow nods.

"The one I legally *can't* have?"

Beckett let out a sigh and glanced quickly at Doctor Lazarus, while Graham patted his aide on the shoulder reassuringly, "We'll see it cleared with the authorities… the more important issue is making sure you're alright."

She scowled and her head throbbed, "Am I alright?"

There was no way to give an easy answer to that one.

She'd been given regen. *Regen*…

Shaking her head slightly, she asked quietly, "I'll always be twenty now?"

"On the surface," Lazarus nodded slowly. "You'll age at a visibly slower rate. You won't hit thirty for… oh, a century. Things go a little faster when you cross 200, but not too much."

Maybe that was good. Sort of good news. Surely, it had to be…

The natural inclination, of course, was to say it was *very* good news, but she'd heard about the consequences of long life before. She'd talked to her family about it. The people who lived three or four times as long as everyone they knew had to go through a lot — friends grew old and died, family went away…

Getting regen was a *decision* — long life looked good on paper, but what about those who didn't get the chance? There was a certain amount of guilt involved, based on what some veterans who'd written their memoirs pointed out. Granted, their pain at not growing old and dying with their comrades was in no small part a component of some brand of survivors' guilt — not only had they lived through the war, they'd been rewarded — but that still left her wondering whether she wanted this, when her family couldn't have it.

What about her parents… her sister? They'd never move to Freetown to get regen, they loved their home too much, and now she'd have to outlive even her little sister by some 200 years. What the hell was she going to do with all the time…

Her life plan had never really been mapped out on the 'centuries' scale.

And now she'd forever look like she was in her early twenties. She suspected she'd appreciate that more as she got older… now she was just afraid of being treated like a youngster forever. And getting carded if she ever went to a club.

Because during a life-changing event like this, *clubbing* was obviously one of the top concerns she needed to worry about…

"Oh my Gods," she said it before the thought had fully registered with her, "my parents are never going to believe why I got this. Never."

She was already capable of speech in full sentences.

Graham frowned, glancing at Beckett and then looking back down at her, "What do you mean?"

"I *mean* this is a big deal, and I always promised my parents I'd talk to them about decisions like these before I made any leaps… but now look at the timing. I get to tell them I'm Top Flight and that they have protection from a coup… and that just happens to coincide with a convenient and yet highly unlikely accident that got me *regen*…" Christine's voice trailed off.

Beckett and Graham exchanged glances again, and then the Earther took his turn to ask the question, "You're worried they'll be angry?"

Christine began to sit up very slowly, but stopped as her mind seemed to reel at the change in angle, "They'll think Graham's trying to manipulate me or bribe me or something... I don't know, but I'm not supposed to do things like this without talking to them first..."

Graham didn't understand any of this, but then he'd never known his parents — Sarah had raised him after theirs had been tortured to death for lack of faith. Worrying about parental approval was completely alien to him... "Well... tell them the truth..."

Christine's blood was tingling again, and she shook her head, "Point to my perfect hair that shows no sign of my brain being irradiated? Tell them I was running to a shuttle, ran right into the *General* commanding Earther marines in this system, and was knocked backwards into a conveniently-placed open conduit?"

Beckett raised an eyebrow, and Graham's face tightened, "Ah. So, they'll think you made it up."

"I can barely believe it myself, and I was there," Beckett added quietly.

"I can send a letter along with you..." Graham offered a bit helplessly, "...explain it all."

Trying to sit up again — this time with more success — Christine shook her head, "No, thanks. My parents aren't the sort to... well, I'll have to sit down with them. I'll... explain it."

Yeah, hi mom and dad. I'm going to outlive all of the family you know by a century or two. No, I got the treatment accidentally. *Please don't disown me. Here's a program that gets you free marine protection in case there's a* coup.

It'd probably be a short visit, and she'd spend half an hour waiting for the bus after it was over. With her bags and their good riddance. Well, maybe not, but this wouldn't be pleasant. Her parents were supportive... but this was a great deal to lay on them and they were going to be upset. She hadn't even quite explained to them about leaving the Panatorium yet. Just sent a note with a new comm number and an "I'll call you."

And she hadn't called. She'd been legitimately busy over the past days...

Well, her family would hopefully rally around her... after a huge argument or two. Or more.

She was subconsciously grinding her jaw when she realized Lupus was eyeing her again.

"Tell you what, I'll take you planetside in my boat and, if you'll have me, I'll back your story entirely — Top Flight included. It'd probably be harder to dismiss as fabricated if I'm there to vouch."

Graham glanced from Christine to Beckett with a significant amount of surprise etched in his expression, "You want to go planetside...?"

Christine was very tempted — this was exactly the sort of thing that would help right now. But she couldn't say yes.

"No, thanks, it'd be an inconvenience. You're a *General* — I shouldn't need to have my hand held when I'm talking to my own parents."

Beckett listened to her words, but his instincts picked up on her near-panic — it seemed quite clear that she'd need some solid backup to avoid being outcast for getting regen. Unsupported, her excuse would probably appear to be a pathetic cover for a procedure she'd undergone merely to satisfy her vanity.

He'd back her up.

"Well... I should also check out the security arrangements at your house to make sure you're not a liability to our Top Flight operations."

That was a good excuse. Total fabrication, of course, since Graham had already had her vetted, but it sounded good.

"Well..."

Graham looked from Beckett to Christine and back, "I think it's a good idea, Christine."

She winced, leaning a little farther forward, "Alright... um... when should I meet you?"

Lupus smiled, "*After* you can stand up. Doc, can you have someone call my wife and get my boat prepped with Sergeant Cuttar's squad. Top Flight business."

Lazarus sounded slightly amused, "You know, I'm really not a *Signal Officer*."

As the doctor paced away, Christine frowned, "Should you be saying that Top Flight stuff out loud?"

Lupus smiled, "You're on *Renown*, remember. We're all Top Flight over here."

Graham's eyes narrowed, "He's just not a particularly modest member."

They shared a friendly glare.

CHAPTER 21

Renown was closing its flight bay doors — having let Lupus' lander exit — when the Sensor Officer on the bridge frowned suddenly. Touching the Sensor Chief on the shoulder, the lion officer pointed at a strange reading on the screen and then looked up at the Sixth Lieutenant, currently officer of the watch.

"We're getting a major e-hyper signature tracking in, Mister Garn. It's a cutter."

The Sixth Lieutenant, on only his first cruise at Lieutenant's rank but still as prudent as any Earther, frowned and turned to the Signal Chief, "Alert the Rear Admiral. Put the ship on heightened alert."

"The cutter has translated… it's sending burst traffic directly to the Chancellors' Directorate… looks like it's going through Sanctity Base."

Sixth Lieutenant Garn flicked his eyebrow, "Decode it."

Sarah reached Command and Control in the basement of her Genesis City Capital Building just behind Fred Thornton.

"Have we got it yet?" the urgent question betrayed the Vice President's impatience.

Sarah simply stood back and waited.

"We just got a quick feed from *Renown*. The Rear Admiral sends her compliments… and 'Dunno'. She's put *Renown* on heightened readiness," the Comm Director for the C&C bunker frowned over the short burst, then his eyes narrowed as the decoded text of the cutter's message scrolled up on his display. He immediately redirected it to the main screen before Thornton and Sarah, and the civilian government officials read it.

It was, again, quite obscure.

Sarah turned away from the screen for a moment, "Someone please contact my husband. And get me Graham on secure link."

Gillian sat on Graham's desk and frowned at the wall screen. She'd come by as soon as she'd heard about the accident with Christine, but she hadn't even gotten to say a word before the comm had chirped to report the arrival of the second of the Faithful's cutters.

Now *Renown's* feed of the cutter's message content was here to be read.

And of course, it was as abstract as hell, totally meaningless unless you knew what it was *supposed* to mean.

"Well, my marines are all on heightened alert. I have the city garrisons forting up, and Second and Third Corps are ready to move out of Lancaster Base if the Crusaders do anything," Gillian folded her arms across her chest and looked down at Graham.

Slouched back in his chair, Graham scratched his chin and frowned, "All my Churchers are at the rift on blockade or at the picket posts. Do you think this is some sort of order though? They can't move without us seeing it — on the ground or out here."

Gillian shrugged, "We have no authority to stop the Crusaders from going on maneuvers whenever they like. I'm just afraid they might concentrate a few Legions on Genesis City. We've only got 20,000 troops in the area, and only 2,000 at Darymanis."

Graham paused as he considered the situation, "If they move a whole legion anywhere, I imagine you'll be all over them. And my Destroyers will be, too."

It was something the Navy — and these two in particular — had long been prepared for. Twenty-odd years prior, sitting up late in bed, Graham and Gillian had mapped out the various offensive actions the Crusaders could manage with the six moderately-equipped legions they were allowed to have operating out of Sanctity Base on the main continent. It was a four-hour run over a single superhighway to the capital from that base, and the trip crossed right through Darymanis City at the halfway point.

Of course, the trip from Lancaster Base — home of the Naval marines — was only three hours overland to Genesis City. Better still, if the shooting started, the Naval marines would be able to move via air with orbital support, whereas any Church aircraft that rose above 500 meters into the atmosphere could be disintegrated safely by orbiting Destroyers.

Altogether, then, the Navy and the marines had the theoretical ability to keep the six Crusader Legions isolated in their Sanctity Base during those years when the Navy provided the city garrisons. Any attempt to seize power while the Navy was in that position would be made virtually impossible by their orbital firepower and by the fortifications surrounding the cities that straddled the superhighways.

Hell, even in the years when the Church garrisoned the cities, the air-mobility abilities of the Naval marines would allow them quick deployment in case of a coup, and the Church could be blockaded and starved.

The theory was perfect. If it *worked*.

Well, they might find out soon enough.

The comm chirped again, and Graham blinked, keying it without looking, "Yes?"

"Message from the President, sir."

"Pipe it down."

•••

High Chancellor Thomas Pious read three words of significance in the message: 'heathen stood forward'. The phrase was mixed in with some flotsam about prophecy meant to disguise it, but it was perfectly clear to him. Those were the key words agreed on years earlier, indicating an Earther move to intervene in sovereign human affairs.

The reply to this message would be simple.

Standing in the Command Center of Sanctity Base — smuggled there quite secretly and replaced with an imposter at his house in Genesis City — he had access to many things the Navals thought were exclusively theirs.

Including a dozen mechanized tank battalions, and 250,000 Crusaders.

Preparations had admittedly been rushed, and plans had to be assembled in rapid fashion from old contingencies, but the new brothers of the Church were not the inept band of weak-willed old men who had fallen to the Earthers, and the plan was coming together.

"I will record my statement to the people now. Send the reply."

Varnia was frowning at the text reply that reached the ailing cutter. A new broadcast feed flew back into the receivers of Sanctity. It was full video, the sensor logs of a Faithful Dreadnought.

"Another e-hyper signature, ma'am. A drone marked from the First Battle Squadron."

Varnia paused momentarily — it probably had something to do with this...

"Put it up as soon as you can. What's the cutter sending down now?"

A screen was drawn in the holo tank, and on it was an image of the First Battle Squadron, with the First Flying Squadron, drawn up in wall formation.

Varnia frowned — the pod's feed must have been put up instead of the cutter's.

"Hold the relay from the drone, I'd like to see the cutter's feed first," she shifted anxiously in her seat.

There was a pause as her Signal Chief leaned over his console and looked at her, "That *is* the cutter's feed."

Then a voice from the screen in the holo tank erupted: "This is not *your* space Admiral Magnus."

Varnia's mind ground to a halt.

"It's *First Lord Magnus* to *you*... Now, there's something you might want to consider... I'm sitting on sixteen of the best ships in the galaxy... You've got a handful of vintage trash... I've got 2,500 guns and a thousand boats... You've got old tubes and twenty fighters... I think you need to ask yourself a question: do you feel lucky... And I mean *very* lucky."

The image cut.

Varnia's muscles tightened.

That couldn't have been the sum total of the encounter… but if that transmission was going to Sanctity Base it meant the Church was getting it first, and they'd say it was a move of intimidation by the Earthers against the interests of the Faith — a unilateral move.

And somehow they'd get to blame the Genesis civilian government for letting it happen.

The Church wouldn't even need a coup to take control… it could turn a vote in Congress to support the little Faithful underdog.

"Put up Fox's signal," Varnia needed the other side of this story.

The First Space Lord appeared on the screen with a frown, "They got around us and set up an ambush for the entire Freetown First Expeditionary, Varnia. I'm guessing you're going to hear the worst about it, but they attempted to engage in an act of war within gunshot of our space. I interposed Batron One and Flyron One and shot down missiles. The entire vid is included from both *Venerable* and *Savanna Felix*. Hope this arrives before their cutter does — and I hope things are holding together."

Just missed the timing on this one, Fox…

"Send Fox's feed direct to Sarah and Graham."

Pausing for a moment, Varnia looked to her Sixth Lieutenant, "Inform Colonel Howler that I'll want his battalion standing by to drop at a moment's notice."

"With that vid they could blow us right out of Congress. We're the ones advocating an alliance with the biggest interstellar bullies… you know that's exactly what Pious will say! Shit. Where is he–"

Sarah put a hand on her Vice President's shoulder, "Easy now, Fred. This is *good* news in some ways. They're probably looking to do this within political bounds."

"You sure about that?" Graham's face was on the monitor, scowling as he listened to his sister's calm tone. "This could be a precursor to a coup. They could use it to fire up their supporters and sway some undecideds."

Sarah shook her head, "Pious isn't ready to deal with the Navy, Graham. We'd know if he was. Without armor they can't even break a city's bastions. They'll be looking for a way to oust me without sacrificing the system, and I think this must be it."

Gillian leaned into the shot, "I'm still going to put my marines on full alert. This could lead to fighting in the streets — civil control–"

"Is a job for the police, Gillian. If we put the marines on full alert, it'll look as though we've got something to hide, or that we're trying to take control for ourselves before this breaks on the news. We'd make Pious' case for him. No, our only hope in Congress is to keep calm. They'll try to provoke us into attacking them, and then they'll discredit us with the Earthers."

There was an interrupting beep, and the Comm Director looked up, "Another feed from *Renown*, looks like it literally just podded in. Response by Fox Magnus..."

Graham was looking off screen too, "Yep, just got it here."

They played Fox's account.

"The Sixth Legion's First Mechanized Phalanx is ready to deploy, High Chancellor."

Pious nodded to the High Shappa who delivered the report, "Very well, confer on them my blessing, and send them on their way."

A single Phalanx — 5,000 men in 500 vehicles — was very little to deploy to any theatre of war. If the Navy recognized the scope and significance of this force as it left Sanctity Base, there would be little hope of it reaching its objective.

But the Phalanx detailed to this duty was one of two equipped with the new stealth technology recently developed in the deep caverns below Sanctity, and its vehicles were built on a design improved from the standard Naval pattern. All of the hover-tanks of the Crusader Mechanized Phalanxes had been built in secret; the Crusaders supposedly had no armor.

It would be a good surprise, and the Navy would not even see it coming.

"We are ready to broadcast the Declaration, Your Eminence."

High Chancellor Thomas Pious turned with a nod to his acolyte, "Very well."

"*No* heightened alert, Graham. I know you want to, but *no*. No provocation. Gillian, tell your marines not to provoke any sort of episode. We'll broadcast our version of the incident near Earth immediately," Sarah was adamant...

And anxious. Very anxious.

This was coming on fast, and suddenly. Years of politics and she was being outmaneuvered, she could smell it. All she could do now was damage control, try to save her government. But it still didn't seem like a coup to her. How could it be one? Even if this vid changed the opinions of the undecideds, the Church had no assets in place that could really get out of Sanctity fast enough to offset Naval control. Then again, Fox had sounded far from pleasant in his tirade. And Earthers always sounded pleasant.

No, if the Earthers had opened fire, maybe the Church could use it to precipitate a public revolution. On their own, though, Fox's words shouldn't be enough to cause problems, and besides, Pious had nothing to fight with...

The door at C&C's rear opened with its characteristic pressurized thump, and Pat walked in slowly, "What've I missed?"

•••

At Sanctity Base, 500 hover tanks deployed their signal dampeners and camouflage.

In the lead machine, Shappa Actan Galtsar spoke into a microphone, “Phalanx, advance!”

At 400 meters altitude, the armor surged southward — riding the super-highway towards Genesis City.

CHAPTER 22

The thick jungle of Genesis had never really appealed to Beckett Lupus — he liked his trees coniferous and his weather cold. Sure, some Earthers really enjoyed an 'island paradise' feel to their environments, but he wasn't one of them.

But that was irrelevant. This was hardly a vacation.

As his dropship's feet lowered smoothly onto Darymanis City's landing field, Beckett stood and nodded to Sergeant Major Cuttar, "Keep an eye on the ship."

Somewhere between offering to visit Christine's family and calling his wife to prep the ship, another good reason for landing on Genesis had occurred to Lupus: with Gillian worried about the tensions in the cities, it made sense for him to use his heightened instincts to get a good read on the situation down here. If there was a real threat, he'd pick up on it.

So that was his official justification for hauling his personal ship and his personal squad to Genesis for a couple of hours.

That and it was faster and more comfortable to travel this way than by the commercial means.

"We can grab a cab over there, General. Um… my house is in the northern suburb, near the edge of town," Christine, much to her credit, was walking steadily and wielding her own bag. The medical monitor on her wrist was humming, and the indicator light on it was green, so supposedly she was fine and healthy…

However, Beckett wasn't letting her out of his sight.

He thus kept close pace with her as he replied, "I'm serious, call me *Beckett*. How do we get a cab?"

The only city Lupus had been to in many decades was Genesis City, so he was taking in his surroundings as Christine walked to the nearby hail post. Keying the cab button, she drew the attention of a prowling hover taxi. As the yellow energy-floater skidded to a halt at the marker, the cabby waved them to the open-topped back seat. Christine pitched her duffle in and then followed it through the open door. Beckett hopped over the opposite side and dropped with surprising agility onto the padded seat.

The driver eyed the Earther suspiciously, but he was drawn off by a winning smile from the younger human passenger. Lupus didn't like the atmosphere

— and he'd been down here for less than two minutes.

"Where to, young miss?"

Christine felt edgy, and it was her blood that was *itching* again. But she knew how to distract the driver from his problem — she was pretty enough to have a winning and distracting smile.

"I'm headed home to see my parents, 511 block nine, northeast."

"Righto, sweetie."

They sped off.

Marshal Joe Greer was sitting in his office in one of Darymanis City's bastions, watching the vid feed as it ran on all the major NewsNets.

"These are the friends of the civilian leadership, people of Genesis. They are *tyrants* in disguise. This sort of infringement upon the space of our friends cannot be met lightly. Do not mistake my meaning: I do not call for war. I assure you that a conflict with the Earthers is not my goal. Instead I suggest we check the government that has allowed — through treachery, patronage and complacency — these Earthers such a free hand."

Joe Greer hated Thomas Pious, but the man was delivering this address well. The feed with Fox Magnus and the Earther guns firing canister replayed, and Greer sighed.

"We will take this to the Congress, and should *our* government prove too arrogant to listen, we will force this fact before them! I ask all loyal *humans* to go to the streets of their cities, not to fight but to chastise the Earthers in peaceful ways. Should any government agent attempt to silence you, it will be the Church who stands against them. We will prove now, once and for all, that this government is a brew of corrupt despots-in-waiting. They have deceived us with their notions of heroism, and lied to us as to the character of their friends. No more! Stand firm, people of Genesis. We will tear the mask off this government!"

Greer expected that to be the end of this disgusting propaganda outburst, but the transmission looped back to the beginning. Oh well. He tapped the screen back to his personal message list. The Church could loop it as much as they wanted, it wouldn't start riots and the Congress would stand...

A new order was sitting on his message screen, from Commandant Hodge to all senior officers.

"Do not provoke any unrest. Do not, under any circumstances, appear belligerent. The President is confident this may be dealt with in Congress," Greer read the words softly to himself.

He shook his head as he read the order again — straight from the top, and dripping just slightly with angst. What was she worried about? He was two hours from Sanctity, with 2,000 marines in seven fortified bastions, all on alert to watch for militant terrorism. He was hardly going to open fire on protesters, and if the Crusaders moved, he'd know about it before the Church did.

No, this was nothing more than a bit of political intrigue for him. Security here was a foregone conclusion, and Darymanis City was almost fully Naval anyway — there'd be no trouble.

Floating through the streets of the suburban city, Lupus found himself surprised by what he was seeing. The houses here had a similar feeling to those on latter-day Earth — they were low and broad, with front and back lawns, pastel-colored stucco coverings, and big windows. There was little to tell them apart from homes he'd seen images of in the history books from human times.

The day was bright and warm, and as such the air had a somewhat familiar summer feel. They'd just passed over the superhighway — a walled silver, twenty-five-meter-wide causeway that effectively divided the city's commercial districts from the residential zone they'd just entered, and the industrial zone to the south.

Lupus found the superhighway to be a fascinating construction. Essentially based on a simple flat channel with walled sides, the highway allowed low-hovering vehicles like the cab he and Christine were riding in to move speedily across jungle terrain. That ease of transit made the superhighway the link that tied together all the old cities of Genesis, and apparently, each city along it was fortified with ground bastions. Beckett had noticed seven of those squat structures around the perimeter of the city on the way down.

There were people on the streets as the cab hummed through them, some with little children, other older retirees. Some were scowling at him as they caught his eye. One teenager pointed and yelled something.

Lupus' expression remained neutral, but his instincts picked up on the increasing tension.

Some — especially the older ones who saw him, waved with smiles... but some made other, less genial gestures, and glared.

That was odd. Humans had never been so visibly rude to him, but then, he'd never been in a city outside the capital.

Christine, for her part, was trying to distract him with small talk, "So the house that my grandfather lived in was torn down thirty years ago when they consolidated the residences on this side of the highway."

Lupus blinked, "Aha. Um. Consolidated?"

Whatever was going on in her body, Christine was acutely aware of the looks the General was getting. And if she knew, he *had* to know. Embarrassment and shame for having brought him were beginning to creep up ever so slowly... so she'd talk just two more minutes, until they got to her house.

"Before Chancellor Bingham's desegregation movement, the Navy lived on the seaside of the city with the landing field, and the Church lived in luxury over here."

Lupus was only half listening as he watched the reaction of more passers-by, but the statement still hitched on part of his mind, "The segregation was that literal?"

Christine nodded, "Back then, yes. But that was easier — you knew who you could trust. These days, we all live on the same side of the highway, but it's a lot harder to pick a solid Naval from a fanatic Churcher."

Beckett's eyebrows went up, but he couldn't think of anything to say. He'd been an Ambassador here for a decade — these were the sorts of things he really should have picked up on by now. But the political sheen that had covered this society was clean and happily focused on Genesis City. He'd spent his time there relaying and advising, he'd never really absorbed the local ambiance — or carefully scrutinizing the mood of the people.

The hover cab made a left turn and glided up a hill. Fences kept the jungle back from open meadows along its slopes, and houses sprawled airily over it.

"We're on the edge of town. You can see just about everything in Darymanis from up here."

Lupus nodded slowly as he looked across to the open landing field, probably fifteen kilometers away by road. The superhighway was fully visible from this high point, until it made a curve to follow a river and was obscured by another hill. Lake Darymanis shimmered pleasantly.

Beckett was seeing the fairytale beauty Genesis had to offer, but somehow he *knew* something decidedly un-fairy tale like was preparing itself in the background.

He should have brought his swords with him from his lander.

The cab stopped and Christine swiped the pay meter with her bank card. Lupus vaulted over the side onto the alloy-plated street and straightened his shirt, while Christine dragged her duffle out the door on the other side.

Lupus' eyes were drawn to the bastions on this side of the city — fortified bunkers lying a few hundred meters beyond the outer fences, tied together by a thin line of walled silver roads and with landing pads on their roofs. From this corner-of-town hill, he could distinguish all of them as he winced against the glare.

Fortifications deployed around all towns… the sorts of things he hoped he'd never have to build on Earth. City fighting wasn't something he liked to think much about… so he wouldn't.

As he observed the houses around him more carefully, he realized Christine was already carrying her duffle up the walk of the second to last home on the street. This was truly the very edge of town — the alloy road stopped at a dead end at Christine's neighbor's driveway and two hundred meters down a grassy slope from there, the fences were deployed against the press of the jungle.

Beckett strode quickly to catch up with his charge, and as she came to a stop in front of the door of the light-blue house, he straightened himself up and took a breath. Time to be diplomatic.

Christine knocked, anxious and headachy. There was a pause, footsteps, and the door opened.

Mister Schaeffer was a fairly tall man, and his hair and moustache were black. Lupus hadn't seen a moustache for quite a while–

The man started to smile as he saw his daughter, then looked past her at the escorting wolf and the half-formed smile vanished. Beckett's ear twitched a little.

"As long as he's not your boyfriend, you can come in."

Lupus' eyebrows nearly bounced off the top of his forehead. Mister Schaeffer's expression was deadpan.

Christine, for her part, was *very* red, "*Dad*, stop it."

Mister Schaeffer suddenly grinned, "So you're dating?"

"I'm actually married to a lovely wolf of my own," Beckett masked his annoyance and offered his reply.

"Ah good, come in then..." he stepped back from the door and Christine led the way into the bright, open house.

The living room was just to the right of the door, and the large main screen was on. As soon as Beckett stepped into the house he heard it — a voice he knew coming from the vid screen.

His head turned slowly and his breathing stopped.

"Dad, this is General Beckett Lupus, of the Earther Marines. I sort of work with him now."

Beckett was sure there was surprise on Mister Schaeffer's face. And Missus Schaeffer, a nice enough looking woman who was already standing in the living room to greet her daughter, paused to look him over.

Lupus had already turned his attention away when her eyes fell on him.

He saw canister shot and heard Fox Magnus, and suddenly the tension he'd felt in the atmosphere on the ride over made sense.

Then the High Chancellor's angry face appeared, and the man spat his accusations at the audience of Genesis.

"...it will be the Church who stands against them!"

With his crimson cloak and intense hatred, this man very much reminded Beckett of Shappa Bactule of the Quest.

And while the High Chancellor was saying this was a matter for Congress, Beckett Lupus knew better. The Church didn't really believe in Congress — not if they could find a way around it.

Christine turned to her guest with a smile — her parents were shocked enough, so it was *his* turn to explain–

Beckett's comm was in his hand, and it was already linking to the Earther embassy in orbit, a response coming over its speaker, "*Renown.* Signal Officer, here."

"Harks, this is Beck Lupus. Put me on with my wife."

There was a pause as the Schaeffers in the room followed Lupus' gaze to the main screen. Christine's smile vanished and her eyes widened. Her parents' faces hardened.

"It's been repeating for three minutes or so. It's just hot air I think…" Mister Schaeffer was kind in his words, but Lupus didn't agree with the assessment.

"The Churchers will use it as an excuse dad…" Christine was frozen as she spoke, then her senses cleared. "I need to call in."

"I'm here Beck," Lupus' comm was loud enough for all to hear. "You got down alright?"

Beckett ground his jaw for a second, "We're here. But I don't like the look of this. Get the battalion prepped and ready to drop."

"They're already geared. I've got the bay doors idling."

A very thin wash of relief hit the General and he smiled just a little, "Should have known you'd be set. I'll keep you up to speed."

"Be nice to Christine's parents."

"I'm always nice."

"Well, you did put her into a conduit head first, dear."

Those words made Lupus suddenly *very* aware of his company.

"Talk later, bye now."

The comm cut and Lupus looked up to meet two pairs of unpleasantly shocked eyes. Then the main screen changed abruptly as Christine keyed it away from Pious' feed, and someone new was there.

"Is everything alright up there?" Christine dropped her duffle and carried the screen remote to the center of the living room. "Do you want me to come back?"

Now filling the screen, Graham shook his head, and Gillian leaned further into the camera shot, "I have orders not to increase the alert status on the marines — we don't want to look belligerent. There's nothing you can really do."

"Have a visit with your family and stay near a screen, I think," Graham nodded. Then the Schaeffer parents moved to stand next to their daughter.

Graham's controlled expression molded quickly into a look of awkward surprise.

"Um… hello there. I'm… uh… your daughter's new… boss."

Christine risked a glance back over her shoulder. Her parents' mouths were hanging open.

"Mom, Dad, there's a lot I have to explain."

CHAPTER 23

Lieutenant Colonel Cadmus Howler let his rifle cradle easily in the crook of his arm, aiming it at the ceiling as he patted each passing marine on the back with his free hand. His battalion was one of the best; *Renown* had been sent to Genesis with an effective combat formation, just in case it ever had to be deployed. These, the troops of the 2nd Battalion of the 54th Regiment of Foot were veterans of Avalon, Amaratsu and Krogg 'A', as well as a number of other, less popular actions.

Even forty years later, many of the remaining rankers were career marines who'd seen action in the Krogg War. As for the non-veterans, well, they were *Earthers*, and as Howler recalled, that had been more than enough qualification the first time Earther marines had seen action against Crusaders. Of course, between the Battle of the Antarctic Plain and now there'd been changes to technology, but when it came down to it, the old Earther training was as effective as ever, if not more.

Five hundred strong, including reserves and specialized units, the battalion fielded fifty single-person pulsars and an equal number of extended-range defense shields. The marines had, by themselves, the ability to effectively seal off a perimeter of some ten kilometers, thanks to the newest versions of the energy shields their engineering platoon had loaded. Shield belts were lighter and about fifty percent stronger, and additional shields were worn on the wrist, with about seventy percent effectiveness relative to the old Krogg War types. Altogether, the marines had the protection of two old shield belts at the cost of one — and a wrist watch.

Not too shabby…

Renown's five assault dropships were filling up quickly, each obviously carrying a fifth of the battalion. These were new as well — craft that were sufficiently shielded to handle fire from fighters and hover tanks, though swift enough not to have to. Indeed, avoiding incoming fire would be the method of choice if a drop was called for today, because fighting in the air was to be handled by another branch of the Navy.

Elsewhere in *Renown's* hull, three full squadrons of gunboats were prepping for launch — two Strike Squadrons mounting pairs of capital ship guns and one Escort Squadron mounting light, quick-firing carronades. These units could in tandem establish superiority over just about anything in the sky, even a

Destroyer or two.

In other words, experience had helped ensure the success of this operation even before it was launched. With the sort of support he could call down, Cadmus Howler was certain 2/54th could stop anything short of a legion.

"There's an Earther in there!"

Beckett could clearly hear the shout from where he sat on the couch with his back to the window, though he couldn't get a sense of the intent behind it. The commotion was growing outside and he knew he was drawing a crowd. Someone had seen him arrive, and now people were gathering to see what he was up to.

He just couldn't tell whether these people believed Pious' broadcast or not. He'd need to go outside to get indications of that...

"There, you're all set. It's nothing anyone will notice, but if the marines light up VIP houses on their panels, you'll look like a small star."

The elder Schaeffers were sitting opposite Lupus, still more than a little surprised at all they'd been told over the past few minutes. Mister Schaeffer seemed initially miffed about the regeneration without consultation, but his mood moderated to one of fatherly concern as Lupus explained the situation.

They were nice enough parents... though it seemed they didn't quite understand their daughter's crazy career choice. The Naval tradition hadn't been passed on through the family — it was something Christine had come to on her own.

As Christine came away from the screen she'd been watching, she paused to peer out the window at the forty-odd bystanders now gathered on the street. The viewers, in turn, focused on the back of Lupus' obviously fascinating head.

"So. Um. Mom. Dad... anything else you want to know?"

The couple glanced at each other and shrugged. They'd been told about Graham's coup-related worries, but a bit of discussion had eased their fear of armed conflict. Pious' statement wouldn't spark civil war; he'd need further provocation to get into a fight, and Gods knew he wasn't ready to tangle with the Navy.

But the evident social unrest was disturbing...

"Well... General Lupus... what is your interpretation of Admiral Magnus' exchange there?" Mister Schaeffer frowned at his guest and Lupus suppressed an urge to correct the gentleman about Fox's rank. He was being diplomatic toda–

The yelling outside drew Lupus' attention before he could answer, and his ear twitched as he turned to the window. The crowd was dividing neatly, and at one front a man in his twenties was bellowing at the seeming head individual of the other — a child of perhaps twelve.

"I think we might want to call the authorities to have this supervised," Lupus said softly, turning back to the Schaeffers. "How soon can they arrive?"

Law enforcement wasn't something the Earthers had ever invested in. Like criminal law and a justice system, these things had never been needed on Earth, and even human settlers on the planet had proven reasonably amiable to that sort of life. So Lupus had no frame of reference when he asked the question, other than what he'd read.

Christine shrugged, "Three minutes, at least."

With a slightly quivering ear, Beckett heard the confrontation escalate into threats. This would have to be dealt with now.

"Call them," he was on his feet and heading out the door before anyone could try to stop him.

As he stepped quickly down the walk, few people actually watched his approach. The crowd was now numbering over sixty, and the middle of the street was densely packed. The older man was yelling unpleasant things at the child, whose face was sour and who was intermittently screaming at a painful pitch in return. The boy was probably trying to actually *say* something, but through the din, Beckett couldn't make out what.

So he did what any peacekeeper would do in such a situation — he walked right up to them and nodded to both. The crowd finally noticed him as he planted himself between the two opposing sides, "Good day."

There were jeers mixed with sounds of relief — Lupus' instincts were getting very mixed messages.

"I'm sorry to interrupt, but I thought I could help," Lupus looked to the twenty-odd-year-old who continued to glare at the child. "Is there a problem?"

Then the child lunged into his side screaming something that he barely discerned as "*Gods damned heathen*."

Well, he'd definitely misread this whole situation.

The boy wasn't heavy or strong enough to shake Lupus' balance, and as the small human smashed into his thigh, he bounced off. The twenty-year-old — Beckett's supporter, perhaps — made to lunge for the child, but Lupus laid a firm hand on his shoulder.

"I appreciate your support, but I can handle this."

With a bit of a hungry smile, the man nodded. Lupus wasn't all too sure what was now expected of him, but the boy's side of the crowd was bristling. And so was the other... *Naval?...* side.

As the boy screamed even more angrily, he threw himself fists-first at Lupus, and the General let him come. Small punches hammered impotently against his ribs, and the wolf looked down with an expression he hoped didn't include bared teeth.

The boy tired quickly, backing up and darting forward in another effort to bowl the General over. By now, the presumably Church side of the crowd was growing embarrassed. Finally the child screamed viciously and turned away, "Heathen piece of shit!"

Lupus frowned as the boy found his mother, who was in turn glaring contemptuously at him. He met her vicious eyes with his disappointed ones, and for a fleeting second a chill ran through him as she looked down at her son and consoled him, "You tried your best."

And then the crowds started yelling back and forth at each other — jeers and insults between people who were probably quite friendly on a regular, superficial basis. It was all very abrupt, a division that had to have been simmering very closely under the surface.

Still no sign of constables. Could there be other such rivalries elsewhere — larger ones?

He'd need to disperse this himself at this rate.

A hand came to rest on his shoulder and he immediately clutched its wrist. He looked back to see Christine, somewhat wide-eyed but quickly composing herself.

"Sorry," he said softly, and she nodded, bobbing her head to the front door of the house. Two wooden training swords sat on the step.

"Just in case we need something."

Then the crowd turned on her, "What are you doing with an Earther, whore?"

"Hey, she's obviously welcoming an honored guest!"

"Honored scum!"

"Because he doesn't believe in bullshit Gods?"

It got worse again, and Christine bristled. She'd never seen people act like this. Sure, her parents had warned her about the 'sort' of neighbors she shouldn't associate with — and by and large she'd agreed. But she'd assumed it was a division based on subtle differences. This was anything but subtle.

"Hey... what's this?"

The voice was only conspicuous to Lupus' ears because it didn't sound involved at all. He scanned the crowds quickly, trying to discern the source, but he couldn't see anyone.

"Mom? Dad? Are my parents alright?"

The question came from the Church side of the mob... No, two teenage girls with shopping bags were coming hurriedly up the grassy slope from the edge of town. He'd managed to pick them out despite the forty yelling people in the crowd between him and them.

A woman in the rear of the Church ranks grabbed one of the girls' arms as she tried to pass, "You've got scum in your house! Little harlot and her Earther-lovin' family..."

Christine was already moving fast around the mass of people, "Get your hands *off* her!"

She was on scene before Lupus had drawn the necessary connections, and by the time he realized what was happening, Christine had heaved the woman accosting the newcoming girl back into the mob. The two teen girls ran to Christine's house as soon as they were freed, the one who'd been accosted looking back nervously as the crowd surged and closed in around Christine.

"Don't touch a pious woman, whore!"

"Your heathen can't save you now!"

"We'll beat the sin out of you!"

"Sinner!"

Lupus decided at that point that he shouldn't have volunteered to come down. Bad idea.

The nearest of a half-dozen people closing around Graham's young assistant grabbed her shirt and tried to haul her into his grasp. Lupus let out a bit of a sigh and heard the crunch and the spatter of blood that signified the breaking of this man's nose.

Christine swung her body into an Earther-worthy unarmed defense stance, and the crowd surged at her.

Then the Naval crowd counter-surged, and the brawl started.

Lupus moved towards Christine with a hint of a defeated groan, flinging people *gently* out of his way. He didn't land focused blows of any sort unless somebody took a shot at him — he was hard pressed to tell friend from foe in this crowd.

Christine, however, was panicked.

She was surrounded and unarmed, and fighting like a veteran. Her blood simmered and her arms flew and she tossed men twice her size around in heated flurries before they could attack her. The crowd wasn't as persistent as it might have been; want of revenge was not sufficient incentive for a shattered nose.

They backed off, turning instead towards the Naval mob that was lashing at them from the other side.

One brave man tried to come up behind her, but as she turned to engage him a sharp crack on the back of his head knocked him out cleanly. A bit sheepishly, the previously-accosted teen from the slope lowered the practice sword she'd hefted and shrugged, "Hi."

Christine smiled despite herself, but then turned away from the younger girl to deliver another nose-breaking punch to someone coming up behind her–

Lupus caught Christine's relatively small fist in one hand and deflected her accompanying kick with the other. He tilted his head, "You really need to stop try to hurt me. One day you'll pull it off."

Christine reddened immediately, and then the faint but welcome sound of sirens started from down the street. The police here were generally Naval — mostly ex-marines and Navy security. This would get cleared up.

Lupus frowned at the slightly shorter blonde girl carrying the practice sword, "Christine didn't say anything about siblings. But I'm willing to bet you're one."

The two girls exchanged glances and the younger shrugged, extending her empty hand, "I'm Claire."

Lupus took her hand and began to nod, but paused again as something besides the mob drew his attention.

No, that doesn't sound like the mob...

He was conscious of how rude he must have seemed as he turned abruptly away from the Schaeffers, but panning the jungle below, courtesy became unimportant. He could see the superhighway from here, and on it he could make out the shape of a crimson tank being trailed by a long file of red-cloaked men.

Crusaders.

His mind took a full second to process this new data, then his hand clutched his comm and keyed it on.

Renown's Signal Officer answered, then Varnia.

"Send Cadmus. And warn Sarah that there are Crusaders at Darymanis."

The cracks of exchanged fire near the bastions below scattered the crowd.

CHAPTER 24

Marshal Joe Greer grabbed his rifle from its stand in the corner of his office and donned his helmet while his aide waited for him at the door.

"You're serious? A Crusader *tank*?"

The woman nodded in reply, "With about fifty Crusaders in file behind it. I've got Jimmy covering it with the mortar team, and I've called up everybody."

Greer nodded, "Good."

They quickly exited his bastion office, checking their ammo as they walked. This was Bastion One, purposefully placed alongside the highway coming down from Sanctity Base, in case something like *this* happened. Whatever these maniacs were up to, they'd be dealt with.

Arriving in the forward firing room, Greer peered through the narrow firing slit at the single red tank and its escort. A junior-rank officer stood before the Church formation, rifle in hand and face as obstinate as one would expect of a Churcher.

"I'll go meet him. Get a company on the upper firing step so they're visible, bring two companies in here — I want to mow them down if they get aggressive."

His aide paused, "You sure, sir? He might want you dead."

Greer waved off the warning as he stepped quickly to the bastion's side door, "A tank. I didn't think they had any — must be stolen. But it's no problem, just keep me covered."

The aide nodded slowly and started barking for companies to deploy to the various firing positions on this side of the bastion. As boots began to clatter on the metal gratings, Greer opened the nearby exit hatch and stepped out into the fresh air, then slowly descended the steps to the ground.

This stop on the highway was set up as a drawbridge checkpoint — if someone tried to breach it, the highway would retract and raise, keeping ground vehicles from crossing. That tank was a proper hover vehicle, though, so it could fly over the gap.

A dozen Navy marines held positions outside the walls of the bastion, four behind information booths for cover and the rest standing nervously across the open highway. A couple released tense sighs as Greer came down the stairs and paced evenly to the center of the superhighway.

Then the Marshal locked eyes with the lead Crusader, "Can I help you with something, sir?"

The junior-looking Churcher glared at him, but said nothing.

Up until this moment it had been a nice day, and Greer wasn't patient, "I'll have to ask you to turn around and go back to Sanctity Base, then. Or I'll have to place you under arrest."

Hearing this, Greer's aide ordered the hastily-deployed company in the bastion to sight their weapons through the firing ports. She drew a bead on the lead Crusader's forehead.

"You will *not* touch us, scum."

Greer cocked an eyebrow, "Is that so?"

In an excellently timed move, one of his marine companies appeared on the bastion's open roof as he replied, and the troops leveled their guns smoothly at the Crusaders standing in the open.

The Crusader grinned.

Tightening her grip, Greer's aide gave her orders, "Get ready. As soon as he flinches."

The lead Crusader made to raise his rifle, but before he could do so his head exploded. Greer dropped to one knee and opened fire, trying to knock down the Crusaders behind the tank. The files of men came apart as the companies from the bastion opened fire, and he got to his feet and scrambled back towards cover. The tank lurched forward in a drunken fashion, and Greer waved the dozen checkpoint guards into the fortifications behind him.

Taking his time, trying to look calm, he carefully squeezed off a few more rounds at a surviving Crusader, then backed up the stairs into the bastion, closing the hatch behind him. Letting out a deep breath, he turned to his aide.

"Inform command! They're not going to like–"

"Gods — *incoming!*"

Forty tanks dropped from 500 meters and deactivated camouflage, then let their main guns spit massive shells at an unexpecting bastion. The fortification was completely unprepared for an attack from above, and one of the shells drove into the armory.

As the first bastion exploded in a bright pyre the mob scattered, screaming. Hundreds of tanks appeared in the sky, and Lupus watched in stunned silence as they swooped down on each of the unprepared bastions around the city perimeter.

Varnia was still on the comm, "Cadmus will be down in two minutes. The city landing field good enough?"

Lupus turned from the gruesome spectacle as a tank came down fast, clearly having spotted his unique Earther form on the hilltop. A machine gun from the tank chewed into the street, and he dove into the Schaeffer sisters and tried to cover them.

"Just get them here, Varnia," he roared over the explosions, getting to his feet and dragging the girls up at the same time. They sprinted towards the front door, unnoticed for the moment.

As the panicked Schaeffer parents ushered their daughters inside, Lupus stood on the porch and looked skyward, quickly assessing the situation.

A half dozen Naval marine tanks had been on standby patrol in the area, and as soon as the Church tanks had appeared, they'd swooped in to attempt to intervene. They died in the attempt.

Beckett raised his comm to his mouth, "Varnia, tell Gillian we're under attack by a mechanized division with significant hover armor, same type as hers. I've got to organize down here, I'll check in when I can."

There was a pause on the other end of the line, then, "I love you."

Beckett's mind stopped for a second; no one had ever told him *that* just before a fight, "I love you too. I'll see you soon."

Already he was keying the frequency to connect to his dropship.

Ernile Cuttar had been sitting on the landing field at the base of the dropship, toying with one of his rifle's power cells. He had ideas as to how to focus the beam and cut power costs, but he seldom had time to tinker.

The dropship pilot was first to sound the alert over the comm, "Whoa — forty incoming! Eighty! More... it's a *division*. Bastion One just went... up..."

Cuttar was immediately on his feet, his rifle reactivated and ready to shoot. But what division was the pilot referring to? The Crusaders didn't have tanks, based on what he knew.

Then Lupus' comm reached his ear, "Incoming *Crusader* mechanized *division*. Get off the ground and get dropped at the top of the hill on the northeast corner of town. Keep the shields up. Cadmus and 2/54th are dropping."

Cuttar didn't even take the time to acknowledge — he was running up the ramp and closing the hatch while the pilot kicked the dropship harshly off the ground in a seldom-practiced emergency launch.

"Shields up, where to Sergeant?"

Sliding to a stop in the rocking cockpit, Cuttar pointed to what he presumed was the appropriate corner of town, "Top of that hill, I think. Rest of the battalion is dropping and this is a mechanized division of *Crusaders*."

The pilot grimaced as she turned her agile assault boat and accelerated over the field. The gunner sitting next to her initialized the targeting computer and turned to Cuttar, "When we're fired upon?"

The Sergeant nodded in agreement, and the heavy pulsars mounted on the exterior of the lander swung to life. Church tanks saw the Earther ship and began charging.

Only a dozen at first, coming on in an open formation, firing rapidly and with some accuracy. Their shells glanced off the boat's shields, and the Earther pulsars replied angrily.

The tanks dropped onto the landing field in smoldering heaps, and the dropship skimmed the surface, driving across the city at irresponsible speeds.

The house across the street from the Schaeffer's exploded. There was no reason for it to be targeted — one of the tanks must have misfired — but it went up with screams and a child. The twelve-year-old boy from the mob, who'd been standing on its porch in awe of the Crusader tanks, was flung bodily across the street, bouncing off the Schaeffers' porch roof and dropping to the front walkway with a crack.

Beckett lunged out the door and hefted his small body, lifting him into the porch and laying him on the ground. He was quite dead, but it might not be permanent — regen was a powerful tool...

Christine's non-military parents were understandably in shock, standing before their living room window and gaping at the spectacle. Tanks were starting to drop lower in the city now, and what few Navy marines hadn't been in their bastions were emerging into the streets, furiously sending random anti-tank shots upwards and spraying the sky with their rifles.

Marine small arms couldn't easily bring down tanks, but they had managed to do it under controlled lab circumstances. Set to armor-piercing, the ammunition was accelerated from a rifle barrel at a shade under the speed of light, and while it took significant time to recharge the magrails that hurled the shell, the shot could potentially punch a hole in a tank.

Lupus had no idea how many Navy marines had been outside their bastions — they were probably guards at police stations and public offices and the like. But the fire from these few marines was drawing the tanks down to low altitudes. Behind this first wave of armor, Beckett could make out APCs — hovering armored personnel carriers — looking very similar to Navy marine designs, which meant they probably held fifty troops each. There were a lot of them coming from the northern horizon, waiting no doubt for the armor to clear out the heaviest resistance before they touched down.

Come on Cadmus...

A hand closed on his forearm and Lupus looked back to the sisters. Christine had her sword in one hand and a longer, regular Earther blade in the other, hilt towards him.

"I bought it at a surplus store a couple of years ago. It still works — I just used it for practice with a regular blade."

Girl has a good cool head.

That was all Beckett could really think as he nodded and took the weapon. It was indeed a second-generation Krogg War canine-sized sword, just like the one hibernating in his closet. He was accustomed to using two blades now, but this was the next best thing. Strapping the sword belt to his waist, he turned back to the front door and narrowed his eyes. His lander had to be coming — Cuttar couldn't have been caught on the ground…

Christine thought her heart had stopped beating. At the same time, though, her blood was *surging*… hopefully from adrenalin and not some side effect of the regen... Trying to ignore the new feelings, she strapped on her sword belt, then realized she was moving without any shaking or other visible sign of panic.

So she almost panicked because she wasn't showing any fear.

Holy Gods, this was *surreal*.

Claire, also standing on the porch, had begun to tremble uncontrollably. Taking her younger sister by the shoulders, Christine turned to her and locked eyes.

"Hey. Look at me."

Claire struggled to make eye contact as what must have been a piece of the neighbor's roof crashed through the kitchen ceiling behind them, but instead found her focus fixed on the puddle of blood that was forming around the dead child on the porch.

How the *hell* had this happened?

"*Look* at me. We'll get out of this. Now get mom and dad back to their senses and grab anything you safely can. We're going to go as soon as General Lupus' ship comes. Okay?"

Claire nodded half-stunned, half-hastily, and staggered quickly towards her room.

Beckett was impressed by Christine's calmness in dealing with Claire… and interestingly, Christine could somehow *sense* Beckett's reaction.

Weird.

"Weird?" Beckett spoke thoughtlessly — he wasn't entirely sure where the word had come from just now, so he elected to ignore it.

There were other matters to concern himself with: here came the Earther lander, with a horde of tanks swarming ravenously around it. Pulsar shots were cutting them down in ones and twos, but if nothing else, the Church was persistent in its hatred of Earthers.

Raising his comm, Lupus took a few steps out the front door and waved his empty arm, "See me?"

"Coming in. Shields down to thirty-eight percent."

Had it been two minutes yet?

The dropship came to hover over the street, its aft hatch opening and Cuttar's squad dropping through the one-way shield with weapons and duffels. Hitting the shattered street first, the Sergeant Major released the safety on his gun and opened a withering fire on the nearest tank, diving aside as its machine guns opened fire.

All the tanks were beginning to take notice, and as the last of the squad hit the street and the dropship surged upward, spraying fire and taking violent evasive action, the tanks continued to focus on the Earthers on the ground. The squad was fast and protected by shields, but enfilading machine gun and shell fire was chasing them across the street.

The squad pulsar hummed into action, and two tanks collided over the smoldering wreck of the house across the street. Focused fire brought down another as the squad tried desperately to get to some sort of cover.

It was jungle or death now — they couldn't re-board their dropship without forcing it to lower its shields. No, they'd need the protection of the underbrush.

The eerily accurate timepiece in Lupus' mind clicked: *two minutes is up*.

There was a deafening roar, and then a fizzling thunder. Energy shot from the guns of capital ship broadsides crossed the sky horizontally and obliterated seventeen of the approaching APCs. Earther dropships hurtled down towards the landing field at dangerous speeds, and right overhead, the Second Escort Squadron, *ENS Renown*, batted the lightweight tanks from the sky with long-carronades.

Enter Cadmus Howler with 2/54th.

Beckett sprinted into the street and helped his squad get their gear into the house.

CHAPTER 25

Sarah couldn't move. Her eyes were locked on the screen as the first images of Darymanis City, taken by an orbiting Destroyer, appeared on her screen. The images filled every monitor in the room, and everyone was frozen.

That was a mechanized armor division.

A *Church* mechanized armor division.

And it was doing *very* well.

Varnia was on the speakers, "Are you seeing this Sarah? Sarah? Hello? Chief, check the comm — I don't know if audio is coming through..."

Sarah opened her mouth to answer, but she couldn't speak.

"Sarah. If you can hear this we just detected another two armored divisions coming out of Sanctity, no stealth. They're heading right for Darymanis, and it looks like there are two or three infantry Legions boarding hover transports to follow."

Sarah hadn't been a combat commander for four decades, and technically, she wasn't one now. But she needed to remember how to snap out of this stunned stillness.

She had to think. Just had to...

So she did: "Comm, I need to make a broadcast to the people *immediately*."

There was a pause and then stammering, "Pious still has us locked out of the system..."

"Break in. Get a line to Gillian, and to Graham too."

That was her veteran combat tone — cool, calm and ready to deal with anything up to and including certain defeat.

Graham's first thought was for his wife — marines were clearly dying, and his instinct was to make sure she was alright with what she was seeing on the screen. He reached back and put a hand on her knee, and she placed her hand on top of his. Then he tapped up a split screen and ordered the fleet to full combat readiness on the right side of the display while she scrambled her six armies of marines on the left.

It was an unthinkable spectacle, but the feeds from the Destroyer *Garstrice* were clear; Darymanis City was being flattened by a Crusader armored division.

And the Church tanks were operating just below the orbiting fleet's fire support ceiling, so Graham couldn't shoot at them. His fighters were next to useless that low in the atmosphere... fighting below 500 meters was the exclusive province of marine hover tanks.

Gillian's territory, and he couldn't really help her with it.

Christine and Beckett are down there.

Graham flinched at the thought and nearly stood up.

Oh Gods... look after yourselves...

But he was already tapping the comm, "Bridge, get a hold of ArcLieutenant-General Rozhestveski. Tell her to start watching the detached Church squadrons for unusual behavior. I'll be up."

"Aye sir... President on the line for you..."

Graham nodded, "Pipe it here."

Sarah appeared on the right side of the screen with barely a flinch of greeting from Gillian — the Commandant was ordering her Marshals into action and getting the Marine Armored Battlegroup online. Her entire Corps had been caught napping.

"We've been fooling ourselves," Sarah said blandly. "I should have listened to you."

Graham shrugged, "No time for that sort of talk. I suggest you prep your shuttles in case you want to move government up to *Genesis One*. I have the Church-loyal ships under watch."

Sarah nodded slowly, "Hopefully it won't come to that, but Varnia's sensors see entire *Legions* loading into hover transports. They're fully mobile."

That grabbed Gillian's attention, and on the screen Sarah keyed a few buttons before her, piping Varnia into this conversation.

The situation was not shaping up well. The concentrated Naval marine armies were stood down at Lancaster Base; the only combat-ready formations were spread across the continent, garrisoning cities along what they'd assumed to be the critical superhighway line — supposedly the Church's only means of rapid travel.

But now the Church had armor, lots of it, and it was mobilized and supported by tens of thousands of concentrated infantry with the ability to go anywhere.

Darymanis City was the only fortress in a position to delay a Church drive on the capital, but with it now overrun, Genesis City could be hit in a few hours, if not sooner. What marines Gillian had on the ground there right now would be slaughtered by the Church's armor.

"Cadmus' boats are engaging. And 2/54th is landing right now."

That was Varnia's voice, and Gillian allowed herself a second's hope. Maybe — just *maybe* — the Earthers could make the difference. She'd been at Antarctica, she'd been at Krogg 'A'. Those Earthers might just buy enough time...

Gillian Hodge hopped off her husband's desk and bent down to kiss him on the cheek, "I've got to get to my office — in case you break orbit."

Graham nodded and took her hand for a second, "Alright. Be safe. Love you!"

"You too."

She left the office, and Graham struggled to control an unfamiliar but potent sinking feeling.

Things at Darymanis appeared to get much nastier.

Under the cover of the gunboats, the Earther marines of 2/54th disembarked from their heavy dropships on Darymanis City's main landing field. The Earthers unleashed concentrated pulsar and rifle fire as soon as they cleared their landers, and the stab of hundreds of energy rifles brought down a dozen tanks in mere seconds. As the battalion scattered across the field to avoid providing an easy target for tank guns, 2/54th's engineers raced out to the edges of the landing zone to deploy a shield perimeter.

The Church tanks were now starting to fall back to protect the APCs that were approaching from the north, but their success so far wasn't startling. The projectile guns mounted on human tanks only weakened shields through cumulative fire, meaning they had no effective way to drive back gunboat attacks. So far none of the Earther boats they'd focused on had been physically damaged...

Though with the amount of fire that was being traded, damage wouldn't be avoided for much longer. Cadmus Howler was soon going to have to start rotating boats back up to *Renown* to avoid actually losing any. Just as the Lieutenant Colonel was thinking that, a Crusader tank dove intentionally into the plated landing field near one of 2/54th's loosely-rallied companies.

The engineers' shields started raising at nearly the same instant, though, and with their deployment a haphazard perimeter went up that would protect this area from strafing. The boats would just have to hold the field's flanks until the rear shield was raised.

Now where was Lupus...?

Cuttar's squad gathered in the Schaeffers' living room and looked over the equipment they'd hauled off the lander in their mad street drop. Extra personal shields were passed out to the humans, and Lupus handed Christine the first rifle from a case holding four, then drew one for himself.

"I... I haven't..." Christine held the weapon in front of her awkwardly, "I've never used a rifle."

Lupus paused and looked up, "Really? Not at the Academy?"

"The weapons option was either rifle or sword. Only sidearm was required training."

Cuttar and Lupus exchanged surprised glances and the Sergeant Major quickly came to her aide, "Point, aim down here, pull the trigger. The regulator's on right now, so the shot will knock whoever you hit into a coma for about a week. Your power cell drops with this blue bar–" he pointed to a small screen on the upper stock "–and an identical indicator flashes on the inside of the sight. It's like a head's up display to let you keep track of your remaining charge if you're sniping."

Wielding his own rifle forward, he keyed a release on the side and pulled the power cell off the weapon, "Each one of these takes about fifteen minutes to recharge on its own. We carry five each under combat circumstances."

The power cell Cuttar spoke of was only the size of two of Christine's fingers, but presumably it worked.

Lupus handed her a pouch with extra cells in it, "That's five. Strap it on your thigh."

Christine nodded slowly, feeling wholly dazed. She was getting a real crash course in marine combat... And her blood hummed. Damn that was *weird*.

"I was in the militia, General. I can handle one of those," Missus Schaeffer stepped forward and pointed to one of the remaining two rifles.

Lupus saw none of the steadiness in this elder Schaeffer that he saw in her daughter... but that seemed to be a hard benchmark for a human civilian to reach. He handed her the rifle and another pouch, then aimed the butt of the last one at Christine's father, "Sir."

"I'm not proficient."

"We'll all need to be armed, nonetheless. Sergeant Major Cuttar will show you the basics."

Claire returned from her room with a kit bag, still walking with the sort of calm panic that exemplified human shock. Christine put her rifle down and tried to steady her sister, while Beckett strapped on his own sidearm and turned to his medic. Kellen Kyra, the newest addition to this veteran squad, was a kindly young wolf who'd been trying to revive the child since they'd gotten through the door and moved his body into the living room.

Now, as she stood and cleaned her hands on a sanitowel, she shook her head, "He's too far gone. I doubt if Elandra Caine could bring him back from this point."

"Stasis isn't an option?" Lupus asked as he checked the cells in his pistol, and Kyra shook her head.

And trying to carry a dead boy to the lines Cadmus was setting up with 2/54th might get more people killed. Well then.

"Alright. Thanks, Kellen... get your gear together, we'll be moving fast."

The medic nodded and turned back to her rifle and pack, both sitting on the couch, then began checking her combat kit.

Lupus turned again to Christine, who was pointing to the button on Claire's belt that would activate her shield.

"Now, the wrist one is your backup. Got it? You can turn it on at any time. I've got mine on now. Okay?"

Claire's gaze was vacant, and understandably so. The sounds of approaching tanks began to resonate in Lupus' ears.

Setting down his own rifle, he took the last three pistols from their case and handed one to Missus Schaeffer. Tapping Christine on the shoulder, he handed her one, and then he caught Claire's eye.

Holding up the last sidearm, he gently lifted one of her hands to take it, "You've got what you want to save in that bag?"

She nodded slowly.

"I'll take it. I'll keep it safe," he slid the sack off her shoulder and hefted it over his. It was quite light. "Now, you watch your sister's back with that."

Claire looked silently at the sidearm and nodded again. She slowly dragged the pistol's holster belt around her waist, then Christine started checking her out on the weapon.

Lupus turned back to the main window and watched as, all the way across town, the rear of the shield wall began to deploy around the landing field. The battalion was down, then, and fortified behind a shield perimeter that essentially formed an open-ended tunnel with its gap at the lakefront. A shield line was probably laid along that open front, but it wouldn't be activated unless there was an emergency. A kilometer long and half that wide, the corridor was a good base of operations...

But Cadmus Howler wasn't going to keep 2/54th sitting inside that tunnel. He was an elite combat veteran of the Krogg War, and here he was only facing Crusaders.

"We need to get moving, Beck," Cuttar came up beside his General, and Lupus nodded.

Tanks swirled in the sky.

CHAPTER 26

"Eight and Nine Companies will hold this landing field. I'm guessing the Crusader APCs are going to ground out in the jungle and will come into town on foot. The boats will keep the tanks out of your way, you keep the Crusader infantry outside this perimeter. We'll probably be trying to evacuate civilians," Howler was speaking in a typically sedate tone, pacing the shield line with a Major, two Captains, and the Regimental Sergeant Major. His microphone conveyed the orders directly to the seemingly chaotic 2/54th, his Earthers responding with their characteristic independent discipline.

The Captains of Nine and Ten Companies were redeploying their troops into squads built around pulsars and stringing them out along the shield perimeter. The battalion would hold this place until reinforcements came, or until they'd been able to evacuate all willing noncombatants.

No Crusaders would move them from this spot — and while that struck Howler as an arrogant thought, he knew it was accurate. This battalion had held back the Queen's own Guards on the surface of Krogg 'A'. No Crusaders could hope to best them.

"Everybody else deploys out into the city. Joyce–" he nodded to a Captain as he passed her, "–Three Company will secure us a straight crossing over that highway, and Two Company will hold a line from the highway to this field. Light, Grenadier, and Four through Seven Companies are coming with me into the civilian district. We'll try to get as many willing civilians back across the highway and out to the landing field as possible."

Howler had received no orders from the Genesis government as to what he was supposed to be doing here — they were probably still scrambling to figure out what was happening — but an evacuation made sense. Even assuming one of Gillian Hodge's Armored Divisions arrived to beat back the Crusaders, there'd be little left of Darymanis City when the dust settled.

And if Howler could get out into the civilian sectors, he'd have a good chance of recovering General Beckett Lupus — something he was particularly keen to do.

"Alright folks, let's move out — double quick!"

He was near the end of the shield corridor, and as the first squad of the 2/54th's Light Company sprinted out into the open, he took a breath and followed at a dead run.

•••

Gillian got to her office just in time to witness an Earther battalion scatter into Darymanis City. It was an impressive sight, and it was complimented by the even more satisfying success the Earther gunboats were visibly enjoying. Four of those small craft had been detached to return to *Renown* for repairs, but none had been shot down in their encounters with the Church tanks.

That was good. Gillian had the benefit of having the very best combat unit in this region of the galaxy — the Earthers — serving as a roadblock on the main road to Genesis City... but she still had to mobilize.

"What've we got?" she passed through the outer office into her C&C, nodding to a few subordinates hurriedly rushing around.

"Six Legions in the open, moving down the highways. They've thrown Mechanized Divisions ahead of them to keep us from flattening them on the road," one of her aides stopped and tapped his pad, bringing up a map of the continent on the large wallscreen.

From Sanctity, there were superhighways leading to Genesis City and Lancaster Base. The former route was choked by Darymanis City, the latter was simply an open highway. Gillian had always expected that, in a coup attempt, the Crusaders would avoid sending an attack directly at Lancaster — the home of the Naval marines on the ground, that facility was a modern fortress.

But with only two armies presently consolidated at Lancaster, the three Legions and six Mechanized Divisions the Crusaders were sending down the road could probably take the base. At the very least, the Crusaders would keep her two Lancaster-based armies — 500,000 of her best marines — on the defensive.

Gillian knew she had to consolidate *something* at Genesis City — Lupus' marines couldn't hold Darymanis indefinitely, and once they pulled out, the Crusaders would be free to run straight down to the capital. But she couldn't risk pulling garrisons from other choke points along the highways... what if the Church shifted to go after other targets...

Who was she kidding? If a *Legion* hit one of the pathetic clusters of bastions that held cities, and was supported by Church Mechanized Divisions, a few thousand marines from the local garrison wouldn't even slow them down.

No, it was time to pile every marine she had out there into transports and get them to Genesis City. They could reorganize and get a mobile force ready to counter the Crusaders if they turned away from the capital and went after targets, but leaving all her marines spread all across the continent trying to defend everything was suicide.

"The good news... ma'am?"

Gillian blinked and looked at her aide. She'd zoned out... "What?"

"Most of their Legions look like they're still tied to the ground. They have some sizable forces airborne, but most of their strength needs to move over the highways."

So they were counting on Mechanized Divisions and APC units to blitz the bastions, to clear the path for a quick highway drive to Genesis. This was a good plan, the sort of thing she'd try in the Crusaders' place.

But she still had an advantage here. Her entire Genesis Marine Corps was Mechanized and Armored. She had tanks and APCs for *all* her troops, giving her a deployment advantage. Once she could get an army or two assembled for rapid counter-offensives, she wouldn't be tied to highways at all.

And she had something else on her side: absolute orbital dominance. Thanks to her lovely husband...

"They've definitely gone silent, sir. All but three of the ships... okay, now two. *Turkoff City* just cut signals."

Graham nodded as he stood before the main screen on *Unity Genesis'* flag bridge. He knew his fleet *very* well. None of the ships left on station in Genesis orbit were reporting any trouble with insurgents — either there were none, or the marines aboard had smartly put them to rights.

But there were still those Church-sympathetic ships in the fleet, the ones he'd isolated out on patrol stations near the Kroggward side of the system and at the hyperspace corridor.

Apparently, isolating those ships was now paying off, as the section of the fleet that was presently cutting its communications and assembling without orders near the entrance to the hyperspace corridor was exactly that group that Graham had expected to cause problems.

He was good.

Now he'd have to remind the traitors of that that.

"I'm guessing Thadeus Morgan is senior out there," Graham turned to his Comm Chief. "Try to get him on the line for me."

A signal beamed out from *Unity Genesis*, crossing the system quickly and tagging the receiver on the Superdreadnought *Caitlin Hargreaves*, flagship of the Third Task Force and doubtless now the flagship of the *Church* force.

There was a pause, and Graham took a breath. Then Thad Morgan, a proper bastard, appeared with a sneer, "Manchester. Surrendering already?"

A real ass, this Morgan character.

Graham smiled politely, "I'm really not sure what I was going to say, Thad."

The ArcLieutenant-General shrugged and narrowed his eyes, "A plea for mercy, I'm guessing. You're tied to your planet. You can't completely trust your ships. You don't know how far we reach..."

"Oh *shut it.* You're a whiny little son of a bitch, Thad. Don't expect me to take you in alive. We can always build more ships."

He waved the signal closed and sighed, turning to a room full of staffers who were smiling very nervously.

"Don't worry, lads and ladies. We'll smite this faithful fellow, I assure you. Send to what we have of First, Fourth and Fifth Task Groups: prepare to break orbit. Second Task Group will hold here in support of the stations and the ground action."

Morgan had only one Light Carrier — an *old* one — but, unfortunately, offset that with the hefty missile complement of about thirty capital ships in a total force of about eighty.

Still, Graham had the numbers; the junior Manchester was moving forward with eighty capital ships, and a dozen Carriers, not to mention escorts.

And he was better than Thad Morgan. There was no question of that.

"Are we in yet?" Sarah turned to the techs hovering around the comm station, trying to adjust its signal frequency to break the Church overrides that had given Pious a monopoly on public broadcast.

One of them looked up and nodded quickly, "We've got *something* working ma'am. We'll have GlobeCast going in about two minutes."

A hand closed on Sarah's shoulder from behind, and she whirled to face its owner. Pat held up her high-collared black suit jacket, cut a lot like her old uniform but devoid of any regalia associated with the Navy.

"You're going to want to look the part."

She nodded and took it from him, pulling it on awkwardly as she crossed the C&C room to her usual crisis broadcast area — a section of the wall with a green curtain draped on it.

As she stopped at the lectern and turned to face the camera, Pat started helping her button her collar, "You know what you're going to say?"

Sarah shrugged. She was very angry and *very* unhappy.

"Nothing diplomatic," she said quietly, and Pat tugged the shoulders of her jacket, gently pulling out wrinkles.

"I've got something you might like to work with. And I don't think you should be in front of *green*... stand in front of the screen over here... we'll get some techs to walk around behind with pads... make it look good..."

Taking his wife by the arm, Pat asserted his theatrical control. He was a historian, not to mention a military hero — he knew what tended to work in situations like this. Or at least he knew better than to have her standing in front of Navy green while saying 'Give peace a chance.'

Earthers were already on the ground fighting for Genesis. Peace was right out of it.

"Ever heard of a man by the name of Winston Churchill?"

Howler was moving along the side of a street in the commercial district, hopping from doorway to doorway, waving friendly civilians towards the landing field and ignoring those jeering his platoon as it moved smoothly up the street.

Then the public address system hummed to life, and the vidscreens in the window of a nearby electronics shop blanked in the middle of High Chancellor Pious' pontification.

Sarah Manchester appeared, and her voice carried over the public system all across the planet and all through the Genesis system.

Howler stopped the squad and watched.

"So much for partnership. The Church is lying to you, trying to tell you that the Earthers who stopped the Faithful's war crimes are the criminals. Now those same Earthers are trying to save innocent civilians being slaughtered by a Church tank division at Darymanis City. A *tank* division. The Church signed a Holy charter promising *never* to arm themselves with tanks. They signed a charter promising no chaos, harm, or dissension. Now we see the measure of their word."

Graham smiled just a little — big sister was on the warpath. This wasn't politics anymore. She was in the old campaign mode that had made her the human bane of the Kroggs.

"I'm sure some of you are on their side, and you're *convinced* I'm a bloody harlot and all that. Well, I'm finished politicking. You're trying to destroy a thriving world — one we've all built together, and I'll be damned if we stand by here and watch you do it. We shall fight you at the highways, at the jungles, in the skies and in space. We shall *never surrender*. Our freedom came at too high a cost the first time — we will not lose it again. And I don't care how much you've lied to us — I don't care how many Legions you bring. You've cheated to gain the advantage, but even now, with the momentum in *your* favor, you *will* fail."

Howler cocked an eyebrow, hoping Sarah's rhetoric would steel some of the civilians he was seeing all around him.

"The human race is free right now, and no matter what we all believe about Gods and prophecy, we do *not* believe in the destruction of our way of life. Be prepared to face that, and be prepared to die for your faith."

Pat winced. Sarah was on the edge and needed to restrain her anger...

"Watch us win, and then decide whose side the Gods are on."

Sarah paused and stared through screens across Genesis.

"No force in this universe will stop our victory. Good day to you."

The link faded, and Pat could almost hear the absolute stunned silence throughout Genesis space.

Well, she'd gotten their attention.

CHAPTER 27

Lupus' old recon squad still had the touch.

They hadn't really been tested since Krogg 'A', and hadn't been so badly isolated since the *Harbinger Bishop* crash. Now they were escorting a small bevy of civilians of differing capabilities through a very hot war zone without support handy...

Welcome back to the deep end.

Most of the civilians they passed elected not to join the group as it shuffled through the streets, carefully picking its way between cover as boats drove tanks across the sky like cattle. The civilians perhaps rightly feared that being seen with the Earthers under these circumstances was probably not a good idea, unless they were firmly on the Earthers' side...

As Lupus dropped to one knee at the corner of a street, covered only partially by a yard fence, he could see the vast expanse of suburban and commercial territory between his group and the landing field. A very long walk... and something told him Crusaders would be coming overland to intercede soon enough.

Howler's marines were deploying across the highway — that much Beckett could make out from the altitude afforded by this hill. The skies were being cleared reasonably effectively, but the boats were hard pressed to fully secure the landing field's air space. They could move against echelons of tanks trying to advance over the residential district, but there weren't enough boat squadrons to establish a proper perimeter around the entire city.

So this was going to get very unpleasant.

Christine knelt behind the General, anxiously squeezing the handle of her rifle. Her head was starting to pound, a throbbing pain worse than much else she'd felt.

"Headaches pass as we get into action, Christine," Lupus looked back and frowned. "You have one?"

She met his eye with surprise, "Um... yes. Actually."

The fact that he'd instinctively picked up on that detail wasn't a great surprise to Lupus, but the fact that he was getting the sense that she knew what he was talking about was starting to register with him. It had to be related to the crash regen treatment... she seemed tuned into Earther instinct in a way no other humans ever had been.

This *really* wasn't the time to wonder. But as to taking advantage of her new abilities, that was quite acceptable.

"Alright, the squad and I don't know this area..."

Christine nodded, "I'll take point."

She was surprised by the ease with which she understood the situation... *Just as if we'd trained together... odd.*

Without another word, she was on her feet and crossing the street with rifle hefted, her eye down the site as she swept across the road. It was unlikely that anything on the ground would threaten them yet, but she was in a cautious mood.

Beckett quickly looked back over his shoulder and nodded to Cuttar and the rest of the squad. The Sergeant waved his marines forward, the humans who'd joined them moving rather awkwardly in their wake.

As Christine lowered herself onto one knee about fifty meters down the sloping road and nodded almost indistinguishably, Beckett got to his feet and carefully followed her path.

Howler was listening to his companies as they started to infiltrate the residential district — Captains were declaring their offer to escort civilians to the evacuation point at the landing field. Three Company and young Joyce Furgus — daughter of the notorious Jax Furgus of fleet fame — had set up a line over the highway, but she didn't have a full shield to protect her position. Instead, she'd used pulsar fire to knock one wall of a building next to the highway across two thirds of the highway corridor to serve as some cover. The building rubble had thus been turned into a rough barricade across the silver, walled channel.

"Alright Cadmus, I see tanks on the highway now, coming forward from the bastion with APCs. Very low level," Joyce was crouching atop rubble with high-powered sensor-optics.

Even as his platoon swept silently forward through a block of lower class small houses, Howler listened closely.

Then a new voice entered his ear, "This is Vern Grange above you, Captain Furgus. I can put eleven boats from One Carronade Squadron along the road if you like." Grange was *Renown's* senior boat officer, and he too was obviously paying close attention.

"Hold for a second Vern... did you read that Cadmus?" she passed the question on, and Howler nodded to himself.

"Go ahead, Vern. Cut them up as much as you can."

"Roger, coming in. Captain Furgus, get your heads down."

The roar overhead suddenly increased markedly, and eleven boats armed with carronades dropped to a dangerous fifty-meter altitude, sweeping down the highway in line ahead. Tanks trying to drop on them from 400 meters were batted aside by higher-flying boats with regular cannon, and the occasional Crusader vehicle that carelessly strayed above the 500-meter ceiling vanished in a brilliant flash as the lasers of three orbiting Destroyers took their chance to contribute to the fight without irradiating the people on the ground below.

Joyce Furgus slid down off the rubble and landed on the silver highway, putting her hands over her ears as a deadly thunder roared.

One by one, the boats peeled up and away, each viciously tearing their targets apart with carronades capable of smashing through the shields of ships of the line. When Three Company's Captain looked back over the crest of the wreckage-barricade, she discovered that much of the highway was gone.

The elevated silver expressway had literally been melted by the heat, with the gap stretching past the bastion and back almost a kilometer into the jungle.

No troops would be entering the city that way, though somehow she doubted the Crusaders were going to give up.

In the civilian district, Howler thought much the same, and he was rapidly given proof.

"Vern here again, I see thousands of red coats in the jungle. I can't get a clean shot yet, looks like they're looking to overwhelm the city perimeter from the north. And now I'm seeing a reorganized battalion of tanks above moving to cover them. We've got to go up. I'll try to give support when the Crusaders get to the edge of the jungle, but they can get into the residential district quickly."

Well then.

"Garth Badger here, Three Gun Squadron. I can light that jungle up if you need me to Colonel Howler, but I'm currently holding the airspace around the airfield."

Howler frowned and actually let himself drop back as the platoon passed him, "Stay in position, Garth. One Gun Squadron, can you get a clean shot?"

A pause, "Sorry sir, we're trying to keep the next wave of APCs back. There are plenty of them up here."

He could call for more boats, but then he'd have no reserve. And this was only the first Crusader division to be dealt with. If Gillian Hodge needed boat support somewhere else, it would be up to *Renown's* group to provide it. Howler didn't want to commit them here just yet.

Lupus' earpiece cackled briefly, and he came to a stop in the middle of a street, tapping it slightly. With the interference of the energy fire overhead, he'd lost clear comm connections. Now, as things overhead cleared somewhat, he was picking up something...

Aha, a friend.

Howler started to walk quickly in pursuit of the platoon, nodding to a passing human family as they hurried down the road towards the highway.

"Cadmus, do you read?"

He stopped again.

"Cadmus? We've had some interference... do you read?"

"I'm here Beck. We're moving half the battalion into the residential area to evacuate willing civilians. Where are you?"

"See the hill in the northeast corner? I'm coming west down the side. What's our status?"

Howler paused and located the hill in his sight, then froze, "I think you're about to get a lot of Crusaders on your right. They've been forced to ground, and we just got a spotting report placing them all along the northern perimeter. Is it just you and the squad?"

"And four humans, Top Flights. One of them is Graham's new aide... she's quite good. Her family is less comfortable out here. Can you get us a platoon in support?"

Another voice cut in, the Captain of Six Company, "Dug Taggus here, General, what street are you coming down?"

Beckett paused, "Long Hill Road. Aptly named..."

"Yessir... I've got a platoon on Short Hill. If you start working your way south you should meet up with them in two or three blocks."

"Understood. Can we get anyone out here to evacuate the civilians on the perimeter? How close are the Crusaders?"

Howler shook his head, again to himself, "They're minutes away. If you try to pull people out you'll get caught in a fight with a battalion or more."

Beckett paused once more, taking a breath and looking down the long street at the neat rows of houses and some of the panicked citizens running aimlessly away from the jungle.

Someone would pick them up, hopefully.

"Alright, turning south. See you soon."

Recognizing now that he was in the middle of an open street, he quickly crossed the rest of the way, coming to a stop on the lawn where Christine was kneeling. As she nodded to him, he pointed southward, "We'll meet up with a platoon from Six Company."

Nodding again, she looked down the road to the next right turn, then rose and swept ahead smoothly, moving with almost Earther precision.

She still didn't know how she was doing this. She felt like she should be panicked, but she wasn't. In some ways it was incredible to be this self-assured in a crisis, in others... well, she wanted to scream and crawl under her bed.

As she planted herself at the street corner, she looked both ways to check the intersection. To her right there was open road, a fleeing low hover vehicle, and running people. On the right–

Damn.

Her rifle swung around as her shield hummed and deflected about a dozen rounds. The squad of Crusaders that had fired on her scattered as she opened up on them, but as they were nearer the city edge there was less cover for them. At 400 meters range, she knocked down each of them methodically, then waved to Beckett to hurry.

More red-cloaked soldiers came from the jungle, and the sound of gunfire started to slowly grow all along the street.

The squad pulsar was suddenly beside Christine, and the Corporal handling it nodded to tell her to drop back down the street, just as her parents began to jog nervously that way.

As the heavy energy weapon began to let loose its lances of energy, Christine fell back, taking shots at Crusaders emerging between houses up the street. Beckett was similarly firing on Crusaders from the other side.

It reminded him of Antarctica in some ways… but was mercifully smaller. And these Crusaders, like those on that icy day, were no match for his troops.

The pulsar sliced across the open street and then hacked through a house the Crusaders had begun firing from, collapsing the roof.

"Displace," Beckett patted the back of the corporal handling the weapon, planting himself to cover the heavy weapon's retreat. "Bayonet charge coming, Christine."

As soon as Beckett said it, a cry erupted from across the street. Forty-odd Crusaders burst out of the houses at a flat run, and another twenty came from the east flank.

Beckett slung his rifle in a smooth action, drew his sidearm and his sword, and crossed to the east side of their tiny position, standing behind Christine. A dozen of the oncoming Crusaders collapsed into comas as they ran into the two defenders' fire, and then a dozen more. But as Christine tried to sling her own rifle and draw her sword another company appeared from amongst the houses.

"This is a fighting *retreat*, right?" she asked loudly over the din.

There was a perceptively long pause as her sword came from its sheath and she uncomfortably hauled out her heavy pistol, and the Crusaders didn't even bother to fire as they bolted across the street with leveled bayonets.

Lupus looked at her with a frown, "You think I'm nuts? Of course it's a *retreat*!"

He was still looking at her as he lopped off the arm of the leading Crusader.

The pair gave ground very slowly.

CHAPTER 28

"Oh, they're not being very polite at all."

Graham sat back in his chair, wearing something of a satisfied — that is to say, smug — expression as his loyal ships formed proper delta-shaped vanguards around *Unity Genesis*. The Churchers were collecting at the corridor but they weren't moving out from their position. Evidently, they wanted to exchange missiles near the corridor's gravity well, hoping to use it as a deflector.

This sort of scenario had been war-gamed a few times, and it had been revealed that missiles could be thrown off by black holes and other singularities during combat, especially when the missiles were fired at long range. This particular hyperspace corridor, unused since the Krogg War, had actually been employed as an example in the war-gaming scenarios.

And Thad Morgan had been a big proponent of the deflection theory that had come out of those war-games.

Prick.

Oops, a bit impolite of me there! Calm down, he'll be dead soon.

Graham's rapidly improving mood was starting to disturb him. He was *finally* going to have a chance to give these Churchers what they'd always deserved — a bombardment — and that was a pleasant thought, even though he knew full well that it shouldn't be one. Forty years away from war had helped him forget some of the worst aspects. The horrors should have stayed with him, but at this moment, all he could think about was getting satisfaction.

"Carriers, prepare first strike wings. Ordnance packages for shooting cruisers — we'll handle capital ships. And keep a good CAP just in case he tries to even the odds with that Carrier of his..." even as he tried to convince himself the threat was serious, the absurdity of the Church position struck him.

One Carrier against twelve. He'd stacked the deck handily in his own favor, no matter what the Church expected of him. Then again, they'd been amply prepared on the ground, so perhaps it was natural that their space preparations had suffered...

No, no Graham couldn't afford to make such assumptions. He felt far too good about this, he had to be aware of the possibility of a trap. If the Freetowners had been caught by the Faithful, he could somehow be caught by the Church. He couldn't risk it. But what to do...

A plan started to form in Graham's mind — a bit of a bastardization of

Earther tactics and one that was entirely untried... In other words, the exact sort of thing Morgan wouldn't expect of him.

"Belay fighters..." Graham's words stopped some of his bridge crew in mid-sentence. "Put in a call to *Renown* for me..."

Varnia's mild surprise was written on her expression as Graham finished explaining his plan. The junior Manchester was suppressing a pleased smile — Varnia could tell he was hiding it, and he knew she could. His plan was, well, interesting. She wasn't sure if she'd be smiling at all given the circumstances, but that was his business. And he was right, she could help; *Renown* couldn't leave orbit without jeopardizing the situation in Darymanis City, but that didn't mean she couldn't play a part.

A *nasty* part, as it were.

"We'll be glad to help, Graham. Just be sure you stay clear."

The ArcGeneral stopped hiding his smile for a moment, "I *know* Varnia. I'll buy you and Beck dinner at the *Pulsar* for this, I promise."

She smiled in reply and nodded, and Graham vanished from the plot.

Turning to *Renown's* Second Lieutenant in charge of the ship's weapons, she offered a simple nod, "Ready hyper charges."

The Lieutenant turned to his ratings, and in *Renown's* depths, heavy weapons dropped into launch tubes.

"They're assembling in a triple van-wall, sir. Outer doors are opening, missiles loaded."

Graham nodded at the report and watched the red icons of the Church ships begin to flash on the front screen. Thad was following the textbooks, hoping to lob debilitating salvoes of missiles at long range while the corridor blocked any reply. He had his back to a subspace corridor, his cruisers scattered forward in screening positions, and his fighters were surging ahead to attack the leaders of the Fleet vanguard moving against him.

Ahh, fighters. Graham had written the book — actually, *three* books — on effective fighter development for the Navy. The human strike craft were *not* Earther boats, though he wished they had been so well designed. Next to Larosian fighters Genesis planes were rather unimpressive: slow, lightly armed, and completely unprotected, with no thought of a ground combat role. They couldn't even maneuver in atmospheres — they were too fragile, so close air support was left to tanks and orbital shooters. Yet despite being quite fragile, fighters were still capable of swarming slower capital ships, even crippling them.

But Graham's overwhelming numbers of small craft would be less effective in the harsh gravity well of the corridor — they'd be slowed to a point where they might be picked off by Dreadnoughts.

So he'd do some parameter changes. There was no way in Hell that Thad Morgan was going to dictate the terms of this fight.

That would be the job of the hyper charges from *Renown*. They'd been known as spatial charges during the Krogg War, but they'd been refined substantially. Bigger explosions, more maneuverability, and lots of reach…

"*Renown* reports ready with four charges, sir. Requesting permission to launch."

Graham sat up straighter in his chair and nodded, "All ships stand by for flank speed. Request that *Renown* opens fire."

Varnia got the nod from her Signal Officer and instantly passed it on to the Second Lieutenant. From the stern underside of her massive ship of the line, four boat-sized missiles launched under the gentle persuasion of energy launchers.

Within seconds they disappeared into tiny hyper points, and accelerated at unnatural speeds.

"Boom."

Graham said the word under his breath, and as soon as he did *Unity Genesis'* bridge began shrieking. There were numerous of alarms denoting the formation of hyper points these days — there was always a concern that the Larosians might try to break quarantine, or more particularly, that some sort of rogue Krogg force might show up to cause trouble.

And when the sort of explosive yields used by the Krogg telepath-bombs at the Battle of Krogg registered on the deep-layer sensors, human ships paid very close attention.

"We're registering four hyper explosions in the third layer, sir. Shockwave inbound."

Third layer meant third layer down relative to normal space — one above regular hyperspace and two or three above the average corridor. The farther down you went in the relative order of hyper layers, the faster things got.

But number three was just right for this job — close enough to normal for the shockwave to be memorable.

"All hands, brace yourselves. Helm, stand by. Ship, charge lasers."

The explosions weren't visible from normal space, but they still had the effect of shaking it up. And they were particularly brutal against small, unarmored ships like fighters.

Graham watched the expanding globe of Church strike craft explode, flight drives being beaten literally out of action by the grav sheer. Their frail and crumpling hulls traveled out with the crest of the shockwaves, so the expanding globe of the blast could be tracked on sensors by the debris it was pushing.

The Church-loyal warships — recognizing the threat these blast waves represented almost as quickly as Graham did — turned their bows directly into the expanding globes. Unfortunately for them, they'd been at a dead stop, meaning they lacked the forward momentum to punch cleanly through.

As the surging crest of the blast rammed into the Genesis Fleet, Graham took a short breath and nodded to his Comm Chief, "All ships ahead .84 cee."

Varnia couldn't help but keep an eye on the situation. Graham was known as something of jack of all trades and though few considered him a *brilliant* Naval officer, that was probably because the war had ended before he'd really come into his own.

The forty years since had given him the chance to go on maneuvers with Earther theorists, dream up doctrine, and scuffle with the occasional raider. Now he was downright dangerous, in a good, Earther sort of way.

As *Renown's* sensors showed the expanding globe of the subspace shock-wave, Varnia nodded to herself. Graham's ships accelerated fast into the front, and punched cleanly through it almost immediately. The Carriers hung back and held their fighters in case of difficulty.

Church-loyal ships, though crewed by effective men and women (mainly men), had been standing still when the wave hit, and were only now firing up their drives to combat its immense sheer. Their formations were gone, one of them even spiraling into the hyperspace corridor. That particular Superdreadnought tried to reverse drives too late; its charged armor acted like a lightning rod, drawing energy lances from all sides of the hyperspace anomaly. In mere seconds, the big ship exploded in a blinding flash.

That was why warships always powered down defensive systems before trying to use a corridor — the conduits that connected galaxies were user-friendly only to a point. The explosion kicked out debris and radiation, the immense gravity of the entrance slowing its dispersion and forming something of a fog bank around the entrance that blocked *Renown's* sensors.

Varnia watched this cloud form before many of the Church ships did, but as soon as they recognized it many dove right in. Graham's fleet surged viciously into the Church ships' disordered ranks, and only those who escaped into the precarious camouflage of the radiation cloud escaped his wrath.

For his part, Graham had become a little more business-like.

"Lasers tracking *Divine Grace*… disabled now. Moving on to *Trelesta Town* and *Mistrale Town*…"

The ArcLieutenant at *Unity Genesis'* tactical console, working closely with the ship's AI, scrolled through targets with the sort of efficiency Graham would have expected from a veteran. Not bad for a twenty-something who'd never seen a real fight.

"Third Battlecruisers, get into that… *cloud*. See if you can't flush them out," the junior Manchester passed on his orders in even tones, and they were relayed out to the appropriate ships.

An exploding Superdreadnought didn't usually make such a mess, but it had managed to blow up at just the worst spot — the so-called 'delta' at the mouth of the corridor, where grav forces were very powerful and equally contradictory. They pulled in different directions to the point that they almost cancelled each other out, leaving a disturbing perpetual energy explosion that was a shade of bright red. No sensors could see through it, so cruisers would have to go in to clear away Church ships that were using it for cover.

At least thirty ships had now ducked into the cloud, the rest being stopped from doing so by Graham's ships. The Churchers were starting to clump together in groups, even as many of their fellow ships were cut to ribbons by the lasers of the Navy's force.

Graham hadn't let a standoff build — he'd charged right in. Thad Morgan must have been very surprised by the move: *Caitlin Hargreaves* was a smoldering wreck, drifting in four pieces. A shame that such a good ship with such a heroic namesake had to go… but.

But.

"They're breaking up sir."

Graham blinked and looked at the Sensor Chief, "I can read the screen, thanks."

The ArcLieutenant reddened and Graham shook his head, "I swear they think I'm bloody senile."

Keep talking to yourself, you'll prove them wrong.

CHAPTER 29

At some point Christine recognized what was happening, though parts of her mind would have preferred to remain unaware.

This was what Beckett had promised: a fighting retreat. Something in the order of a company of Crusaders was lying in the street, missing limbs or bleeding copiously from slashes and stab wounds. And that was just the pile of bodies she and Lupus had created.

The squad pulsar was playing hell with the Crusader flanks, and as she and Beckett backed slowly southward down the street, only a limited number of Crusader bayonets were getting near enough to engage them.

Christine was relegated to something of an internal spectator as her body seemed to instinctively move in the ways it had been trained. She'd gotten into a combat 'zone' before against holos, but this felt much different. Her opponents were real now of course, but it was more than that.

Her blood was burning, and she was demonstrating the ability to get past a thrusting bayonet with incredible speed while bullets from afar bounced of her shield, or to put a Crusader down with one or two flicks of her arm and the atom-sharp saber she loved to practice with.

That all said, she was *nothing* next to General Beckett Lupus.

At some point Sergeant Cuttar had tossed Lupus a second sword, and now he was moving with the sort of incomprehensible speed Christine had seen in the sparring chamber.

To him, both swords were like extensions of his arms, and he was able to move one in a flash during the half-millisecond before it could have collided with the other. Flurries that might have other people lopping off their own arms for lack of timing were his *norm*, and he had half a mind to actually advance against the Crusaders with his two blades.

But the last time he'd counterattacked that way, it had been against Krogg Queen's Guards. He'd never been proud of the incident — he'd *really* lost control.

These adversaries, even though Crusaders, were still humans, and they'd given him no reason to slaughter them with prejudice. He was taking limbs wherever possible since such wounds were presumably non-lethal, even in the absence of Earther regen. Bullets were occasionally striking his shield, but most shots at him missed by whole inches.

He honestly had not wanted to ever again do battle with humans. And even while he fought, that disappointed thought recurred in his head. He'd been at Antarctica, and that had been enough.

Now... They were trying to kill him, and he obviously wasn't going to let them.

Christine was doing well. But he could sense a sort of uncertain angst building in her as she knocked down more and more Crusaders. She'd known she was good with her sword, but equating that sort of skill with the ability to kill dozens of men was something entirely different.

She had to be asking herself what Lupus and many other Earthers had long ago asked: what manner of creature was she, who could kill so *well*.

Lupus sighed and kept his two swords moving. The Crusaders were starting to back off a little, it'd soon be time to break and retreat under cover fire.

He'd wonder about what manner of beast he was later, as he always did after a fight.

What seemed like another Crusader company appeared in the distance, and Beckett accelerated the pace of his fallback.

Lieutenant Ellen Arbear was a relative newcomer to the marines, but she was no slouch. Hers was the platoon of Six Company moving fast up Short Hill Road, intending to link up with the General's party, and already they could see the energy flashes in the distance. Humans were running past them in huddled family groups, carrying whatever they could as they kept children close.

One little boy threw rocks at her squad before Arbear's deep glare scared him off, while others chanced a stop to cheer on the advancing Earthers.

There was no consistency among the humans, but that was to be expected.

As the private at the head of her quick-moving column slowed at an approaching intersection, Arbear waved her sixteen marines into an open line across the road and onto lawns. Ahead, Lupus' squad was clearly visible now. Three armed humans made up its rear, and they were running for Arbear's platoon.

The eight Earthers of the squad were far more deliberate as they gave ground, and far ahead of them Arbear could see the General and someone else using swords in a rearguard action.

"We'll need to give them overwhelming cover to allow them to back off. Sergeant Cuttar, can you hear me?" Arbear found a hedge and knelt behind it, her black-bear head and shoulders clearly visible atop the greenery.

"I'm here, who am I on with?"

"Ellen Arbear, Second Platoon, Number Six Company. We're on the road down here, ready to give the General all the cover he needs as soon as your squad is in a good position to contribute."

Cuttar's Recon squad disappeared from the road as soon as she said it, taking tentative cover and leveling weapons at the oncoming Crusaders. Even by Earther standards it was a fast reaction — but then, the General's personal troops were the very best.

"Hit it. Watch your targets. Don't shoot anyone with a sword."

Cuttar's orders precluded any from Arbear — although technically junior, he had the superior experience with the situation, and he was a seasoned veteran to boot.

Twenty-four Earthers opened fire with twenty-one rifles and three pulsars, and immediately swathes of the carelessly deployed Crusaders were thrown back.

Lupus recognized the din of the bombardment, and without thought he turned and ran southward down the road.

Christine was less attuned — as she had no earpiece, she hadn't been privy to the dialogue between Cuttar and Arbear. She was also quite distracted by her own abilities... so Lupus turned around, ran back, and tapped her on her shoulder.

She made to swing her saber into his stomach but recognized him half way around, and instead thrust the curved blade into its sheath and sprinted down Short Hill Road. A Crusader came at Lupus, but even with swords sheathed he was able to disarm the man and break his arms before following Christine in her rapid flight.

Bullets started to nick both of their shields more regularly as the Crusaders that remained standing took their chance to get some retribution, but Earther energy fire — accurate to a fault — slashed back at them, often swinging across the street in a wide arc, pausing only to allow the fleeing rearguard to get past.

It didn't take long for the men of the Church companies to scatter from the street and shelter themselves between houses.

Of course, that left the Earther flanks potentially open — with the Crusaders moving behind the houses instead of through the streets, they were much tougher to keep an eye on. In many ways it was remarkable they hadn't taken to backyards as soon as they'd reached the city.

Even as Lupus was skidding to a halt at the hedge over which Arbear was firing, she was speaking, "Alright, pull back to Second Main Street, we'll meet back up with the rest of the company."

The Earthers quickly dropped back down the street by half squads and silently ushered the friendly humans before them as best they could.

At the city's edge, over 5,000 Crusaders began to press in to catch them.

CHAPTER 30

Lancaster Base was a mess of action, but despite the confusion of the rapid mobilization that had been launched less than an hour before, two marine armies had finally shaken themselves into some order, and moved into to their prepared defensive positions. Three Church Mechanized Divisions were on their way, backed by three Legions of infantry and still more tanks.

There had never been a fight like this in Genesis history — humans against humans, with state-of-the-art mechanized vehicles and tactics flung at each other in an open air pitched battle.

But even as Gillian watched the massive preparations on her main screen, she was more concerned with getting transports to Darymanis City than with Lancaster's condition. The Earthers were, through sheer firepower, holding the Crusaders at bay in Darymanis, but it was clear they couldn't maintain the position for long. Weight of numbers was already forcing them to contract, and while they were doubtless capable of a fast exit from the situation when the time came, the civilians they were trying to escort out of the city weren't so lucky.

Unless Gillian moved transports in to grab them.

Only three sizable civilian transports were on the city's landing field. Most of what cluttered Darymanis spaceport were light craft and personal jumpers — nothing capable of removing as many as 12,000 innocents.

No, that sort of moving power could only be found with the military forces in orbit — Gillian's heavy dropships and landing craft. The latter vessels, larger but less well protected, were probably her best bet for extracting the willing, but in the unstable situation it was the smaller dropships that seemed more likely to survive, as they were well-designed for first strikes and attacks on defended targets. That said, they carried only 100 people each; the landers could each cram in as many as 1,000 persons.

Well, the Earthers seemed to be faring well enough in the skies… why not trust their air support and use both?

"Drop Wing Eleven and Transport Wing Eight, make ready to boost from *Genesis Four*. Orders to evacuate all willing humans to the capital. Wait there for further orders. Put the Sixth and Thirteenth Transports on standby for drops to the capital as well… in case it looks bad."

The orders went out smoothly, and Gillian narrowed her eyes at the overhead shots of Darymanis. Out on the fringes of the residential area, eight-marine Earther *squads* were doing all they could to keep entire Crusader *companies* back, but they were inevitably giving ground.

And there was an entire Legion coming down the road from Sanctity, with two more behind it.

Genesis City needed to be fortified… quickly. She couldn't only focus on Darymanis and Lancaster, she had to defend the seat of planetary power. The defenses had to be strengthened at the capital.

And Gillian had half an army there to start the work.

One of Arbear's marines had been knocked flat by a lucky artillery round, and had been carried back minus two legs by a Sergeant. The lost limbs would be regenerated aboard ship, of course, but it'd be a long and difficult recovery.

The sight of seriously wounded Earthers was not new to Lupus — casualties had been unpleasantly common against the Kroggs, and he'd been one of them.

But now the sight of a legless cat being carried off by a tan wolf jogged his mind, "Cadmus, how are we doing for casualties?"

They were almost all the way down Short Hill Road, getting ready to dig in at the main cross-town road to hold it in support of the squads further to the east that were still falling back. This route was their surest connection to Joyce Furgus' highway line, so platoons were setting up at every intersection to keep it safe.

Howler was west of Lupus, holding one of those intersections against what appeared to be a battalion of determined Crusaders. His mind needed full seconds to find the answer, though his sighting and his firing never slacked off.

"One dead, eleven wounded at last check. We lost Corporal Dirks of Six Company, Beck. She got hit in the head by a lucky shell."

Lupus winced and nodded to himself, "Alright. Everybody better be falling back right now — I think any civilians we weren't able to reach have gotten the message. Anyone who wants to run from the Crusaders is moving."

There was a round of acknowledgements over the comm, the experienced company commanders of 2/54th having long since come to the same conclusion.

"Alright, you all know who's farthest east. We'll break contact from that side, and roll back down the highway. By the time we reach Joyce we'll have a half-battalion together again. Get civilians moving down the road as fast as you can… hopefully Gillian has transports coming down for them," Beckett hadn't actually thought to ask the Commandant about her preparations, though he had faith in her presence of mind. Still better safe than sorry…

Beckett tapped his comm again to redirect the signal skyward, "Varnia, do you read?"

There was a brief pause, "I'm here, what's up?"

"Make sure Gillian has transports coming down for civilians, and put a few more squadrons of boats with them. I think we'll be out of here soon."

"Okay. One of the boats is gone, but we've got the crew. Gun overloaded in the upper atmosphere, but their bridge pod cleared the blast."

Lupus nodded to himself again, "We're doing alright then. As well as can be expected under the circumstances."

"As long as you get out of there."

Lupus sighed, quickly leveling his rifle and firing at another foolish charge up the open road.

If we can get out smoothly...

Christine had wanted to stay with Lupus.

Who was she kidding, she had wanted to *run*. Far and fast.

No, she had actually wanted to do both, and instead she was settling for a bastardization of the two.

Civilians fled down Crosstown Street, heading for Joyce Furgus' crossing over the superhighway escorted by a ragged band of humans with guns. Some Navy marines had survived the tank onslaught — altogether about thirty, only fourteen with all limbs and organs fully intact. Then there were the constables... all six of them she'd seen... and civilians who'd picked up guns and were acting as irregulars.

She didn't like walking down a street with them, but it was necessary, because the Earthers were spread too thin to keep the line absolutely secure. Crusaders could hop through backyards, go through sewers or houses... anything to bypass the Earthers' defensive lines. Worse, though, were the Church civilians who were finding guns on dead Genesis marines, and who were acting in support of their Holy warriors.

She'd sent two of those sorts of people into comas, and many others had been blasted apart by the less sympathetic human rifles.

A long walk was still ahead of them. Half an hour at this pace...

Claire was half-stumbling beside her sister, pistol dangling from her right hand. The shock hadn't really worn off, but that was hardly a surprise. She was keen on being a journalist or a writer... military action wasn't for her.

But circumstances demanded.

The elder Schaeffers were just behind the sisters, a bit more hunched as they walked, trying to cover all sides with their rifles, even as a tide of panicked humanity flowed down the street beside them.

Then a loud shot cut through the air.

It was *close*, from a nearby house. Blood glanced off Christine's shield as a man crumpled in the street beside her, but she was already dropping to one knee and opening up on the windows of the nearest home. People scattered behind her, and her parents instinctively latched onto their flank, running but turning their rifles on the line of houses they were passing, hoping to offer cover to the unprotected crowds.

Another shot exploded from the house Christine had been targeting, this driving straight at her face.

The bullet impacted angrily against her shield, dropping its already weak field to virtual non-existence in an instant. She'd taken too much fire with Lupus back at the edge of the city...

So she clamped down on her rifle's trigger and sprinted for the house, unable to tell precisely where the shot had come from but deciding the shooter's head would stay down if she tore the windows apart.

She was right, and as she blasted through the front door and sprinted into the porch, the rifle carrier bowled into her, clearly and carelessly trying to escape through the back door.

Christine's rifle was knocked form her hands, and before she could really register that fact her arms were flying around, snatching the shooter's rifle and pitching it out the front door. A knife swung at her and she slid out of its path, kicking in reply, then drawing her sword smoothly.

The knife found her shin, the last of her shield thinly deflecting the slash. She responded with a swing of her saber, backing quickly into the house's incinerated living room. The attacker followed fast, unimpressed by Christine's longer blade, and dove inside her guard. The young Schaeffer's eyes followed the short knife as it dove for her breast, and with a speed she really didn't expect to have, Christine slid aside and hacked down hard against the attack.

Her saber made no sound, the atom-wide blade simply cut through the unshielded person, who collapsed bloodily to the rug with the back third of her head on the floor beside her.

Christine took a moment to retch, but her mind was screaming at her as staggered back from the corpse. She seemed outwardly calm as she deactivated her sword and sheathed it. Her movements were controlled as she picked up her rifle.

Then she stopped as she saw Claire standing in the doorway.

The younger sister was staring at the body, long blinks punctuating a seemingly disinterested stare, "She was in one of my classes at school."

Christine turned and looked at the dead shooter. Sure enough, a teenage girl. Good Gods.

Good *Gods*.

She wanted desperately to collapse... maybe to sob or maybe to scream. But Claire was starting to tremble, and there was still a long walk to the space port.

So she laid down her rifle and embraced her sister.

They left the house wordlessly, the boiling of her blood fortifying Christine...

CHAPTER 31

In a bunker in Sanctity Base, images taken by stealth tanks told the story of the Earther evil.

They'd all heard the stories of the demon Earthers on their icy hell plain on Earth, but they'd never suspected this sort of tenacity. They had assumed the Kroggs to be weak in faith — thus more easily defeated — and the Earthers powerful only when deployed in large numbers.

In retrospect, that seemed short-sighted, but Thomas Pious could not dwell on that now. No matter what they'd thought of the Earthers, the Chancellors' Council had not predicted such a rapid intervention, both on land and in space.

There were still contingency plans — that much the Chancellors had learned from the failures of Bingham and his followers during the Quest. At this moment, the Council could summon the help of the Commonwealth of the Faithful, but that would not arrive in time to retrieve this situation. No, the Church of Genesis would have to deal with this on its own.

"Release the Seventh Legion to run straight down against Genesis City. Don't use the highways."

Seventh Legion did not, publicly speaking, exist. The Genesis Naval Marine Corps had six armies, the Crusaders had six Legions... on paper.

But when building illegal vehicles in copious numbers, there seemed little to lose by recruiting an extra quarter million men. It had not been easy, but by hiding them on registers as altar boys, clerics, and monks, they'd pulled large numbers together over the past decade.

It would now pay off.

"Things look like they're stabilizing a bit," Pat pointed to the screen and Sarah nodded darkly.

"Beckett's saved us. Somehow I'm not surprised."

Now that victory seemed to be at hand, Sarah was starting to feel more self-depreciating. How naïve could she have been — of *course* the Church would try a coup. They'd almost wiped out the crews of the fleet in Sol space half a century ago, and the new brand of fanatics were far less passive than Bingham had been.

The coup had only been going on for a few hours, and she was already turning hindsight against herself.

As well she should, because she'd missed any signs this was coming — and for the Church to hide that much armor, she *had* to be incompetent…

"If you're beating yourself up, stop right now. I'll have none of it," Pat had leaned in close and was speaking quietly. "They fooled us all, even Varnia and Beckett by the sounds of things. But we've got them–"

"We've got them over a bloody barrel, Sarah," Graham's voice cut through the room unannounced, and Sarah blinked and looked to the secondary screen.

"What's left of the bastards are hiding in the energy cloud in the delta, just over the corridor. I'm leaving a good piece of the fleet nearby to handle them, but I'm coming back. How is it on the ground?"

Gillian's face split the screen immediately, "I've got a hodgepodge forming a defensive position north of Genesis City. Lupus is getting ready to evacuate Darymanis now, and I've got armor moving to meet three Legions coming down the road at Lancaster. Still trying to pull it all together, but I could use a squadron of Destroyers for high cover."

Sarah felt entirely like a bystander, because neither were talking to her. Directly, anyway… It was their fleet and army, not hers. She was a civilian.

In a twisted way she was very disappointed by that… though it wasn't all so difficult to figure out why she might be. She knew what she would do if she were Graham. It wasn't what Graham was doing, but that didn't matter.

She almost wished she had the choice again — Congress and bureaucrats were getting to be too much for her. But there wasn't much else for her to do just now.

"You'll have two squadrons then," Graham was saying. "I'm sure once Beckett gets out he'll provide you with boats for closer support."

Gillian nodded and there was a sense suddenly that things were under control — or getting there. More and more armor was arriving from the bastions all around the planet, taking high arcs at dangerous speeds to reach the capital in a timely fashion. Unlike the Church tanks, the marine armor had nothing to fear from the Destroyers above, so their flight ceiling was six kilometers, not 500 meters.

And then there was yet another alarm.

Sarah wasn't surprised, her eyes simply crept back to the main screen. Ah, a new Legion. Cutting over the jungle at high speed, only an hour and a half from Genesis City, cruising at a safe altitude just above the treetops.

A long column of crimson armor, ready to come down onto Gillian's roughly-deployed defense, while three Legions beat their way down the highway.

"We'll need the boats," Gillian said after a pause. "Think *Renown* could come down with them?"

•••

Varnia's ear twitched as she watched the last of her husband's companies pull back to the crossing point protected by Joyce Furgus. From above it seemed like such an orderly operation, but the comms were adding to the suspense.

The marines of 2/54th weren't panicked, by any means, but the great hordes of humans fleeing behind them to the landing field were terrified. They were escaping a war zone — narrowly, and doubtless with many casualties.

Gillian's transports were landing safely under the shield of *Renown's* second wave of thirty-eight gunboats, the first forty-five having been thrown forward to keep the heads of the Crusaders down during the evacuation. Earther companies were lining the route from the superhighway back to that field, but theirs was a scarcely visible khaki line when seen from above. The Crusaders were a great hammer of crimson — one growing more ominous by the minute. It would take at least an hour to get the human non-combatants out, so that meant a long holding operation at the field... and there was nothing *Renown* could do but watch.

Then Varnia's other ear — listening to the human feeds in orbit — twitched too. *Renown* go *down* there? Of course it had been a joke. Varnia was watching as new images filled the holo plot, and Crusader tanks whisked over the jungle.

That'd be a problem...

Wait, go *down* there?

Renown had a crew of 4,400, including boat crews and marines. That left a good 3,600 at Varnia's disposal, and among them many who were proficient enough with the rifles and swords. She'd read somewhere that old Royal Navy landing parties had included selected men of the ship's company... so why not...

She turned to her Flag Captain, Bev Kirby, in an abrupt whirl, "What do you say to sending down some reinforcements."

Kirby smiled, "I'll take them myself. Master-at-Arms, break out the small arms!"

Howler was forming a crude command post in the landing field's main terminal building. Marines were hustling civilians who'd been waiting at the field aboard some of the human transports that had arrived. They'd filled a lander already, and sent it on a hop-run to Genesis City.

But there were thousands more trying to get to the field, strung out from the highway and coming down many unprotected streets in their quest for a shortcut. The entire battalion was on the west side of the city now, and about 350 Earthers were massed to stop the advance of the Crusaders over the highway.

But their flank would be turned any minute.

It *had* to be.

The two companies at the north edge of the landing field could slow down the advance, but the shield wall only went so far, and it could be flanked easily as well. He needed more troops, more boats... *something*.

Cadmus Howler wasn't in the business of wishing haplessly for the impossible, but sometimes circumstances demanded a little help. The Crusaders had to be looking favorably at an approach in force from the north on the *west* side of the highway... down Lupus' left flank in the commercial district, and almost right onto the field.

Well, maybe Gillian could divert some reinforcements.

"Varnia, I need a line to Gillian," Howler went to a window and looked north as he spoke.

"We've got it covered, if you mean what I think. We'll have 1,100 troops on the ground in ten minutes. You've got eight minutes until Crusaders hit your flank... best call Beckett back to the field."

Howler instinctively looked upward, "Alright... thanks."

He could almost hear her smile, "No problem."

Well, Earther timing — Fox Magnus' favorite subject — was paying off again.

Long may it remain so...

CHAPTER 32

Beckett dropped to one knee and squeezed the trigger. The first Crusader in the rush had been flung back, and Lupus' energy burst knocked the second down. The General was draining his second cell, but he was close to the landing field…

The rest of the squad's fire intensified enough to drive the Crusaders back, heaps of bodies building up where the flow of the retreat was blocked by a fence. The rest of Six Company had joined them now as well, and the marines of 2/54th were once again proving their reputation as the steadiest around.

Well, the Guards would obviously dispute that… as would the 95th, given the opportunity…

Lupus shook himself and almost let some scorn seep through — the nearness of escape was causing his intensity to slack just a little. He had to stay focused, these were the times when casualties were most common.

"We've got volunteers deploying on the northern frontier. The Crusaders are starting in on them now, Beckett. I think they'll hold."

Almost eight kilometers away from the General, Captain Bev Kirby was waving a file of rifle-wielding ratings into a rough, open line, then she stopped to snort amusedly.

"That's us, General Lupus. Bev here, and I've got 1,100 *Renowns* with me. We won't disgrace you, will we folks?"

There was a roar of agreement — and it was cut short as the first smattering of machine gun fire traced up and down the lines of irregular troops. Earther spacers, midshipmen and Lieutenants leveled their guns in reply.

Lupus fired smoothly as he dropped back, and he smiled thinly to himself at Kirby's attitude. The Navy had been a little cavalier ever since their famous boarding actions at Krogg, and it wasn't an unqualified sentiment. Their predatory ancestry had given all Earthers the general propensity for ground combat.

Those who'd volunteered for the landing party were doubtless the best in the crew — one characteristic of Earthers was their typical good sense in dealing with these matters. No one incapable of handling a rifle would be on the ground.

A human ran past him towards the landing field, screaming — literally — "bloody murder".

Well, there are no Earthers *on the ground who can't handle themselves...*

Suddenly he wondered about Christine.

"Inside — *quickly*. Come *on,* move it!"

A man was holding up the entire line as he searched haplessly for something he'd dropped. Christine ungraciously grabbed him by the collar and hauled him through the lander's hatch — whatever was missing could be replaced.

The writhing tide of humans tried to force its way up the ramp again, and with her rifle leveled, Christine began to organize the civilians into a line. She was helping dozens of other Earther-aligned personnel sort these people quickly into the ships, and no delay could be accepted.

Even a crack unit like 2/54th could only buy so much time, no matter what sort of power they had in the air. There was a crushing hammer of crimson on the way.

"Keep it *moving*. Steady there! No shoving!"

There was clearly panic in the crowd, and she saw it every time she locked eyes with anyone in the growing mass, but they were taking her orders. Maybe it was her rifle, or maybe it was the confidence in her voice. Though that would be remarkable — she was convinced she was going to throw up any moment now... she *had* to break down soon, surely...

But for whatever reason, she *was* able to forget the killing and destruction surrounding her, and the destruction of her home. Her mind, or at least the productive part of it, was dismissing all that as melancholy and useless. Getting these people to safety was what mattered for the moment...

Her blood continued to boil.

She'd analyze it all later, not right now.

But she'd have to hurry to get to later.

"We're facing about three battalions now, and we're falling back," Kirby's voice was even as she smoothly fired her rifle at the oncoming Crusaders. Christine tried to pay attention to the report in the earpiece she'd acquired, but it was meant mainly for others.

Beckett finally turned to face the field as 2/54th opened itself into a long skirmish line at the spaceport's perimeter. There was a short lull, which probably meant a heavier attack was imminent. The Crusaders were regrouping in the wreckage of the commercial district, and they'd drive the thin khaki wall of the Earther Marine Corps back onto the open field...

Where civilians were still milling around, trying to get aboard transports.

Artillery was growing more intense now, too — medium guns were firing beyond the city, sheltered from boats by the thick canopy of the jungle.

Two more Earthers died in the next dozen minutes, one Private of 2/54th and a Bosun's Mate from *Renown*. Both Earther fronts slowly contracted over the open field, and the shield tunnel laid down by Howler's troops when they landed was deactivated and redeployed to offer some cover to the civilians.

As the Crusader thrust started the first human transports were beginning to rise into the air, holding approximately half the gathered civilians. The Church troops came with at least 4,000 men spread across the entire frontier, with concentrations in spearheads aimed to exploit the narrowing gap between the flank of 2/54th facing east and Kirby's *Renowns* facing north.

Boats drove the assault back, carronades hissing and burning the air, slicing swathes of Crusaders from their path. The Crusaders pressed harder — they knew as well as Lupus did that this was the moment of Earther weakness.

Now that 2/54th was tied to a position, easy to find and even easier to outmaneuver…

"We need to get out of here, Cadmus. How are the evacs coming?" Beckett was walking slowly behind the ragged line of Six Company as he spoke, his rifle never silent, his shield deflecting hordes of bullets in a dangerous cacophony.

Christine's crowd was thinning fast, the people terrified further into cooperation by the nearing sounds of gunfire. She stopped speaking and simply waved, and they herded into the lander.

To the north the *Renowns* gave ground doggedly. Despite their lack of special ground training, they were more than capable of hammering Crusaders in open line.

The Crusaders, however, kept coming — they liked doing things in waves of ten thousand, and that left the volunteer Earther defenders with little more to do than give ground slowly. The perimeter was still shrinking.

Christine tried to count quickly, and decided those left in her area could be crammed aboard the lander she was currently loading. It was only a sub-orbital hop, they could stand to be over-crowded…

Shells started landing closer and closer, and panic was quickly beginning to set in among the milling civilians. They lunged for the lander ramps in a seething mass, trampling a few unfortunates to death in the process of getting aboard. Christine left them to it now, as she moved away from the lander hull and raised her rifle.

Crusaders were coming on the flank, just about to enter her range. They were giving hell to a retreating Earther platoon.

She waved to the other marines loading landers nearby and then walked evenly in the direction of the crimson advance.

They were cutting this very fine.

•••

Gillian watched as the last of the landers filled and rocketed upward into a swirling line of gunboats, then flew southeast under the shelter of orbital Destroyer lasers. The Crusaders were pushing *very* hard now, and they were nearly crushing the thin Earther line.

But the Earthers were falling back smoothly — accustomed to working under this kind of pressure — and both 2/54th and the *Renowns* were beginning to coalesce around their own dropships. They'd have to turn their backs to get aboard, though...

Gillian blinked a few times and took a deep breath.

Beckett was running down his fifth cell as his marines backed into a close square with the volunteers from *Renown*. They were dropping back faster than the Crusaders could advance, and in their fallback to their dropships they'd actually managed to substantially widen the gap between Earthers and Churchers. The trick would be keeping the Crusaders back while the marines and *Renowns* disengaged to board.

But Garth Badger's boats were overhead, and without an order, the boat officer knew exactly what to do. The gap opened by the retreat made close air strikes a bit safer for Earthers on the ground, so the boats of *Renown's* six squadrons fell to hover only dozens of meters above the ground, and then proceeded to demolish the Crusader Army.

Thousands were coming in open order from all sides — it was impossible to miss. As the first guns flared, the *Renowns* broke from their rough lines and sprinted back aboard the landing craft that had delivered them, the process taking an entire minute owing to their inexperience with such operations.

Christine found herself with Joyce Furgus, who had been reduced to using her sidearm after a lucky shell had breached her shield and unpleasantly burned her arm. The company Captain was ignoring her injury, firing steadily with her sidearm as though nothing at all was wrong, "Keep it steady everyone. Not long now. Mark targets... that's the style..."

Christine was surprised on many levels, not the least of them the one that pointed to the Captain's attitude as a reflection of her own — obscenely calm under pressure. But the Captain clearly wasn't nervous on the inside...

For some reason Joyce paused to frown and look Christine in the eyes. Neither knew precisely why they were looking at each other, but Christine shook her head and went back to firing.

Howler watched Bev Kirby board the last Navy lander and then patted Lupus on the back, "*Renowns* are lifting off, Beck. Our turn."

Beckett, only paying attention with a third of his mind, nodded, "Your battalion, Cadmus. It's your honor."

Howler nodded and looked up at the collapsing bubble of khaki-clad fighting Earthers, "Evacuate *now*."

The battalion waited until those words came, then vanished into their own dropships in scarcely more than the blink of an eye. The dropships lurched upward, and then together the Earther boats and transports hurtled skyward, marking a course directly back to *Renown*.

On the ground beneath them, Darymanis City was awash with red.

Crusaders and blood.

CHAPTER 33

Narosh was awake.

He was in more pain than he ever remembered feeling, and blood was seeping from his eye onto his armor.

His remaining eye was still and his mind was quiet, but he was awake. He hoped that 'Natosh' didn't realize he was, in fact, conscious. Whatever it was that dominated the brain of his old friend was highly capable.

"Of *course* you're awake, Narosh."

Natosh was standing at the helm, and he turned on the Admiral-of-the-Fleet, "I can read your mind, you should know better."

Narosh cursed himself–

"Now now, self-cursing is for the weak… sorry to cut off your thoughts like that, but I'm in a cheerful mood. We're about to reach our destination. Your friends won't see us coming, and even if they do, their useless ships won't be able to stop us."

Anger started to bubble in Narosh's mind–

Excellent imagery — bubbling anger!

–a sort he hadn't felt for many decades… one long associated with his hate of the Kroggs. Caine had helped him control it before… but now…

Aha, Caine…

His only chance was to stop all thought… his Earther DNA was not dominant, but perhaps it could be of use…

"What — do you seriously–"

Narosh flung himself out of his chair and staggered quickly to the nearest hatch — one leading to the Captain's day cabin. Natosh followed him with blinding speed, but he had indeed been surprised, so he moved a fraction of a second too late. Narosh slammed the day cabin's hatch shut and attempted to seal it with a stroke of several keys.

Remarkably, the heavy alloy door cycled and locked correctly, leaving Narosh trapped in a small box of a room… with no alternate exit.

Oh, poor fellow. Guess you can stay in there for now, I must take the helm. Hold tight though, it might get bumpy. Especially if they try to shoot at us… oh that'd make me laugh! They've always been so foolish — creating me and whatnot…

Narosh fell painfully to the deck, trying not to think but desperate to do something.

Something caught his eye… he immediately erased it from his mind, then rolled slowly in its direction.

There would be no more thinking, only instinct and action.

The mood aboard *Savanna Felix* was becoming relaxed as it orbited Io, even though the run-in with the Faithful Fleet had been only eight hours before.

Ed Jeffries realized the real time as he looked at the chrono, then sighed. It felt as though he'd been here much longer, but that was probably due to the earlier stress. Getting First Expeditionary into Earther space after their near miss hadn't been too difficult — Fox Magnus had been kind enough to offer a Battle Squadron and a Flying Squadron to help with that. No, it was the lengthy conference with Audrey DeBrooke that had made it feel so *long*, because she was miffed.

That word was too polite — she was *pissed*. And it was a fair reaction to the trap the Faithful Churchers had used to lure the cream of the Freetown Fleet into what would have been certain death, had it not been for the Earthers.

And Freetown, not to forget Freetown.

There were two 'fleets' currently guarding Freetown, but neither contained anything more than Battlecruisers and some lighter vessels. Old Battlecruisers, well-crewed and well-upgraded, but hardly a match for Faithful Dreadnoughts that seemed to be equally well equipped.

This day had soured a whole lot.

But Ed Jeffries was nothing if not an optimist… *Felix* was about to be joined by four sister ships and a flagship, all rushed out of the of the yards by Earther builders who seemed eager to prove they could finish advanced Battlecruisers in *hours* instead of days. He could almost picture veteran dock crews remembering the glory days when they'd been asked to produce a squadron a week, starting at the keel and finishing right up to the guns. Now they had their chance again, slapping the last electronics into hulls they'd been working (purposefully) ponderously on for almost a year.

It was a good thing, because *Setter Caine, Andra Ursla, Varnon Broadpaw,* and *Fox Magnus* were already taking crews aboard, as was the far more formidable vessel in the arsenal: *FRS Republic*. This ship was quite unlike anything else in space — armed to the teeth with enough hybrid firepower to smash a Dreadnought, it carried a complement of 64 boats in eight combat squadrons.

The boats themselves weren't quite a match for Earther boats, but they were more than a match for fighters, being shielded and armed with light carronades and missiles. They were thinly crewed and highly versatile, and they were massively superior to anything Genesis R&D had developed.

Which meant that the new Freetown Fleet would have a major edge next time the two colonies ran into each other.

Unless, of course, the Faithful got to Freetown before the new ships did…

"And that's exactly why we're taking on crew so fast," Jeffries said to himself with a nod, and a number of bridge crew looked up with confusion.

Jeffries blinked and looked around with a shrug, "I talk to myself. So what?"

That would have been a good moment to abandon the narrative, but the Signal Officer was stirred by a low beeping on her panel, so she picked it up, "Sir, pod from Genesis coming in."

Jeffries frowned briefly, "Signaling?"

The Lieutenant was keying her console quickly, "Just a minute... it's riding hot, sir, carrying information from only thirteen minutes ago. Looks like it lost some of its comm computer in a high-speed translation."

Jeffries swung his chair, "It must be important then."

The Signal Officer nodded slowly, "Very important, sir."

Chancellor Pious appeared on the main screen.

Audrey DeBrooke had to admit she liked her new chair — the Earthers made extremely comfortable furniture. Still, she missed *Grendelsbane's* bridge, and the feel of the Light Cruiser. *Republic* was a spectacular ship — it had the same feel as an Earther ship of the line — but it wasn't her old gallant command of four decades.

She'd grown attached to *Grendelsbane City*, but now duty demanded she occupy the fleet flagship, at least until they got this augmented First Expeditionary Force safely to Freetown.

"How much longer?"

She'd asked the question only fifteen minutes earlier, but half-hoped that by asking again she'd get crews to their posts faster.

"Another hour and a half, ma'am, at least."

She wanted to say it wasn't good enough, but that would have been a joke, and a bad one — they were moving at an insane pace, crewing ships right out of docks without shakedown cruises, and essentially sending them to battle.

An unfamiliar droning beep started, but Audrey ignored it — it meant nothing to her on this new ship. Somebody's cabin door probably didn't open all the way...

The new Signal Chief, standing with his Lieutenant and the instruction manual, frowned and awkwardly hit a few buttons on the panel.

And then High Chancellor Pious was in the main holo tank.

Audrey looked up — as did the entire bridge crew — and listened to his words, and then to the familiar ones of Fox Magnus.

"Oh my Gods," someone gasped.

Pious finished saying something inflammatory, and then the projection remolded into an overhead view of deploying Crusader Legions...

Great Gods, a coup.

And it was triggered by the Faithful. They'd wanted a fight near Earth space so they could use it as a spark to overthrow the Genesis government.

Audrey DeBrooke got chills. This was all so much better coordinated than she'd thought possible. Suddenly it looked as though every bastion of human civilization was under serious, *serious* threat.

By the *Church.*

Gods dammit — how did those incompetent damned fools pull this off?

Well, first, they'd managed to maintain an image of stupidity, and that had led to Naval overconfidence.

Freetown would be in trouble, then. The Faithful had this opportunity to attack openly, and possibly to get direct reinforcement from Genesis.

But only if the civilian government and the fleet caved immediately...

Could she count on the Manchesters?

No way to be sure.

"We're leaving in forty-five minutes, get the word out," Audrey's brain changed gears. "Get a pod ready, we have to warn Freetown."

CHAPTER 34

Setter Caine and Andra Ursla were civilians, which in official terms meant they were no longer part of the Earther government's decision-making process.

But the Earthers never much believed in letting official structure interfere with doing the right thing, or asking the right people for help.

So both Setter and Ursla stood in sad silence in the war room under Admiralty House as Thomas Pious' message was repeated. It had arrived in Earth space thirty-seven minutes earlier, and the Freetown force was on the verge of departing.

Standing next to Caine, Lab Forepaw and Fox Magnus were agitated.

Fox was particularly miffed, "They try to start a war five minutes from my driveway and they expect me to sit by and *watch?* I've got half a mind to put six squadrons in their lap… no, *ten*. Send to Garvin and he can put the Gibraltar Squadron in their space too."

The little red fox was venting and he knew it, but he was entitled. He was being used as the excuse to start a rebellion, after all.

"I'm not sure we can do anything," as always, Forepaw's voice was much cooler. "They've got us over a barrel — we send ships to help Audrey and Ed, they get evidence that we're interfering in their affairs. We go to Genesis and… well… there's no doubting we're involved."

Varnon Broadpaw was standing next to Ursla, "Yes but we're *always* involved. They should recognize that!"

Caine took a deep breath, "We've kept a very low profile, though. We trade with Genesis through their dealers, we use their currencies and their measures… and remember it's a different generation out there, Varnon. We all remember the war, but most of them only grew up on embellished stories and movies that make us out to be different than we are. They won't acknowledge us as helpful."

Varnon scratched behind his ear and sighed deeply, "Yeah, probably."

"We can't help. Or look like we're acting against *any* human interests," Ursla's words concluded the disappointed commentary, and the five Earther leaders watched the message again.

"Hail from *Republic*."

Forepaw blinked at the report from Rawden Coggs, "Right. In the main tank."

Audrey appeared with a resolute expression, "I'm shipping out now, with everything."

Both Lab and Fox shook their heads simultaneously, and Caine spoke quietly, "Until we get a better read on the situation, we can't move with you. If this is just bluster, it might blow over — we could give Pious exactly what he needs to keep it going and make it much worse if we're not careful."

Even through the tank the Earthers could see the surprise and fear that flickered across DeBrooke's mind, "You're playing politics?"

Broadpaw shrugged, "We don't want war. This might be the only way to stop it right now."

A silent Audrey looked between the five with a darkening expression.

"Safe journey… good luck," Ursla's words were quiet, and Audrey vanished from the holo.

There was another uncomfortable silence as the five stood and watched the Freetown Fleet, minus its transports, accelerate out of the system in a hastily-formed line.

Caine folded his arms across his chest. He was trying to understand what he'd just done… the *safe* thing… and why he'd done it…

He obviously hadn't been making combat decisions for a long time.

Then Varnon cleared his throat.

It was almost comical, the way the four other Earthers looked at him at once, and he frowned, "If I know my son-in-law… and I do, because he married my little girl… And if I know her… and I do… they've already gotten into it if the Church is serious. And if it's not as serious as it looks, we're okay to move."

Ursla cocked a thoughtful eyebrow, "It's a free universe. The fleet can go on maneuvers whenever it likes."

"A little training does good for the soul!" Fox nodded. "I'll be getting back to my ship–"

Caine held up a hand — he was a civilian, but he was unquestionably the senior leader in the room, and the other four were glad of that fact. He was the best.

"They're not stupid. They might catch on when Fox annihilates the Faithful Navy with a Battle Squadron."

Forepaw blinked twice, "*But…*"

Caine looked to his old Flag Captain, and Forepaw smiled. Of course the Earther Navy couldn't go to battle against the Faithful, but there were plenty of third line units floating around… left under the orders of the Naval Reserve.

The new First Lord turned to Coggs, "Call up the 11th and 15th Reserve Squadrons."

Turning back to the other four senior Earthers, Forepaw gave one of his uncommon but greatly appreciated broad grins, "I've got them on standby from storage. They're ready to go, as soon as we get their full complements aboard."

Caine matched his fellow's grin, "Glad you got that rearmament going. I guess you'll want old-timers in command… no one official"

There was half a glimmer of hope in that comment — Caine wouldn't have *minded* boarding a ship of the line for a job like this, but he couldn't. His was too high a profile to make a maneuver like this subtle.

Forepaw smiled, confirming his old commander's judgment, "Neither you nor Ursla could pass as real civilians, even now."

Caine nodded with his friend, "We'll need someone on short notice…"

"I've got a name," Varnon was already grinning to himself.

Ursla frowned, "I'd say Artie Tigar, but he's out in New Halifax…"

"No no… someone much more colorful."

"I'm old. Let me sleep Varnon. Or I'll slap you around. It's 03:00 in the *morning* here."

Admiral (Retired) Jax Furgus, the old firebrand, yelled ungraciously at the comm on his bed table.

His wife poked him in the back, "Shhhh."

"See Varnon, you woke the wife. I'll walk into Government House tomorrow and whup you."

The speaker cackled, "Are you getting more crotchety then?"

"Yes, I am. Old, remember."

"You're only 187. Setter's 209 and he's *much* more civil."

"Yeah, well he's enlightened and I'm crabby."

There was a brief chuckle on the other end of the comm and Furgus groaned and tried to paw it off.

"Well, anyway, I've got a squadron of modernized 74s and one of 44s loading up with reserve crews. I want you aboard in forty-five minutes."

Jax Furgus' eyes opened.

This wasn't the average crank call.

He sat upright in bed, "I'm dreaming."

"No, you old cat, you're awake. You're too grumpy to be dreaming. And make that forty-four minutes, now."

Furgus frowned, swinging his legs out of bed, "I can be crabby wherever I want, dream or otherwise. We won a war, remember?"

Varnon laughed.

The Earther ship of the line *Aboukir* was a veteran of the Krogg war, and now it sat at the head of sixteen-ship group of modernized vessels of similar vintage.

In the command chair, Jax Furgus sat happily…

Wearing a housecoat and eating a croissant, "So they've got two hours lead on me, with good drives, eh? So I can't catch 'em?"

In the plot, Lab Forepaw smiled, "They're *fast*, Jax, but they're still slowed by some old flux drives. You could run them down in hours if you wanted to… but don't."

Furgus indelicately smeared butter on the greasy bread and raised his eyebrows, "Right, it's about the appearances. Get them to fire on us first and all."

"I doubt it'll matter that you're from Fleet Reserve and not a front line squadron — we'll still get blamed for sending you," there was a bitter edge to Fox's tone, and Jax looked up.

"So why aren't we *all* going? Penny and pound… or whatever," Jax handed the butter to a nearby — unexpecting — First Lieutenant.

"Spin doctoring purposes. It looks better if their old ships get smashed by our old ships instead of our new ones. Sarah and the Genesis government might be better off that way. Be delicate, though."

Jax Furgus stuffed the whole croissant into his mouth and started his cat jaws chewing, "Mm thma nghing ugh smflll."

Forepaw and Magnus exchanged glances and Furgus scratched his neck and stretched his arms over his head with a guttural groan.

"What was that?" Forepaw asked amusedly.

Furgus swallowed and donned a frustrated expression, "I *said* I'm the King of subtly. What do I have to do, paint a picture?"

Fox started laughing outright and Lab sighed, "You're crotchety and old. Behave yourself."

Jax Furgus smiled, "I'm just grumpy, Lab."

He didn't need to say anything more, because his hunger for command and the excitement at having a couple of good old squadrons under his orders were kicking his old instincts into high gear.

Crabby or friendly, the old Jax Furgus — bane of the Kroggs — was wide awake.

"Safe journey," Forepaw smiled in reply. "We'll be here if you need us."

The link cut and Jax Furgus ordered his squadrons to energy drive.

CHAPTER 35

James Stanton read the personal note a third time and took a deep breath. He was barely conscious of his surroundings as he walked through the corridors of *Archangel Sword*, but then it could hardly be expected that he'd be paying attention to details at the moment.

He'd received a pod about the ambush of Audrey's ships only hours ago, and that had brought enough terror to satisfy him for the rest of his anticipated 200 years of life. As much as he thought himself accustomed to the threat of losing his wife to combat, he was never really prepared for the reality. Maybe because he'd never needed to be — she was too good, and he had always been right there...

But that had been during the old renegade days before Freetown had been a solidly established, strong colony. In the interim, he had to admit he'd grown a little complacent, a little too comfortable being young and free and happy on his own personal planet.

Maybe that was pushing it a bit, but he was still happy where he was. Happiness had a way of making him nervous — it so easily could turn into despair — as the message from the Admiralty so aptly demonstrated.

So Audrey had been ambushed, which was the first piece of bad news, but the pod contained a second: it suggested that the coup on Genesis, the warning of which had come from *Renown* four hours ago, was going to lead to a direct assault on Freetown.

It reported that the Faithful who would lead the charge had at *least* three Dreadnoughts, one of them reasonably modern, with which to launch their strike.

Audrey was coming home as fast as her elite force could move, but if this had all been mapped out as neatly as it appeared, the Faithful Fleet could very well reach Freetown first.

And that would be catastrophic.

James emerged onto *Sword*'s bridge and was hit with a sudden wave of nostalgia. He'd turned the ship over to its new Captain decades ago, electing to run the government instead of remain with the armed service.

But he was still a military governor, and that meant he had absolute control of the fleet during a crisis. So *Archangel Sword* and the rest of the First Defense and First Battle Fleets were directly under his orders.

Six Battlecruisers, two Heavy Cruisers, three Light Cruisers, and seven

Destroyers; eighteen ships, six of them reasonably powerful, though not nearly a match for Dreadnoughts. Once Audrey got back, someone might call a full fleet-to-fleet battle an inevitable near-run thing, with the superior Freetown skill deciding the engagement…

But then, the Faithful's recent ambush had proven that their skill level was far beyond any expectations he'd held for them. As much as it bothered him, James was seriously beginning to think Freetown would need Earther support to weather this storm. It was bitterly ironic, then, that this was the first time — the *first* time — in their mutual histories that the Earthers had refused absolute support to the Freetowners. They thought they could stop a coup…

It was like a waking nightmare.

James had done what he could. The planet was under a declared state of emergency, its militias arming with Earther-built energy weapons and shields, its reserve Naval personnel scrambling to augment the crews of the standing fleet… for whatever good it would do. The battle would come in space, and James was certain that hiding children in bunkers and deploying Freetown Home Guard would be a futile move.

The Faithful would irradiate the planet from above.

So Audrey would return in two days, but the Faithful could arrive in as little as a day and a half. If Paine decided to move quickly, Freetown could be on its knees or simply gone when Audrey arrived.

James took a deep breath, set that possibility aside in his mind, and nodded to *Sword's* Captain. The Governor of Freetown then took his old command chair.

"Take us to standby alert," he said quietly.

Grand Chancellor Paine meant to finish Freetown before the heretics could consolidate, and the strategy was no secret. The Carrier *Glorious Prophecy* and the Redemption Fleet were even now rendezvousing with Chancellor Leo's force, turning to run at high speed to the heathen colony. Four capital ships were with that force, as well as eight Battlecruisers, four Heavy Cruisers, four Light Cruisers and eighteen Destroyers.

They would reach Freetown before the scum hiding in Earth space could possibly move to assist, and barring Earther intervention, Leo would have the heretics on their knees long before DeBrooke and the bastard-ships showed their faces.

That was very good news, but better still was the silence from Genesis.

Sitting in his office under Ecclesia's orange skies, Paine smiled to himself as he thought of the inevitable chaos in Pious' realm. He had ordered the cutter that had delivered Fox Magnus' ultimatum to Genesis to report back to the Faithful colony if the storm of Holy fervor failed to start a coup, and now that almost ten hours had passed, it seemed highly unlikely that a peaceful settlement had been reached.

Paine had faith that his brother Chancellor Pious had control of the situation on that world. Because the Gods sided with men of Faith, and because the men of Faith had tanks and stealth technology they weren't supposed to have.

The plan had at last come together, and soon a united Genesis would stand against the Earthers once again. This time, however, it would be a Genesis of the Faithful, unimpeded by the Krogg War and the Navy heretics.

Their space fleet would be led by men of true Faith and brilliance like Chancellor Leo, and the Earthers would have no chance to use treachery as a means of escaping their inevitable destruction. Redemption after forty years... a long wait, but justice at last.

It would all begin in thirty-eight hours, when Leo arrived in Freetown space.

Gregory Paine steepled his fingers and began thinking of life on Earth...

Audrey DeBrooke marveled at *Republic's* construction, walking almost aimlessly through its corridors. The ship was a wonder, to be sure. She was still very attached to *Grendelsbane City,* but as she saw more and more of this great ship, she came increasingly to the conclusion that she didn't want to be aboard any other vessel just now.

Those Dreadnoughts would have no idea what hit them.

With 100 augmented missile tubes, long carronades, and the advanced boat wings all built to Freetown specifications by Earther yards, it seemed doubtful there were more than a handful of Genesis *Navy* ships in existence that could handle *Republic*. Just as the designers had hoped.

The only problem lay in getting this magnificent ship to Freetown before the Faithful attacked. Audrey knew it wasn't an easy proposition, so she was taking a risk. Despite the danger of splitting her force, the First Expeditionary — beloved *Grendelsbane* included — was being left in the wake of the faster Earther-built ships.

Republic and its five fast Battlecruiser escorts were hurtling ahead at 3,290 pls, the old upgraded cruisers and Destroyers making only about 3,000 pls. The speeds, once entirely unthinkable, represented the cutting edge of Earther engine technology. Not many ships in space could hope to keep up.

And that would hopefully put the new First Assault Squadron of the Freetown Navy into its home space before the Faithful could intervene.

If it didn't... well, Audrey wasn't going to think about that just now.

They'd come up with something. Even if the Earthers weren't there to help...

Jax Furgus stretched and yawned cheerfully.

Yes, that seemed like an oxymoron, but grouchy old cat that he was, a good yawn was actually a cheerful gesture.

"They're splitting up, then," Ronax Hobbes, Jax's recently-recommissioned reservist Flag Captain made a point of announcing his observations. The slightly younger cat had once commanded *Monarch*, one of the original rebuilt carriers of the old Earther gunboat arm, and had gone into retirement to enjoy astronomy and conduct historical research on space flight.

Now he was Captain of *Aboukir*, and Jax Furgus' right hand. The crotchety Admiral was still wearing his pajamas and house coat, but was slightly more pleasant than he'd been hours before.

"Yes, they have split. So we will too, I suppose..." Jax grumbled and stuffed his hands into his robe's pockets. He turned to the Signal Officer, "Contact Commodore Locke: Flying Squadron to keep watch over the First Expeditionary."

The eight 44s of Tom Locke's squadron would be a match for the entire Faithful Navy, or at the very least they'd be able to cover First Expeditionary's retreat if the Faithful somehow fell in with that formation. Meanwhile, it was time to see how well these upgraded 74s really accelerated.

"So Ron, you think we can do better than 32... what was it, 3,290?" Jax's question revealed his good spirits, or at least a sliver of them.

Hobbes smiled, "Hold onto your housecoat."

Turning to the Cruising Master, Hobbes offered a nod, "Make speed 3,400 pls. Steady increase."

Jax allowed himself a bit of a crotchety grin, then nodded to the Signal Officer, "Repeat that to the Battle Squadron."

The pair of cats made their way to their side-by-side chairs on *Aboukir's* bridge, then sat down. With only a slight shiver, the upgraded 74 began to accelerate to its maximum cruising speed.

"Think a *Venerable* would be faster?" Jax asked happily.

Hobbes paused and pursed his lips, "Well, probably. I've heard Fox gets 3,500 on hard drives."

Furgus frowned and harrumphed, "He doesn't get to wear his housecoat on the bridge, though."

Hobbes smiled again, "Life of a reservist... can somebody get some donuts up here?"

CHAPTER 36

Christine Schaeffer took a few deep breaths and rubbed her head. It had started pounding again about twenty minutes before, almost as soon as she'd stepped off the lander onto *Renown's* deck. She'd hitched a ride up with the General, hoping to rejoin *Unity Genesis* as soon as the Superdreadnought docked with *Genesis One*.

Her brain was apparently starting to register all that had happened to her… all of it, in its gruesome detail. She didn't want to think about it — not that her desires mattered — but her mind was already well-entrenched in its determination to review and feel guilt.

She realized she hadn't even said goodbye to her family… in fact… wait, she didn't even remember loading them onto a ship.

Someone must have… they had to be in Genesis City now…

"Christine?"

Her mind stalled and she turned to face the speaker. Beckett Lupus frowned at her, "You're pale. Feeling alright?"

A very long pause preceded her words, "I feel… sick."

Beckett's frown deepened and he stepped closer, putting a gentle hand on her shoulder, "Alright, you're twenty, you just came out of a bloody fight, and you've got so much unassimilated Earther DNA in your system that your body's trying to shut itself down to adjust. I can understand sick."

Christine bobbed her head exhaustedly, leaning forward a little and casting her eyes on the floor.

"But what else?"

She let out an exasperated sigh, "I don't *know* Beckett, just leave me alone. I've got to find my family. Then I have to get back to *Unity*. Okay?"

Lupus cocked an eyebrow, "I'll have those things taken care of. Go sleep. Or go see a doctor… whichever you prefer, but do one of them."

Looking up with a mixture of contempt, relief, and plain exhaustion, she nodded, "Where's a bed?"

With a quick nod, Lupus signaled a nearby marine, "Get her to guest quarters."

The bear helped Christine stumble off the flight deck, and Lupus ground his jaw. Formidable as the young human was, she was definitely in over her head — or at least she had been, and now she would undoubtedly need a lot of time to make sense of everything that had happened.

•••

High Chancellor Thomas Pious was satisfied.

The Earthers had put up quite a fight, to be sure, but they hadn't stopped the advance of the Crusaders outright. They'd fled before the Legions of Crusaders, unable to defeat the red fury that had almost overrun them. He was under no illusion that, with anything approaching even odds, his Crusaders could handle Earther marines, but they didn't need to. A battalion was all the Earther ship of the line in orbit could offer, and that wasn't nearly enough.

Now, the Crusader mechanized legions were sweeping down towards Genesis City, ready to overwhelm the meager defenses desperately put in place by Gillian Hodge's Naval Marine Corps.

Another tough fight would come of this encounter, but with the momentum they'd gathered at Darymanis City, it seemed impossible the Crusaders would lose this battle.

After so long, the Church would be restored.

Pious resisted feeling excited by the prospect of this victory — even now, he felt a certain wariness when it came to overconfidence. Instead he turned away from the main screen of Sanctity Base's control center, and faced a cluster of Chancellors and Crusader Shappas.

"Brothers, we seem to be doing well."

There were some reluctant glances exchanged among the Crusaders, and one spoke up softly, "We lost most of the tanks and troops that were sent into Darymanis, Your Eminence. The casualties might be as high as 5,000 men."

Distantly listening to the words, Pious nodded, "Yes, that is true. But consider, that was the strongpoint held by *Earthers*. If we could defeat them ten-to-one, we shall have little difficulty with the capital."

The Shappas seemed reluctant still, the one who had spoken earlier taking a step towards the screen and pointing up, "Enhance the capital city."

With the order, one of the nearby Crusader technicians enlarged the view of Genesis City, revealing almost an entire Naval army dug into the jungle around it.

"The weight of their force, Your Eminence, is well-placed to meet our head-on assault. I fear an attempt to flank now would only allow them to assault our rears as we turned to redeploy," the Shappa bowed his head as Pious looked to the screen and then turned to glare at him.

"You can more than double the force they have?" the High Chancellor demanded.

The Shappa nodded, "We can, Your Eminence, but I fear for our success if our forces are decimated in this attack. It might become impossible for us to maintain control of the capital, or any of the other cities we've occupied.

The High Chancellor, despite his previously bright spirits, scowled, "Well what of Lancaster Base. Will we be able to capture that?"

Another deep breath delayed the Shappa's answer, and then he shook his head very slightly, "It will not be easy, Your Eminence."

Thomas Pious slammed his palm into a nearby console, "That is simply unacceptable, Shappa. You *will* take both of our objectives, and you *will* do it in the planned timeframe. Or you shall burn as a nonbeliever. Is that understood?"

The Shappa nodded uncomfortably, then retreated to his fellows' company. Pious whirled back to the main screen with clenched fists, eying the capital city that was destined to be his very soon. Presuming his Shappas could *fight*...

It seemed ironic to him. Harvey Bingham, a man of pathetically weak faith and higher purpose than even Pious, had squandered the advantages of a superior Shappa in Elias Bactule. Now, as another wrong was in need of correction, a much more faithful Chancellor was being forced to act with only nervous men for Shappas.

A divine challenge, it seemed — Pious would be forced to prove his own abilities to the Gods before he could properly save his planet and his race.

But the challenge would be dealt with properly, even if he had to handle it himself. In the meantime, there was much to consider about the state of orbital control. He'd witnessed the defeat of the Church-loyal Naval force at the hands of Graham Manchester, but honestly, Thad Morgan's loss had been of no surprise to Pious.

It had kept the Navy occupied long enough to keep the main body of shipboard marines from landing to make nuisances of themselves, and the threat of further strikes against the Navy by the surviving Church vessels would adequately distract Manchester from assisting his wife at Genesis. But to be sure of that, Pious would have to force his faithful Navy men to continue attacking Manchester's ships — to keep them tied up...

"Communications, locate the senior faithful warship on your screens and signal them. I wish to speak to the new commander."

The Navy would not be ready for the onslaught about to be unleashed — on all fronts.

"We're in good shape now, I think," Graham offered a reassuring nod through the screen, and Sarah took a deep breath.

"I could use your shipboard marines on their flanks... give their divisions some hell as they try to come up," Gillian occupied the other side of the screen, and her husband nodded.

"At your discretion. We'll drop them wherever you need them."

Pat looked from Sarah to the pair on the screen, "That settles it then, we can hold them short of the capital?"

Gillian frowned briefly and then nodded, "We should be able to hold them. I've got a good front thrown up, and Glen Vincent has the army command.

At the very least we'll break two legions. If they send more I can't promise anything..."

"But they shouldn't send more because they also have to pin down your forces at Lancaster," Sarah held up her hand. "Very well. I still want arrangements made to start ferrying civilians to Murdock Island. I don't want eight million innocent people caught in this. Graham, can you drop pinnaces to make it quicker — if they do it with orbital hops it'll be twice as fast."

The junior Manchester nodded to the senior, "I'll send the station craft down... that should be close to 600 craft. They should be able to move over 50,000 in a single run. I'm not going to strip the fleet though, since we may be dropping marines on the attack's flanks."

That was good. Sarah's mind had a good grip on the situation now. This was what she'd done for a living a long time ago, after all. No matter how tactically thoughtful, the Church should have known better than to cross her militarily.

Unless the Earthers switched sides, there was absolutely nothing that would stop her getting her revenge.

As soon as the thought crossed her mind, she started to regret it.

New alarms flashed.

"Chancellor!"

Pious whirled to the main screen and his eyes widened.

The Gods... what was this...

Sarah rushed to the main screen, then came to an abrupt halt, Pat accidentally skidding into her from behind.

"Oh Gods wept. Any time but now..."

CHAPTER 37

"Hey Narosh, how you feeling?"

The yell was colloquial, and Narosh forced his mind to remain blank.

"You're getting good at this, aren't you? Must be all that Earther DNA in your head! No Praaxus-loving Roshie pureblood could stop thinking like that. I should know… haha!"

But the Admiral-of-a-Fleet kept ignoring 'Natosh' and continued instead to tear the last of the circuitry from the message pod.

"Message pod, eh? Oh it's a valiant thing, you trying not to think, but trust me, I'm still getting stuff out of you. How about this, you come out willingly and I don't torture you. You can watch as I take over that planet you care so much about. I'll even let you take a cut!"

Natosh's comments were brutally pedestrian — they lacked the sophistication of a Larosian. He was baiting the Admiral, trying to force him to think…

And it worked, didn't it Narosh?

Narosh ground his jaw in a very humanistic manner, then pulled the last live conduit out of the pod. The floor was now covered in various sorts of internal equipment, including the pod's anti-matter reactor. The power source that, if properly handled, could take the bridge right off the Warcruiser…

And deal with 'Natosh'.

See, you're not even trying to hide your thoughts any more, are you? Well it's a noble plan, blowing me up and all…

Shanavorous began to shudder.

"…but it's too late. The acceleration is up way past anything you idiots could ever pull out of this ship. You'll never have that thing rigged before we hit the planet. And damned if I'll just stay out here and let you incinerate me when I've got a people to harvest. Sure you don't want to watch?"

You will die, Narosh thought plainly.

"Well that line must've taken a while to think up. Fine."

The sound of footsteps moving away from the door reached Narosh through his brutalized senses.

Shanavorous' shuddering increased, and Narosh recognized the sensation of acceleration. The Warcruiser was close to home… and it would be a Trojan horse, carrying this… *thing* to the Larosian people.

You think I'm going to 'bring it' to the Larosians? You're more of an idiot than I thought! Not that you're privy to my timetable, but 'bringing it' is hardly my goal. Let's see, I need slaves. So there's that. But maybe there'd be more joy in just wiping them out. Not like I have to worry about it right now. *Got some time to think, eh?*

The sound of dark laughter filled Narosh's mind with that comment, and the Admiral-of-a-Fleet gingerly dragged the anti-matter cell across the floor towards the door. Stopping in the center of the room, he reached back and clutched two hefty conductor rods.

Shanavorous seemed to surge against hyperspace, and Narosh gritted his teeth at the unnatural grav sheers. The old Warcruiser had been close to coming apart as it was... this explosion should do much more than take the bridge. If he placed the charge correctly it might blow the power grid, and force a crash translation to normal space that would disintegrate the ship.

That was all he could hope for right now — there was nothing more he could do.

"There *is* something more you could do — you could watch!" 'Natosh' yelled from the bridge. The flippancy in his voice would have turned Narosh's appetite, had he one to begin with...

Appetite? Well there's a human expression! Oh come on Larosian, you can't do better than stealing from a human? You ever wonder how those useless cattle are doing now? I'm guessing their society is shattered and they're trying to haul the Earthers into a pointless war.

Narosh's mind snarled back. *Keep trying, thing. I don't care what you say, if Laros falls the humans or the Earthers will defeat you. Count on it!*

There was a pause from the bridge as the turbulence grew more violent and then settled. The Admiral took the chance to connect the two conduits to the nodes on the reactor, then connected the free ends to the secondary inputs.

It was a crude feedback loop... the fail safes in the power plant would probably try to stop it. So he'd have to disable those quickly. Flipping open the top panel, Narosh forced his ailing hands to claw at the circuitry.

Finesse... "Finesse! I don't like it when someone tries to kill me, Narosh. I've got a bad history with it. But if you're going to try, at least do a good job!"

I will do a very good job — you will die.

There was a sigh, "I tire of this. Do you want to know the truth about your beloved Earthers and humans. See what I'm seeing in my mind's eye right now..."

And then images suddenly began to flood Narosh's mind, halting his hand and forcing his remaining silver eye to open wide. Humans killing each other, Earthers killing red humans in defense of green ones... ships and explosions, small craft and Superdreadnoughts...

"What..." it was a torn rasp, but it was all Narosh could muster.

How can you see this? Across a galaxy — no one is that powerful.

There was laughter in his mind again, and Narosh's good eye screwed shut against the pain it inflicted.

"Maybe I'm that powerful, or maybe you're just a close-minded idiot. Anyway, hang on a minute, I have to decelerate."

Narosh marshaled his mental strength and forced his hand back into the reactor control casing, trying to trip the release on the fail safes...

And stop that you ignorant fool.

An unseen hand grabbed the back of Narosh's armor and threw him across the room. He slammed into the outer wall with an unhealthy crunch, silver blood spattering the floor. A sharp vocal scream escaped him as he came down in a heap on the edge of the beacon pod.

The two-meter cylinder had been built to be jettisoned at the ship's destruction, with copies of the logs and records from the ship. Gutted of its power, it was little more than an empty shell now. He needed to set the explosion...

"Oh *stop it* already!"

A sharp jab to Narosh's throat knocked him into the pod's now-hollow interior, and the lid slammed shut and sealed.

Better hold your breath. And in case you're wondering, I used the power of my mind to throw you into that overblown black box. Still think your friendly humans can kill me?

Narosh's body ebbed with pain, and in the dark interior of the pod he realized he was trapped... for the last time.

That's the style. Finally gives up... I was getting a bit worried. So you don't want to watch, that's alright. Think about your family... your people. Next time you see them it'll be over coffee with Praaxus, I'll wager.

Narosh tried to lift his head off the cold silver-alloy wall of the pod, but he couldn't raise it anymore. The tremors running through *Shanavorous* faded, and Narosh realized the ship was decelerating.

"Good God, I must talk to housekeeping. There's all sorts of debris around here. You really should see it Narosh — maybe talk to your friends about proper maintenance of the hyper lanes. But I suppose they weren't expecting such distinguished guests."

He had failed. Fighting as hard as he could, he had been no match for this thing. What had been Natosh. Now his people would pay...

In a roundabout way, you're exactly right. You're vastly inferior, and you'd have done well to remember that. But oh well, you get the glory ride with me. It'll be fun. Now if you'll excuse me, I've got a planet to...

Narosh's ears barely picked up: "What the hell?"

Where had this thing learned its dialogue? Not even Novash was so fluent in colloquial human! Its mental powers must extend far enough to witness life on Genesis...

Now who leaves this sort of EM delta at the mouth of a corridor. Humans... I hope they're as entertaining...

Narosh's mind seized the words, but they made no sense to him.

All he understood was that *Shanavorous* had translated shakily into normal space, and that his death was imminent.

Well, it's been fun Narosh. Have a nice crash!

And in his mind's eye Narosh watched as *Shanavorous* kicked into rapid acceleration, lunging at almost light speed at the single planet in the Larosian home system... and the force of this unnatural acceleration snapped the grip of the launcher clamps. The pod he lay in snapped off the hull and somersaulted out into the deep blackness of space, and Narosh blacked out.

But just before darkness consumed him, he realized one important thing: the Larosian home system had three planets, not one.

CHAPTER 38

Renown's alarms blared just as Beckett reached the bridge. The Church was probably mounting a raid–

Varnia came out of her chair and her husband stopped beside her in front of the main holo tank.

A silver icon that had hurtled out well beyond the opening of the corridor was heading for the planet at incredible speed, shedding debris as it flew through space. Since the Krogg War, no force in the Earther database had been assigned silver icons, out of respect for their allies...

"Collision in... forty seconds."

The report came laden with the disbelief felt by everyone on the ship of the line's bridge.

"Can we get our guns on it?" Varnia turned to her Second Lieutenant, but the officer's head shook silently.

"Coming from too far around the arc of the planet — we couldn't break dock and get there in time."

Beckett Lupus looked from the tank to his wife and then back, "Point of impact?"

Varnia looked from the holo tank to her Sensor Officer.

"It'll hit Sanctity and spray Lancaster with debris. The force of the impact will probably plunge the planet into darkness."

"Warn the capital. Release docking clamps and prepare to maneuver."

A name popped up next to the speeding silver icon as the computer finally detected its transponder. Beckett's eyes widened.

He waited a few seconds for someone to confirm his fears, but no one was paying attention. So as *Renown* went through the minute-long process of slipping its locks, Beckett looked at his wife.

"It's *Shanavorous.*"

She nodded solemnly.

Graham came to his feet.

"Anything positioned to intercept?"

"*Genesis Three* is getting a laser lock now... it's moving too fast for more than a few seconds of engagement though, sir."

"*Anything*. Tell them to take the heat off it. Warn the capital."

• • •

Sarah stood aghast at what she was witnessing. Helpless. Unable to do anything to prevent it. Too wrapped up in local affairs to remember galactic duties…

And now they'd pay for it.

"Pray Gods the plague doesn't survive impact…" Pat whispered.

Genesis Three sprayed the Warcruiser with laser fire, blasting away some of its hull and scattering more to skitter off the atmosphere.

But the main hull dove into the atmosphere faster than it could be tracked.

From staring at the monitors of Sanctity Base, Thomas Pious turned his eyes upwards. He began a prayer to the Gods, and he wondered why they had forsaken him. As he opened his dialogue with the Unity National, a blinding light overcame him.

The anti-matter explosion was stunning.

Dust that should have been kicked into the atmosphere to block sunlight was erased as matter and anti-matter canceled each others' existence, and Genesis' main continent shuddered.

The surface life of the northern third of the landmass was erased.

Sanctity was gone, as was Lancaster. None of the armies or Legions racing to do battle for those installations had a prayer of survival. If the impact wave didn't kill them, the concussion did. If by some miracle they survived that, the radiation was almost surely lethal.

And failing that, their fate might be much, much worse.

Sarah stood completely aghast. The ground was still trembling, and half the monitors in her command center had gone dead… more were getting filled with static. There were reports of pandemonium everywhere — even *worse* than before, as the Church-friendly civilians and the Naval-friendly ones stopped trying to kill each other and fled in terror…

Sarah still stood, completely disbelieving — what sort of Gods-damned cosmic farce was this? There was no way it could be *real*…

Pat's mind was a bit more willing to take what he saw for truth, though he didn't know why. He simply grabbed Sarah's elbow roughly and tugged, "There's no staying on the surface now, Sarah. We *must* get up to *Genesis One*."

She didn't hear the words at first, but the insistent tug on her arm forced her to pay attention. Looking to Pat she nodded, "Yes… yes…"

There was no telling what was on the Warcruiser, though Sarah couldn't conceive of whatever it was surviving the massive explosion. Best not to take any risks…

She turned to the Communications Chief, "Scramble bio-containment units... redirect anything that's on the ready landing pads up to the Genesis stations right now. Keep them clear in case we need to begin mass evacuations."

Pat turned to one of the junior clerks nearby, "Have our luggage sent up to *Genesis One*, eh? Make sure the swords get packed."

The clerk nodded and rushed off, and Sarah looked back at Pat, "I should make an address..."

Pat held up a hand, "We've got no idea what was in that thing. You wait until you're in space first."

Sarah considered overriding her husband, but he was right. She was the head of the civilian government, apparently the only government that had survived the crash. Survival was key...

On landing pads all through the capital city, transports that had only minutes earlier arrived from *Darymanis City* began to depart, clearing the way for local craft that might need to launch. The Genesis stations could accommodate hundreds of thousands of unexpected guests on short notice, so for the time being the wayward survivors of the battle would be put aboard the orbitals.

But some had already begun to unload, so they'd be delayed getting off the pads as they re-boarded their charges. Transports unwilling to wait, boosted only half-full, and the Schaeffer family was caught out as they rushed from the capital's main terminal building to try to reach the transport that had delivered them.

Their craft soared high and accelerated into space, and they looked on as it went.

Still in shock, Claire Schaeffer watched it go silently, eyes slowly floating over the other ships at the terminal. None seemed to be on the lift-off line — she and her parents would have to wait for the next one going up... try to get to the head of the lines before mobs of panicked people overran them...

Or they could try to take advantage of their elder daughter's new friends.

Missus Schaeffer went to find a car, while her husband and daughter stayed close together and held their weapons in case of trouble.

There was still a coup, after all.

CHAPTER 39

Sarah watched her capital city blur past as her heavily-protected convoy floated quickly through the streets. Some of the roads were eerily abandoned, others flooded with panicked people. Her city… her *planet* was in chaos… she should have been leading it, not abandoning…

Almost as soon as she had the thought, Pat's hand settled on her knee, and she looked at her husband with a taught expression.

He nodded to her silently, and she sighed. They were close to the main terminal.

Renown's engines hummed slightly as the First Rate floated free of *Genesis One*, and the ship quickly lurched forward to examine some of the debris that had flaked off *Shanavorous* during that ship's final run.

"Look for anything remotely biological," Varnia knew she was stating the obvious, but to be honest, she was completely in shock.

That Warcruiser had come out of *nowhere* — how could anyone have expected it?

She just hoped that wasn't part of the plan… presuming there was a plan.

Beckett was standing next to his wife, eyes settling on the reports that were now scrolling through the main holo tank, "It's chaos down there… I don't think there's any order left…"

His words drew a nod from his wife, but he steeled himself against the next inevitable statement: he *couldn't* re-insert the 2/54th. They were shot up and replenishing… they couldn't be ready for at least another half hour.

And as the tumult spread through the entire planet, what could his few hundred marines do? The lion's share of this duty fell on the Genesis marines… and some were still tied up with surviving Crusaders.

The rest… well…

"Ma'am... hold on..."

Varnia's ear twitched and she turned briefly to her Sensor Chief. The experienced noncom was frowning, "Yes ma'am, I definitely have a Larosian bio sign in the debris… it's far out, near the rift. Looks like it came loose almost on reentry. I don't see anything abnormal with the bio reading, but that's certainly not an escape pod he's in…"

Beckett and his wife exchanged quick glances — neither willing to believe a

Larosian would do this intentionally, or even allow it to happen by accident. He *had* to have been infected... which meant he was a biohazard. And that meant the Earthers were the best ones to deal with him.

"Inform ArcGeneral Manchester, and mark course for it. Make your speed 300 pls, Cruising Master."

Unity Genesis slid keenly into position next to *Genesis One*, not yet ready to dock with the station, but set to defend the President's convoy as it came up from the surface.

For now Graham just sat in his chair and stared at his screen.

The devastation didn't even begin to register — most of the central continent had been irradiated. There were no signs of the virus, but then, how could there be? Under the Church, an explosion like that would probably have ranked high on the emergency decontamination solutions list if a Genesis city had come down with the Larosian plague.

Nothing had survived, and now chaos was reaching new heights. It wouldn't be long before the civilians swarmed launch sites and piled into small craft... many could be Church sympathizers, posing a threat to Sarah and the Genesis government.

They'd have to move her to *Genesis One*, perhaps even *Unity Genesis* if refugees turned out to be militant.

The situation was flying apart. And only one woman had the resources in position to attempt to control it.

Gillian Hodge refused to process the loss of Lancaster Base. She still had almost 300,000 marines under her command, and over half of them were near enough to the capital city to at least maintain order there. She was ordering everyone into biohazard gear in case the worst happened, but she doubted it would be an issue.

Looting, mob violence, terror, and fear would kill many more than some damned Larosian plague.

Junior Commandants were moving to assert control now — martial law had yet to be declared, but Gillian's tanks would be in the streets of the capital very soon. And she still had the rest of the planet to consider...

Well, it wasn't too bad: the other cities on the continent had been taken care of by that blast.

Gillian's mind froze — the cold tactical insight made her feel wholly ill. Her hand began to tremble.

Perhaps a hundred million were dead... no, maybe *ten times* that many...

But the tactical instinct shut down her compassion, and her trembling hand balled into a fist. She had orders to give, and had a few lives left to save.

Marines drove towards Genesis City.

Sarah's personal guards forced a corridor from the vehicle convoy past the terminal to the landing pads beyond. Panicked civilians were screaming and begging and charging the line of marines, and shots were fired on several occasions.

Trying not to think about it, Sarah rushed through the causeway with her guards, and sighted her official pinnace on the tarmac as she drew nearer to it. The ship's drives were already alive, charged and ready to make the run up to *Genesis One*.

Marines were forcing people to stay away from its invitingly open entry hatch.

She wanted to close her eyes, but she forced them to stay open as she finally reached the bottom of the ramp. The marine accompanying Sarah looked up at the President as she boarded the ship, "It'll just be a minute as we grab your luggage, ma'am."

Sarah nodded very slowly, and as she retreated into the relative silence of the pinnace's cabin her mind whirled at the very thought — *luggage*? With so many lost souls on the ground…

But she silenced her mind for now. Her people would be safe in the end, she knew that for certain. It was a matter of maintaining order… and given the highly unstable situation, she couldn't do that from the surface.

She expected Pat to say something calming–

Sustained gunfire erupted outside, and her eyes jolted back to the cabin door.

Pat swore something unintelligible as a group of men opened fire on the car he was pulling two bags from. He tossed the duffles to a nearby marine and then hefted the last two items, the family blades, out of the vehicle's trunk.

He tossed Sarah's sword to another marine, then attached his own to his belt. Marines around him were spraying the opposite side of the street with bullets, and a couple of civilians in the terminal joined the Presidential Guard in firing.

Gods wept, I can't tell friend from bloody foe out here…

"Sir, time to go."

Pat turned to see the middle-aged marine who'd taken Sarah to the ramp standing with her rifle poised.

He nodded, took his old coat and hat from the top of the car where he'd laid them, and turned to follow the marine in her retreat.

Bullets flew all around, and as screaming civilians scattered and fled to cover, the Presidential marines began laying down portable breastworks to establish a perimeter.

Then an anti-tank missile hit the car.

Pat was far enough away not to die in the blast, but it flung him into the air in a blur of surprise and pain. Someone behind him had blocked the shrapnel...

As he hit the carpeted floor of the terminal, he recalled the pain he'd felt back on the Antarctic Plain, when he'd been fool enough not to outrun Crusader shell fire. At least he'd been good enough to make fun of himself then... he'd have to do the same this time, though he wasn't badly hurt.

He was still a robust twenty-nine-year-old in body, after all... obscene as that fact felt at this moment. But his coat was burning, so he tossed it aside as he forced himself to his feet. Turning, he found the ground littered with dead marines, and a horde of gun-wielding maniacs trying to force their way across the street. Enough guns were firing to keep them back, but he had to hurry.

Even though his ears were ringing... and he felt slightly deaf. That'd pass...

Then someone with a rifle was in front of him, saying something–

Pat's mind, battle hardened and no stranger to the din of ground fighting, snapped itself into reality, "You *are* Pat Conroy? Sir?"

He nodded, hand drifting to the hilt of his sword. It was a civilian with a rifle — a man carefully keeping his teenage daughter on the safer side of his body as he fired blindly at the attackers.

"I'm Mark Schaeffer... my daughter's Christine... she said you know her..."

Pat didn't know what the hell... oh wait, of course he knew, and he nodded, "Graham's assistant, right? What are you doing here?"

The fire intensified briefly, then slackened slightly as a few more guards got better firing positions and sprayed rounds into the renegade fighters from above. The lull let the man turn to Pat with determined eyes.

"We were in Darymanis... we missed the transport when it reloaded and shipped out... please..."

Finding form again, Pat's mind quickly connected the dots, "Yes of course, come on. You can come with us..."

Mister Schaeffer held up a hand, "I won't go without my wife, sir... she went to find a car... well, we'll get off when we can. But take Claire, my daughter. She's still in shock from the fighting... please just get her up there."

Pat found himself at a loss for words, and bullets began to nick the carpet around them as the fighters on the other side of the street took new positions.

After a very long second, he nodded, "I will."

Schaeffer closed his eyes for a second in relief, and gently guided his daughter forward with his hand, "Go Claire. We'll come up later."

She looked up vaguely at her father and nodded, "I'll... see you soon, daddy..."

It was a small child's reply, and Pat immediately recognized the girl's dire state. She was traumatized — she never should have seen the things she had.

Mister Schaeffer bent down and kissed his daughter softly on the forehead, then looked at Pat, "Take her, sir. And tell Christine I love her too, please… if I don't get to…"

Pat was nodding and gently taking Claire's hand in the same instant, "I'll tell her. But you survive — I don't mean to write a sad ending into my book on this thing just for you."

It wasn't the best thing he could have said, but it was all he could think of, and it drew a nod from the Schaeffer father, "*Go*, sir."

Pat took Claire and quickly rushed towards the gate, Presidential Guards giving him room to get through. There was another roar of fire and he looked back from the landing pad. He couldn't even see Mark Schaeffer through the mess, so he turned again and rushed up the ramp.

Sarah stood as he entered, and frowned at the girl who stumbled stunned into the quiet cabin, "Who…?"

"Claire Schaeffer, Christine Schaeffer's sister… missed her ride to *Genesis One*…"

A slow nod was all Sarah could manage as Pat helped Claire settle into a chair and buckle in. He put her battered duffle on the seat next to her, then turned back to his wife, "Her father's out there helping the marines… he doesn't know where her mother is. He wouldn't leave, but he wanted me to take her."

Sarah's eyes filled with a sort of appalled terror she wasn't sure she'd ever before felt. This was a monumental tragedy, but at least she was helping one girl escape it. And a Top Flight family member…

"How do you find these people, Pat?" she asked in a rasp after a moment.

He shook his head and shrugged, clenching his jaw and forcing down any urge to get emotional. The pinnace hatch shut and the craft lifted jerkily from the pad, quickly accelerating upward towards *Genesis One*, with a half dozen escort vessels forming around it.

In the confusion, no one even noticed the fighter as it descended towards the main terminal of the capital city's landing fields.

It was silver, a bit scuffed and in poor repair. It made a grating noise as it shifted from an angular craft into a roughly humanoid robot form, and then it let its feet rest on a landing pad.

A disc descended from the underside of its cockpit, and a smiling Larosian stepped off it onto the tarmac. No, it wasn't a Larosian, it had black eyes… and something about it was different…

'Natosh' smiled and paced across the pad, noticing the loud firefight with some amusement. The humans were at it again — they seemed to make a habit of killing each other. And he always reaped the rewards.

Ahh, but it was good to see humans again — it'd been a while since he'd seen anything remotely human-like. Narosh *excluded*, of course… ha!

Strolling past firing marines into the terminal building, 'Natosh' began to chuckle to himself, and as he stopped paying attention to the humans, they all began to notice him. Fire slackened, then stopped as he paced into its path — no one quite knew what he was, but they knew he didn't belong here…

A marine approached him slowly, rifle up and eyes narrowed.

"How did you get here?" she demanded plainly.

'Natosh' grinned, "Come closer, let me tell you."

The marine stopped and raised her weapon, "Hands on your head then, Larosi–"

"*Don't* call me that."

'Natosh' moved with blinding speed, and the marine found her throat in his waiting hand. He smiled at her as she struggled to free herself, and he lifted her off her feet with one hand. Around him marines opened fire, but none of the rounds seemed to even come close to him. Something like a shield stopped them.

The marine hit and kicked and struggled… it was amusing.

Using his free hand, 'Natosh' drove fingers into her eyes, and gripping the bone of her skull, twisted the head from her neck in a single, terrifyingly smooth motion.

He tipped her body up and started to drink…

The crowd stood silent in utter disbelief, and most looked away to gag or scream. Not even the Kroggs had produced such displays of absolute horror…

"Kroggs are amateurs," 'Natosh' dropped the headless corpse and smiled at the collected humans. For the people watching, it was a nightmare of unimaginable proportions.

"This is reality, not a nightmare, ladies and gentlemen," he said firmly. "But fear not, I've better things in store for all of you."

No one moved… no one believed they could.

'Natosh' wiped some of the blood off his mouth with the back of his hand, leaving much on his face and armor.

"Mmmmm… have to admit though, you humans still do have that winning flavor. She tasted *good.*"

For no reason they knew of, every Earther on *Renown* felt a sudden chill.

CHAPTER 40

Jax Furgus still wore his housecoat, though he'd changed his clothes underneath the shabby thing so he looked marginally more professional. He was wearing sweat pants and a t-shirt now, and everyone on the bridge took some comfort in that.

In between chuckles, anyway.

"They're now forty-two minutes behind," Captain Ron Hobbes pointed to DeBrooke's First Assault Fleet, still making its maximum speed but being left in the collective wake of *Aboukir's* fast squadron of 74s.

Furgus nodded slowly, his mind waking up to the strategic realities that he'd slowly been mulling over for the past hours. They were still almost a day from Freetown, but the old cat had a feeling the Faithful were even closer.

Something in the back of his mind made him worry — the Church had executed their ambush so well…

Even in leaving the Freetown ships forty-two minutes behind, the coarse old Admiral was taking a major risk, since they could be hit out in the open without the support of his guns. He'd decided to lead the way into danger, but now he had to be very careful about how he handled things.

"Ron, you think we can squeeze anything else out of these engines?" Furgus made the question a distant one, and the Captain's eyes narrowed thoughtfully.

It was risky, but if crotchety old Admiral Furgus thought it necessary…

"Well, it's a maximum *recommended* speed. I'm sure they built in a buffer. Want me to go for 3,500 pls?"

With a deep breath and a frown, Jax nodded, "Tell anyone in the squadron who can to keep up with us, but signal *Fundy* and *Bismarck* to stay back with the Freetowners. I've got a bad feeling."

There were quick nods from various members of the bridge crew, then *Aboukir's* drives began to hum a little louder.

The Earther squadron of 74s surged ahead.

Chancellor Leo's hand was clenched into a fist, and as much as he wished to calm himself, a mix of nerves and excitement held him firmly in its grasp.

They were but twenty hours from Freetown, and if this gambit proved a success, the Faithful at last would crush their nemesis, as the Church of Genesis was crushing its own.

Four capital ships would be more than a match for the pathetic defenses Freetown could offer, and then the planet would be irradiated before the reinforcement bastard ships could arrive to save it.

Nothing could stop them now.

In less than a day…

Unable to sleep, James Stanton paced the decks of *Archangel Sword*, examining the old ship's fittings and panels, watching its veteran crew, and remembering the gloried days of its past.

The hybrid ship had been a trendsetter, and it'd been through every great battle of the Krogg War save for the battle for Krogg 'A' itself. Now it was the flagship of what was being dubbed the 'Home Fleet', and James couldn't help but fear its inadequacy for the task.

Freetown had for too long been arrogant and overconfident in the abilities of its vintage Genesis ships, and had waited too long to take the Earthers up on the offer of new construction

If even two of the *Felix*-class advanced Battlecruisers had joined the fleet now, this story would be a very different one.

But they hadn't.

Six Battlecruisers — including *Sword* — two Heavy Cruisers, three Light Cruisers, and seven Destroyers. And only the Gods themselves only knew what was coming for them… and how soon.

There'd been no more recent news from Genesis or Earth. James could only hope that the Earthers hadn't actually left Freetown without the help it might so gravely need. Not after such a long friendship… how could they?

But it did seem as possible as not. Everything good that had been built over the past forty years seemed to have unraveled almost overnight, and all thanks to the arrogance and damnable skill of the Faithful. A week ago the universe had made sense…

James ground his jaw and laced his hands behind his back. Somewhere out there Audrey was racing back to Freetown, with enough ships to make a difference. She couldn't be much more than a day away, but where were the Faithful?

He didn't know, so James Stanton waited and worried.

Republic didn't even shiver as it made its way between star systems.

Audrey DeBrooke sat on the bridge, feeling unable to be anywhere else and tapping her foot restlessly on the deck.

She was all that stood between the Church and victory right now, and even as she edged her advanced ships past their recommended speed limits, she kept feeling as though she was losing time. There was no way to know for certain, but something in the back of her mind kept insisting she was too late.

But Audrey DeBrooke had lived through far too much to believe that she was too late. She'd read Pat Conroy's books, she'd *lived* them. She knew about Earther timing… she knew everything always worked out.

She just wouldn't be satisfied until it actually did.

"ETA Freetown?" she asked absently, and the Cruising Master looked up at her with a frown, "Just under a day, ma'am. About twenty-three hours now, I'd say."

Audrey nodded with a deep breath. Well, she'd know relatively soon.

For better or worse.

Setter Caine sat silently on a large rock on his estate's beach and watched the pounding waves as they drew back and threw themselves at the shore. He felt unsettled… something somewhere wasn't at all right.

There was a burning in his blood — very mild but very insistent. It was as if his instincts were telling him that a change was about to occur. That the rules of the very universe were somehow being rewritten.

But that didn't make any sense…

"Dad?"

Setter blinked and turned himself on the rock, smiling at Phealan as his son paced over the beach towards him. Phealan really was turning into a fine Earther…

The oddity of that thought struck Caine, and he almost wanted to frown as Phealan came to a stop beside him. Something inside his body quite literally felt different, and Setter Caine knew that something was wrong.

His son's instincts picked up on the discomfort immediately, "What's going on?"

Setter frowned and looked back at a collapsing wave, offering a weak shrug, "Wish I could say. Jax is out there looking after Freetown, Beckett and Varnia are helping out at Genesis… and I can't shake this feeling that it's all destined to end badly."

Phealan cocked an eyebrow, "*Destined*? You don't believe in predestination — not after all you've been through."

A small smile crossed Caine's face, "You're right. It's just an odd feeling, I suppose. Maybe I've been out here in the wind too long."

The junior Caine put a hand on his father's shoulder, "That sounds about right. You are getting old, after all…"

Setter donned a mock frown and glared at his son, and Phealan held his hands up defensively, "Hey, I don't want trouble. Don't want to beat up the old man…"

With a chuckle, Caine glanced back at the water before standing, "Alright. I'll go watch some holos like a good retired war vet."

"That's better. I need advice too…"

Setter and Phealan headed into the brush towards the house. As they went, the veteran First Lord and First Consul managed to forget his discomfort of moments before.

Of course things would work out — they always did.

CHAPTER 41

Christine leaned against *Genesis One's* corridor wall as *Unity Genesis* locked into its airlock, and in a haze she watched the pressure hatch slowly draw aside. The corridor around her was awash with civilians, only the first batch of thousands and most from her home town, at least for now.

Maybe she shouldn't have left *Renown* without sleep. No, she couldn't have stayed on that ship… it wasn't where she wanted to be. She needed to attend to her duty… or something. Of course, she'd still managed to doze in and out of sleep while leaning against this wall. But she was being saved from her dreams now. Reality wasn't as bad as what she was seeing in her sleep.

Someone had tried to explain to her what had happened. A Larosian ship had crashed into the planet… it didn't make sense, but running people — *terrified* people — did. Because there was a coup and now probably a civil war brewing.

Whatever it was, she had a job to do…

Her eyes closed slowly as she tried to order her scrambled thoughts, and then a hand grabbed her shoulder. She flinched and her eyes flew open, one hand finding her saber and drawing it part way from its sheath.

When did that *become my natural response to human contact?*

"Are you alright? Come on now Christine, look at me. Let me have a look at you. You must've gotten some sleep — Beckett wouldn't have let you off *Renown* without rest. *Christine.*"

She was having a hell of a time focusing — it felt as though she needed to reestablish the connections in her mind… to *wake up*. Sleep had brought only terror, mainly, and horror. Things she hadn't dealt with hours before were bubbling right up to the surface.

"George, hand me that bucket please. Yes, *that* one. No, go *fill* it then, man! Come on now… *Christine.*"

It was a lot to take in… and her blood seemed to tingle every time she tried to assimilate it. She might never escape this feeling of dispossession… it was so *alien* to her, so not human.

She'd recognized something deadly in herself down on the planet, something she had to come to terms with. And always wonder whether it was put there by the Earthers. Suddenly the burden of the Earthers made so much more sense to her…

But she didn't want *plight* — she wanted out, she wanted frivolity. To lie in bed and read… to go shopping… to *gossip*, even though she hated that. She was too young to have been so–

Graham took the bucket of water from ArcEnsign Rumpsfeld and indelicately tossed it in his adjutant's face. Her eyes bolted open and her sword came from its sheath in such a blur that the ArcGeneral didn't see it — and the bottom of the bucket fell to the floor while the top stayed in his hands.

He looked from the halved bucket to Christine and tried to lock eyes with her, "I'm not taking resignations today, actually. You alright?"

Christine took three long blinks and her mind slapped her subconscious ungraciously back into its place, "I'm so sorry — I didn't even think... it just happened..."

Graham looked at the remains of the bucket in his hand, fighting down his first urge to leap away and yelp. Christine wasn't herself — she hadn't done that intentionally, and he hadn't been *halved*, so now wasn't the time to call her on her highly irregular behavior...

He tossed the bucket to Rumpsfeld, "It was a bit impressive, actually. Scared the living hell out of me, but you managed to cut the bucket without gutting me... so you've either got impeccable motor acuity, or you missed and you're rather mean."

Looking from the ArcGeneral to her saber, Christine swallowed nervously, then shrugged, "I'm nice, I think."

Graham nodded, "Good. Sarah's coming up and I'm determined to get her onto *Unity*. Nothing personal, but I don't trust these Darymanis refugees any more than I'd trust Thomas Pious. And with this *new* situation..."

Christine frowned, her mind finally ticking over at its usual interval and her self-doubt being silenced by sheer determination. The arrival of that Larosian Warcrusier made the surface a very questionable place to be even though it probably hadn't delivered a virus in its incinerating blast.

Apparently her mind had been listening to the news reports, despite its chaotic state.

"So the President is coming up... I should try to find my family too — they must have come aboard somewhere. Can I get them guest quarters aboard *Unity*?"

Graham offered a quick nod, pointing down the corridor, "All arrivals are coming from Gates 35 through 60. If they're here they'll be that way. Sarah and Pat are coming in on secured Gate 28. Come down this way with me and we'll have a look while we wait, alright?"

Christine offered a nod, and dropped her duffle on the deck with a quick glance at ArcEnsign Rumpsfeld. The tired young man nodded and collected the bag, bringing it inside the lock for safe keeping.

"Lying sixty points off the port beam, ma'am. There's definitely a regular Larosian biopattern aboard and I still don't see any signs of a plague."

Varnia nodded in reply to the Sensor Chief's report, frowning at the silver cylinder as it tumbled through her holo plot. There was no telling what could have possessed that Larosian to do what it did — indeed, if it was a disease virulent enough to defeat Larosian science, it might be undetectable.

It could be like the Omega 'Virus' — a super-plague, self-aware and hiding itself from scans. Varnia ground her jaw at that thought. It was very unsettling to think about intelligent plagues like that, given the history of the Earther race.

But it had to be considered.

"Alright," Beckett turned to his wife, "Take it into bay ten. I'll take a dozen marines and a medic with me, and we'll go shielded. See what we find… and be ready to space it."

And that was an even more disturbing concept. Varnia frowned and turned to her husband, "That's a *lot* of risk–"

Lupus held up his hands, "Don't worry, I've got no desire to die. But somebody with firsthand Larosian experience ought to be there. *I* need to be there."

With a sigh, Varnia offered a slow nod, then turned to the First Lieutenant, "Bring it into bay ten. And make sure you entirely isolate it with deck shields when you do."

Graham wanted to see Gillian, but he'd get to that later. His wife was probably much too busy to be disturbed… his sister was a tougher case.

It wasn't that the younger Manchester sibling didn't believe his elder sister to be a highly capable woman, she obviously was. No, it was that suicidal penchant of hers — the will to charge the guns that seemed to have mellowed only very slightly with age — that worried him the most.

He absolutely had to get the President aboard the Genesis Fleet flagship, and then he had to close the locks behind her. That made the most sense — there was no more secure location in the solar system, save for *Renown,* but running the government from an Earther ship would definitely create the wrong impression.

Keeping a quick pace, Christine and Graham reached the secured gates section of *Genesis One's* planetside airlock bank only a few moments before the lights over Gate 28 blinked green. A party of marines was keeping watch, and the President and her bodyguard edged from their craft.

As Graham stopped to watch the opening hatch, he wondered how much of Sarah's staff had come up with her. Surely she'd have taken a dozen marines — from what he'd heard, things had gotten rather rough in the capital.

But the opening hatch revealed one man with a pistol and drawn broadsword, cautiously eyeing the terminal area before stepping into it.

"Pat!" Graham quickly crossed the floor to the hatch, "Where are your *marines?*"

The big Irishman looked very weary, and he shrugged slowly, sheathing his sword and putting his pistol awkwardly in his pocket, "They had to cover for us... things in the capital have gotten bloody bad."

Almost as if on cue, sounds of commotion came from one of the nearby corridors, as passers-by recognized Graham and Pat in the distance. Marines stood their ground, politely trying to send them on their way, but the people desperately wanted *something* to make sense of — a leader to tell them what was going on.

Sarah was second through the hatch, silent and grim as Graham locked eyes with her. Graham immediately recognized the pain on his sister's face. However he'd seen her in worse states, and at least Pat was still here to help deal with this one.

Graham was opening his mouth to speak to his sister when a teenage girl stumbled slowly from the Presidential pinnace, carrying a filthy and crumpled duffle. He frowned first at Sarah's blank stare, then at Pat's tired eyes, then realized Christine had edged ahead of him.

Pat blinked and looked at the gaunt face of the elder Schaeffer, "Your father sends his love, dear. Said he had to find your mother and he'd be up presently, but given the heated situation we left behind, he wanted your sister up here."

Christine found herself nodding very slowly, and then Claire seemed to wake up to a little more reality — not so much as Christine had with the help of cold water, but enough to recognize her sister.

Graham watched the siblings as they edged closer to each other and finally embraced, and found himself wondering briefly why Christine hadn't mentioned her sister. Then he thought about himself and Sarah. His sister was a handful... speaking of which...

"Well, we need to get to *Unity Genesis* before we get mobbed."

The five humans headed back towards the military locks in silence. Aside from the flight crew, no one else had been on their transport.

Lupus forced his heart rate to stay low, and he glanced anxiously at Howler as they stood in *Renown's* tenth landing bay. It was relatively small, but more than large enough to handle this Larosian canister and the Earther examination team.

Doctor Lazarus had elected to join the party herself, having saved the life of an Admiral-of-a-Fleet once and thus being acknowledged as one of the most Larosian-savvy medics in the Earther service.

Now, she'd have to determine how threatening this Larosian was. And if he was a threat, the marines would see him off the ship as smoothly as possible. Given their surroundings, that meant venting the bay into space.

The reception committee all wore personal shields, keyed to a field density that would be medically acceptable to protect them in situations involving potential biological contamination. And just in case, the deck chief was guiding the cylinder into an energy-shield shaped like a box that was atmosphere-tight.

Already, the space doors were beginning to close behind that cylinder, and Lupus tensed. The battered capsule obviously hadn't been pressurized, though it may have held atmosphere long enough to keep the occupant alive...

"Ready arms," Howler's words were soft as the cylinder came to a halt in midair.

The marines of 2/54th leveled their weapons, as did their Colonel. Lupus took a step forward, breathed deeply, and waved to the Deck Chief. The grav anchors released the Larosian cylinder, and it clattered noisily to the deck.

Edging closer to the shield that contained it, Lupus watched and waited as the tube rolled back and forth under its own power. If the Larosian was alive, he'd logically try to get out.

And fortunately, this Larosian was being logical. After what he'd seen so far today, Lupus didn't have the patience for much else.

With a painful shriek, the hatch swung open, and a Larosian hauled himself over the side. Covered in silver blood, the alien hauled himself free of his escape ship and painfully dragged himself around to see his location.

Lupus watched, standing perfectly still, trying to decide if the Larosian had any defining features. Nothing seemed to stand out, but then its blood was masking a lot of detail. As the alien's face slowly came into sight, Beckett frowned.

Wait — it had only one eye... and it had clearly been beaten badly... but...

"Great Earth," the General rasped, "*Narosh...*"

And with a feat of titanic strength, the Admiral-of-a-Fleet lifted his head to look at Lupus, "Beckett Lupus... help me..."

Beckett moved forward out of instinct, but stopped himself abruptly. Narosh tried to use his arms — one without a hand — to drag himself towards the Earther, but found his energy depleted.

"The writing is on the wall..." the Larosian rasped painfully, "The plague... is with Natosh... and the human world is in danger..."

The phrases sounded almost strong as the Admiral said them, but then his face flopped forward onto the deck. Lupus found himself staring open-mouthed, then nodded to the Deck Chief, "Drop the shield. Doc, give me good news... please..."

It was Narosh's ignominious return, and it did not bode well.

CHAPTER 42

Renown's medical bay was silent as Doctor Celia Lazarus moved around Admiral-of-a-Fleet Narosh. The Larosian had survived the depressurization of his chamber remarkably well, but he was still ailing from the many injuries that had seemingly been inflicted on him during his cruise.

Beckett silently watched the unconscious Larosian. The Admiral's words had not inspired confidence... Lupus just had to hope it was mindless blather, brought on by a delirious, pain-driven state of mind.

But they'd prepare for the worst, just in case...

"I'll wake him, General," Celia Lazarus looked up at Lupus, and he blinked.

"You can do that? So soon?" Beckett hadn't expected to be able to talk to Narosh for quite some time — for some reason he held that all too stereotypical belief that, unless forced, doctors never wanted to release their patients from the safety of unconsciousness.

Lazarus offered a mild shrug, "The UDRC I put into him during our last encounter seems to be holding his system together. A lot of the Larosian antibodies in his blood have been irradiated somehow, but the old AB-114 seems to be holding firm."

For his part, Lupus understood some of that. He'd read the incident reports from *Orion's* flight deck. Forty years before, Narosh had crashed in a very destructive accident, and Doctor Lazarus had injected him with Uniform DNA Regeneration Compound — an Earther catchall healer — to stabilize him on the flight back to his flagship. The treatment had saved his life, and evidently, the Earther DNA remained in his system even now.

Well, we've apparently got some tough genes. Funny, I feel like I'm soon going to really need them ...

"I increased his dose with some AB-264. I should be able to grow a new hand and eye for him, too, since his immune system will likely accept our gene templates now..." Lazarus' words slowed as she watched Lupus' frown deepen. Well, she could boil it down even more. "Long and short, General, I think he's going to be fine. A bit more Earther than before, but fine."

Lupus took a thankful breath and nodded, "That's good to hear. So let's wake him up..."

Turning away, Lazarus collected a silver instrument from a tray behind her, then held it over the Larosian's head and keyed it to life. After a few seconds

Narosh twitched and the doctor drew the device away.

Opening his one unbandaged eye — the other socket covered by a folded sterile cloth for the moment — Narosh tried to sit up, but was stopped by some instinct even before Lazarus' hand could restrain him.

His one good hand rose to his face, feeling the cloth gingerly and then patting his face in an odd manner, "I feel... weird."

Beckett Lupus cocked an eyebrow at the Larosian's choice of words, "Well that's to be expected. We just pumped a new set of Earther DNA into you... Doc Lazarus here thinks your Larosian immune system is pretty much gone now. It's all Earther."

Narosh's head turned towards Lupus, and a small smile came to his face, "It does me good to see you, Beckett."

Lupus offered a quick nod, "Kind of you. I wish the circumstances were better. *Shanavorous* did a lot of damage when it crashed... can you explain that?"

Narosh's smile vanished almost immediately, and again he tried to sit up, this time being halted by Lazarus' hand.

"You'll bleed to death if you don't stay flat, Admiral," the doctor said frankly, and Narosh tilted his head at the comment.

"Very well... but Beckett, beware of 'Natosh'. He was infected by the plague, and we tried to cure him with Krogg DNA, but instead the cure took control of him and he became an... *abomination*..."

Urgency began to invade the Larosian's weak words.

"We were using *Shanavorous* as a laboratory... Natosh was my friend, so I came aboard to bear witness, but I was trapped. Natosh... *it* killed the scientists, but it said it could not infect me because *Earther DNA* was impregnable to it. So it is the plague that controls Natosh, and that guided *Shanavorous* here. For the entire journey it taunted me, made me think it was going to Laros... evidently, it wanted humanity for some reason..."

It took a lot of effort and self control for Lupus not to show his concern. This was not good...

"So it's crossed with Krogg DNA and it's become some sort of... *intelligent* virus?" Beckett's words were quiet.

Narosh bobbed his head painfully, "We thought it was of Krogg origin, and our scientists believed only a Krogg cure could kill a Krogg disease. We tried to use raw Krogg cells to break its defenses. It was folly."

"And Earther biology is immune?" Lazarus leaned closer to her patient with interest. "Why didn't you try that sooner? I remember sending drugs back with you last time..."

A long, thoughtful blink punctuated Narosh's thoughts, then, "Those drugs... I believe they were destroyed with our hospital ships at Krogg 'A'. And we would not have thought to try such cures, in any case... I am the only Larosian with Earther DNA, but until now, I was never exposed."

Grinding his jaw, Lupus glanced from Lazarus back to Narosh, "So, it's an intelligent plague, and it's occupying Natosh. You make it sound like it's got control of him."

"It does. It was 'Natosh' that inflicted these wounds on me… for pleasure, I think. He had extraordinary telekinetic and telepathic abilities… and physical strength beyond anything I could have expected. He spoke with many human colloquialisms… to taunt me, I believe. He professed his desire to survive the crash…"

Lupus frowned, "Nothing survived, except for you, Narosh."

The Admiral-of-a-Fleet turned his head to the General, his one silver eye staring at Beckett's two amber-yellow ones, "Check again."

For a moment the Larosian's stare froze Beckett Lupus' mind — there was something almost Earther in the alien's gaze.

It seemed they were dealing with an *intelligent plague*. They had a great track record with those…

The very thought of Omega sent a chill through Lupus, but he steeled himself against it. Whatever this one called itself, the Earthers would deal with it.

Varnia turned to her husband as he emerged onto the bridge, and she frowned immediately at the anxiousness he was projecting, "What is it?"

"Narosh wasn't the one who crashed the ship. His old Captain Natosh got taken over by some sort of Krogg-mutated intelligent plague," the bridge dropped into silence as Beckett crossed to the main battle tank. "We need to take a very close look at the planet — Narosh thinks 'Natosh' would've found a way to survive. And if he did, there's no telling what the plague could do…"

There was more silence, and the bridge crew began to exchange unsettled glances. Varnia found her mouth open, but she forced it shut and turned back to the plot for a moment.

"Well," she said after a pause, "I'll have to let Graham know… he can start looking first… Is there any *good* news?"

Beckett heaved a long sigh and shrugged, glancing at his wife, "Well, Narosh was saved from infection because of the Earther DNA we shot into him on *Orion* when he crashed. The thing told him it couldn't infect Earthers… so that gives us an edge."

Varnia frowned, "So humans might be alright then — a lot of similar DNA…"

Lupus shrugged, "I can't say. I… well, I don't know. We can hope."

The husband and wife exchanged worried glances, then Varnia turned to her Cruising Master, "Time to *Genesis One?*"

"Five minutes, present speed, ma'am. Shall I increase speed?"

She ground her jaw thoughtfully, nodded, then turned to the Signal Officer, "Get me ArcGeneral Manchester."

CHAPTER 43

It was very strange.

Gillian Hodge sat on the edge of her desk and watched the satellite scans scroll across her large screen. As much as it felt as though things were almost coming together, it also felt as though they weren't. The capital city had gone silent, and much of the planet was doing the same…

But her marines were clearly taking control of the situation. Hi-res satellite feeds showed them restoring order in cities across the continent, calming the people, and putting down firefights with what she presumed to be Church sympathizers.

And yet no one was contacting *Genesis One* with reports.

It was confusing, and worrisome…

Containment teams were in the air, scouring the continent for signs of Larosian wreckage. There was no sign of debris thus far, and no indication that anything had survived the massive anti-matter blast.

Again that thought forced Gillian to pause. She'd seen a lot of fighting in her time, but it was still hard to conceive of the scope of the death caused by that single blast. It was so much worse than the millions of Crusaders lost in Earth space…

Civilians and marines, millions dead in a single brilliant flash that should never have been allowed to happen, but for the Gods-damned Churchers and their ambitions.

It took another deep breath to force the thoughts out of her mind. She couldn't afford to worry about that until everything was back under control, which, by the look of it, would be reasonably soon.

Thank Gods…

A knock came on Gillian's open door, and she looked up and nodded at the adjutant who stood there, only slightly pale-faced. The young man almost stuttered his first words, but steadied himself with a breath, "Sorry, ma'am. The last of the Darymanis City survivors are coming up, as are a lot of refugees from the capital and some other continental cities. Contact with a few of them, but a lot seem to be flying quiet."

Gillian frowned thoughtfully, "There must be some sort of interference from the blast…"

Or, it was a Church trap. They were putting on a good show, trying to get troops aboard the orbitals...

Better safe than sorry.

"Alright, give them clearance, but spread them evenly among the stations, and order each orbital to put a company of marines at every airlock they use. Watch for Churchers trying to get aboard."

The adjutant nodded slowly, "Yes, ma'am."

As he left, Gillian frowned and turned to her screen again. She should comm Graham and make sure his ships separated from the stations... if some of the orbitals were somehow carried by boarding, the ships would be vulnerable.

She turned to her keypad and sent a message to *Unity Genesis*.

Graham kept looking nervously over his shoulder. He wasn't sure why, but he was getting an uncomfortable feeling as he passed through the last corridors to *Unity Genesis'* lock. The crowds were being kept back by marines, but their pleading, some of their jeers and some of their cheers all came through... it felt so awkward.

Half of his planet's habitable land had just been devastated, and he was more worried about a handful of people than the millions of dead.

Prioritization. Truly fun stuff...

Ahead of him, Christine and her younger sister leaned against each other as they walked, the elder seeming to have found some of her composure as her sisterly instincts took hold. That was good, Graham decided. She had something left to really depend on, even after all she'd been through. People needed crutches like that sometimes... Graham certainly had his.

Sarah, however, was walking very determinedly by herself, Pat flanking to one side with his hand on his sword. Those two had seen many rough times — they were accustomed to being composed and distant during crises... much as Graham himself was being. Indeed, all the old veterans, like Gillian for instance, had that ability...

Speaking of which, a company of Naval marines appeared ahead of them, jogging back down the docking deck in single column. Sarah and Pat shifted out of their path, as did the rest of the entourage, and Graham watched them pass with a slight frown. Were they dropping reinforcements?

Well, he'd find out from Gillian in a minute now — as soon as he got back to his office.

Hopefully everything was going alright, relative to the circumstances, that was.

Gillian was about to go back to her C&C when the adjutant reappeared in her door, "The first wave of ships is about to dock now, ma'am. There's at least a company at every lock on every station."

She nodded with a deep breath, "Good. How many craft to what stations?"

"We and *Genesis Three* are each getting two, the other four are only getting one for now. Things seem to be quieting down planetside, ma'am. I'm guessing these are panicked upper classers from the capital."

Well, at least a bit of confidence was resurfacing in the young man's voice. Gillian nodded, "Okay... well, keep me updated. I'm still trying to get in touch with my husband about cutting his ships loose. Send word to station C&C's to order their ships off the dock on my authority."

"Yes, ma'am."

The adjutant disappeared, and Gillian found herself looking at the sat scans again... it was damned irregular down there. Her marines had visibly secured most of the capital city's streets... there was no way that many Naval marines could be replaced with Crusader impersonators.

And the Church wasn't tampering with her scans — most of these feeds were coming not only from defense satellites but from the orbiting Destroyers as well.

Gillian shook her head and made to leave again, but the comm chirped. Ah, that'd be Graham —*finally*...

The signal kicked into her main screen as she tabbed the nearest acceptance key, and Varnia Lupus appeared with a concerned expression, "Gillian, double check your sensor logs. We've recovered Admiral Narosh, and he says there was a plague-infected Larosian controlling *Shanavorous.* Worse, that plague was *intelligent* — Narosh is certain it was in control of the body, and it was telling him that it meant to survive."

Altogether the words came far too quickly to process, and Gillian held up her hand, "Hang on a minute, check the *sensors?* That's Graham's depart..."

She froze as everything sunk in, and she looked up and met Varnia's eyes, "I've lost contact with everyone on the ground... but I'm sure they're my marines in control down there. Except..."

Varnia looked off screen for a second, "You have *small craft* coming up right now? Stop them Gillian, you have to stop them!"

In a very uncharacteristic moment of panic, Gillian looked from Varnia to her door, then back. A second later she jammed her thumb on the intercom.

"C&C here," a voice said on the other side.

"*Stop all small craft immediately! Don't let them dock!*" Gillian's voice was rushed, and the staff officer on the other side seemed to pause in confusion.

But orders were orders, Gillian's mind roared. *Come on, stop the damned things already!*

"But ma'am, it's too late, they've already locked on with us and–"

"Cut them *loose!*"

"Ma'am... they could be *civilians...*"

"*Gods damn you!* Don't let the atmosphere mix!"

And somehow she knew it was too late.

• • •

Unity Genesis broke seals with *Genesis One* just as the station's emergency lockdown alarms began to blare. Graham reached the Superdreadnought's bridge a moment later, frowning at the various warnings scrolling across the large screens.

"What the devil..." he frowned and glanced at *Unity's* ArcColonel.

"Dock Control ordered all ships to cut loose about a minute ago, just before that flock of small craft docked. Seem to want to keep us out of harm's way in case there are Churchers piggy-backing."

Graham nodded slowly... "There must be. Look at the alert on *Genesis One*... that's full–"

"Message from *Renown*, sir."

Turning to the system map projected on one of the larger screens, Graham frowned at the First Rate as it edged in to dock with *Genesis One*, "Put it up."

Varnia Broadpaw appeared with an expression on her face all too familiar to Graham. He'd seen it on Earther faces at Gibraltar and Krogg, back in the war time. *Oh Gods...*

"Narosh was on *Shanavorous*, Graham, but he got off. He says it was a plague ship, and that the plague was actually intelligent. It was controlling a Larosian, and he's sure it survived the crash somehow. Gillian lost contact with her marines shortly after that, and she didn't have any contact with those small craft..."

For some reason, it all came together immediately in Graham's mind. Gods' mercy, this was...

"You think the stations have the plague?" Graham's words were colder than anyone — especially he himself — could have expected.

Varnia nodded, and a collective gasp of shock captured *Unity's* bridge.

The thoughts jammed through Graham's mind — he turned quickly to his Comm Officer, "Get all ships to cut loose *now*!"

"Earther DNA beats it, Graham. Narosh couldn't be infected because we shot him full of regen compound when he crashed at Krogg 'A'."

The message in that, Graham understood immediately, was that his wife was immune. Varnia couldn't say that so plainly in front of a bridge full of men and women who'd probably lost entire families with the news.

And even though the thought occurred to Graham, he wasn't focusing on it right away. Somehow, duty came first...

"How many of our ships are still docked?" he whirled on one of the Sensor Officers, and the woman quickly checked her lists.

"Still eleven, sir... no, only ten now..."

The Comm Officer quickly inserted himself into the exchange, "Sir, I just lost everything from *Genesis Two*... and *Four* now. And *Five* now..."

Graham's mind locked. *Gods no.*

"*Six* and *Three* sir... and *One*. I'm getting absolutely nothing from those last ten ships either... sir, they're all dead."

That remark, while referring to the status of the comms on those orbitals and vessels, felt suddenly very real to Graham — and to everyone.

Gods help them.

Almost the entire human race was...

"Gone..."

Gillian said the word weakly as she edged out of her office, looking around the corner into the C&C. Three of the crew there were on the ground, their bodies spasming. Two more were standing in dead-faced tableaus, and one seemed to be moving abnormally... too fast.

They'd been infected.

A pang of guilt was shrugged aside only by one of terror as Gillian tried to decide what to do. Backing silently into her office, she closed the door. She hadn't been infected.

Why? What was different... Why hadn't Narosh been infected...

Well she'd had Earther regen. Other than that, there were no substantial differences between her and everyone else. Maybe she could get away... get to the Earthers. *Renown* would be immune...

She could get out, then. She just had to get to an escape pod.

A sinking feeling clutched at Gillian's stomach — absolute terror, entirely unlike anything she'd ever felt — but she suppressed it. She was doing that a lot today. And she hated it.

Poor baby.

The thought struck her as odd and foreign, but Gillian ignored it as she opened her desk drawer and drew her sidearm. There was no telling how skilled or fast these infected humans could be. If they'd managed to pass themselves off as her marines from sat scans, they had to be good enough.

Wise deduction! But really now, you think that's all? These things are always faster and meaner, aren't they?

Inner cynicism wasn't something Gillian was accustomed to, and she again forced it away. Her eyes instead turned to the wall behind her desk, and the sword that was mounted there. It was patterned after an old Chinese straight sword, and was quite elegant. She didn't use it that much, but she was passable with the weapon — as good as her husband, at least.

Undoing the buttons on her tunic, she tugged the heavy green jacket off and dumped it in her chair. Her undershirt would grant her more range of motion, and it wouldn't be nearly as conspicuous.

Oh very nice physical specimen... I can see why Graham enjoys you so much! He must've had fun making that baby of yours...

That thought stopped Gillian in her tracks —- what the hell was putting these things into her head...

Don't ask, just move... mmm...

She took the sword from the wall, quickly clipping its sheath onto her belt. With a last look around, she got ready to move–

There was a knock at the door.

Gillian whirled with her pistol drawn, lining up the door in her sight.

"Please be Beckett... or Graham... please..." she whispered to herself, and she heard a laugh from the other side.

The door was ripped from its frame almost casually, and a mutated Larosian with black eyes and an awkward smile leaned in.

"Ah, good day! I'm here to wipe out your civilization. Might I come in?"

Gillian emptied her clip at the creature... the bullets pounded through its flesh but it didn't flinch.

No good dear. See, it's me who's been peeping. The Larosian stepped fully into the room and smiled.

"You'll be an interesting challenge. All Earthered-up, aren't you? Hmm, we'll just have to have a *lot* of fun..."

Gillian tried to draw her sword, but found her arms locked in place.

"That'd be my mind doing the motion-locking..." 'Natosh' rubbed his hands together expectantly, and he slid across the floor to stand before the Commandant. "Right, I don't have much time, but I should be able to enjoy this anyway. I really have missed this."

Looking into the black eyes of her captor, Gillian Hodge felt terror pierce her soul.

Graham I—

There was an explosion of pain.

CHAPTER 44

Graham was very calm — he wasn't just pretending, he was totally *calm*. And it scared the hell out of him.

His mind had a full grasp of the situation. He was coming up with alternatives and trying to figure out what to do. He was in command.

He gave the orders that got the Genesis Fleet out into open space away from the orbitals' weapons, and sent Destroyers and cruisers to pluck crews off the nearby shipyards and the more distant asteroid mining stations.

Anything that refused to communicate with his ships was incinerated.

And so *Unity Genesis* drifted away from *Genesis One*, and Graham left his wife behind, even though she was immune...

What am I, nuts?

"Send to ArcLieutenant-General Togo. He has fleet command. He is to stay clear until he gets further orders."

Even as he was saying the words, Graham was leaving his bridge. The crew watched him go with wide-eyed surprise, themselves only barely controlling their fear and desperation. He was their leader, and he was abandoning them?

Graham knew it was patent dereliction of duty, but suddenly he understood exactly how his sister had felt one day at Gibraltar, many years ago.

Claire was staring blankly out the windows of the observation lounge, watching as *Genesis One* slowly shrank. *Renown* was floating just off the behemoth station, making for quite a spectacle.

Christine sat next to her sister on one of the lounge's couches, keeping an arm around her and making as many reassuring comments as she could. The elder sister paid little attention to Sarah and Pat, both now standing uncomfortably behind the Schaeffers, watching in shock as contact with the orbital was cut off.

For Sarah it was almost impossible to fathom. She'd been President of a productive world only forty-eight hours ago... how had it all gone so horribly wrong?

Pat's hands slipped around her waist, and he pressed against her back to offer some semblance of comfort... but then he was only barely holding his own desperate shock at bay. If this was as bad as it seemed, it would mean *billions* taken by a plague.

But even if it was that bad, wouldn't the Earthers surely find a cure?

The door to the lounge opened abruptly, but no one present could force their eyes off the vision of *Genesis One* and the planet slowly falling away. They stood without taking notice for a minute, and then Graham rounded them all and stood in front of the glass.

"Gillian is alive over there," he said almost coldly, and four pairs of eyes shifted to him. "She's protected by regen, and so are we. So we're going to go get her, before that plague thing gets a strong grip. Alright, let's go."

He didn't make a single request, and the orders seemed to bounce off everyone assembled.

"Come on you two," he said, eyes settling on Sarah and Pat, "she's *family*."

Sarah met his eyes, and her refusal was written in her expression. Graham clearly wasn't thinking–

He came around the Schaeffers' couch and stepped right up to Sarah, his face stopping a few inches from hers, "You're not moving."

His words were almost a snarl, but Sarah's cold expression didn't change, "Graham, it'd be suicide. I can't risk it... I'm responsible for too much..."

"*Bullshit*!"

Christine's head whipped up at the word, and she saw her ArcGeneral quivering with anger. His sister stared him in the eyes, and Pat edged quietly out beside his wife.

"Graham," Pat's soft words were clearly meant to calm, "we can't. We have to organize. The risk to a *President* is too great."

Graham turned his deathly glare on the Irishman, "You're a *coward*. Don't hide it Pat, you're Gods-damned afraid. Too much time with the books, I think."

The Irishman bristled, and Sarah held up a hand, "Graham, you're very upset, just–"

In a flash Graham had his sister by the collar of her green suit jacket, "Don't *tell me what I am, damn you*! You went after him–" he bobbed his head at Pat, who was closing as Graham spoke, "–back at Gibraltar. Gillian is my wife, she's carrying my *daughter*–"

Pat's big hands yanked Graham's from Sarah's collar, and the Irishman forced himself between the two, "You better calm down now, brother-in-law. That's no way to–"

Graham's hand landed instantly on the Irishman's throat, and Pat lost his balance and his grip at once, being kept upright only by the junior Manchester's hand. Too shocked to move, Sarah simply stared.

Christine placed a hand on Claire's shoulder and stood. She didn't know why, but she felt compelled to do *something*. She owed a lot to both Pat and Graham... and she could almost feel the junior Manchester's pain.

And he was right — they *could* do something. After what she'd done at Darymanis, she was sure she could do anything… and at least saving Commandant Hodge would repay some of the debt she owed these people for saving her sister.

Graham released Pat's throat, then stepped back from the two with his face twisted in an expression of disgust unlike anything he'd ever before worn, "I'll go alone then."

"No you won't," Christine spoke almost without thinking.

Whirling, Graham eyed his new aide suspiciously, "Meaning?"

Christine steeled herself, "I'm coming."

Graham's face neutralized immediately, and he nodded somewhat humbly, "Thank you… let's go then."

Nodding, Christine took a second to kneel in front of her sister, taking both of the younger girl's hands in her own, "I'll be back soon. I'm sure Pat will look after you while I'm gone, but I'll be back soon."

Claire nodded vacantly, and Christine hugged her beloved little sister quickly before standing and rounding the couch to stand at Graham's shoulder.

Sarah and Pat watched them both in utter disbelief.

With a last glare, Graham began to step around Pat to get to the door, but the big Irishman interposed himself again, "I won't let you kill yourself, Graham."

The ArcGeneral clenched his jaw, then glared into the eyes of his brother-in-law and one-time friend, "Move, Pat."

Taking a breath, Pat shook his head, "No."

The Irishman's hand found the hilt of his sword, still on his belt from the flight up. Instinctively, Christine found her hilt in hand.

But Graham's eyes bored into Pat, "*Move*."

Pat opened his mouth to refuse again, and Graham's fist found the Irishman's chin. The bigger man lurched aside at the blow, and as he did Graham swept past him, Christine following closely.

Sarah moved to intercept, but Christine's blade automatically came up, the promise of the point keeping the President at a distance.

"Graham," Sarah's words were almost pleading now, "don't make this mistake… I can't lose you too. She might be immune, that doesn't mean she's alive…"

A cold steel filled the junior Manchester's eyes. He turned from the door, looked down the line of Christine's saber, and met his sister's desperate stare, "Some President you are, sister dear. Lost a coup. Lost a planet. Lost a *race*. I won't let you take my *family* from me too. I'll see you in hell. Sure hope you're not running the place."

With that, he turned and surged from the room, and more than slightly shocked at the exchange, Christine followed him. She wasn't sure how those fences would be mended, but it could only happen once they got Gillian out of *Genesis One*.

And she'd just left her sister...

Christine ground her jaw and joined Graham as they jogged towards his quarters, in search of his sword.

Sarah dropped to her knees, staring blankly at the door as it closed. Pat, completely at a loss for words, simply knelt down in front of her, and they held each other close.

Claire watched the Genesis station and the planet, both of which had now swallowed her family. And her mind still refused to process anything.

CHAPTER 45

James Stanton could remain passive no longer.

The Faithful were on their way, and he couldn't simply stand by and wait for them to come. His Home Fleet wasn't a brawling force, it was a quick raiding group, comprised of the best cruisers in this sector of space. And it was time to take the initiative.

Turning to his Navigator, the Governor of Freetown came out of his aged chair, "Give me a straight base course out towards the Faithful. Whichever one you think they're most likely coming in on. Remember they've probably rendezvoused with the ambush force."

The Navigator looked up from her plot in surprise, "Uh... aye, sir."

James turned back towards his chair, eyeing the main chronometer. Audrey was probably going to be in Freetown in twenty hours. If the Home Fleet could slow down the Faithful enough to let her arrive first, things would go well.

As long as they didn't pay too high a price in the process...

Well, it was a risk James was willing to take. He'd had his fill of the static defense he'd been trying to mount.

"Signal Officer, send to the fleet to spin up flux drives. We'll be moving out to intercept the Faithful within one half hour."

Somewhat prepared for the order, the Signal Officer simply nodded and began keying the message. James retook his seat, staring for a moment at the disposition of his ships displayed on the main screen.

They were as elite a group of cruisers as had ever been assembled, and now they'd get their turn to do what they did best. Freetown would depend on them.

"Course marked, sir. Relative 344 port, up angle 122."

James offered a nod to the Navigator, then turned his chair again to the Signal Officer, "Tell all ships to mark that course, battle echelons by ship class. Destroyer Division One will advance ahead at standard picket distance and fan out to search for the enemy. Division Two will remain in close escort position."

The Lieutenant at signals didn't look up, but typed as he nodded to each of James' stipulations.

"Ships to accelerate at my order," James turned back to the main battle plot on the bridge screen.

This was right out of the blue, and he knew it. He just hoped it would pay off...

"All ships, accelerate."

"*Cressy* is dropping back, sir — its drives are nearly shaking themselves apart."

Jax Furgus nodded slowly, then glanced at Ronax Hobbes, "We're driving them awfully hard, eh Ron?"

The Flag Captain nodded in reply, "They'll hold together. And even if only four of us get there in time, we'll be enough."

Furgus offered a dashing grin, "Yes, we will." He turned then to the Cruising Master, "How long for us, Cruising Master?"

There was a pause, then the Master turned to face the veteran Admiral, "I'd make it about eighteen hours at this speed, sir."

Furgus nodded again, then took a deep breath, "Well, I'll go to bed for now. You too, Ron. We're too old to fight a battle having not slept in thirty-six hours, I think."

Ron Hobbes tilted his head and smiled wryly, "Speak for yourself, Admiral Housecoat, sir."

Furgus chuckled and waved as he left the bridge.

The Earther Naval Ships *Aboukir, Hogue, Revenge, Excalibur,* and *Justinian* hurtled through space in search of the enemy.

Behind the Earthers, and entirely unaware of their presence in space, Ed Jeffries sat on the bridge of *Savanna Felix*. The Battlecruiser was leading a long column of advanced human ships, with *Republic* cruising in last position behind *Caine, Ursla, Broadpaw,* and *Magnus.*

They were managing extraordinary speeds, but Jeffries wasn't too confident in their chances of arriving at Freetown in time.

For the first time since... Gods, since the Quest, Jeffries found himself uncertain of his own ships — of their ability to patently outclass the enemy.

And there was no safety net this time, no Earthers.

They'd picked a hell of a time to get politic...

"Skipper?"

Jeffries looked up with some surprise, turning quickly to the Sensor Officer who stood frowning at the main holo plot, "What is it?"

The Lieutenant turned to him and pointed into the three-dimensional projection, "I'm seeing some odd energy eddies. They're above us to starboard, and they seem to be holding speed with us."

Frowning in puzzlement, Jeffries came out of his seat and paced to the plot, "Any indication what they're from?"

Tapping the keys next to the tank, the Lieutenant shook her head, "No sir.

I thought they might be a bug in the receivers for a while there, but they drifted overhead from port to starboard, then accelerated to make sure they stayed in formation."

Jeffries stiffened slightly. Were they being tailed by the Faithful? That wouldn't make a great deal of sense — once First Expeditionary had gone off the back of this Freetown formation, it would have been madness not to strike the separated halves.

Unless they only had a couple of Destroyers watching...

"Report that to *Republic.* Let's beat to quarters."

Captain Alix Tarkam stood next to his plot aboard *ENS Bismarck*. The veteran 74 was currently his flagship, such as it was. *Cressy* was coming back from Furgus' advance group to join both *Bismarck* and *Fundy*, the pair of 74s left to protect the advanced Freetown unit. It was tense work — they kept eyes glued to battle plots, watching for the Faithful ships, and tried to drift by the human ships entirely unnoticed...

"Sir! *Savanna Felix* is charging carronades... *incoming!*"

Tarkam turned on his heel to look at the Sensor Chief, then his head whipped around to the Cruising Master, "Evasive, Master. Alert *Fundy* to stay clear."

Cruising with its field at 250 percent extension, making 3,300-odd pls, *Bismark* felt a little unstable as it shifted to avoid the long carronade shot, and Tarkam frowned unhappily at the holo tank. So *Felix* saw something out here... well, the ship did sport Earther sensors, after all...

"They're evading!"

Jeffries nodded at the report, then bobbed his head to the Signal Officer, "Relay that to flag. Lieutenant, bring all forward carronades into action. Bracket one of those ships please."

Six of *Felix's* forward long carronades fired handily, attempting to box in the unknown eddies.

"They're *bracketing* us, skipper. We've definitely been seen."

Tarkam let out a sigh as *Bismarck* skipped sideways and then climbed slightly. Energy fire hitting its drive field might cause some problems, at least while the field was so widely extended.

Well, it wouldn't be politic, but they might as well just give in.

"Alright then," Tarkam turned to *Bismarck's* Master, "Reign in the field to 100. Signal Officer, give me *Felix* please."

"Oops."

Jeffries looked first to the Sensor Officer and then to the plot. Earther transponders popped up as two drive fields drew into tight energy balls. *Bismarck* and *Fundy*, recommissioned 74s from the reserve...

"Signal coming in from *Bismarck,* skipper. Captain Tarkam."

Jeffries nodded to the Signal Officer, and the face of a tan wolf appeared in the holo tank. The Earther frowned in a genial fashion at his dark-skinned human counterpart, "Be so good as to stop firing at my ship, would you?"

As *Cressy* was picked up by the advancing human force, tightbeam signals were passed between *Bismarck* and *Republic*.

Audrey DeBrooke wasn't sure whether to be elated or furious — why hadn't Forepaw told her he'd sent so much help? But it didn't matter now. She had five veteran 74s going to the rescue of Freetown which meant she had the opportunity to take a chance with her new ships.

They were patently faster than any Faithful ships... perhaps running down on the Churchers in open space would give *Republic* and the advanced Battlecruisers a chance to bleed the Faithful short of their goal.

So *Felix* led the Freetown line-ahead formation in a turn to starboard, and headed for the Faithful Fleet's projected course from Ecclesia.

Under orders to protect the advanced Freetown forces, *Bismarck, Cressy,* and *Fundy*, turned with them.

CHAPTER 46

Graham sat silently at the helm of his personal pinnace. The pilot didn't have regen, so Graham had dismissed the man immediately upon boarding the craft. He wouldn't let anyone die on this quest of his.

Well, that wasn't precisely true. Some *might* die, but they wouldn't die running away. He'd go in fighting, and with a lot of courage and a little luck, he'd find Gillian. The Earthers always managed to pull through on timing, and he had enough Earther DNA in him to know that he could manage it too.

And to hell with Sarah and Pat — Gods damn them for refusing to help family!

At least some were loyal to their Top Flight fellows. Some of the youngest among the elite group. Some like Christine.

Graham's anger hadn't faded, but he knew well not to direct any at his adjutant. She was sitting tensely at the engineers' console next to him, watching *Genesis One* grow before the pinnace, her pulse surging faster as she watched it. She'd left her sister to come with him, and that's something he wouldn't soon forget.

There was a chirp in the cockpit, and one of the screens on the forward console switched immediately to the face of Varnia Lupus, "If I'd realized you'd try this, I wouldn't have said anything about regen."

Christine stiffened slightly and looked across at Graham. Her ArcGeneral's glare might've shattered glass, and he cast it down at the monitor, "You mean to stop me, then?"

Varnia cocked an eyebrow at the vicious remark, "You might want to tone that down a little, Graham. We were already planning to put 2/54th aboard *Genesis One* to confirm our guesses. You can join them if you like... I wouldn't recommend landing alone though."

Graham tilted his head slightly, expression softening very little, "Sounds like a perfect way to restrain me, now doesn't it? Oh come aboard and we'll all go togeth–"

The screen split and Beckett Lupus caught Graham's eyes in a steely stare, "You watch your mouth Graham. I'll take 2/54th in after your wife, but you better respect mine."

Lupus' eyes left Graham with little doubt of his honesty, "So be it. We'll be aboard directly. Have shields for us, please."

Graham cut the comm as Beckett opened his mouth to say something. He shifted his eyes from *Genesis One* to *Renown*, the First Rate now edging up to its usual docking berth, using grav anchors to stabilize the approach.

He appreciated the fact that, despite his anger, Beckett would still help. The Earthers were good people — better people than most humans.

Sarah and Pat… doomsayers…

But not all humans were failures, he reminded himself. He ground his jaw against frustration but was unable to calm himself with a deep breath, but did manage to look across at the small-seeming young woman in the seat next to him.

Christine noticed his change in focus, and she met his eyes. They held so much anguish and pent up fury she almost found herself short of breath.

"Christine…" Graham's words were labored, "thank you. For supporting me. And for helping save my family."

She didn't react for a second. Then she nodded slowly and solemnly, and Graham looked away. They would be even then…

Christine's mind was hazy. She couldn't think clearly…

My parents must be dead.

It was a realization that she'd suppressed, and she forced it down again. Her sister was alive and safe. She had a debt to repay… and she did feel a kinship to this man and his family.

They would save Gillian.

Beckett stood on *Renown's* third flight deck, thoroughly checking his rifle as Graham guided his pinnace into the bay and let it come to rest on the deck. It wasn't a great landing job, but no one cared.

Slapping his power cell into place, Lupus slung the rifle over his shoulder, keeping it behind and clear of the two swords that hung from his hip. He watched silently as the pinnace hatch opened and the ramp dropped, then let out a sigh as Graham and Christine descended.

It was extremely strange, he realized, that he'd literally run into the girl. That accident and the following regeneration had changed so much… it had put him on the ground with 2/54th, and it brought her here now.

Graham stepped determinedly towards the General, clipping his long, straight, mortuary-hilt sword to his belt. Lupus cocked his eyebrow as Graham came to a stop before him, then handed the ArcGeneral a shield belt.

Slowing too, Christine took a belt from Lupus, nodding to him in greeting, "General."

"Beckett, remember," Lupus nodded personably to the young human. "You're feeling alright, Christine?"

She frowned at the question, "Yes, why would you…?"

Lupus shrugged, "You came from Darymanis exhausted and then I presume you didn't sleep."

Graham glanced at his aide and then looked at the General, "You know how it is when there's work to be done, Beckett. Like *now*."

The two met each other's eyes again, and Beckett Lupus saw a determination he hadn't seen in many years deep within the terrorized eyes of his old friend. A *fury*...

"Well then let's go. I'll have rifles at the lock for you if you want them."

Lieutenant Colonel Cadmus Howler stood with his officers at the lock as it cycled through its pressurization sequence.

Even after Darymanis City, 2/54th had about 400 marines in condition to fight, but the Colonel didn't mean to march them all into the station at once: "Joyce, you'll be the anchor. Your company holds this corridor and keeps intruders out. The rest of the companies need to disperse until we locate some survivors. Make sure you know your routes back, though — we don't know what's going on there. From what I understand, this *plague* literally took control of a Larosian body, so you might face... *infested* humans..."

There was a ripple of discomfort at that thought, and the officers exchanged glances. Joyce Furgus swallowed awkwardly and looked to her Colonel, "And if we run into them...?"

Howler's eyes hardened. He'd fought alongside humans many times, and he had the utmost respect for them. These circumstances demanded a sort of ruthlessness that wasn't easy.

"If you get a chance, hit them with UDRC... that may well cure them. But there aren't any guarantees, so if that doesn't work, try to put them into comas. I don't think bringing anyone aboard will do us much good if we have to throw them in the brig anyway — if one ever broke out it could be a disaster. But if you can knock them down and take some bioscans and some small samples of their blood and DNA, if might give us something passive to work on."

There were some nods from the Lieutenants, Captains, and Majors of 2/54th. But Joyce still met Howler's eyes, "And if we can't put them down on low settings?"

Was she supposed to kill infected humans?

Reluctantly, Howler nodded, "If they're a deadly threat, you must defend yourselves."

The sound of footsteps in the corridor beyond marked the arrival of Lupus, Graham and Christine, and Howler took a last look at his officers, "I'm going with Sergeant Cuttar and the General. We'll be following bioscans from the bridge until we find Commandant Hodge. She'll be immune to this thing because of her regen. But for you all this is still an exploratory mission — find out what this thing is, and we'll make sure we know how to kill it."

Final nods came as Beckett and his human charges rounded the corner to the lock, followed closely by Cuttar's recon squad. Standing along the walls of the long corridor to the lock, the marines of 2/54th snapped to attention out of respect for their commander, and he nodded thankfully to them.

Together, the elite human-Earther force tasked with finding Gillian Hodge paced up to Howler, and the officers dispersed to their units as Beckett stopped next to his longtime friend.

"Ready, Cadmus?"

The Colonel nodded, and Lupus took a deep breath. In front of him, the light above the airlock hatch turned green. It opened.

CHAPTER 47

Graham followed Lupus out into the abandoned corridor, one hand on his sword hilt and the other clutching an Earther energy pistol.

It was silent. The lights were the same as usual and there was no sign of anything out of the ordinary…

Except for the feeling of… *death.*

The veteran recon squad — one well accustomed to looking after the Manchester family — swept ahead now, rifles leveled, and led the way. They'd start at the boardwalk and go from there; according to *Renown's* scans, that was where human bio readings seemed to be the most numerous.

Though it was impossible to say what *human* meant to the Earther sensors just now.

Behind, hundreds of Earther marines spilled from the lock, heading in every direction. One platoon followed the search squad down the corridor a ways before breaking off and taking its own route. The Earthers would be all around, Graham realized with some comfort. There'd be help at hand if things turned unpleasant.

What a word for it, given the circumstances…

Beckett was walking silently, his eyes narrowing very slightly as he followed his troops down the corridor. Somehow the air felt wrong… not *alien*, just *wrong*. His instincts weren't even heightened… only agitated.

Something was very unwell in this place.

Varnia narrowed her eyes at the holo plot. A significant part of the giant projection was now displaying a complex model of *Genesis One*, with green icons marking the positions of the Earther marines (and their human guests).

Red denoted the human signatures on the station, but there were very few. For some reason, *Renown's* sophisticated sensors were having a hard time picking humans out.

All they could see for certain was a massive cluster on the boardwalk, hovering around the *Bloody Pulsar* and the nearby shops. That's where Beckett would start looking…

A chill seemed to touch the base of Varnia's spine, and she halted a shiver as it tried to surge through her.

Why was she so very nervous about this?

The thought that Beckett might get caught out on the station forced its way into her mind, but she resisted it. They were Earthers — they'd pull through this.

They always did.

Lieutenant Ellen Arbear took her platoon of Six Company up a level through the zero-gee service chute near *Renown's* lock, and silently came out on what should have been a bustling deck. She dropped to one knee and leveled her rifle down the corridor in one direction, the next marine out covering the other.

The entire platoon climbed out onto the silent floor, and nothing seemed to be around them...

"Lieutenant Arbear, Six Company, to *Renown*. You told us there were some humans up here?"

There was a pause as her microphone carried the question to the First Rate, then one of the Sensor Ratings replied, "Yes ma'am. I see them down the hall from you... about 100 meters in the direction you're facing."

Arbear frowned, "I don't hear anything. They're stationary?"

Another pause, and as the members of the platoon waited for the report — all hearing the feed through their own earpieces — they began to reorient themselves in the direction of the human signature.

"No ma'am, they're moving around as if they're working... I think."

That was disturbing — they were being awfully quiet.

"Keep an eye on them for us, *Renown*," she said in low tones, then waved her platoon forward.

There were no words — the veteran unit moved silently as a mass, sixteen Earthers of all species edging their way down the corridor. Arbear kept her position near the front of their ranks, her rifle held level and her eye trained down its sight.

These humans couldn't be much farther away–

A hiss filled the air, and from one of the intersecting corridors a blur erupted. It slammed into one of the cats near the rear of the platoon, knocking the marine flat. Then the blur stopped over the fallen Earther.

The blur had been a human.

Had been.

It was crouching in an almost-ape like pose, holding some sort of crude blade over its head, evidently preparing to decapitate the downed Earther.

Six energy blasts caught it in the chest but it didn't flinch. It looked up at its attackers and Arbear caught sight of its face.

Its eyes were black, its face seemed to bulge unnaturally in some places and to be drawn tight in others. What once had been a woman no longer looked like a woman... the gaunt figure was horrid.

"Reset your rifles!" the Lieutenant roared, already keying her own weapon to full power.

A second blur slammed into the platoon, this time from Arbear's side. A wolf next to her toppled, but as the next mutated human stopped menacingly over its victim, Arbear's full-power shot flung it back against the wall.

The first attacker was similarly batted off its victim, and both the fallen Earthers began to stand. Arbear released a sigh and lowered her weapon, edging towards the 'human' she'd shot. She realized half a second too late that she shouldn't have lowered her gun.

The 'human' surged from the wall and hauled the gun out of her hands, swinging it like a club to catch a nearby cougar in the cheek. Though the marine's shield absorbed much of the shock, the sheer inhuman power of the strike knocked the Earther to one side, forcing him to a knee.

"*Swords!*" Arbear didn't even hesitate in giving the order. Indeed, hers was out and humming to life before she'd finished saying the word.

The 'human' swung her heavy rifle at her but she slipped aside and dropped as low as she could. Her blade flashed through the air, and the 'human' lost both its legs below the kneecap. It fell backwards and flailed.

Now two other marines turned on the first attacker, and as it came they evaded its blindingly fast strikes... barely. Their swords lunged after it, but missed. The 'human' surged into the center of the platoon, tore a sword from one of the marine's belts, and made to decapitate the surprised Earther.

Again, the marine's shield proved her salvation. As the blow glanced up and over her head, she hammered a fist into the 'human's' gut... but hit a solid sheet of bone and winced as her hand was almost broken.

The 'human' was standing still now, and swords flicked through the air. Its legs and one arm were severed. As both 'humans' fell to the deck, both of the platoon's medics hurled themselves on top of the unfortunate mutated beings, pinning them and injecting them with UDRC shots.

As those medics got to their feet and backed away from the flailing creatures, Arbear turned quickly to her platoon, "Everyone alright?"

There were nods and Arbear turned back to the fallen 'human' she'd dismembered. It was flailing no differently... and as she leaned in very slightly and eyed its stomach, she froze. The blast from her rifle had indeed disintegrated the man's skin and flesh, but beneath was what might only be called a plate of subdermal armor.

Black, *bone* armor.

That matched the black eyes, and made her — and every Earther — think of Kroggs.

One of the medics stood next to her with a scanner, and he shook his head slowly, "It's as though he's been taken over by Krogg DNA. Our stuff doesn't seem to be getting through his defenses — any effect would be immediate."

Arbear frowned and then nodded, "Collect samples. We don't have time to waste." Addressing herself then to the battalion as a whole, she slowed her words, "We're seeing some sort of Krogg armor under their skin here. You need swords to bring them down but they're *very* fast. Be careful. Guns even on full won't do more than slow them."

As Beckett Lupus heard these words he and his group were stepping onto the boardwalk.

He froze.

As did Howler, Cuttar, and the rest of the squad.

And Christine.

Graham narrowed his eyes, drawing to sword and dropping his gun. He wouldn't be stopped by–

He caught sight of them.

All of them.

And then from the center, 'Natosh' waved a friendly greeting, "Why it's the cavalry! Good to see you all, though I think you might look better in pieces!"

It was, in Graham's estimation, a terrible line.

But a seething mass of perhaps a thousand 'humans' stood there, on the boardwalk, filling it wall to wall.

'Natosh' would get his wish.

CHAPTER 48

Varnia's claws dug into the rail around the plot as she listened to the Larosian's voice come distantly through her husband's head set.

This was not going as it should…

"We need every company here *now*," Howler's voice came over the comm quietly, and Varnia heard laughter beyond.

By the Earth, what was this thing?

"Every company, Cadmus? That's an awfully big gesture isn't it?" 'Natosh' pushed his way to the front of the crowd, coming to a stop at its head.

Perhaps ten meters separated the Larosian from the front line of the recon squad.

In a smooth motion, rifles were dropped to the deck and swords were drawn. This squad wouldn't be caught out.

'Natosh' grinned at the Earthers, then raised his arms to emphasize his own force, "Well, you guys sure do *look* good when you do that! But come on, you'd all be dead if I wasn't feeling a bit playful right now."

Beckett edged forward into the Earther line and stared at the Larosian, "You're a bit over-confident, I think. Perhaps you'd introduce yourself — Narosh told us you're no longer a *Larosian*."

'Natosh' dropped his arms and shrugged, "He's right, Beckett. But you don't need to tell *me* that, I don't think. Maybe you'd like to take some guesses as to who I am… come on, the longer you stall the more time you give that marvelous 2/54th of yours to rally!"

Beckett's brow creased, "Not really in the mood just now…"

Something… some*one* caught his eye. She was hanging with a cord around her waist in the window of the *Bloody Pulsar*… by the *Earth*…

"…but we do know you're the plague. The Krogg one — you've proven that already with those 'humans' we encountered on the deck above. But your amour isn't a match for our shields, you should know that…"

'Natosh's' grin broadened, "I like it when you do the big talk, Beckett. That's pretty funny. And you're partly right, I must admit — but those *humans* upstairs, and even these here, are only a few hours old. They haven't even been fully adjusted yet. They'll be much better armed and armored soon enough."

Lupus slid slightly sideways — getting between the Larosian and Graham's line of sight — and drew his two short swords. From behind Graham frowned, then realized the action was intentional.

He sees your wife, Graham dear boy! She's strung up in the Pulsar, just have a look. That's a lot of blood, I know…

Graham froze as the thoughts entered his head, and looked quickly to Christine. She frowned, her grip on her own saber tightening. What was–

You left your sister? Ha! Well I must say I'm glad though. You're nice and young… I can have fun with you. I mean Gill was great, but she was disciplined and such. You're just a sweet, innocent little kid. Oh my, you must have lovely skin. I might like to redecorate my face with some of it…

Christine was stiffening as the voice pierced her mind… and somehow Graham was overhearing the thoughts. *All* of them…

He touched Lupus on the back and bobbed his head towards the *Pulsar* as the General glanced back. So they'd have to try to move that crowd of 'humans' back far enough to get to the restaurant.

"Oh come on already," 'Natosh's' tone smacked of arrogance. "She's obviously the bait I've been dangling to get you here in the first place. Let's not dawdle. Haven't had a really good fight yet."

Lupus and Howler exchanged quick glances, neither of them optimistic.

'Natosh' looked at them both, "Oh come on, boldness kids! Didn't daddy breed it into you? What about storming Darymanis? Or how about joining that Krogg War, hmm?"

Rolling his swords into a ready position, Lupus narrowed his eyes at the creature, "We're not eager to fight such unfair odds."

Another inappropriate grin covered the alien's face, and he stretched his arms out again, "How about your squad against me. I'll hold my minions back for now — except for, oh, say fifty who'll try to stop Graham getting his wife. We just fight for a little while. Haven't had a good fight at all, you see. Could do to raise the heart rate… assuming this body has a heart…"

Howler's eyes narrowed as he lowered his center of gravity further, his sword sweeping formally up over his head, "You're a lying–"

"Maybe. But either way we're about to dance, aren't we, Cadmus? You better hope I keep my word, or you'll be dead pretty quick, won't you?"

Lupus and Howler exchanged anxious glances. There was nothing more to do…

So the pair surged forward in flash, Howler leading.

Graham saw them go in one instant and was sprinting for the *Pulsar* in the next. Christine was still so shocked she could barely follow, but somehow she managed to. Her saber came up out of instinct, and the point of Graham's sword led the way towards Gillian. And just like the abomination of a Larosian said, only some of the 'humans' tried to stop them.

Graham's mind was filled with a fury entirely unlike anything he'd ever felt, and it drove his sword around viciously. He stabbed through the mass as quickly as he could, slicing his way towards the restaurant window, leaving Christine in his wake to keep the humans occupied. And with the same terrifying precision she'd found on the streets of Darymanis City, she struck now. Her saber hacked through dozens in elegant motions...

It was almost too easy — as if the 'humans' were merely trying to slow her down, but not stop her...

Ooh, now there's a smart one. Mark me, girl, you'll be tied to a table one day soon. I'll think of all sorts of lovely things to do to spice up the occasion. Like scented candles?

The Earther blood in her was keeping her fighting, but that cold voice in her mind still tried to petrify her humanity. Wasn't Lupus keeping that thing *busy*...?

Howler hit the wall so hard he spat blood, but he was on his feet quickly. He hadn't even seen the kick coming...

Cuttar rushed to take his Colonel's place, and two more squad members came forward with their Sergeant. Lupus stood off quickly, letting the well-coordinated trio try their skill. But 'Natosh' was so blindingly fast — he was ahead of even these marines. Swords came from impossible angles — there was no way he could evade...

Which meant he did.

As the last five of the squad's marines made to charge, Beckett held up his hands. Cuttar and his two compatriots were flung to the deck meters from their opponent, and 'Natosh' looked to the General, his frightening black eyes marking the wolf.

"Make it good, Beckett, or I'll kill you all, right now."

Lupus wasn't about to be bested by an abomination.

The words had barely come out of 'Natosh's' mouth when the General was in front of him, his two swords working as a single unit. Beckett Lupus was the best Earther sword-wielder alive. There might only be one or two in the universe capable of matching him...

And here was one.

Blades that would easily have killed any creature missed 'Natosh', and the Larosian evaded and danced with an impunity that was unlike anything Beckett had ever seen. A blow came in reply, but Lupus managed to slide out of its way with difficulty. He backed off quickly and then surged forward again, trying to bracket this creature with his swords.

Graham decapitated one last human and then dove sword-first through the glass of one of the *Pulsar's* windows. The point of his blade shattered the window ahead of him, but the shards scattered off his shield.

You're being regular Mister Action Hero today, aren't you? Sure you still want your little lady there Graham? You do have this pretty young blonde at your disposal now. And besides, I've had Gillie for a while, and I think I've left some surprises in her you won't like. It's so much fun to be a monster, you know. Ever heard of the Marquis de Sade? Love that guy's work...

Ignoring those thoughts, Graham climbed fast to his feet and turned to the hanging form of his wife. His sword flicked and the rope that suspended her let go. She collapsed to the deck, and Graham quickly scooped her unconscious body up into his arms, struggling as he realized her sword was dangling from her hip. With effort that he didn't even feel, he hopped out through the shattered window, and ran with her towards the recon squad.

He passed Christine, and his aide continued to fight, backing away slowly but without lessening her effort.

Lupus forced himself to focus. This Larosian couldn't simply be a match for him — no plague could best an Earther. Not even Omega had been able to. This Krogg-infested creature would be–

The blow to his stomach sent him back into two of the members of the waiting squad, and Howler and Cuttar went forward again in his absence.

Lupus tried to shake off the shock as he landed, but found himself paralyzed for seconds as he regained his senses. By the Earth...

Graham stopped next to him and laid his wife down, propping her up against the wall. He turned back to Christine, "Let's *go*!"

Christine heard the order distantly, took a mighty swing to demobilize her immediate foes, and then turned and ran towards the squad. Lupus forced himself back up just in time to have Howler and Cuttar land at his feet.

"Time to leave," the General said quickly, and he thankfully heard the boots of a company coming up behind him — at last.

Graham was waving to Christine as she ran when a hand clasped his ankle, "Graham."

It was Gillian's voice.

Graham hadn't realized how desperate he'd been to hear it until that moment. Now it was all worth it — they just had to get out of here...

As Christine safely closed the last distance to the corridor, Graham turned to look at his wife.

First he saw the appalled faces of the Earthers standing opposite her.

Then he looked down.

And his heart stopped.

Christine was slowing to a stop next to Graham as she tried to catch her breath and free her mind of that *thing*...

She looked down into the black eyes of Gillian Hodge. And at the feral smile.

The Commandant surged to her feet in a swift motion, grabbing Christine by the throat and lifting her off the deck. Gillian... *not* Gillian... looked at Graham and grinned, "Glad to see me, honey?"

Graham couldn't move.

Gillian looked back up at Christine, "This your little whore then, hubby? Hmm, a bit young for you, isn't she? I'd be jealous... but I'm sure her hide will make a nice *skin* suit for me someday..."

Grinning, the Commandant threw Christine across the corridor, but Howler managed to catch her light body without too much difficulty.

Turning now, Gillian moved closer to her husband... no, it wasn't 'Gillian' now. Gods.

Her black eyes peered into Graham's stunned brown ones, and she leaned in and tried to kiss him. He flinched away, and laughter erupted from the boardwalk as 'Natosh' watched with a smile.

Told you I left a little something in there...

Graham tried to open his mouth, but Gillian's finger pressed his lips gently to keep them shut. Her other hand took Graham's empty one and placed it on her stomach, "Guess who didn't have the Earther DNA shot into them yet, eh honey? You know a pregnant woman is damn near ruled by a baby... now I really am."

Any color that had been left in Graham's face drained away.

"See, I couldn't infect her directly," 'Natosh' called helpfully, "but it was awful fun getting at that baby. Once I infected that it was a natural foothold — let me right past all those Earther immune cells. Oh I'm proud of myself!"

Gillian smiled sweetly at her husband, and then in a blur drew her sword. Graham was unable to do anything. Now at least he'd be out of his misery...

Six swords swung at Gillian's arm, and the first to strike was Christine's saber. The Commandant's hand dropped to the deck with the sword in its grasp, and Cuttar grabbed it quickly. Prying the weapon away, he dropped the hand into a sealed bio container.

Gillian looked up at her stump and frowned, "Not very sporting, you little witch..."

Beckett's fist crossed Gillian's jaw so fast few saw it, and as the Commandant was knocked aside, the General grabbed Graham by the arm. Christine quickly picked up the fallen sword, and the squad turned to run down the corridor.

Beckett had to drag Graham — he was entirely unresponsive.

And then Joyce Furgus' company was all around them. As a seething mass of 'humans' moved to give chase down the corridor, withering energy fire knocked them forcibly back. Somewhere a pulsar hammered at the plague's minions.

The Earthers fled.

And Graham's wife was... gone...

CHAPTER 49

The Earther marines were madly falling back all around Graham, sheets of energy forcing the 'humans' back for the moment. They were close to *Renown's* lock, and 2/54th was retreating into its ship as quickly as possible.

It was almost unthinkable — Earthers retreating — but then Graham couldn't process the level of shock he should have felt.

Because this sort of thing could never truly happen. No thirty-six hours in history could so thoroughly destroy his home, his race... his *family*.

He'd sacrificed everything to come here.

And he'd *failed*.

The daughter he'd always wanted had turned his wife into a puppet. Of evil.

He couldn't even bring himself to ask *why*...

Beckett pulled the ArcGeneral steadily down the corridor, nodding to marines as he passed them. He wouldn't lose anyone else here today... as he'd lost Gillian...

"They're forcing from all sides now, sir. We've got shields up to try to hold them back, but they're finding ways around them. We've gone to sword."

Beckett couldn't make out the identity of the speaker from the cackled voice in his earpiece, but it didn't matter.

"Keep falling back in order. We're close to *Renown*... we want to leave immediately. No one will be left behind."

"Yes, sir."

It was all too much... he'd had it all under control.

Now... some damned *plague*. What kind of cruel joke was that?

How and why... this never happened to the people in Pat's books. The Earthers could stop anything. They were the great heroes, the moral titans. And even if they died, their families and the people they were helping lived on.

No planets had been destroyed before. The Earthers hadn't annihilated the Kroggs. Humanity had progressed — albeit painfully — and now the hammer of fate was still falling...

I'm no hammer, thanks.

Graham's mind screamed as the thought invaded it.

Come on, fall down now. I need to talk to Beckett.

His knees buckled for no reason at all.

Beckett tried to haul Graham to his feet, but the human suddenly seemed to weigh ten times more than was possible. The General sheathed the single sword he had in hand and crouched, trying to get the junior Manchester to keep moving.

But Graham stared vacantly at the ceiling.

It had to be a combination of some sort of telepathy and the massive trauma of the day — Lupus knew the mettle of the Manchester family, and in combat they seldom failed to deliver stellar performances.

But this was less combat and more terror.

The marines continued to fall back all around, but Graham wouldn't — couldn't — move.

Christine forced herself against the tide of the 2/54th retreat, letting instincts she shouldn't have had guide her actions. Her saber still in hand, she knelt next to Graham and looked at Beckett, "We can't leave him..."

The General nodded, "I wouldn't anyway."

And the 'humans' were coming closer...

Varnia almost wanted to throw herself into the battle plot as she listened to the exchange over her husband's voice comm — this plague was more than a match for the Earthers. They'd already lost Gillian... he *couldn't* stay.

And yet he had to.

He couldn't leave a friend, she couldn't either.

She ground her jaw and tightly held the railing around the main battle plot. Hoping against hope.

"Keep falling back," Lupus said with some finality. "We'll make do."

Captain Furgus looked down at him with some disbelief, "Excuse me? Not likely — we can hold them a bit longer..."

Beckett shook his head, "No. I'm not leaving him, but you'll all die if you stay. So go."

"No I–"

Varnia's voice came clearly through every Earther's headset, "Follow the orders."

Beckett froze, then blinked a long blink. He wanted to say goodbye, but he couldn't. He hadn't given up yet...

Furgus' company backed away, and the 'humans' drew nearer.

Lupus looked over Graham's anchor-like body at Christine, and she met his eyes, "I'm *not* going. I came here with him, I won't leave unless he does."

"Your sister?"

Christine's expression didn't waver, "I... she'll be alright. I can't help her now..."

"What you *mean* is that you'd rather die than try to live, right?"

No, of course Beckett Lupus hadn't said that.

The 'humans' stopped their advance, and 'Natosh' emerged from their front rank with a seemingly more somber expression on his face, "You're afraid of living after seeing my work, aren't you little Christine? Hope I'll end it quickly for you, so you don't have to go look after your little sister while I tear your universe apart."

Lupus' eyes narrowed and he came to his feet, turning to face the creature.

"No Beckett, I'm right. I schooled you today —- that can't make these shitty little humans feel very good, can it? They're all terrified for their lives, but that's not what this has really been about... I think you know that."

Beckett smoothly drew his swords, then brought himself to combat stance. 'Natosh' smiled and shook his head briefly.

"No, no, no... see, I'm not going to kill you yet. There's a lot you and your beloved Earthers need to see first. No more sheltered 'hero-always-triumphs' crap. You're all going to watch me pick you apart — all these humans first, 'cause they're easy. Then your friends. And your little cosmic presence..."

Christine slowly stood, turning and sinking into a proper stance as well. 'Natosh' caught her eye and smiled, "Not yet for you, pretty girl. I wish I could watch you trying to tell little Claire that everything will be alright after seeing what you have. It'll be *brilliant*."

Swallowing hard and taking a deep breath, Christine brought her blade up to face the monster. She refused to let its thoughts and words take hold in her, even if it was right.

"Anyway," 'Natosh' looked back at Lupus, "I think I have to send a message home with you in *Renown*."

Beckett titled his head slightly, "Is that so?"

"And I'll let you all live too... so I think that wife of yours can stop worrying. Too bad I can't get into *her* head — she probably doesn't know what to think right now... ahh I'm *so* good."

"You don't understand us," Beckett said coolly. "Your *message* will be received with about as much fear as the Kroggs were."

'Natosh' smiled, "Oh ye of little faith. But at least you're playing along, I suppose. See, I knew you'd be cooperative with the message thing. You lot always seem to be..."

Lupus frowned deeply, drawing himself up to stand straighter. There was little point to maintaining his readiness now — he'd either die, or the abomination would do as before and be true to his pledge.

"Good that you trust me, Beckett," 'Natosh's' smile clashed with his black eyes, and Beckett forced down a feeling of dread. This *thing* was hideous.

"Tell Setter Caine that his great-great-great... hmm.... one more *great*, I think... well, anyway, his however-great *granddaddy* is back. Tell the Earthers their *God* is back. Tell them that after spending *seven centuries* trapped in your blood, castrated by an immune system of my own design, watching you be the fucking boy scouts of the universe, I've come back to my ranch. I'll be having some revenge on my cattle, I think. And *I* am in control. All of your beautiful Earther timing wouldn't have been so bang-on if I hadn't been there to help it along."

Lupus stiffened and his frown set deeper, "What...?"

'Natosh' smiled, "Come on Beckett, how many intelligent plagues do you think are kicking around in this universe? We're not exactly in a position to unionize."

The eyes of every Earther listening to the conversation widened and their heart rates raced. Beckett peered into the black eyes of the Larosian and tried to shake his head, but the creature's smile turned instantly into a snarl.

"Say the word, Beckett. Say my name."

Beckett's voice was gone.

"Oh come on, please," 'Natosh' taunted.

It took every scrap of self-control Beckett Lupus had to allow him to whisper the word.

"Omega."

"There you go!" 'Natosh' grinned. "I'm coming for *all of you*, Beckett. And none of you will stop me in the end."

With that, Omega turned its Natosh avatar around, and its minions parted before falling into step behind the Larosian shell.

The Omega 'Virus' left its pet Earthers to return to their ship.

CHAPTER 50

"Lock closed, ma'am."

Varnia almost didn't hear the report, but part of her mind remained engaged enough to make a response, "Break seals. Get off the station... all hands to action stations. Ready a broadside for *Genesis One*."

Renown smoothly broke free of the massive orbital, and as the great First Rate's drives kicked in and it slid through space away from the infested station, the crews of the ship's 250 guns rushed to their weapons.

"Run out the guns," Varnia continued in very low tones.

Ports opened and the advanced energy cannon slid through them, giving the ship's beam a painfully serrated look.

"Ready at the guns, ma'am."

A slow nod was all Varnia could manage at first, then she ground her jaw, "Very well. Keep guns trained on the station until we can clear weapons range. Prepare to roll... Master, be so good as to plot a course to *Unity Genesis*."

There was a pause, the Second Lieutenant looking up with a frown from the gunner's station, "Shall we not destroy the station then, ma'am?"

"No point, Kirsta," Varnia glanced at the Lieutenant sadly. "We might yet be able to cure those humans... and I can't see 'Natosh's' existence making a real difference now. The plague... *Omega*... has all it needs with the humans on the planet. It serves no purpose to kill a few thousand..."

The solemn words silenced the bridge. There was no way to hide the shock of what had happened — no way to bury the horror. Today's rape of Genesis would go down in history as singly one of the most destructive and appalling actions of all time.

And the arrival of this thing... this self-professed God...

...of Omega.

It scarcely bore thinking about. The universe had changed.

Beckett shut off the pleas for sense that dominated his thoughts — even he was finding himself overcome by this *horror*. He'd thought he'd seen enough in his years to be able to make sense of anything... but what of this Omega creature?

He wanted to believe 'Natosh's' proclamation was a lie... but his blood knew better. Something within him hummed at the thought of the return of that plague. Somehow it all made sense, now that the last component had been dropped into place.

It made terrible, horrific, damning sense.

Now, however, was not the time to worry about that — they had faced dark days before, and he'd found that such times were always much more comprehensible in retrospect than in the moment. The Earthers would figure this one out, there were too many great people among them not to.

The immediate goal had to be *escape*. That was his wife's job, but he still had to see Graham right.

The ArcGeneral seemed dead to the world. Simply staring at the floor as Lupus and Christine helped him hobble along, Graham looked almost as though he'd suffered a stroke. Perhaps he had — there was no telling what Omega had been able to do to his mind...

Graham, barely aware that he was moving, could feel only shock.

Disbelief.

It was to him as unbelievable as everything else that day... Gillian was gone. She and the rest of Genesis. *Gone*.

Because of a centuries-old plague, back to revenge itself.

A plague that had seized his mind and battered his body.

Such great evil should not have been able to exist — who could have conceived of it? After such a time of tranquility. After the Earthers had done so much to bring safety.

But at least, Graham realized, he was beginning to think again. His mind had frozen entirely... Omega's thoughts had chilled it, but his thoughts were beginning to thaw...

"Where am I?" it was a pained rasp, and it drew glances from both Beckett and Christine.

They slowed to let Graham get better control of his feet, and as the ArcGeneral lifted his arm from around his aide's shoulder, he rubbed his eyes uncomfortably, "Gods. *Gods*... I must... I must get back to *Unity*. That is my place..."

Beckett released a pent-up breath at the words — Graham was in great pain, from which he might never recover. But he wasn't catatonic, and his well-developed Manchester genes were driving him to the thing he knew best — duty. He would look after his ships, do his job, and break down later.

And there would be a breakdown — how could anyone escape it?

Lupus made sure his friend was ready to stand on his own two feet, then stepped aside slightly, putting a hand on his shoulder, "Varnia's taking us that way now. We'll be alongside *Unity* soon."

The flag bridge on *Unity Genesis* was as silent as a tomb. People weren't thinking about all they'd lost, they were staring at their screens. Sarah and Pat stood silently on the deck, watching the feeds from various ships and sensors throughout the fleet.

What remained to them of the Genesis Navy hovered in close order, weapons armed and ready to engage the orbitals, but no one had the heart to order an attack. They wouldn't kill the men and women on those stations — not in an age such as this, not when Earther medicine could fix so much, not when Earther DNA had already been proven a vaccine to this plague.

No, they would flee as soon as the last few garrisons were collected from the space yards at the asteroid belt. A pool of commercial vessels was already forming around them — hundreds of ships that had been safely away from the planet during the coup, now seeking whatever refuge remained.

They'd be ready to go in two hours... less, perhaps.

To Freetown or Earth or somewhere...

Gods only knew...

"President Manchester!"

Few seemed ready to make exclamations given the circumstances, but the call's urgency turned Sarah fast on her heel, "What is it?"

"The ships that were lost when docked with the Genesis stations... they're going through the decoupling cycle."

Sarah's eyes widened — that was *impossibly* fast. This plague's progress was entirely unthinkable, "Warn *Renown*. Fleet to stand by — all evacuating persons expedite measures to leave immediately. We mustn't get caught out!"

Varnia was just turning to see her husband, Christine, and Graham emerge onto *Renown's* bridge when the Signal Officer's console bleeped. In that same second, the main battle plot shifted focus, black icons coming to life.

The Sensor Officer was first to open her mouth, "We have about a dozen Genesis ships coming online docked to the stations... they're preparing to disengage."

Lupus and Graham skittered to a halt on the bridge deck as the report came, and Varnia whirled to the plot. Things were moving so impossibly fast — Omega was operating with a voracity the Earthers couldn't seem to match.

"Prepare a spread of e-hyper drones for Earth, Freetown, Gibraltar, and Krogg. Dump everything we've collected in the database over the past... say... fifteen hours into the banks, and copy the feed to *Unity* just in case," Varnia's orders came as a surprise, and they muted the Signal Officer briefly as he cleared the drones for launch.

Graham steeled his mind, pacing past Beckett towards the plot as the ships that had once been his cycled clear of their stations. Gods only knew what those things would try.

"President Manchester for you, ma'am, from *Unity Genesis*," the Signal Officer turned back to his report, and Varnia nodded.

Sarah appeared life-sized in the holo tank, her eyes shifting quickly between Varnia and Graham, "Was the operation a success?"

Her cool words stung the junior Manchester, but Varnia shook her head before he could reply, "You're getting it all in your buffers right now. But this… *this* is much worse than any of us could have thought. It's–"

The signal flickered for a second, and then a second figure appeared in the holo tank, splitting the screen on *Unity's* bridge. Omega stared through Natosh's eyes at the bridge crews of both ships, offering a chilling and alien grin.

"Why it's Sarah Manchester! Good to see you, good to see you!"

Varnia looked quickly to the Signal Officer, and he shrugged almost invisibly as he hammered at his controls, trying to cut the feed.

"Don't bother with cutting the link, Varnia," Omega's eyes seemed to settle on the Vice Admiral, and she stiffened, her eyes narrowing.

"You've got no control over my ship," her words were solid, even if she was wrought with fear.

"Who the hell are you?" Sarah's words were sharp, and her expression was dark.

Omega smiled at her, "They haven't told you yet? Here I was assuming they'd shared the story — I guess they haven't. Very impolitic of them, but it is their *shame* after all. I, my dear, am *Omega*. Once known as the *Omega Virus*, though I should take offense at being called a 'virus'. If you'd like to look me up in one of your dear husband's books, that might clarify the issue."

Varnia could see Sarah's visage freeze, and then Beckett was suddenly beside her again, "So you're calling for a parting taunt, are you? Or to set up a new game with those ships you're moving?"

A feral grin formed on the plague-avatar's face, "Would I do that?"

Both Beckett and Varnia glared, and Omega chuckled, "You're being intimidating! Oooh I'm frightened, what with two Earthers glaring at me… Oh wait no, I beat dear Beckett bloody hand-to-hand, and I've already got an army numbering around two billion in human minions. So no, I'm not *actually* frightened."

Sarah was separated by ship hulls and the void of space from Omega's telepathy — unlike Graham, her mind was processing this all with a desperate alacrity. And it was driving her to fury… a fury like the one Thomas Pious had instilled, but so much worse.

Her face reddened and her eyes set in a dark, penetrating stare, "We'll have our planet back, *Omega*. You best surrender it now, save yourself the pain."

It didn't feel like an empty threat to her — the Earthers had come up with solutions to so many problems before…

"Oh well, in that case," Omega offered a fresh grin to the President, "that's fair. Why don't you all just come right back and land on the planet. I *promise*, no infecting… only rape, pillage, murder, and feeding."

Sarah seethed, and in her eyes Varnia could see her self-control, well worn by these days, snap.

"Your regrets will be *remembered*," she almost hissed, then turned to face someone outside Varnia's view through the tank. "All ships to advance in echelon. Destroy the stations and his ships. We'll take control of orbital space!"

That order set Varnia back — Sarah had to be insane. She had only about 150 ships at her disposal, almost three times that many civilian vessels hovering around her… and the Genesis stations, such as they'd been hours earlier, could potentially wipe her from space.

And that was all in conventional combat terms — there was no telling what Omega had waiting for them…

"I'll be glad to take over your ships then," Omega's voice was so sickeningly close to sincere…

Sarah would not be swayed, "Damn your impudence, we'll see you dead in a–"

Nothing seems rational anymore.

Graham's mind came to the conclusion in a near-vacuum of thought. He was on the verge of feeling the weight of his wife's loss. His sister, only recently sensible enough to refuse his effort to get her to join a rescue mission, was preparing to charge the guns blindly, as had always been her habit.

And Omega had risen from the ashes, after seven centuries, to be the bane first of the Larosians, and now the humans and Earthers

Graham's mind focused — not froze, *focused.* He refused himself anything beyond what he knew was happening. The emotion of all that had just occurred was isolated, quarantined in his mind. He forced himself to think rationally and calmly.

He looked up at Sarah in the tank as she began her next set of orders, his face hardening into a blank slate, and he forced his voice to reach its most commanding level. Damned if he couldn't repress pain.

"Get my fleet away from here, Sarah. Take the survivors and move out immediately."

Omega and Sarah's eyes turned instantly to the ArcGeneral, and he met their gazes evenly, "Leave immediately. Or by Gods I'll have Varnia blow *Unity* to pieces and get someone else to follow orders."

The statement was so cold, so unfeeling, it pierced Sarah's flushed mind. She blinked, remembering her decision not to board *Genesis One*, then slowly nodded. Before she gave any further orders, she cut the link to *Renown.*

Omega grinned, "The voice of reason? Well *done* Graham, now I don't have to waste my time on them. And you've not been castrated after all! That's impressive too — made of that stern Manchester stuff are you? Well I'll leave you to it… but Varnia, I'll send you a little message to pass on in those drones of yours. Nothing harmful, I *promise*."

The feed cut, and the Signal Officer turned to his Chief in charge of received messages, who immediately found one in the buffer from *Genesis One*, "He sent us something ma'am. Scans show it to be harmless… simple holovid."

Varnia nodded slowly and took a deep breath, watching in the restored plot as *Unity* and the Genesis Fleet turned away from their homeworld, urging the civilian vessels to scurry away before them.

She glanced at Graham, "We'll have to wait to get you back aboard your ship."

He nodded silently, refusing to take his eyes from the plot.

Locking eyes for a second with Beckett, Varnia turned again to the Signal Officer, "Attach Omega's holo to the drones and send them. Let's prepare to move out. We'll head for home… there'll be much to plan–"

"Omega's ships are moving!"

Varnia turned to the plot without missing a beat, then watched the dozen formerly-Genesis ships slowly accelerate, and her eyes widened.

By the Earth, he *couldn't* mean to…

But of course he did. Omega played by different rules.

CHAPTER 51

Bismarck raced far out ahead of the advanced Freetown ships, with *Cressy* and *Fundy* in close formation. These 74s had no need of stealth now, and collecting their drive fields to full concentration, they were pushing themselves to speeds nearing 3,500 pls. They'd find the Faithful first, and make sure anything Allied in nearby space caught sight of them as well.

There'd be no gallant defense of Freetown alone — the advanced human ships would tear through the Faithful Fleet in open space.

Captain Alix Tarkam kept his hands behind his back as he watched time tick down in *Bismarck's* plot. The line-of-battle ship had enhanced Earther sensors, doubling the detection range of an average Krogg War 74-gun vessel. Those detectors would certainly come in handy… projected intercept time, given comparative base courses from Ecclesia, stood at a little under an hour.

There would be broadsides crossing soon enough.

Archangel Sword seemed to surge against an invisible wave, the force of FTL travel finding its way through the decks of the ship. The old Battlecruiser was protesting its high velocity, but despite over forty years of constant duty, it remained intact.

Still, the shudder didn't much comfort James Stanton. Long ago, *Sword* had proven itself better than a well-crewed human Superdreadnought and its escorts. Now the vessel would have to make its mark again, but this time against a carrier and as many Dreadnoughts as the Faithful had commissioned.

But at least this fight would be on the Home Fleet's own terms.

James sat silently in his chair, watching the monitors as the Destroyer group ahead sent back continuous telemetry. They were quite a ways out of Freetown now — they could potentially run across the Faithful at any moment, though he expected it would be a number of hours yet.

Then it would be up to the Home Fleet to slow down the Church bastards… nothing he hadn't already decided. He just hoped that, whatever happened, his home would be safe, and that the Earthers would come through — as they always did.

Labrador Forepaw stood and looked out over the city of London. The First Lord of the Admiralty had been grimly reflecting on the situation, wondering whether Earther *politics* were appropriate after all.

They could check the Church with scarcely any effort — all he had to do was put a squadron of the line off Genesis with sufficient cruiser cover. That'd give the sector a presence of around 5,000 marines, more than enough to batter a Crusader front, given Lupus' display at Darymanis.

But what would the humans think? The Earthers would indeed be meddling in Genesis matters...

It was a bitter brew. Labrador Forepaw believed in helping those who needed help, and among the Earthers that was a very simple and effective system. But if he were to help the Genesis government so heavy-handedly, he couldn't count on the population's support. Humans could be indecisive... perhaps even fickle... in giving their support.

The Earthers knew well what was best for Genesis, but what gave them the right to intervene?

And that was the roadblock that stopped Forepaw's thoughts. How could he do anything without subjecting the Earthers to human scorn and denial? Sometimes he half wondered whether the Earthers should even bother trying to help the humans.

But alas, he couldn't honestly ask himself that question. The Earthers had been granted so many advantages by their genetics that, as a people, they were obliged to share their good fortune. Some old humans considered such sentiments imperialistic, but those humans had been forced to factor the concept of corruption into the equation. Humans claiming such a position in history as the Earthers might today had lorded over their 'subjects' — the Earthers meant only to guide and help.

Forepaw's young race possessed a paternalism that he personally believed in, and he couldn't rightly stop the help he could offer because some who didn't know better thought it impolitic.

Church be damned.

Turning away from London, Forepaw keyed his intercom, "I need the Comptroller and the First Space Lord on comm immediately. And send for First Consul Broadpaw, too."

Sub-orbital flights being as quick as they were, the trip for the three high-ranked officials of the Earther Navy and Consulate took only fifteen minutes.

Fox Magnus was the last to arrive in Lab's office, slowing as he saw the Earthers assembled in the room. He glanced between Broadpaw and Nightclaw, then looked up at Forepaw, "Well, I do like the looks of this."

Forepaw offered a neat smile, "I thought you might."

Varnon craned his neck around, looking up at the First Space Lord with a grin, "Would you like to go show the flag at Gibraltar?"

Magnus wasn't surprised by the suggestion — he'd long been troubled by the Earthers' inactivity, "Gibraltar's seen the flag. I wouldn't mind showing it to the Church, though."

Lab's eyebrow arched, "What route you take to Gibraltar is your own business. Far be it for me to tell the First Space Lord his business."

Fox grinned, "Well that's kind of you. What'll you give me?"

Nightclaw turned in his chair to address the red fox, "I'll give you six squadrons of 74s, two of Second Rates and one of Firsts, plus a mixed force of 120 cruisers. But you'll have to build them when you get to Gibraltar."

Fox's eyebrows had begun to rise, but they dropped into a frown at the suggestion of reconstruction, "I'm going to show the flag as stamped on the side of a boxed 74?"

Forepaw smiled wryly, "We meant to move them out to Gibraltar anyway... a gesture of our interest in the Genesis situation. *I'll* give you two squadrons each of *Venerables* and *Cerberuses*. And a squadron of sloops."

A light came into Fox Magnus' eyes, "That'll remind the Church to step into line, I think. When do I leave?"

There were smiles exchanged between the other three Earthers in the room, Fox's youthful enthusiasm reminding them of younger days.

Forepaw tapped a few keys on his desk and a glowing holo displayed the assembling squadron of cargo haulers detailed to carry the disassembled fleet to its new home in Gibraltar, "It'll take them a day to prepare, and I want to send enough personnel to form skeleton crews for these ships too. I'm calling up more volunteers from the reserve... should have them aboard some transports by tomorrow at 07:30.

With a nod Fox took a step forward, frowning silently at the holo. The haulers were all reasonably fast — each capable of over 3,200 pls... as were the transports, rated at 3,360 pls. This would be a very fast convoy, though it would still be an eight-day trip to Genesis, and would probably take over two weeks to get to Gibraltar.

"Well, I'll return to *Venerable* then. We'll have to prepare–"

"Sir..." an adjutant swung quickly in the door, quieting herself as she saw the impromptu assembly of high-rankers, "Pardon me."

Forepaw held up a hand, "It's quite alright, Ellie. What is it?"

"A drone from Genesis sir, just being picked up off Pluto now."

Varnon, Fox, Lab, and Dran Nightclaw exchanged quick glances, then the First Space Lord nodded to his aide, "Bring it in as soon as you have it."

She nodded and left the doorway, giving the officials time to plan their involvement in the new campaign.

CHAPTER 52

Renown edged around as the Omega vessels formed a cluster over Genesis. The human ships under Sarah were backing away at a steady speed now, the merchant and civilian vessels moving with them in a massive, chaotic horde. It was in some ways unfortunate that, in the days since the Krogg War, Genesis space had become more than an almost exclusively military theatre. Now so many miscellaneous civilian installations needed to be abandoned... but at least they were yielding survivors.

The humans who remained free continued to move quickly, desperately trying to avoid the peril that had swallowed their world. A few hundred thousand remained, perhaps.

From billions of inhabitants.

Those staggering numbers were still so hard to believe. Beckett found himself continually repeating them in his mind, but they simply refused to take hold. No tragedy of such scope had been witnessed by Earth-borne eyes.

But then, perhaps this was just a slim slice of the pain the Larosians had faced for decades. An empire overrun... An empire of those infected, but not *possessed*.

At last a fresh thought carved a foothold in Beckett's mind. Omega had come in a single experimental body — a body that had granted it great physical and telepathic powers in the comparative 'outside' world.

Humans certainly seemed to serve it well as fodder, but were it to lay hands on more Larosians... or luck forbid, on *Kroggs*, the erstwhile God would have a force so powerful, the universe would be his playground.

It was a chilling revelation, but Beckett was certain it was Omega's plan. A creature so depraved, so vicious as the 'virus' seemed to embody all the evil the Earthers could conceive of. Maybe even more.

Varnia, standing next to her husband, was frowning into the plot at the cluster of black icons hovering over the planet. She meant to keep *Renown* between those ships and the rest of the human armada — if these vessels could somehow rig weapons to infect human ships, none of the Genesis survivors might escape.

But against twenty ships, many of them capital, even *Renown* might be troubled.

"Varnia... they must be preparing to head back through the *corridor*... at least some of them," Beckett's tone was low and grim. "They must want to capitalize on their Larosian victims. If they can get back through to Laros and break the blockade..."

It took less than a second for Varnia to process the statement. He was absolutely right. They had to contain the spread of this... of Omega... before he collected the raw material he needed to build a mighty army.

The human abominations were tough enough to deal with as it was. More Larosian minions would be a disaster.

"We have to warn Gibraltar — the Kroggs would be a good target, and the corridor on that end of space must be watched. But this one... can we close it?"

Beckett looked to his wife with a frown, "Not my area. I think we should if we can–"

Varnia was beginning to nod when the plot started to bleep.

Renown's scans tracked the progress of half of Omega's ships out of orbit at *600 pls*. They accelerated faster than should have been possible, and hurtled towards the corridor at dangerous in-system speeds.

"Interesting," Graham was standing a few feet away from Beckett and Varnia, and now he paced forward to the plot's surrounding rail. "They intend to go after the Larosians."

His words were still cold, and there was a hint in his voice that they might never warm. For some reason entirely apart from its meaning, Graham's observation disturbed Beckett. His longtime friend was not himself. Not even *close* to himself...

Beckett cut off the concern and watched distantly as his wife ordered *Renown* to pursue at 650 pls.

"Prepare another e-hyper pod," she was ordering now, approaching the console cluster of the Signal Officer. "Send to Gibraltar as soon as we slow to launch speed. Warn Admiral Jardaw that the Omega 'Virus' will likely come after the Kroggs... for raw material. Inform him that *Renown* is making chase of Omega ships in order to stop infection of Laros. Advise him to increase the guard at the hyperspace corridor at Krogg A's flank."

The Signal Officer nodded to his commander even as two of his chiefs transcribed it and dumped it into a drone.

As Varnia turned back to the massive holo tank, the Cruising Master looked her way, "They're slowing now, ma'am. Obviously planning to enter the corridor."

She nodded and paced back to the rail around the plot, "Classes?"

"One Superdreadnought, two Dreadnoughts, five Battlecruisers and four Destroyers. They're ignoring us."

Varnia ground her jaw and glanced at Graham. His eyes flicked thoughtfully between the icons in the plot, but his mouth remained tightly closed. It was

Varnia's ship, after all.

"Decelerate to match. Guns target the capital ships first… Lieutenant Sarta, arm hyper charges and stand by for launch."

Perhaps on a normal day there would have been some surprise at the last order, but the Earthers aboard *Renown* had seen too much in the past thirty-six hours to find anything surprising. Varnia almost regretted the lack of response, "Graham, you think four charges will collapse the corridor?"

He didn't take his eyes off the plot, but Graham nodded evenly, "It is our best option, I think."

There was no hint of emotion, feeling, *pain* in those words. They were icy.

"We'll be alongside one of the Dreadnoughts in twenty seconds. Guns standing by."

Renown coasted through the silent vacuum, erupting from energy drive alongside its desired target. The starboard broadside — 100 guns with as much power as *Orion's*, but only half the physical size — hurled their shot at the once-human capital ship.

And it maneuvered almost completely out of the way.

Perhaps a third of the broadside caught the ship's superstructure, but what should have been a crippling blow served only to damage.

Then *Renown* trembled as lasers cleaved at its shields, and the Omega ships gave the First Rate a few heavy salvoes before abandoning the action in favor of their approach to the corridor.

It happened as fast as any Earther maneuver; *Renown* was now more than aware of the surprising caliber of its foes.

"Master, make speed 95 pls. Let's have all guns prepare for steady fire. Get us into that corridor ahead of them," Varnia's orders set the Cruising Master to work, and orders streamed through *Renown's* bulk.

The First Rate's acceleration was enough to send it into the midst of its opponents, and lasers viciously lashed out at it. Replying broadsides batted a Destroyer aside and maimed a Battlecruiser — a poor tally, given the energy expended in shot — and yet the Omega ships continued to fire. The Earther ship's shields forced off the blows, and at such speed as it was making, *Renown* hurtled into the corridor at dangerous speeds.

A couple of Earther sloops and frigates had made test runs through these corridors about thirty-five years ago — just in one side and out the other, to see how Earther ships would withstand the strain. But *Renown* was the first capital ship to attempt the crossing.

Lowering its shields and closing its gunports, the First Rate surged ahead. The decks bucked and trembled as the Master eased *Renown's* cruising speed back, hoping to bleed off some of the painful sheers of the spatial layer.

"The Omega ships are beginning translation," the chasing vessels were highlighted with a yellow flash on the plot, and Varnia took a deep breath.

What she was about to do, she realized, would destroy *Renown*... or leave the ship hopelessly trapped between galaxies or layers or subspace.

Well, it had to be done.

"Stand by to drop charges in our wake. Master, we'll need every scrap of speed we can carry to clear the blast wave..."

At last, something drew cautious glances from the bridge crew.

"We can't let any of these new Omega cells near Laros. The additional firepower he could pick up would be too incredible."

There were almost invisible nods around the bridge deck, and the Master caught Varnia's eye, "Ready ma'am. I'll bring us up to 760 pls... I shouldn't like to risk much more."

She nodded, "Very well. Lieutenant Sarta..."

For some reason she didn't want to go further with her orders... she didn't want to take a chance with *Renown* like one of her mentors had once taken with *Tonnant.*

But damned if she had a choice, "...release charges. Full speed ahead, Master."

The launch of four charges from *Renown's* stern caught the pursuing Omega vessels slightly by surprise. A Destroyer, a Battlecruiser, and the Superdreadnought managed to weave around the oncoming warheads, surging ahead to get past their blasts...

Breath caught on the bridge of *Renown*.

It'd only be seconds before–

The explosion couldn't be physically heard through the vacuum of hyperspace, but the concussion traveled faster than light and hurled *Renown* ahead of it in a shower of energy.

As the force of the blast carried the First Rate towards a new galaxy, half its reactors failed.

The First Rate ship of the line *Renown* tumbled into regular space in a new galaxy about a minute later.

CHAPTER 53

It had been over ten hours since *Sword* had accelerated out of Freetown space, and still there was no sign of the Faithful.

That was starting to worry James Stanton.

He hoped he hadn't misjudged this maneuver — going out to meet the enemy was a good theory, but what if he'd called it wrong, and the two forces had passed each other in space.

He'd left his homeworld undefended, and though Audrey's forces were on their way, he couldn't be certain of when they'd arrive. The Faithful could win because of his gambit. His impatience and his impetuousness could–

"Sir, the Destroyers are detecting a large force coming this way. ETA… four minutes."

Well that was good timing…

James turned his chair to *Sword's* main bridge screen, "Let's see them."

The display quickly switched to a battle plot overview, marking a force that had to be Faithful as it closed with the Freetowners. Three Dreadnoughts, a Carrier, eight Battlecruisers, four Heavies, four Lights, and eighteen Destroyers, all making about 2,600 pls on their run to the free human colony.

Cruising with James against these attackers, the Freetown Home Fleet was an unimpressive six Battlecruisers, two Heavy Cruisers, three Light Cruisers, and seven Destroyers. Well, it could have been marginally worse for the Towners… *marginally.*

"Orders to Fleet," James didn't let the situation's gravity drag his mind to a halt, "stand by to engage. We'll operate in uniform class units. Destroyers to strike fast against their opposites, Heavies and Lights to make fast runs on the Faithful BCs, and our Battlecruisers to focus fire on that Carrier."

A charge of energy seemed to run through the words, and *Sword's* bridge filled with the sort of atmosphere that had once been so familiar to James Stanton. They were about to go into battle.

"We don't need to stand and fight too long, just do as much damage as possible and then evade and return to Freetown. Let's see if we can't wear them down a little, though."

The orders were broadcast to the Home Fleet's eighteen warships through *Sword's* Signal Officer, and battle alarms rang through the Freetown force. Missiles loaded into ready-fire positions and magazines prepared to feed more.

Laser crews went to their weapons, central fire control was routed to ship AIs and networked through each homogenous squadron.

Range closed smoothly.

Chancellor Leo caught sight of the approaching forces a minute after James Stanton detected him.

"They are three minutes away, closing to do battle, sir."

Leo offered a slow nod in reply. This was an unexpected and admittedly wise deployment — presuming there was more to it than he saw on his screens. That unimpressive Freetown force had no chance of surviving under the fire of his capital ships.

No, the Freetown scum, for all their heresy, weren't fool enough to send such a substantial portion of their force into action without properly supporting it. These were bait — the new Earther-built vessels had to be nearby, waiting to pounce on his open flank.

So he would have to deal with these infidels thoughtfully…

"Battlecruisers forward! Support them with nine Destroyers, and hold Heavy Cruisers in reserve. Light Cruisers and the balance of the Destroyers to screen around the capital ships."

James' reaction was less one of disappointment, more one of plain surprise. The Church commander had deployed his forces properly given what he saw, and probably based on what he assumed he *didn't* see.

So a force of ships not *quite* a match for the Home Fleet was surging ahead of the Faithful armada... but the heavy force supporting that unit was more than enough to blast James' small offering apart.

He'd have to smash the advancing picket and then run…

"All ships, change of target. Focus all fire on their advancing line, mainly the BCs. Let's try to put as many out of action as we can."

Before he realizes I've been fool enough to come out here alone!

"Got the tail of *First Defense Fleet* on my scope, skipper!"

Ed Jeffries slid forward slightly in his chair, eyes narrowing as he scanned the plot. What the hell was First Defense doing out this far... unless James had taken them out to harass the approaching enemy. That was very possible, come to think of it.

But had they *found* the enemy? Audrey had relied on James' presence at Freetown when she'd decided to make her own move — now it'd be up to Jax Furgus' ships to close that door…

Hopefully the Faithful hadn't passed First Defense in space.

"They're decelerating skipper! Battle ready — I think they found the Faithful!"

Ed came out of his seat. That was a quick assumption… they might be just slowing to turn around. But he couldn't be sure; what James' ships saw was beyond the range of even *Savanna Felix's* sensor grid — its range didn't extend beyond ten minutes ahead, at this velocity.

Well, if they had found the Faithful, First Defense and whoever was with it would have to hold out as long as possible. Help was on the way.

Sword reached normal space velocity smoothly, and the rest of the Freetown Battlecruisers came alongside their hybrid flagship in a long line abreast. The other cruisers and Destroyers formed lines above and below, their weapons standing by.

Hurtling towards an enemy that was only now beginning its deceleration, they made 84 pls on their approach, and veteran crews and their old but reliable AIs planned the first missile salvoes of the engagement.

James didn't intend on making this too complex.

"Missile range in thirty-four seconds."

He nodded and took a deep breath. This was going to be interesting. He tried to run over the plan in his mind again, but it wasn't substantial enough to kill half a minute.

So he watched the range close, and the time tick down.

Five... Four…

The Home Fleet seemed to brace itself.

Three… Two…

Sword prepared for its first action in decades.

One.

James Stanton's lips curved down and he delivered the order, "*Fire*."

Leo watched with a silent frown as the first large salvo of missiles rippled into space, racing towards the leading line of his fleet.

Counter-missiles erupted from Faithful Destroyers almost immediately — counter weapons designed to splinter and detonate as many missiles as possible — and lasers stood ready to accept more fire.

The Holy Battlecruisers, however, saved their tubes for offensive fire… which came instantly. Warheads rushed from their blessed tubes, charging towards the Freetown scum, determined to give the heretics the fiery deaths they deserved.

Counter-missiles erupted onto the plot from Freetown Destroyers.

"So that's how the game will be played," Leo offered a feral smile. "Very well. Send the Heavy Cruisers forward, and order *Saint Tobias Janus* and *Saint Michael Darwin* to prepare long-range salvoes as we close range."

As warheads accelerated past each other in the space between the closing forces, more Faithful ships mounted their charge.

•••

This didn't look good to James at all. They were definitely calling his bluff...

But Freetown missiles were beginning their final runs at last. Faithful point defense was disturbingly proficient, but some of the weapons still got around lasers and missiles and hammered into the Faithful Battlecruisers.

Two took minor hits, one moderate damage. Not too bad for a first salvo, but they needed to do more than bloody three Battlecruisers. They needed to *cripple* at least that many...

"Maintain fire and continue to close — we'll go to energy range but run before the Dreadnoughts engage."

Orders were again passed through the Home Fleet, and then Faithful missiles arrived. Veteran point defense teams took down many, but two Battlecruisers and two Light Cruisers were hit, one of the latter significantly.

James didn't pay attention — he *needed* to close range, and to get the Faithful Battlecruisers out of the picture so his ships could focus on the Dreadnoughts once they reached Freetown.

The second salvo of missiles erupted from *Sword's* tubes, and the veteran ship lurched sideways and down slightly to avoid the fire of the Faithful ships.

Now those damned Heavy Cruisers were getting into it, launching a salvo at extreme range. The missiles weaved around the Faithful front line, and surged towards the Freetown echelons.

James grimaced. Whoever was running this Faithful force wasn't leaving much chance to pick it apart. *Damn damn damn...*

Well, the Home Fleet would have to settle for doing what it could.

"Prepare to break formation. We're presenting too big a target..."

For some reason, James stopped in mid sentence, then narrowed his eyes at the main screen. Two things caught his attention.

First, there was the abrupt appearance of three *74s* — bless the Earthers, the Home Fleet suddenly had a chance!

The second was a Heavy Cruiser missile that stumbled past *Sword's* point defense. James only had a few seconds to follow its course with his eyes before the alarms started. He thrust himself to his feet and began to shout a warning to his crew...

Then the warhead sheared *Archangel Sword's* bridge cleanly off its hull, shattering it into thousands of pieces.

Captain Alix Tarkam only had to nod to his First Lieutenant and *Bismarck's* guns released their formidable shot. The target was the Faithful Carrier, and as *Cressy* and *Fundy* joined the salvo, the Faithful recognized the new threat.

Destroyers flung themselves into the path of the ninety-odd bursts of energy, but even though the diminutive vessels sacrificed themselves, some of the shot rained through. The Carrier bucked spectacularly with a massive gouge in its upper hull, and then the three 74s put their second broadside into space.

Running over six minutes ahead of the human force, Alix Tarkam had been quite surprised to see other Freetown ships in the vicinity. But now there was a very good chance to rout the Faithful far short of their goal, and to do it without putting the new human ships at a defensive disadvantage.

They'd just need to coordinate with the Freetowners to put these upstart Faithful to bed...

"Contact *Archangel Sword*. Let's get coordinated with their forces."

There was a pause as the Signal Officer spun up her comms, and then another as she frowned at her comm grid, "They're not on my grid, Captain."

Tarkam frowned and turned to the Lieutenant, "You're sure?"

A slow nod answered the inquiry, and as Tarkam turned to question the Sensor Chief, that rating held up a hand, "*Sword's* bridge is gone... and no one's taken up the flag yet."

Tarkam blinked — that was an unpleasant surprise. Seldom did such bad fortune seem to strike the Earthers and their Allies. Well, there was no time yet to dwell on it. He could only hope that the bridge crew had escaped safely, and that the ship would be manageable on auxiliaries.

"Link all Freetown ships into our grid. *Cressy* to finish that Carrier, *Fundy* to keep the Dreadnoughts preoccupied. We'll go after those Battlecruisers..."

Leo's teeth bared angrily as the meddling Earther ships split up and made their attempts to hurt him. But without their flagship, the heretic Freetowners were back on their heels for the moment... he needed only to bloody these Earthers and his victory would still be at hand.

"Dreadnoughts focus fire on the 74 attacking them. All Light Cruisers and Destroyers attack the 74 targeting our Carrier... Heavy Cruisers change target to the last 74. Battlecruisers and Destroyers on the front line maintain engagement with the Freetowners... we'll yet win this."

Cressy's broadsides flashed through space, batting the swarming escort vessels aside as it dove into carronade range of the wounded Carrier. Fighters began spewing from the cumbersome ship, but canister hit them as they tried to form, scrambling their systems and destroying their cohesion.

The 74 drove into close quarters and its carronades finally spoke. Great beams of energy carved through the lightly-armored hull of the Faithful ship, decompressing large flight bays and sparking explosions in internal magazines.

In the course of a few dozen seconds, explosions began deep within the big ship. Containment systems managed to partially hold them in, but the ship's bottom swelled and bulged unhealthily as sections of the ship were sacrificed to save it from utter destruction.

Falling from formation, the vessel limped away, and *Cressy* let it go, turning two broadsides of canister against Faithful missiles now stabbing at *Fundy*. The Dreadnoughts were indeed a threat, so together the pair of 74s closed the range and exchanged fire.

Bismarck dove into the Heavy Cruisers sent against it, and three of the human ships were crippled or destroyed in the exchange. The ship of the line made its goal obvious as it left the surviving Heavy Cruiser in its wake, Tarkam's ship pressing close to the rear of the Faithful Battlecruiser echelon. Those ships could *not* fare well with an Earther capital ship behind them…

Chancellor Leo's face contorted in fury — Gods damn these Earthers, even their *old* ships were performing so well his forces were left wanting. He could still carry the day if–

"Sir, I'm detecting the advanced Freetown force at extreme range! Five Battlecruisers of the *Felix* class and a *Carrier*."

Leo blinked.

This was not the right time then — the Gods would yet deliver opportunity into the hands of the Faithful, but patience and rebuilding would be required.

They would live to fight again.

"All ships disengage."

Tarkam was standing at the plot, watching the second Faithful Battlecruiser come apart, and then the rest turned hard towards *Bismarck* and raced into flux drive. The speed of departure caught the Captain slightly by surprise — he still wasn't used to seeing human ships with that sort of agility, but then there had been many advances since the Krogg War.

"Let them go," he said quietly. "Let's take stock, see what we've lost."

Audrey DeBrooke sat anxiously forward in her chair as *Republic* slowed behind its screening line of advanced Battlecruisers.

It seemed that James had come up with similar ideas to hers — and he'd done well, thanks admittedly to Captain Tarkam's intervention. The Faithful were running, and she doubted they'd rush to return.

So things could settle down again, or perhaps she could rally with First Defense and go after them. Lay siege to Ecclesia and force a peace.

Well, she'd talk that over with the Governor.

A small smile twitched to life on Audrey's face, and she turned to the Signal Officer, "Raise *Sword* for me."

The Lieutenant began to nod, then paused as the console bleeped beneath her nose, "Pardon ma'am, Captain Tarkam on the line."

Audrey shrugged, "Sure, put him up."

Tarkam's face was grim, "I'm sorry for your loss, Admiral. It happened before we got here..."

His voice trailed off, and Audrey frowned. She opened her mouth to ask, and then the Sensor Officer's pale face caught her eye.

She froze. No, it wasn't possible.

It went against all the rules they'd learned during the last war — it couldn't *be*.

But her eyes turned back to the holo plot, and there was *Sword's* icon. With the red ring around it. Significant damage. And no pennant.

Anywhere.

Audrey DeBrooke couldn't quite breathe.

CHAPTER 54

Setter Caine straightened his arm and dipped at the knees, extending the point of his long dragoon saber out before him. One arm stayed seemingly precarious, hanging immobile at his side, but his eyes warned all viewers that he was keen on this weapon of his.

The Admiralty-awarded sword had been left on a wall for the first two decades after it was received, but since then Caine had taken some pride in developing skill with the long, only slightly-curved blade.

"So... *balance* is key?"

Today he wasn't hefting the sword for himself, though.

Phealan frowned at his father, mirroring his stance but feeling much less comfortable with a standard off-the-shelf saber in hand.

Caine nodded to his son, "You'll get different ways of standing from every different sword holder, I think. But the trick is to keep focused on your target. Deflect with the flats of the blade and don't over-commit... you'll leave yourself open."

Managing a thoughtful nod, Phealan guided his saber in a slow approximation of a parry, then a quick lunge.

Caine cocked an eyebrow, "Not too bad at all, you see."

Phealan drew himself up to full height and shrugged, "It's partially instinctive, I admit. But I don't think it's what I was built for."

A smile formed across the elder Caine's face as he came to full height, sliding his weapon into its sheath, "And that's fine with me, as you well know. Next time we see Pat, though, I'll get you two to have a sit-down about the history-writing profession."

Phealan grinned, "Definitely."

Sheathing his own sword, Phealan turned with his father and they paced out of the Caine Estate's large sparring chamber, built into the second sub-level of their house. Climbing the stairs past the den on sub-level one, they emerged into the bright living room on the ground floor.

It was a foggy day today — at least for this particular Newfoundland cove — but the fog was glowing with the light of the sun beyond, so it'd probably burn off soon. For now it was a comfortable shroud, seemingly keeping the world out.

Phealan watched his father, feeling just a little worried. Setter had seemed *uncomfortable* since he'd come back from Admiralty House the day before. Word of coups and Faithful ambushes, along with some sort of instinctive dread...

It didn't make sense to Phealan, but he was well aware that he hadn't lived through the trials his father had survived. Something in the Earthers' greatest hero was warning of impending darkness. And all Phealan could do was try to take citizen Caine's mind off the workings of the universe.

Setter was at the refrigerator, and as he drew two water packs from the open door he tossed one to Phealan, absently tearing the other open for himself. A feeling of uneasiness was still saturating his senses...

He wondered if it wasn't just a response to inactivity. It was his great fear that he would feel incomplete without the duties he'd once held, that his retirement would be nothing but torture and futility to him.

Perhaps he missed command.

"There are... yikes, *eleven* messages. Want me to check them?" Phealan paced over to the comm panel near one of the living room's couches, but his father shook his head.

"Not now... I'm really not in the right state of mind, I think."

Phealan frowned, "That's not something I often hear."

As the son turned to the father, the latter shrugged slowly, "Hard to explain, I suppose. I'm just starting to feel like a fifth wheel. Mightn't be the best thing for me to hear more things I'll brood about..."

"But there could be news of the coup..."

Setter came from the kitchen, draining the last of his water pack, and nodded, "There could be. But right now I'd think too much on it... try to decide what *I'd* do. And if I said anything I might undermine the authority of both Varnon and Lab. I won't do that — they're both perfectly capable of handling the Church."

Phealan processed those words for a few seconds, and he slowly lowered himself onto the couch, looking over its back at his father, "So that's what's been on your mind? For the first time in ages you aren't in command... and now's the worst possible timing."

Setter paused, then nodded, "That'd be it."

Phealan took a few long breaths, slowly beginning to shake his head, "Well there's no way I can tell you what to think. But I do know you'll sort it out. You always do."

Smiling at his son, Setter paced forward to the side of the couch and keyed the comm panel. Just as the holo of Varnon Broadpaw was glowing to life in the center of the living room, both Caines heard someone coming up the front lawn.

Frowning simultaneously, they glanced at each other. Setter tapped 'pause' on the comm panel, and they went to the front windows to wait by the sliding door.

Through the glowing fog, Varnon Broadpaw and Lab Forepaw appeared.

They walked slowly through the thinning banks of mist, and as Setter caught sight of their faces something in him chilled.

Phealan slid the glass door open as the leaders of the Earther government and Navy climbed the steps to the broad patio that ringed the circular house. The young Caine held up a hand in greeting, and they did the same out of courtesy...

But neither looked happy to be where they were.

As Setter's two successors stepped into the living room, slipped their shoes off, and turned silently to face their old leader, Caine straightened himself. There was nothing good in the air around these two.

They exchanged quick glances, then Forepaw, as close a friend as Caine had, met Setter's eyes.

"We haven't been able to get you. Have you checked messages?"

The grim question forced Setter to point to the frozen holo of Varnon on the other side of the living room, "Was just about to."

Lab nodded, "Well, better we tell you before you see it third hand."

Setter frowned, "The coup's gone badly? Freetown's been lost?"

There was much genuine concern in his questions, but Phealan detected a different level of... *despair* on the part of the current First Consul and First Lord.

Still silent, Varnon walked to the comm panel, rounding the image of himself on the way, and then began to strike keys quickly.

"Everything's different now," Forepaw said quietly. "All the rules have changed."

Setter's frown deepened, and he looked past Lab to Varnon, "I don't see how they could have changed so much as to–"

In the living room's center, Varnon's holo was abruptly replaced by a Larosian, and Caine's mind halted its line of thought. What was a–

As Varnon tapped the controls, the projection rotated to face Setter, Phealan and Forepaw, and as it came around Setter saw the differences — the black eyes, the abnormal contours in the face... the *emotion* behind that snarl.

Around the figure, now, various other holo images were imposed. A Warcruiser, badly beaten, emerging from hyperspace, Earther marines in darkened corridors, sat-vids of people on the surface of Genesis... what was all this?

And then Varnon hit 'play'.

The holo came to life, and its alien eyes seemed to find Setter's, "This is an open letter to Setter Caine and all his lovable Earther people..."

It was not a Larosian's introduction.

"...from, yours truly, your God..."

A confusing statement to say the least. The thing must have been delusional...

"...the Omega 'Virus'."

Caine's muscles snapped tense, and the dread he'd been feeling swarmed his nerves.

"That's right, Setter, Earthers, I'm back at last. A bit of a hiatus I know — but that's your fault, see. Now I don't want to take up too much of your time, but I've got to give you something to chew on while I chew on these humans of Genesis... yum, by the way — it's good to be eating human again."

Setter stared.

"Now, let me explain. I created you — you've all managed to figure that out, at least. And now you're all past it and philosophically secure because Andros Grieve died with some pretty words killing a Queen. Woo. That's *so* important. But I digress. Anyhow, you never got rid of me. I'll give you credit... because I designed you... you did succeed in messing me up. That super immune system I built into you was meant to keep other viruses from muscling in on my cattle... you all just managed to castrate me with it."

The brutalized Larosian face smiled sardonically, "I've never left your blood. Your immune systems hit me hard, killed my ability to infect terrestrial biology. But it didn't *kill* me. So I sat and waited. That's right — in your blood, I bided my time and hoped I'd find a way to get back to glory. And then you went off to play interstellar do-gooders. And you found the Larosians for me."

Now the dark smile descended into a darker scowl, "Their civilization was very accommodating. All you needed to do was share blood with one of them back during the attack on the Queen's Hive in Genesis. I was in — right past their defenses. The Larosians are still paying for that. Paying for being your friends. I couldn't infect any terrestial biology, but theirs was totally defenseless."

"And then they were really intelligent — set a thief to catch a thief, they thought. Hit me with raw Krogg DNA, figuring it'd kill me because they thought I was Krogg-built... nope. I'm good at manipulating biology, so I took that Krogg DNA, mutated it, took over this nice body here, and haven't looked back."

It was a horror story.

Phealan had read so much history, but none of it so vile as this.

"So that'd be what... oh, between Larosians and humans now, call it twenty-five billion dead... all of it the responsibility of the Earther race. You thought your killing of a few million was bad, Setter? Get used to the new game. Your race has been my Trojan horse. While you managed to take away my power seven centuries ago, you've still been great cattle. Brought me all sorts of new opportunities out there, I have to say. I sure scared the hell out of the Queen and her telepaths at Krogg 'A', so I figure I've got a bright future out here.

"But now, *now* you'll pay for making me wait. For making me watch. You have no concept of how torturous it was, to watch things you grew for *food* first castrating you and then doing the exact opposite of everything you believe. But now I have the means, and you're all going to pay. Not as food, I'm just going to kill all of you."

"You're an experiment gone wrong—you're fuckin' Frankenstein monsters, except you're too stupid to recognize yourself as overblown teddy bears. So like every bad experiment, you'll be cleaned away. And I'm sure you'll get your guts together and try to stop me — I *invite* that. But remember, I made you. And I've ridden in all of your blood since the beginning. I know how to crush your bodies, and I certainly know how to beat your junior high strategies.

"Earthers no longer reign, Setter. I am *Omega* — I'm not just the hand of God, coming to sweep you away… I *am* God. And I'm back in color and high def. Look forward to seeing you. Kiss Elandra for me."

Another feral smile formed on Omega's face, and he held up his hand in a wave, "Ta-ta for now!"

The holo froze.

And there was silence.

Setter Caine's mind spun.

The rules of the game… had changed.

CHAPTER 55

Varnia tugged at her husband's sleeve, but he didn't move. Favoring her broken arm, she gingerly shifted her weight forward and used her good hand to cover his nose. When his next inhalation was interrupted his mind kicked him into consciousness and he shook his head.

"What the–"

He caught sight of Varnia immediately, and a sudden sense of relief hit him — preempting what might well have turned into panic. Detecting a tingling sensation in his back, Beckett quickly realized he couldn't use his legs. Couldn't even feel them.

"Dammit," he muttered as he propped himself up partway on his elbows, "Paralyzed from the waist down again.

Varnia frowned, "Same old injury?"

He nodded, "Feels familiar enough. We can deal with it later, though — what's going on? Where are we?"

Looking around the bridge, Beckett could see many of the bridge crew trying to collect themselves in the flickering dim of the emergency lights. He forced down a cough and frowned at his wife, "You alright?"

She shrugged uncomfortably, "Just my arm. As to where we are, I think… though I might be wrong… that we're in the Larosian galaxy. I'm hoping we rode the shockwave out the other side, that we're somewhere with some sort of civilization around. We're a long way from home."

Lupus nodded gruffly, "Yes, we are."

Graham was suddenly next to them, fully upright and seemingly unshaken. He looked down with a disinterest that almost bordered on contempt, "Are you two alright?"

Varnia looked up at the ArcGeneral, "Battered and half-paralyzed, but nothing that a few hours in a regen chair won't fix."

"Good," the clipped word was all the junior Manchester offered before stepping over the pair.

Beckett and Varnia exchanged puzzled glances, and General released a short sigh, "He's going to have a long road back… if he ever wants to come back."

Varnia nodded slowly.

•••

Christine groaned at the ache in her head. Blood seemed to be sloshing around in her veins — it felt *heavier* as it went to work repairing the many centers of damaged tissue marked by her bruises.

She tried to force herself up off the bridge's cold deckplates, but found herself pinned by a pressure on her back. Dammit, she couldn't get up. Failing to roll over, she just let out a long breath and resigned herself to waiting for help.

After so much chaos and death, she didn't want to have to do anything more. She wanted to go back home. She wanted to crawl into bed and complain to her sister and read a book. She wanted a life worth living.

And instead, she'd survived an apocalypse. With nothing to comfort her and nowhere to go.

Damned if anyone could show her a bright side to that.

The weight came off her back abruptly, and forcing her fears to be silent, she rolled over. A human hand extended down from the smoky air above, and she took it. Graham helped her indelicately to her feet, then quickly looked her over.

"You're alright?" he asked in quiet tones, his eyes meeting hers.

Christine could see little sign of anything but deadness in those eyes.

"Yes. Yes, I'm fine..." she let her words fade, as they weren't wholly true.

Renown slowly, painfully, began to right itself.

Unity Genesis hurtled through space well ahead of a mixed formation of Genesis refugees. Most of the Genesis Fleet was to the rear of that formation, ready to respond in case Omega ships chased the slow-moving convoy on its escape run to Freetown and Earth. *Unity* needed to get to the Earther homeworld with all possible speed.

There were many contingencies that needed to be considered.

On the bridge of the Superdreadnought, Sarah Manchester, President of a dead world, sat silently in a chair, watching the time tick by. The shock of all that had happened wouldn't wear off for a long time — that was for certain. But her mind was fully in charge of her faculties again, and now all she wanted to do was find Liz Hastings or Setter Caine, to sit down and ask profound questions with the voice of a child.

She felt betrayed by the universe, and she knew full well she'd let her people down. It was because of her that the coup had been allowed to begin, and in turn, it was her fault that Omega had gotten through...

Her responsibility.

It made her understand the guilt Caine felt for the Crusaders and all the death of the Krogg War.

More than abandoning her post to rescue Pat, this was a true failure on her part. She had no excuse but incompetence... and it hurt.

It hurt so much.

But she couldn't let that hurt show — unlike most people, she'd personally only lost her brother. So many had lost so much more...

The promise of Graham's death struck her anew every time it crossed her mind. He'd been lost in the corridor, having known nothing but disappointment in his sister during his last hours of life.

Her little brother was *gone*.

It was too much to think about. She had to lead from a distance... she couldn't dwell on it. Caine would have the answers... there was none wiser in this universe. He'd make it make sense for her. In the meantime she'd refuse to think about it. And she'd lead.

Pat had been through a lot in his life, and yet the scope of this tragedy was too great for even him to absorb.

Walking the decks of *Unity Genesis*, he knew that Sarah needed time to gather herself. She always grew distant when she felt she'd betrayed those loyal to her... he'd try to help her more actively once she got the survivors to safety.

In the meantime, all he could do was wander.

He'd written the history of the last war. The way things had happened then — the *character* of that conflict — had been so different from what he'd just seen. And that was hard for him to accept.

Of course he wanted to believe the Earthers would pull through, save the day, find a cure and restore Genesis...

But a goodly portion of his mind didn't believe it was possible. Not with Omega lurking. Their creator, and humanity's old destroyer... back for another round.

Pat focused on keeping his pace even, passing silent spacers in the corridors. The ship felt like a tomb.

Finally his destination appeared down the corridor. The single door at the end of one of *Unity's* long passageways was entirely nondescript, but behind it waited the youngest girl on the ship, without a single family member left in the cosmos.

Damn Christine for having left young Claire with no one. Now Pat felt obligated to be the father-figure, Gods help him. The youngest, the *only* Schaeffer had nothing else, and for the traumatized teenage girl that was acute problem.

Coming to a stop at the door, Pat collected himself with effort. He couldn't be cheerful, but he'd do his damndest not to appear depressed. Gods only knew what he could do for this girl.

Hopefully she'd be alright... one day.

Maybe they'd all recover...

Yes.

Yes, Pat believed they would.

CHAPTER 56

Jax Furgus stood at the main plot, Ron Hobbes next to him.

They watched the Freetown force, accompanied by *Bismarck*, *Fundy* and *Cressy*, reenter their home system.

Commodore Locke's Flying Squadron had escorted the Freetown First Expeditionary Force, including *Grendelsbane City*, into the system about two hours before. Now it felt like a great reunion — the entirety of the old Freetown Fleet, combined with the new ships, and joined by two Earther squadrons... it would all have been quite a happy scene, but for two factors.

First, of course, was that lovely pod they'd gotten from *Renown*. The one that seemed to have promised the death of Jax Furgus' daughter on that ship, when it went corridor-busting. It also brought a new player into the game, one Jax Furgus had no interest in facing.

Omega.

All cheer and good feelings among the Earther ships of the line had instantly disappeared when they'd heard. And there would be no more relaxation. Jax was now in full uniform on the bridge of *Aboukir*, and he meant to remain formally dressed until they defeated the damned plague.

The second bit of news was the loss of Governor James Stanton, to an abrupt and senseless stray missile. No Battlecruiser had sustained as much damage as *Sword* in that engagement, though many more had been wounded.

Of all the people to lose...

It felt wrong to Jax Furgus. He'd had half a dozen ships blown out from under him without too much detriment to himself in the last war, and yet another old great hero of the past had been assassinated by fate. Or just really bad luck.

Jax Furgus didn't mean to try to justify or explain the loss... but it was hard not to wonder about mortality some days. Like on days when you only had a faint, tiny sliver of hope for your daughter's survival. And when your creator just came back out of the blue, ready to smite you.

Audrey DeBrooke had received *Aboukir's* pod detailing the destruction of Genesis and the revival of Omega three hours after her husband's death was confirmed, so she just kept trying to soldier on.

There had been so much death.

Many Towners still had family on Genesis... perhaps some had survived with the fleet. There were many thousands of refugees...

But no, the likelihood seemed very slim.

And now Freetown was changing roles, becoming a frontline defensive position for Earth. Because this Omega 'Virus' was back.

So she'd try to stop the plague. As a widow.

Thank Gods for shock suppressing my emotions, or I'd have crumpled to the floor hours ago.

She'd have to find a way to cope — everyone would have to find a way.

The reality that had killed so many would finish the job if every human and every Earther didn't quickly pull together.

Fox Magnus and Dran Nightclaw sat silently across the former's desk from each other. Admiralty House was bustling outside the door — things were being moved quickly to war footing. Battle had been expected, as Lab Forepaw had kept a careful eye on the Church situation for many years.

But now a whole different sort of war was being promised.

Fox couldn't conceive of such a great loss as the planet of Genesis and its entire population. But he knew fully that his thoughtful inability to conceive of the loss didn't make it any less real to those much closer to it.

Omega's message, though...

Well, it made Fox furious. And afraid, he had to admit. He'd spent a long career in action against ridiculous odds, and he'd seen good friends lost on too many occasions. But he'd always found a way to win.

Now he'd have to do that again. He'd have to...

Dran Nightclaw was, as always, very cool under pressure, and as Fox forced his reflections aside he looked at the panther, "So you think only weeks for everything?"

The Comptroller nodded, "We're running every work crew in the system at 130 percent. We'll have the old fleet back online quickly..."

Fox leaned back in his chair and scratched his chin, "*Renown* sent warning to Gibraltar and Krogg. That's Chronos Claw and Lang Sandpelt out there — two of my old *Flame* crew..."

"And Garvin Jardaw and Karl Kandam," Nightclaw added smoothly, "all excellent officers."

Fox nodded, "So you think we need to put any more brass out there to give them a hand? They've got two squadrons of *Venerables* and the eight *Champions*... plenty of frigates and sloops. We can give them a lot of help..."

"I'd say give them 128 recommissions," Nightclaw said slowly, "and send Jax out with them. He's already out at Freetown — he could pick up with the convoy and escort it with his squadron."

Fox looked thoughtfully at the desk, then shook his head, "No... no Jax needs to babysit Freetown. He'll be the nucleus for the force we put out there. Someone else needs to get out to Gibraltar."

Nightclaw leaned back slightly and frowned, "You want to go."

With a blink, the First Space Lord looked up, "Lab can handle things here. The whole point of a *First Space Lord* is to be mobile. *First Lord of the Admiralty* can stay home and look after the defense..."

"He won't like it. You're the best commander we've got."

"Excluding yourself, Lab, Andra and Setter and many others. But Gibraltar's cut off and we can't let Omega have Krogg. They need me out there..."

Nightclaw let the Space Lord's words fade, then offered a slow nod, "But you can't take *Renown*. We only have three squadrons of *Venerables* out here."

Fox nodded — that was true. They'd have to work out actual defense numbers later, but for now Earth space would need every front-line ship it had. That left those aged third-line ships that could be fully re-crewed in short order.

"I'll take the *Chimeras*, and we'll get a crew convoy in tow. Every recommissioned ship we have will have to serve as escort for the haulers."

Nightclaw blinked and nodded slowly, "Very well. I'll issue the orders for your ships and supplies."

Fox took a deep breath and nodded, "Good. I'll call my wife..."

There would be moves to check this Omega. Even if they were desperate moves.

Lab Forepaw was taking a call from Admiralty House, Phealan was talking on the other line with his mother, still at work in Sydney, and Varnon Broadpaw was sitting on the couch, leaned forward with his chin cradled in his hands.

He'd been trying for the longest time to deny the possibility that Varnia had been lost. But she and *Renown* had been doing a very risky thing in aiming to collapse that corridor. The right thing... but risky.

If she and his son-in-law were dead... that'd be hard. Very, very hard. Krogg 'C' had almost spelled Varnia's end, but she was saved by Savanna Felix. Now... well, the second time worrying about his daughter's survival was no easier than the first.

He had the consolation of knowing it had been her choice — indeed, her very order — to take the risk. But how the hell did that qualify as consolation today?

Setter sat across from his friend, staring grimly at nothing as his mind sifted through all he'd been told. Of all the loss and the danger... it was beyond comprehension in so many ways. He was fighting with himself, forcing the thoughts to come, the ideas to form.

There would have to be leadership for Earth and its allies now... and Varnon was in poor condition for it...

"Alright, Fox will be taking about 200 ships out to Gibraltar… some recommissioned for escort, the rest still packed up 'in ordinary'. He'll leave this afternoon."

It was a two-week trip to Gibraltar, assuming the haulers were fast, and it was another six days at least to Krogg from the Earther Naval base. The First Space Lord would have to move quickly to beat Omega's deployment on that front… assuming the virus moved as fast against those installations as it had against the Genesis orbitals.

"I'm going to head back to Admiralty House for now — Setter, will you come over later?"

Caine nodded slowly to the First Lord, "I will. See you soon, Lab."

Forepaw took a deep breath and nodded, then stepped to the front door, patting Varnon on the back once on the way.

As the First Lord headed back into the woods, on his way to landing site for his sub-orbital craft, Setter looked back to Varnon.

"Will you be alright?"

Varnon took a long blink and looked up, then breathed deep in a vain attempt to clear the hopelessness, "I… don't know. Should be… I suppose."

Phealan and Setter exchanged a quick glance as the First Consul spoke, and the younger wolf got the message to head out for a while. Setter needed to speak privately with his old friend. Moving silently, the young wolf took one of the side doors out onto the deck, then walked towards the shore.

Setter sat forward in his chair, heaving a mild sigh, "What can I do, Varnon? I'm… at a loss."

Broadpaw cast his glance from Caine's eyes to the floor and back, "Make sense of it for me, perhaps. All of it. You're going to have a lot of people asking you, Setter. They'll want to know why and how. How the timing was so obscenely right for him. Why a planet of humans died…"

His voice trailed off for a moment, and Setter let out a long breath, easing back some in his seat.

"And we'll all want to know whether it's really our fault. Omega's pushing our buttons, and by now everyone on this planet will have heard. How can we *not* feel responsible? And what can we do to fix it? You answer those questions and I'll be satisfied. But I won't be happy until I see my daughter again. You bring my daughter back to me and I'll never be unhappy."

Caine's brow creased as he sensed the pain in his counterpart's voice. It was hurt that was all too familiar to so many Earthers.

"So I'll go make a statement, and I'll organize and administrate, because that's my job, Setter," Varnon's words were tougher now. "But I won't know what, how or why things have happened. I'm a wise wolf some days… but this is beyond my scope. The sheer size of this is…"

"Unthinkable."

Varnon concurred with a slow nod, and Caine rubbed his eyes slowly.

"We have to face our creator—all of a sudden. And he's got the momentum… *and* he's Omega," Varnon's voice was almost defeated in its tone, and Caine understood the sentiment. He'd been there.

He was the only Earther who'd really been there.

Which put the ball in his court.

"I'll take an appointment of Supreme Consul, Varnon."

The First Consul looked up slowly, and met Caine's eyes.

"What's that?"

Caine raised his eyebrows and shrugged, "I don't know. But we'll make it up. I'm as close as we've got to someone with experience in this. If only for… *morale* reasons, I'll take another turn at the helm."

Varnon's head was moving in a slow, persistent nod, "Yes. That'll do us all quite a lot of good. You should make a statement on vid soon… we'll need to give everyone something to strengthen resolve. And that's you."

Caine nodded slowly. That was his duty.

So he'd become the leader again.

EPILOGUE

Andra Ursla skittered to a halt behind the camera just as Setter Caine began his speech. She'd been on safari, of all places, when she'd heard.

All this worried her, but she'd reflect after she heard her best friend deliver a statement to calm the universe. Omega's message had been a brutal one, but their longtime leader couldn't open his mouth without being compelling.

Setter Caine smiled and offered a tiny nod to his friend, then looked into the camera. The feed went live to the entire system.

"A long time ago I took the job of First Consul, and on my inauguration, I promised that the future was unwritten. That we were going to face challenges, but that I knew we'd overcome them. Because of what Andros Grieve, my good friend, pointed out one dark day on Krogg. We do what we say we'll do in a way that reflects us. And yet now, when this new challenge comes, it's a simple matter for each of us — all of us — to forget that strength."

Renown lurched forward under its own power, coasting into the blackness of a new galaxy. Graham watched in silence through his cabin window, the lights off and his thoughts still. He felt as though he had no emotion any more, and was glad of it.

"Omega has mounted a challenge today. It... *he* means to call us cattle. He means to shock us with death and terrorize us into capitulation. We've witnessed in the course of thirty-six hours the most heinous atrocities we've recorded in this galaxy... and yet, we must remember something: there have been worse."

Christine watched space go silently by from her own cabin in *Renown*. Somewhere else on the ship, Beckett Lupus practiced walking with his new spine, and Varnia watched and made sure he didn't fall.

"The Kroggs wiped out planets as a matter of course — that's why we stopped them. And the Larosians have been ravaged by Omega — he was under another guise, but he was Omega all the same. The loss of Genesis is the loss of a single planet. And in the grand scheme of things, some will say it's irrelevant. We know better."

• • •

Pat sat silently in a chair next to Claire's bed as the girl tried to sleep. *Unity Genesis* raced through the stars, Sarah on its bridge, hoping to be comforted by something.

"Genesis is so close to us because it's been a part of us for as long as we've been Earthers. And Omega knew that. That's why he took it so viciously. But that's not my point. History has seen greater loss, more complete destruction... the stories simply haven't been told. No one has been left to tell them."

Fox Magnus boarded ENS *Chimera* and set about pre-departure checks for his run to Gibraltar.

"But we're here. And we've told the story of one war. We've made that story — we've made sense of it all and moved on. We know the price we've paid for carrying our philosophy to the stars, and now we'll have to do it again. One day the story of Genesis will have to be told. The story of senseless loss, and of epic survival."

Audrey DeBrooke walked through her empty house on Freetown, trying to stay composed as she collected her things for space duty. A long road lay ahead.

"That story will be told," Caine's eyes seemed to pierce the camera. "All *our* stories will be told. But only if we win. We'll either make a great fight worthy of conspicuous tales, and come away from this alive, or we'll fail, and all our stories, and the meanings of all our lives, will be lost."

Caine's mind surged with thought. This was his forum — *his* medium, and he knew it.

"I don't mean to let go my life's legacy. None of us do. Omega wants to take it from us, and he claims he has the power to do so. Maybe he does, maybe he doesn't. All we know, here and now, is that it's our job to defend what we have..."

Aware of the people around him, Setter's mind pressed on, "We could stop but we will not. We could fail but we *shall not*. There are always ways to be defeated. Denying potential failure is courting it. But damned if we'll let it come without a fight. To arms. To war. However you say it, get ready. The universe isn't waiting. We must face it with what we've got. Nothing more can be asked of us."

This would be it, then, Caine decided.

"The rules of the game have changed," he said more quietly, "but it is the *same game*. And we play it well. Omega means to take from us what we hold most dear — he hopes to change our ways, and to make us weak. But we hold firm. Because *no one, no thing* will intimidate us out of hand. We'll live or die as we are, but we won't break. That is our lot — we can adapt but we'll never fully change. Not for Omega, not for anyone."

Caine's last thoughts came as he caught Ursla's eye, and he felt an absurd smile trying to surface as he did.

"That's the difference. He's changed… had his *genesis*… and we remain what we've always known we were. That's the way we deal with the metamorphosis we've seen — the changing of the rules. We are the constant in this whole formula. No factor will move us."

Ursla, standing aside, saw the revelation coming. And she smiled at last.

"That's another of the famous equations, I think..." Caine smiled, "...one that grounds us in the face of change. We're still here... we're still who we were, despite this horror. And, my friends, I'll call that..."

He felt stronger.

"…the *genesis* equation."

APPENDIX A: CHARACTERS

It's been forty years since the end of the Krogg War, and with that much time it's probably not a surprise that many Earthers and humans have moved on to different roles. Some new faces have emerged, other familiar names remain ever-present. Just where are the people we know, and what are they up to?

Arbear, Ellen – Lieutenant
A marine with Cadmus Howler's elite 2/54th aboard *Renown*, Ellen is the daughter of venerable Krogg War Captain Esther Arbear. While her mother retired, Ellen elected to go into the marine service, feeling the open air of a land battlefield better suited her height than the command decks of a frigate. She is a rising star in 2/54th's ranks, and seems destined to be as successful as her mother.

Broadpaw, Varnon – First Consul
Varnon Broadpaw, with his trademark bad sense of humor, has left the Earther Navy and is now taking over for Setter Caine as the First Consul of the Earther people. He is, in fact, now the leader of all Earthers, as Setter was for thirty years after the Krogg War. Some joke that it's a scary thought, though in fact everyone knows that Varnon is very well-equipped to handle the job. The wolf remains one of the most respected veterans of the war, and he still likes fish cakes.

Caine, Elandra – Doctor
Since the end of the Krogg War, Elandra's been quite busy. She led the team that developed regen treatments for humans (doubling their lifespans and granting them prolonged youthfulness) and making many advances to Earther medical genetic technology. Earther genetic panacea drugs are now common, wherever they aren't banned by the Church. She still operates out of Fengate Hospital in Sydney, Australia, and her work has saved millions of lives in countless ways.

Caine, Phealan – Citizen
Phealan is over forty and about ready to move out on his own, though he still hasn't settled on just what career he wants to make for himself. He's fairly certain military leadership isn't for him, though Pat's history writing does have a certain appeal. He'll make his decisions in due time, and in the interim, he remains at home, spending a good deal of time with his now-retired father.

Caine, Setter – Citizen
Setter Caine remains the patriarch of the Earther people, having led them to wartime victory and peaceful prosperity. After thirty years serving as First Consul, he's elected to retire, turning the Earther state over to the capable hands of Varnon Broadpaw. Now he'll be able to spend more time with his family, to rest some, and to decide how to spend the half-century or so he has left.

Conroy, Pat – Good grief, he's a Historian now
Pat Conroy has left fleet life and post-war celebrity behind, trading in the glamour that the press tried to heap upon him for a rumpled trench coat, a beard, and a job writing the best-selling *Equations* books — histories of the Krogg War based on interviews with his friends and a great deal of additional research. He attempts to cook on a regular basis, failing consistently, and supports Sarah, his beloved wife, in everything she does as President. Regen treatments have granted him at least two more centuries of life, a concept with which he has yet to fully come to terms, but he looks forward to finding out just what the future will bring.

Cuttar, Ernile – Sergeant Major
Ernile Cuttar could have taken a promotion to Captain or even Major in the Third Guards Regiment on two occasions, but he's elected to retain his non-commissioned rank and command of the recon squad that he'd fought with during the Krogg War. That squad — first Beckett Lupus' and then Cadmus Howler's — has found another exceptional leader in Cuttar, and as it serves as a special guard force for Lupus, it remains perhaps the most elite eight-wolf section ever assembled by the Earther Marine Corps.

DeBrooke, Audrey – Admiral
Thanks to her regen treatments, Audrey remains young and quite fit to retain command of the Freetown Fleet. Flying her flag from her old Heavy Cruiser, *Grendelsbane City*, she is the senior Naval officer in the Freetown Navy, and remains attached to James Stanton, her co-founder. The two are married by common law, though not formally, as the Church has no place on Freetown.

Forepaw, Labrador – First Lord of the Admiralty
Lab Forepaw is probably the best officer ever to serve in the Earther Navy, and now he's taken up the top job in the Fleet, becoming First Lord with Andra Ursla's retirement. The canine's job description has changed slightly from Setter Caine's Krogg War mandate; the First Lord of the Admiralty now shares powers with the First Space Lord, a setup designed to allow the Earthers to have a Fleet commander in two places at once. Lab doesn't mind; the division of the powers

of the old First Lord position gives him more time at Earth, allowing him to better manage the new Navy as it develops.

Furgus, Jax – Admiral (Retired)
Before leaving the Earther Navy twenty years after the end of the Krogg War, Jax Furgus worked his way up to the rank of full Admiral, and commanded the first mobile striking force of *Chimera*-class ships when they were relegated to second-line status. Since that time, he's gone into a passive retirement, spending long lazy days sitting on his porch in his housecoat and reading letters from his daughter. He's happy to be an old curmudgeon, even though he happens to be younger than a number of his contemporaries, like Setter Caine.

Furgus, Joyce – Captain
Commanding a company of Cadmus Howler's elite 2/54th based aboard *Renown* at Genesis, Joyce is one of the junior officers marked for rapid rise in the Marine Corps. Quick-thinking and quite adept, she doesn't share in the grumpy demeanor of her father, the famous Jax Furgus, though few would doubt that she's inherited her father's tactical sensibilities.

Hodge, Gillian – Commandant
Gillian Hodge has retained command of the Genesis Naval Marine Corps since the war, working to turn it into a force that truly out matches the remaining Crusader armies in all areas. Developing effective hover tanks and better projectile weapons, she has drawn on the experience of the Krogg War to better her troops' ability to cope in combat, though Church regulations have denied her the use of Earther equipment in that effort. Now nearing 70, she is getting ready to retire, and thanks to Earther regen, she is also preparing to have children with her husband, Graham.

Howler, Cadmus – Lieutenant Colonel
Cadmus Howler had commanded Beckett Lupus' old recon squad on Krogg 'A', and since then he's remained at Beckett's side, turning the recon squad into a special escort unit for its former Sergeant, and eventually taking over command of 2/54th, turning that entire battalion into what might be unofficially termed "Beckett Lupus' Personal Guard". Under Cadmus' watchful eyes, 2/54th's effectiveness has only improved since its harrowing stand at Krogg 'A', and the unit and its veterans now rival both Guards Brigades in reputation and renown.

Jeffries, Ed – Captain
A veteran of Pat's Pirates, Ed left Genesis shortly after the end of the Krogg War, displeased by the conservative influences of the Church. Arriving at

Freetown, he was immediately recognized for this skill, and was appointed a senior Captain in the privateer squadron. Forty years on, he remains a Captain (a veritable flag rank in that small Navy) and has been appointed to command *FRS Savanna Felix,* the first newly-built hybrid Battlecruiser purchased by Freetown from Earther yards. Having received regen treatment, he continues to appear to be about thirty-four years of age.

Kudlee, Karyn – General
A distinguished veteran of the Krogg War campaigns at Avalon and Amaratsu, Karyn has worked her way up from her old command of 2/49th to her current post, General commanding the defenses at Earth, which she holds while Beckett Lupus — her only superior — serves as a diplomat in Genesis space. Karyn is decidedly aware of how her last name is pronounced, and she uses her considerable bear size to make sure no humans give her grief for being a 'cuddly' bear.

Leo, Thomas – Chancellor
Serving with the Chancellory of the Commonwealth of the Faithful, Leo is the primary fleet commander for the small fleet that the Church has assembled there. With Dreadnoughts and even a Carrier at his command, Leo is in an ideal position to take advantage of the Naval strategic expertise he gained from years of study, and he hopes to one day command the whole of the Genesis Navy in a new Quest against the Earthers.

Lupus, Beckett – General
Beckett Lupus has risen to the top of the Earther Marine Corps in the forty years since the end of the Krogg War, though he has stepped aside from overall command, offering it to General Karyn Kudlee while he takes up one of the two ambassadorial posts the Earthers maintain in Genesis space. Based aboard *Renown*, then, Beckett is one of the two diplomats to whom the Genesis government turns for an Earther perspective. The other diplomat, of course, is his wife Varnia. Beckett remains one of the most formidable hand-to-hand specialists among the Earthers, and he's taken it upon himself to help show Graham how to use a sword. That particular effort... well... could be going better.

Lupus, Varnia – Rear Admiral
Varnia (Broadpaw) Lupus married Beckett despite (feigned) reservations on the part of her father, and was thus banished from Earth space... to take up the most important diplomatic post in Earther history. Thus, while her father takes over the Consulate at home, Varnia and Beckett together serve as the elder Broadpaw's eyes and ears in Genesis — a crucial job, given the growing tension

with the Church. Varnia flies her flag from the *Venerable*-class *ENS Renown*, and is considered the 'senior' ambassador to Genesis — though such titles are rather irrelevant in practice.

Paine, Gregory – Grand Chancellor
The patriarch of the Chancellory that runs the new Commonwealth of the Faithful, Paine is a quintessential Churchman with a slight difference: he is a student of strategy and tactics, on par with the best of the interwar ArcGenerals. Determined to bring down the Earthers and fulfill the Quest, he has made it his mission to defeat the Freetown colony, and to help spark a revolution that will return Genesis to the control of the followers of the Unity National.

Pious, Thomas – Lord High Chancellor
After a line of progressive Chancellors in Bingham and Argyle ended with the latter's death, High Chancellor Thomas Pious (son of Chancellor Andrew Pious, one of Bingham's conservative contemporaries) has taken control of the Chancellory, and wields it as an effective weapon against Sarah Manchester's civilian government. Working together with Paine, he is laying the groundwork for a military insurrection the likes of which Genesis has never seen.

Magnus, Fox – First Space Lord
The intrepid Fox Magnus remains his adventurous self as he takes up the post of First Space Lord. Tasked with commanding large scale fleet operations far from Earth (allowing the Admiralty to retain its First Lord, Lab Forepaw, at home while such operations are ongoing), Fox has the best job he could have asked for. Ostensibly flying his flag from the fleet flagship *Venerable*, he's actually found he's spending a lot of time in Earth space, with maneuvers being the most excitement he sees.

Manchester, Graham – ArcGeneral
Graham's come a long way from the young ArcBrig who fainted the first time he met Andra Ursla. Now commanding the Genesis Fleet, he's a veteran 70-odd-year-old in the body of a 27-year-old man. He fathered the Genesis Carrier program, has reorganized and improved the fleet's logistical and research sections, and overseen the development of a new breed of conventional Genesis warships with combat capabilities beyond anything the Navy had before maintained. Now married to Gillian Hodge, he's living a happy life in Genesis space, though he remains wary of Church interference.

Manchester, Sarah – President
Accepting a twenty-year term as President of the Genesis civilian administration had never seemed a particularly appealing assignment for Sarah, but she took it

at the request of her predecessor and mentor, Liz Hastings. Now attempting to keep the influence of the Church over political affairs at a minimum, Sarah is growing ever more frustrated, and is looking forward to the century and a half of rest that her regen will afford her, after her term is up.

Narosh – Admiral-of-a-Fleet
Commander of the Larosian Fleet at Krogg 'A', Narosh has a unique perspective on his people and the Earthers, thanks to the Earther DNA now floating through his silver blood stream (a result of treatment after his accident aboard *Orion*). Narosh headed for home after the victory at Krogg 'A' on a mission to defeat the Krogg-devised plague that was ravaging the Larosian Empire. In the time since, things have not gone well, and now only his homeworld, Laros, remains safe behind a quarantine force of patched-up Krogg War veteran ships. The responsibility for protecting the last survivors of the Larosian Empire thus falls squarely on Narosh's shoulders.

Natosh – Captain
Narosh's Flag Captain during the period of the Krogg War, Natosh became a senior officer in the defense of Laros, but was infected by the Krogg plague when an afflicted Larosian, acting in a fit of madness, rammed and boarded his flagship. He has since become a test subject for the experimental treatments devised by Larosian scientists.

Nightclaw, Dran – Comptroller of the Navy Board
Acknowledged by one and all as the greatest frigate officer who ever lived, Dran has taken up the often forgotten but crucially important position of Comptroller of the Navy Board. It thus falls to him to organize the operational aspects of the new Navy, from its logistics to the production and maintenance of its powerful new ships. This panther's influence on the growth of the new Navy has been quiet, but without him, it's unlikely great ships like *Venerable* would exist as they do.

Schaeffer, Christine – Senior Cadet
Christine Schaeffer is an unassuming fourth-year cadet, soon to be graduating from the Genesis Fleet Academy. She's spending her summer break working a part-time job at the Genesis City Panatorium to build up some spending money for her final term, all the while studying and practicing to become the best fleet officer she can be. Granddaughter of Krogg War hero Bill Wallace, she is an excellent sword-handler, and routinely wields the blade presented to her family by the Earther Admiralty for his contributions during the Krogg War. She has a bright future ahead of her.

Stanton, James – Governor
James Stanton has moved smoothly from his place as commander of *Archangel Sword* to the role of Governor of the Freetown Colony. Having undergone Earther regen treatments, he remains young and vital, and is enjoying his time as the leader of the tropical colony. With his common law wife Audrey at his side, he has helped turn Freetown into a thriving new place to live, while staring down the challenges issued by Gregory Paine and the Commonwealth of the Faithful.

Ursla, Andra – Citizen
Andra Ursla took over the Admiralty twenty years after the end of the Krogg War, with Lab Forepaw as her Second Lord and Dran Nightclaw as Comptroller of the Navy Board. Though she'd never take credit for it, she built the new Navy from the ground up, crafting it into an effective force that could meet the demands asked of it. While she remains concerned about some of the fleet's numerical shortcomings, she's elected to hand operations over to Lab Forepaw, trusting in his incredible abilities to polish the reorganization she carried out. She's now just citizen Ursla, a very tall tourist, and of course, Setter Caine's good friend.

APPENDIX B: THE EARTHER NAVY SINCE THE KROGG WAR

Forty years have passed since *Orion*, *Agamemnon, Engadine, Atlas, Cerberus* and *Flame* (to name a few) fought their way into Krogg space and did harm to the Queen's armada… so what's happened in the meantime? Well, the Earther Navy has certainly rebuilt itself, learning from its experiences during the war to create a new breed of ships. But just how different are things as the Faithful and the Church rear their heads and plan to attack Earth?

Let's say *pretty* different.

New Ships

The most obvious evolution between wars has come in the realm of Earther capital ships. As you might recall, the Battle of Gibraltar and the introduction of gunboats to the battle line produced some complications at the close of the Krogg War; Setter Caine was left scratching his head as to how to employ these new weapons.

With the help of Graham Manchester, he concluded that boats should be placed aboard all fleet ships, but the resulting deployment was far from ideal. Boats weren't allowed full service crews, decks were overcrowded, and accidents happened (recall Narosh's crash on the deck of *Orion*). Along with that problem, think back to the end of Draco Maximane aboard *Engadine*; some of his last words to his dear friend Garvin Jardaw suggested that future Carriers be tougher gunnery platforms, because the *Engadine*-class had proved as vulnerable in a gunfight as one would have expected.

As the dust settled after the Krogg War, the solution to both these problems seemed evident enough: Garvin Jardaw arrived at Fleet R&D and spent a full ten months on detached duty, working with designers to come up with a hybrid carrier-capital ship. Historically (in human sea navies) such ships had never proved successful, and the idea of a hybrid had been abandoned, but the realities of three-dimensional combat are different in space than on the ocean. Boats didn't need the 'flat top' of a seagoing aircraft carrier. What they *did* need was a lot of hanger space.

Remember the cavernous size of *Orion's* gun deck from the tour Liz Hastings took right back in the beginning? Indeed, that's the challenge: guns are big, and gunboats are bigger, and even a ship the size of *Orion* couldn't handle vast numbers of both. During the post-war fleet modernization (the process by which all surviving Earther ships were put into drydock and had their boat-carrying capacity enhanced) it was found that there really wasn't much room to add to a capital ship's boat wing without crippling its broadside. The challenge was thus set: build a hull that had sufficient hanger space *and* still had room for a considerable broadside.

This proved to be a more difficult task than Garvin Jardaw had hoped.

The first attempt at a hybrid capital ship came eight years after the war, with the *Chimera*-class, a line of vessels that featured the mix of 94 guns and 30 boats. This class of ships retained the pedigree of the 74- and 80-gun ships that had decimated the Kroggs, but in terms of extra boat capacity they were limited. Essentially, they were ships of the line purpose-built with extra deck space, but not proper hybrid battleship-carriers. Along with the *Chimera*-class came the *Pallas*-class frigates and *Match*-class sloops, designed with a similar philosophy and equally gun-heavy.

Following in the footsteps of *Chimera* came the new *Champion*-class, being begun about fifteen years after war's end, after extensive research and development. Featuring a more balanced lineup of 100 guns and 60 boats, the *Champions* succeeded in providing the Navy with its desired hybrid. The *Active*-class sloops, similarly designed, were equally successful. The Navy Board's plan had been to build forty-eight of these ships (to form six squadrons, two squadrons more than had been built of the *Chimera*-class), but the order was cut short when a new development in gunnery technology entirely changed the rules of Earther design.

Thirty-two years after the end of the Krogg War, scientists at Earther Fleet R&D finally cracked what came to be known as 'Compression Pulsewave Field Technology', a means to reduce the size of both the reactor and output conduit required for the emission of an energy burst. In English: they found a way to build guns one third the size of Krogg War weapons, but packing *more punch*. The advent of these slim guns and the development of 'long-carronades' (carronades that could match the distance of Krogg War guns) revolutionized ship design, and led to the development of a class of ship that was a true hybrid: the *Venerables*.

Appropriately named, the *Venerable*-class ships are the most powerful vessels ever to have put to space (at least in known history). Their firepower is epic: 250 guns, each with an output approximately fifty percent greater than the maximum output of *Orion's* guns, with better range and better handling. Together with this mighty broadside is a *Venerable's* boat wing: the ship carries *115* boats. The hybrid concept has truly been realized in the *Venerable*-class, and its accompanying *Cerberus*-class frigates and *Flame*-class sloops. It is believed that a *Venerable* could easily crush an elite squadron of 74s, and could quite possibly break the heavy stations that defended the perimeter of Krogg 'A' during the final battle against the Queen. The Earthers maintain forty-eight of these (forgiving the pun, but, well, it's in the name) venerable ships.

So technology came a long way for the Navy in the interwar period... but what's that, the sound of the other shoe dropping?

New Organizational Reality

As a peacetime fleet with no expectation of a visit by humans determined to take Earth away, the Earther Navy has considerably downsized since the days it fought the Kroggs, or indeed, since the days when it waited patiently for the Church Quest to arrive. The main fleet has thus been reduced to 178 ships, along with 112 reservist vessels and 256 mothballed Krogg War ships, ready to be mobilized in case of crisis. The breakdown is as follows:

Front line:
- 6 squadrons (total 48); *Venerable*-class ships of the line — *250 guns, 115 boats.*
- 3 squadrons (total 24); *Champion*-class ships of the line — *100 guns, 60 boats.*
- 6 squadrons (total 48); *Cerberus*-class frigates — *58 guns, 20 boats.*
- 6 squadrons (total 48); *Flame*-class sloops — *24 guns, 8 boats.*
- 3 squadrons (total 24); *Active*-class sloops — *20 guns, 5 boats.*

Reserve (second line):
- 4 squadrons (total 32); *Chimera*-class ships of the line — *94 guns, 30 boats.*
- 8 squadrons (total 64); *Pallas*-class frigates — *50 guns, 8 boats.*
- 2 squadrons (total 16); *Match*-class sloops — *18 guns, 2 boats.*

Mothballed:
- 14 squadrons (total 112); improved *Atlas*-class ships of the line — *74 guns, 16 boats.*
- 18 squadrons (total 144); improved *Acheron*-class frigates — *44 guns, 4 boats.*

TOTAL: 560 ships (all ages)

In addition to these 560 vessels, some 1,500 ships that had fought the Krogg War (primarily 44s, 74s, 80s, and First Rates) were packed into floating crates, or 'boxes', ready to be reassembled in short order should circumstances demand. All older ships (be they Krogg War veterans or *Chimeras*) were over time modernized, but they have *not* received the new guns. The integration of that new technology into older power grids was deemed too risky to attempt — it wouldn't be good for an old 74 sporting 140 new guns to go into a fight, only to explode the first time its power grid caught a back-surge from one of the broadsides.

The reality, nonetheless, is that at the dawn of the new Church challenge, the Earther Navy is much smaller than it has been in centuries. Even counting the packed ships, it barely outsizes the fleet that met Bingham on the Pluto Orbital Plane in terms of numbers, and while it is true that the quality of the ships has grown astronomically, the size of space hasn't decreased.

Deployment and Exploration

As the senior Allied partner left standing after the Krogg War, the Earthers took it upon themselves to look after much of the charted galaxy after the dust settled. The Earther Navy thus finds itself spread thin by the time the Church resurges, with New Halifax, Earth, Gibraltar, and Krogg 'A' being the points of concentration of force. This vast territory would be extremely difficult to defend against a concerted attack from Genesis, owing to Genesis' position right at the midpoint of the long line.

In addition to the established bases, too, new exploration has been ongoing since the end of the Krogg War, with the Earther Survey Service, a quasi-military organization, being established. Under the Service's command, converted 64s and 28s that survived the war have been turned into explorer ships, moving out across space that the Kroggs once had dominated (between Gibraltar and Krogg 'A') and studying whatever is found. The Survey Service is a mixed-species force, with humans and Earthers operating in a single command structure. The organizational model has met with great success, perhaps because the humans involved are often the likes of Jessica Forbes (formerly of *Harbinger Bishop*) or Liz Hastings herself. Former Carrier skipper Farley Karr has joined the service as well.

With this ever-broadening star map to contend with, how have the Earthers deployed their ships? From New Halifax up to Krogg, here's the allotment:

New Halifax (32 ships):
- 2 squadrons of *Champion*-class ships of the line (total 16).
- 1 squadron of *Cerberus*-class frigates (total 8).
- 1 squadron of *Active*-class sloops (total 8).

Earth (144 ships):
Mothballed ships not included in tally
- 3 squadrons of *Venerable*-class ships of the line (total 24).
- 4 squadrons of *Chimera*-class ships of the line (total 32).
- 2 squadrons of *Cerberus*-class frigates (total 16).
- 3 squadrons of *Flame*-class sloops (total 24).
- 4 squadrons of *Pallas*-class frigates (total 32).
- 2 squadrons of *Match*-class sloops (total 16).

Gibraltar (95 ships):
• 2 squadrons of *Venerable*-class ships of the line (total 15 — *Renown* stationed at Genesis).
• 2 squadrons of *Cerberus*-class frigates (total 16).
• 4 squadrons of *Pallas*-class frigates (total 32).
• 2 squadrons of *Flame*-class sloops (total 16).
• 2 squadrons of *Active*-class sloops (total 16).

Krogg 'A' (32 ships):
Includes ships blockading hyperspace corridor to Larosian galaxy
• 1 squadron of *Venerable*-class ships of the line (total 8).
• 1 squadron of *Champion*-class ships of the line (total 8).
• 1 squadron of *Cerberus*-class frigates (total 8).
• 1 squadron of *Flame*-class sloops (total 8).

Conclusion

So there we have it: the Earther Navy has more powerful ships than Setter Caine could have imagined by the time the Church rears its head, but fewer of them, and much more territory to look after. What will they do when the threat from Genesis materializes into something more horrid and frightening than anyone could have imagined? Well, you'll have to wait and see… because by the time *The Vengeance Equation* is done, this neat set of charts and figures will be flying out an airlock somewhere. Hold tight to the Earthers' battle plot, because this is going to get rough!

ABOUT THE AUTHOR

Born in 1984 in St. John's, Newfoundland, Kenneth Tam holds both a Bachelor's and Master's degree in history from Wilfrid Laurier University in Waterloo, Canada. His MA thesis examined the creation and operation of the Caribou Hut, a hostel for Allied servicemen in St. John's during the Second World War.

In 2006, Kenneth received a prestigious Canada Graduate Scholarship from the Social Sciences and Humanities Council of Canada. He was also awarded a Balsillie Fellowship at the Centre for International Governance Innovation during 2006-07. In that capacity, he worked for Mr. Paul Heinbecker, Canada's former ambassador and permanent representative to the United Nations. He presently serves as a Communications Consultant for Kitchener–Waterloo's federal Member of Parliament, Peter Braid.

Since releasing the first *Equations* novel in 2003, Tam has promoted his books across Canada, speaking with junior and high school students, delivering writing workshops, and doing book signings at bookstores and Iceberg-organized events. He frequently appears as a guest author at science fiction events across the country.

Kenneth is a partner in Iceberg Publishing, the company he and his family started in 2002. He has authored many of the company's existing titles, and is also responsible for graphic design, including the company logo, website, banners, advertisements, and other marketing materials. He acts as a primary contact with printers and suppliers, and is also key in new author development and recruitment.

He remains very lazy about writing his author bios. When they told him to make this one longer, he mostly copied and pasted it together from the Iceberg website, www.icebergpublishing.com.

www.ingramcontent.com/pod-product-compliance
Lightning Source LLC
La Vergne TN
LVHW091031080826
845145LV00002B/442

* 9 7 8 0 9 8 6 5 0 1 7 5 3 *